WHITEWASHED JACARANDAS

BOOK ONE: THE UMZIMTUTI SERIES

Diana Polisensky

Cover illustration by Lynette Hirschowitz.
Cover design by Rogenna Brewer.

Whitewashed Jacarandas / Diana Polisensky. -- 1st ed.
ISBN-13: 978-1515366829
ISBN-10: 1515366820

Library of Congress Control Number: 2015950418

To the Memory of My Father

...for the secret of the care of the patient is in caring for the patient
Francis W. Peabody, October 21, 1925

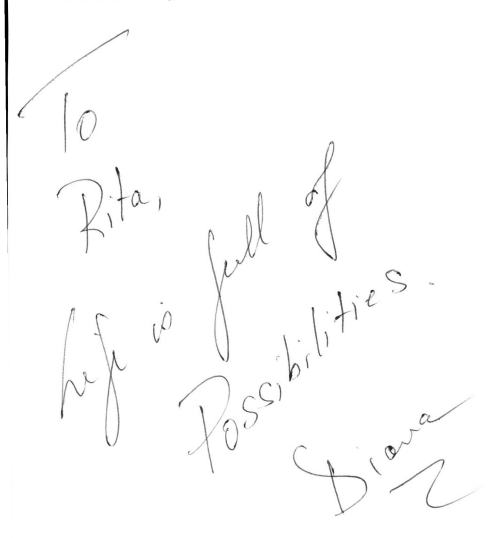

To
Rita,
life is full of
Possibilities.

Diana

CONTENTS

The Fifty-First Prospect _____ 1
Heaven or Hell _____ 9
Securing a Contract _____ 20
New Life New Land _____ 28
Leah's Tea Party _____ 37
Clearing the Air _____ 46
Clearance _____ 49
Brandied Marmalade _____ 52
Confronting the Matron _____ 59
A Day's Work _____ 63
Temps _____ 66
First Successes _____ 69
Settling in the Turkeys _____ 74
An Incident at the Bar _____ 77
Going Underground _____ 83
Rejection _____ 89
Showdown _____ 91
Spinning Yarns _____ 96
Explanations _____ 99
Doris Comes to Town _____ 104
Doing the Conventional Thing _____ 108
A New Addition to the Family _____ 115
Homecoming _____ 120
House Calls _____ 125
Leah's Bid _____ 135
A Lawsuit in Umzimtuti? _____ 145
A Tidbit _____ 147
The Little Village that Could _____ 148
Paying Homage _____ 161
The Hospital Christmas Tea _____ 164
New Year _____ 174
A Special Delivery at the Railway Station _____ 181
Hitting the Headlines _____ 188
An Official Visitor _____ 190
The New Governor _____ 198
Fate and a Fete _____ 203
The Warning _____ 212
Consultations _____ 213
Anticipation _____ 217

Fifty-One Steps from Wildest Africa _____ 223
On a Wing and a Prayer _____ 232
A Proposal and a Recovery_____ 238
Just What the Doctor Ordered _____ 244
Railroaded_____ 250
Heartbreak _____ 263
Waiting Up _____ 271
Competitions _____ 273
Poker Night_____ 277
The Aftermath _____ 288
The Smallest Municipality in the World _____ 296
For or Against? _____ 299
Last Minute Canvassing _____ 301
A Plea _____ 303
An Unexpected Victory _____ 306
A Setback at the Town House _____ 307
The Sin of Omission _____ 313
Preparations for the Royal Visit_____ 316
Capital Affairs_____ 318
The Governor's Ball _____ 320
Is the Town Ready for the Tea? _____ 324
A Watering Stop_____ 328
New Joy _____ 337
A Whale of a Treat _____ 340
A Long Night _____ 342

CHAPTER ONE

The Fifty-First Prospect

Dr. Sunny Rubenstein swung neatly up into the last railway carriage, with his small bag in hand. He stood at a corridor window and shouted back to stocky, wild haired, Dr. Michael Gelfand. But their parting words were lost amongst the noise and chatter of last minute boardings from the brightly lit platform of Salisbury Railway Station. They waved. The Garratt steam engine was panting hard and on cue from the stationmaster's shrill whistle, the train pulled out.

Sunny leaned on the windowsill and looked out eagerly to take in Southern Rhodesia's capital city lights. But almost as soon as the train left the station it was swallowed up by the black void of Africa. He pulled the window up and turned to rap on the compartment door ajar behind him before he slid it open and entered.

He slung his suitcase onto the luggage rack above, then caught a glimpse of himself in the small beveled mirror inserted into the leg of the hinged table fastened up to the post between the windows. Steel-gray eyes behind round glasses looked back from a big egghead. He removed his military cap and tossed it on the bunk. With both hands he smoothed back his mop of fine black hair. Even with the lateness of the hour he scarcely needed a shave. His youthful looks had plagued him all his life: he hardly looked his thirty-one years.

"I caught the train just in time," he said as he sat down opposite a very blonde man already settled into the compartment holding the newspaper close to his nose.

Bending the paper down to peer over it, with big blue eyes magnified in the thick lenses of his spectacles, the man said, "I'm a bit hard of hearing and eyesight's not so good either. I see you're still in uniform."

"I'm a doctor," said Sunny leaning forward, raising his voice, "and I've been kept on in Pretoria to vet the disability claims of South African troops returning from Burma. It'll soon be done and I'll be demobbed myself."

"I noticed Dr. Gelfand saw you off."

"I only just met him—by chance."

"Then you've stumbled on the very best professional association you could've in Southern Rhodesia."

"I'm desperate for a posting. He gave me a lead—even gave me a lift to the station. I'm on my way back home from Kenya where I had to turn a partnership offer down from my wartime CO—such a disappointment. The war has set me back five and a half years in private practice."

"I was too young for the Great War and almost too old for the Second. Initially the Rhodesian army turned me down because I'm practically deaf and blind, but I certainly wasn't going to be shut out of the war. I paid my own passage to England and hoodwinked my way into the army there. I've come back to my farm in ruins, starting again at forty what I began in my early twenties."

Sunny shook his head. In the silence that followed he peered out of the window. Besides the moving rectangles of vegetation vaguely lit by the carriage windows and obscured by the reflection of the cabin interior, he caught only the occasional view of the coach windows fore and aft and the red embers of the Garratt's furnace in the small engine cabin lit a cheery yellow, as the train curved up ahead.

The man folded his newspaper and said, "Whitehead's the name. Edgar."

"Rubenstein. Everyone calls me Sunny."

They shook hands.

Reaching for his pipe, Whitehead said, "I'm going all the way to Bulawayo."

"I'm due in at Umzimtuti at 2.01—such an uncivilized hour to disturb you. My apologies."

"I could have motored down but I enjoy the train and the people I meet along the way. There's a tremendous need for medicine here," reassured Whitehead.

Sunny pulled a box of cigarettes out of his breast pocket. A match flared and he lit up. Whitehead dipped the bowl of his pipe into his pouch, gave it a tamp or two and drew on it before he lit up, too.

"I've found my amateur doctoring on my farm is the best way to get to know my Native workers, build their confidence, get them back on the job and incidentally call into question their superstitions without offending them," said Whitehead.

"When I treat Natives it's almost always under pressure of time and numbers. Very often they don't come in until their disease state is far advanced. I work through an interpreter. They usually present multiple maladies but beyond that I hardly have time to consider them personally."

"Pity," said Whitehead, "but I fully understand: it's the same all over Africa—the demand's overwhelming. But here, we'll get a grip on it. What we need are more people like you to settle."

"I don't see much."

"One rainy season I was holed up at my farm for six months and never once went into town. I was studying a tremendous amount about economics in the evenings—such a welcome change after the daily farm work. Since not one of my farmboys spoke a word of English, I started reading aloud just to hear the spoken language."

Sunny said, "I don't speak a word of any Native language and don't intend to." He looked out and thought *it doesn't look as though there's a single soul out there of any sort to talk to.* He drew on his cigarette. What could there be in any prospect here for his family?

"As soon as I arrived in this country, since there was no written language, I started to create my own dictionary so I could begin to meet them on their own level."

"You speak their language to get the job done but in the long run what helps them most is to insist they learn English so they can get ahead. You see the sad thing is ninety percent of their diseases are preventable. Education's key."

"No, the economy has to come first: exploit our natural resources and industrialize. Then we'll have the funds to bring them along."

Whitehead sucked his dormant pipe, before he tapped out the ash and began to load it again.

Topping 40 mph, perhaps, the Garratt lumbered its way across the vast land. The coach swayed clumsily, clunked and squeaked. But the timbre soon changed as the train was reined in and slowed to a crawl.

"There's precious little to see," said Sunny. It was obvious Whitehead enjoyed debate.

"That's exactly it—it's all wide open for possibilities," Whitehead puffed thoughtfully on his pipe. "We deliberately caused unemployment on the outbreak of war so that men could join up and now the war is over we are reversing the process. Back then we reduced internal purchasing power deliberately to avoid inflation by restricting imports and we increased tax enough to pay for the war without resorting to borrowing. So now, there's not much debt. We concentrated on producing goods for the war effort or to replace essential imports. So, we're ready to forge ahead."

"What are the possibilities then in Umzimtuti?" said Sunny, as he reached inside his breast pocket for a cigarette and they both lit up again.

"I know it quite well. I was apprenticed to a chicken farmer about forty miles away in my early days. I paid him five pounds a month for tuition, board and lodging. Took what I learned after two years working there to strike out on my own farm, Witchwood, in the Vumba— the Eastern Highlands."

"So you didn't settle in Umzimtuti. What can I expect?"

"Well, not much right now besides a rich gold mine, the Cheetah."

"That's it. They're looking for a doctor to fill in on the mine. The current one wants out."

"That's not where the future lies."

The bedding steward rapped on the compartment door. They stepped out into the corridor. Sunny leaned his elbows on the windowsill, still searching the night for life—at least a recognizable landscape or better yet the rectangular outline of a farmhouse or a tall stand of blue gums signaling a mining community, but saw nothing, while the bedding was rolled out and crisp white sheets neatly turned down by the steward.

Turning back into the compartment, Sunny glanced at the beds. They looked inviting but he doubted he would sleep that night. He reached down and unlaced his shoes, switched on the bed light, propped up the pillows and leaned back with his arms behind his head. "So," he said, "where does the future lie if not in gold?"

"The Cheetah Mine has been exploiting the gold there for fifty years but," said Whitehead, drawing on his pipe, "there's a lime works nearby and a high grade iron deposit. It's pretty unusual to find the two together: perfect for a steel complex. That's where you'll want to get a contract. It'll be the industrial hub of the country with a model residential community." He puffed on his pipe, which never really lit up properly. "I drew up a financial plan for Southern Rhodesia before the war broke out and Prime Minister Huggins had me refine it while I was holed up incognito at a hotel in Twyford between assignments during the war. The government's purchased the Lime and Iron Works. If Huggins can win another term it'll be big—I'll see to it plenty of money is made available. Get in on the ground floor."

He reached down into his briefcase and pulled out a block of Hershey's K ration chocolate. "Terry's All Gold, my favorite, was taken over as a shadow factory in the war—one of our great sacrifices. We'll have to make do with the Yankee version I picked up at Fort Leavenworth." He broke off two generous hunks.

Sunny thanked him and they chewed on it thoughtfully.

Whitehead said, passing the newspaper to him, "Here, I've read the important part—the sports page—cricket in particular. I managed to take in the three Victory Tests at Lords before I returned. But I like equally to follow and promote the local chaps."

"I had a reputation at one time for googlies," said Sunny.

"Ah, a man of surprises. A good man to have on your side."

Sunny opened out the *Rhodesia Herald*. "How do you feel about the Prime Minister holding office so long?"

"Almost thirteen years. Huggins is a fine man. I had to resign my parliamentary seat as a backbencher when I signed up for the war but I'm hoping to get re-elected next year. Huggins wants to give me the cabinet position of Finance Minister but there's been a shift to the right and strangely enough there isn't much regard for returning exserviceman."

"Churchill lost the election even before the war ended. I believe Smuts might well lose the next election in South Africa too. The Afrikaner Nationalists may well take over. I'd like to move. If this job looks halfway promising I'll take it, but to be honest Southern Rhodesia's not too impressive in the dark."

"It looks brighter in the sunshine."

Sunny pulled down the window and stuck his head out. He listened to the wheel beats slowing over the track joints as the bluster of the wind declined. Ahead, the headlight beam lit up a sheet of corrugated iron painted white with black lettering in capital letters, announced Lochinvar. With a jangle and a hiss the train came to a halt.

There was no platform. A couple of sacks of mealies and a few milk cans waited in the dim light of the train for pick up. The sound of voices carried over the night air as Natives got on and off. Sunny was impatient with the clatter and scrape of baggage as it was loaded. There seemed an interminable delay before the fire was stoked, gray smoke belched into the night, pistons pushed and pulled and they were on their way again.

"Family?" asked Sunny.

"I'm going to welcome the first batch of children to Kingsley Fairbridge's Child Migrant Program to the now vacant RAF training base at Induna, outside Bulawayo. They'll provide me with as rich a family as I could ever want. My sister Frances and I have worked hard to bring them here. I couldn't do justice to both family and politics full-time."

"Free and entirely independent then?"

"Yes, farming affords me that privilege, though it's tough: weather, plagues, labor problems. But I'm always my own man. I'm puritanical about politics, so I'll never work for or own shares in any company."

How Sunny wanted to be 'his own man,' test himself in civvy street, after all the years of answering to his old man, buckling down to his choice for a career instead of following his true love of physics at university. Then, taking orders in the army for five and a half years. He said, "The new trend, now that the war is over, is to specialize but I'm feeling guilty about my wife, Mavourneen, and little son, Douglas. He's been very ill. They've been holed up in a succession of pokey flats in Pretoria all through the war. Stability is what they need—desperately. Still, I don't want to land up with one of those boring G.P. jobs referring out all the time. I want to see my patients through their difficulties and have a free rein in surgery—I've had plenty of war casualty experience. So to be honest—I've turned down a few offers. This is my last chance on this trip before I go home empty-handed."

"The need for medicine is tremendous here. There is no shortage of opportunities."

They forged on, pausing at the sidings of Marimba, Hunyani and then Norton. Here at least there was a shed, a bench and two lamps to light a platform. The men he'd just met, Gelfand and Whitehead, were very impressive but the emptiness of the night contradicted them. Could this backward place offer him the independent and interesting life he was searching for? He looked at his watch as they approached Lydiate, where a post bag and a crate of fowls were loaded and a group of women with babies on their backs, bundles on their heads and small children at their sides clambered onto the third and fourth class coaches.

There was no denying the slowness of this rural society that he'd seen all the way up Africa; time was measured in two seasons: the rain and waiting for the rain, not the passing of the hour and the urgency of the moment. The ponderous train and the meager luggage of the Natives epitomized the clash of cultures in an ancient but young land.

They swooshed and rocked through a railway cutting.

Sunny unbuttoned the table, lowered it down and folded out its leaves. He pulled out a map from his breast pocket, smoothed it out and looked at his watch. There was so much further to go: Kutama, Makwiro, Selous, Madzongwe, Gadzema, Hartley, Chigwell, Martin, Gatooma, Rimuka, Leighfield, Umsweswe, Battlefields, Umniati, Sherwood and Shamwari: all these stops in the middle of nowhere before he reached his destination. He looked up and caught Whitehead's eye and said, "There's such a mixture of English and Native place names, do you think this country will evolve into a common society?"

"That's the hope: time is on our side."

"Where're you from—originally?"

"Coming out from England my first time, I celebrated my twenty-first birthday on the train in the Karoo. '26 it was and I've never hankered for England since. This country's mostly free of class-consciousness—but I owe a lot to England. I was educated at great expense at Oxford and I intend to put that education to good use."

An Oxford man! His open necked collar was frayed, his trousers rumpled and his shoes dusty. Sunny recognized that he had received a very whole impression of Whitehead—and a valuable evaluation of the country—and its promise—in their conversation.

Whitehead lifted his battered briefcase onto the table to extract a file and sucked on his dormant pipe.

They settled into a comfortable silence. Sunny closed his eyes and dosed fitfully on top of the bedding.

Finally, Whitehead said, "Your stop's coming up."

Rain was coming down in sheets. A pair of lamps dimly lit a small Dutch gabled station building. "All the best in your election and plans for national expansion. I'll follow your career with interest in *The Herald*," said Sunny, having tied his shoelaces and straightened up.

Whitehead shook hands firmly and said, "The future's especially bright right here. Stake your claim."

Sunny picked up his suitcase and adjusted his cap. The only white passenger to disembark, he moved quickly towards the shelter of the station.

A hulk of a man in a glistening mackintosh stepped out of the baggage claim and extended his black umbrella to him. "Dr. Rubenstein?"

"Yes," said Sunny. "You must be Dr. Gidney Palmer. I'm sorry to have got you out at such an ungodly hour. My humble apologies," he bowed ever so slightly.

"The late arrival's routine. Your belongings?"

"This is it," he said, raising his overnight bag. "I'm traveling light."

Palmer turned and led the way hurriedly to his car.

This terse welcome contrasted with his earlier experiences that day. Could he put it down to the rain?

CHAPTER TWO

Heaven or Hell

Doctor Palmer looked dubiously at the lightweight traveling light. He held the umbrella over Rubenstein and caught a glimpse of his boyish face, his eyes framed in heavy round-rimmed glasses, which glinted off the car interior light. Rubenstein slung his bag onto the back seat and got in. Palmer rounded the car, collapsed the 'brolly, shook it, tossed it in the back and drove off.

The African downpour demanded Palmer's concentration and drowned out any possibility of conversation as they drove up to his house. He had left his house lights on and they hurried onto the long enclosed verandah, which encompassed the low-slung house. Palmer's yellow dog, Bundu, greeted Sunny with enthusiastic wags. The rain drummed noisily on the corrugated iron roof so that conversation was still confined to clipped shouts of the barest necessities.

The tea tray had been set in the lounge, and even at this late hour Palmer's servant, Leonard, appeared with the cozy-covered teapot and egg and Marmite sandwiches set on shredded lettuce. Bundu flopped down at Palmer's feet. He offered Sunny the plate. Before the tea had time to draw, he leaned just beyond the border of the Axminster rug and poured Bundu a saucer of milky tea, plopping in one lump of sugar. They ate in silence as the tea slopped and the saucer slid around on the hard concrete floor as Bundu's tongue worked on it, around it and under it. Rubenstein's head was so big Palmer wondered if he had been hydrocephalic at birth perhaps. Imbecile or Einstein? A few minutes passed before he asked, "Black or white?"

"White, please," said Sunny.

Passing a hot, strong cup of tea to him, he noticed Rubenstein's smooth skin and the gap between his front teeth which did nothing to change his first impression: he hardly looked old enough to support Gelfand's telephoned recommendation. Still, his short, taut frame sprang from broad shoulders, so that he carried his disproportion well. This was a tough mining town. He'd be on his own with no one to fall back on, Palmer mused. He was only too painfully aware of the times he himself had missed the support of a partner or consult. Presuming Rubenstein possessed the medical skills, would he be able to command the respect and confidence of the community? He was a Jew and a South African. Would he follow company policy in the interests of British shareholders?

Palmer wanted out desperately. He'd not so much as a nibble of interest even though he'd advertised extensively. He drained his teacup and dropped the crusts of his sandwich to Bundu. The man before him was his only hope. He'd keep an open mind.

He ushered Sunny into the guest bedroom.

Sunny lay back, enveloped in the comforting cocoon of mosquito netting, lulled by the throb of the wet African night. Family ostracism on both sides had pressed down on his marriage to Mavourneen that even the advent of Douglas had not broken. Robust at birth and for the first few months, his deteriorating health that stretched into years had seemed a reflection on their marriage. But finally, abruptly, thankfully, the marathon of anguish had come to an end recently following a timely article in *The Lancet*. How grateful he was to Mavourneen for encouraging a trial treatment: Douglas had never looked back. The angel must surely have been on his shoulder but Mavourneen had been stifled by confinement, impermanence and loneliness in a succession of shabby flats and his long absences during the war. Now the responsibility of a second baby loomed ahead, weighing the burden of duty more. He had been far from either the companion or provider he had wished to be. He keenly hoped to make an accommodation here, even as a locum tenens for six months, to tide them over. He knew so little except that Gelfand and Whitehead had urged him to take up this post. But he needed to be careful: the English never showed their cards and drove hard bargains.

With the rain percussing on the roof, Palmer lifted the ghostly shroud of mosquito netting that hung from the metal frame of his bed and swayed to the close breath of the ceiling fan, and dropped into bed. His little daughter Samantha's illness was a riddle neither he nor the Rhodesian pundits had been able to diagnose. His wife, Jean, mad with worry, had gone back home to England with her to find a cure. He longed to follow. He lay restlessly. The drumming of the rain, like the drumming on Saturday night in the mine compound, was as foreign to him now as it had been the day he'd arrived, before the war: primitive, relentless, monotonous. He yearned for the soft mist that shrouded the sharpening chill of England's winter and in the summer the brass band that played on a Sunday afternoon on the village green.

This land, the people, and the things in it were exotic and untamable: volatile and unpredictable like the rain. Oh, how he longed for rain in the stifling heat of October. But then how menacing it was when it came, like now, deafening, spawning all those detestable 'things' as Jean called them. The mosquitoes and ticks sucked one's sap, invaded the blood stream and even the very marrow with deadly organisms. Worms and flukes burrowed beneath the skin and penetrated the vital organs. Oh, the rains meant work alright in the weeks to come. At one time, he had looked forward to seeing textbook cases in the flesh, but with familiarity came boredom.

He felt heavy and dull with fitful sleep ever under threat from the telephone. He wanted out just as soon as he could. The war was over now, and despite the remoteness and discomforts, this had been a safe and profitable berth. He wanted to be back in civilization and specialize in obstetrics and gynecology. He'd offer this fellow a locum for one year and then bow out of his responsibility altogether.

Sunny woke to the whine of the mine hooter at seven. He heard the screen door of the verandah slam. He rose and dropped his flannel pajamas. In underpants he went through his muscle control exercises. That was the beauty of them, he could do them anywhere he went and they gave him a sense of mastery over himself. He perched on the edge of the bed pushed back the bedside lamp, placed his elbows on the table and his palms on his head and went through his routine: First the right, then the left, then in unison, each bicep popped like a calabash. Next, the triceps, long and slender, pulsed back and forth. Straightening up, the deltoids and pectorals rippled singly and in combination. Standing, under tight, smooth skin, he played his hamstrings opposite his quadriceps, then his glutes pulsed singly and in unison. Squats, sit-ups and knee bends followed. He was nothing like as fit as he'd been in the field. Although unsure of himself after six years of obeying orders and getting paid every month, he was desperate to find a way to civvy street.

Flexed, toned and alert, he dressed quickly and stepped out. Bundu was there to greet him as he took in the highly polished red cement floor of the verandah, the white sanitary pails of sword ferns standing like sentries to salute his arrival in the cool, sparkling early morning. He could see his son careering around on the tricycle in the corner, while he and Mavourneen had early morning tea out here on the screened-in East verandah. Heart shaped leaves of coral creeper grabbed the gauze with twisting tendrils, pink sprays of tiny blossoms shot from every angle to provide privacy whilst filtering the breeze. Perhaps they could even move their beds out here to catch whatever breeze there was on hot summer nights.

Bundu joined him as he wandered in the garden shaded by jacaranda trees, Mavourneen's joy in summer, clothed now in soft green lace, diamond studded after the rain. A child's swing waiting for Douglas hung from one of them. Whitewashed stones framed the expansive front lawn, the walkway to the gate and the driveway. How happy Mavourneen would be with the beds of flowers that bordered them. She would know all their names. A Wendy house nestled among a clump of poinsettias in the farthest corner: waiting for a girl. A grape vine covered a pergola leading to a small green gate and the Cheetah Mine Club beyond. And this was just the front garden.

This was just the job. It would suit Mavourneen, Douglas—and the new baby—very, very well. He fancied himself as quite a singer and their song welled up within him:

"I was born without a silver spoon.
But in my heart I've got a golden tune...
I've got a pocket full of sunshine
And a heart full of song..."

The shadow of a U shaped cocopan passed over the lawn as it whirred on the cable overhead which carried ore from the shaft to the mill, day and night, seven days a week, every day of the year, except Christmas probably. He paused. Would he be able to accommodate mine management attitudes aimed at maximum efficiency and at the same time protect mineworker's health and safety? The mine almost certainly employed a doctor simply because it was more efficient than government service, not for any humanitarian reasons. He was now more anxious than ever to see the facilities, assess working conditions and meet the management.

Palmer had not slept well. At seven, as the mine hooter wailed, he began Sick Parade at the Cheetah Mine Native Clinic before returning home to call Sunny in from the garden for breakfast.

Leonard served an English breakfast of fried eggs glazed with grease, bacon transparent with fat and fried tomato softly disintegrating. As Palmer and Rubenstein settled into the meal, Palmer inclined his head to a silver frame on the sideboard which held a photograph of a beautiful young woman with a curly haired child sitting on her lap. "That's Jean, my wife, and our little girl, Samantha. Samantha's ill and Jean's taken her home, to England. We haven't been able to diagnose Samantha's illness. The only clue is a number of small tumors of the skull but we've failed to find the primary," he said. He noticed Rubenstein politely skirting the bacon but was not about to apologize for the oversight of not instructing Leonard about it.

Rubenstein mixed bleeding egg with tomato pulp. "I'm sorry to hear that," he said, "biopsy?"

"An undifferentiated primitive cell structure. No clues," Palmer volunteered. "Toast?"

"Thank you," said Sunny as he lifted a slice from the silver rack onto his side plate, spread it sparingly with butter, thin shreds of marmalade and took a sip of tea. "Have you explored the kidney?"

"Kidney?"

"Yes, it's rare, but I once had a case of hypernephroma, with the usual skull secondaries."

"Goodness me no! Not a malignancy! It's nothing like that." Palmer felt his temper rise, his cheeks flush: this cheeky little upstart Jew.

"Forgive the suggestion," said Sunny.

"You don't presume to better Rhodesia's specialists, do you?"

"My humble apologies, for my telling habit, after such a short acquaintance."

That was better. It was good to see this young man back down. Abruptly, he got up and the color drained from his cheeks. He had to keep an open mind if he wanted to get out of here, "Let me show you around the European surgery for a start."

"Very good," said Sunny, pushing his teacup away. His white serviette dropped to the floor as he followed Palmer out.

Sunny understood Palmer's parental ordeal better than he knew: he and Mavourneen's long agony over Douglas had come right, but to offer assurances that Palmer's troubles would do the same would be false if his diagnosis was correct. He had blundered thinking Palmer was really seeking a professional opinion from him. But in his rebuke Palmer had shown his cards: he was desperate to leave. He would not jeopardize his departure because of his prejudices.

On the other hand, he was desperate too. His marriage, his whole future, depended on this prospect. The house and garden would exceed Mavourneen's wildest dreams. If the surgery setup measured up he'd be a fool not to take this job.

Outside, away from the bacon smells, the atmosphere lifted as the men approached the garden's encroaching brittle web of rubber hedge. When meddled with, it had a poisonous white sap which oozed. "The proximity of the surgery is very much a double-edged sword," Palmer said, opening the gate that led onto the circular driveway marked with whitewashed stones that encircled two spreading peppercorn trees. Their pink, papery beads, sodden with the rain, had accumulated in little drifts. He stepped up heavily to pull open the flimsy, spring-loaded fly screen door onto the surgery verandah. It banged behind them.

Sunny frowned as he took in a single bare tube and wire-mesh bench.

"Outpatients" Palmer gestured. "It's cost effective."

On the left there was a small cubbyhole and behind it, consulting took place in a small dispensary room, between bottle-laden shelves, a wash-up sink and a dispensing counter that also served as a writing table and was stacked with recording files and stationery. There was no examination couch, nor room for one. Presumably, the patient perched on one high stool and the doctor on the other, to lift a shirt to listen to a chest or feel an abdomen, or through the clothes, in the case of a woman.

Sunny realized with disbelief that with the dispensary door and cubby routinely open, auditory and visual privacy was jeopardized, to say the least, clinical examination and taking histories reduced to a minimum. "What about a proper examination?" he exclaimed.

"Oh," said Palmer, leading the way back past the bench and on down the length of the verandah, "if recumbency is absolutely unavoidable, the patient is taken into either of the two wards. I must tell you, too, custom has it," he continued, "that Coloured and Indian patients wait around the corner, here on the side veranda. They are only seen after all Europeans have been attended to."

"I say," protested Sunny, "is that fair to the patients?"

Sunny saw Palmer's irritation in the thick dark lifted eyebrows, the black eyes lifted heavenward, as he replied, "It's only fair to the Chee-tah that their workers get back on the job as quickly as possible." He waved as he entered a four-bed ward, "This mobile screen provides all the privacy anyone needs."

"We're almost at the half way mark in the 20th century. It'd all have to change if I took over," said Sunny.

Palmer's jowls flushed. "Look, I inherited this system and it's worked well for me. Nobody's complained—not a single person. If an-yone warrants admission we have these male and female wards. You've always got to bear in mind the Medical Benefit Society and whenever possible save on Government hospital charges on patients that don't require twenty-four hour care or special treatment." Turning abruptly to face Sunny and looking Sunny's uniform up and down he said, "Being an army man, I don't expect you know a *thing* about the practical running of a private practice."

"I'll agree," said Sunny evenly, "service to keep the world free has set me back five and a half years in practice."

Palmer was breathing harder and looked away. After a pause he said, "The success of the mine is dependent on a healthy labor force at minimum cost. Mark my words, *if* you're offered the locum, always bear it in mind when making decisions."

"What about qualified staff?"

"Sister Barbarus oversees it all and lives in two private rooms at the very back. Surgery is a misnomer, really. She's no theatre sister."

"Surgery is my forte and I could save the Benefit Society a great deal by referring out as little as possible." Sunny could not contain his irritation of what was obviously antiquated, unprofessional and inade-quate.

"Surgery is entirely out of the question here. Sister Barbarus doesn't do anesthetics or any assisting so you'll have to refer out, I'm afraid," said Palmer.

Sunny inclined his head and scowled.

Palmer went on, "She's always been here. Divorced with two chil-dren. I warn you, she's somewhat of a battle-axe. She comes with the territory and you're not going to change her."

Sunny looked up at the lazy ceiling fan in the center of the high pressed ceiling. This roomy converted house was full of possibilities. He wouldn't hesitate to change the arrangements.

Palmer was saying, "She'll be at Holy Communion now. Count on her as your general factotum. The consolation is she's made Jean feel secure...you know what I mean."

What a reason to keep an incompetent nursing Sister on, thought Sunny. Why would Jean have cause to worry? Mavourneen certainly would not. For his part he was committed. It occurred to him that although Palmer was heavy, with gross features, he would probably be attractive to some women who liked a big self-indulgent man. He said nothing.

Palmer suddenly attempted to mollify him, saying, "The New Government Hospital, quite a long way beyond the railway tracks, actually in the bundu, is properly staffed with Sunshine Girls newly qualified from England. Know their stuff all right and so easy on the eye—every one of them. The theatre there is fully equipped, and I'm the only one availing myself of it. The GMO and Medical Superintendent, Maxwell, is of the old school I'm afraid and quite past it. As GMO of course, he's responsible for all the Native cases free of charge. In a surgical emergency he calls on me and I've been happy to oblige. The only other doctor, Eckhart, refers out to Bulawayo or Salisbury. It's all yours so long as you can justify the case to the Medical Benefit Society."

"What's the fee structure?"

"Mine Medical Benefit patients are not charged for service or the medicines I provide. Private patients pay a consultation fee of seven shillings and sixpence. If I don't make it myself, their scripts are dispensed by the town's chemist."

By now they had reached the back of the building and looked out into the grounds beyond. "Private Native patients wait outside," said Palmer, "on these two old tree trunks. Cookie here, our illiterate Native takes all the histories, interpreting, and assisting. He's quite indispensable. He prides himself at engorging a suitable vein for intravenous injection and indicating the insertion site. He always carries a rubber tourniquet draped around his neck as a symbol of his position. He also collects the cash: one shilling and sixpence includes a bottle of medicine, half a crown includes an injection or a dressing."

Sunny said nothing but he thought, *I've seen this symptomatic quackery in Sophiatown. It's exploitive, hypocritical and soul destroying. To live with myself, I'll have to put this on a proper footing. Examining rooms...* He could see that Palmer recognized his disapproval.

Palmer said, "You've a lot to learn. You see, the GMO service is free; they can always go there. I'm offering this reluctantly as an alternative. They *choose* to come here and pay."

Sunny clenched his jaw. He knew he had said too much already and antagonized Palmer. This was wholly and completely unsatisfactory, but he'd be his own man here and could change everything. First he needed to secure the position. Did Palmer know how much he wanted it?

Finally, they entered the kitchen converted to a sterilizing room, presided over by Cookie doing the Sunday laundry. He was hot from the press of steam rising from a white cotton sheet at a huge ironing table, while the stainless steel sterilizer hissed. He pulled on both ends of the rubber tourniquet around his neck and flashed a welcome smile. Sunny liked him instantly.

Palmer drove Sunny over to the whitewashed Cheetah Mine Native Clinic. A Union Jack drooped from a flagpole at the center of the wide whitewashed circle of stones. Under a nearby clump of blue gums, he held Sick Parade at 7 am daily. "It's not always easy, but almost a sixth sense develops over time, to weed the sick from the loafers," Palmer said.

"I'm familiar with it," said Sunny, "I'm currently vetting the troops returning from the Burma Campaign. Some of the cases are genuinely tragic and deserving, but it's amazing what others hope to get away with."

They were both silent as they walked the neat pathway of white-washed stones which led to the Mine Native Hospital beyond. Sunny accompanied Palmer as he made rounds with the portly, bush jacketed, pith helmeted P.Q. Oosterhuizen, the enthusiastic Compound Manager, who, though he had no medical background, ran the hospital and operated the Siemens Global Portable X-ray machine and made a point of showing it off proudly, which impressed Sunny. There were no qualified nursing sisters but medical orderlies had elementary training.

"Here, the theatre's all mine," said Palmer.

Conditions were primitive and sparse, but the hospital was clean and adequate.

The Native compound was hidden from the European residences by the mine buildings and workings, tucked away to the northwest, and backed up to the flat-topped slimes dam of mine tailings. The compound took the brunt of the fine dust from these dumps when the prevailing winds blew. Single mineboys were housed in a quadrangle of cement barracks. On the periphery, married quarters consisted of a motley array of small dwellings, varying from whitewashed wattle and daub one-roomed huts to a few of brick construction as well as corrugated iron shacks. Ablutions and toilets were communal. A beer hall and school were the only amenities.

Turning into the driveway of the house Sunny said, "Thanks very much for the tour. The only thing we haven't done is go down a mine shaft."

"A mine shaft? I've never been down in all my years here."

"Isn't that the only way to assess worker conditions?"

The mournful wail of the mine hooter signaled the noon shift change. As the noise abated Palmer switched off the ignition and said, "It's time for lunch."

Sunny was relieved to return to the cool of the house to reflect. The curtains were drawn in the dining room against the heat of the noonday sun. Bundu lay with his back legs splayed out on the cool of the cement floor.

Palmer doled out Bombay curry from a tureen onto a bed of hot fluffy rice.

Sunny swallowed hard on the burning curry, washing down mouthfuls with gulps of water. His nasal membranes began to stream. He stretched to retrieve a handkerchief from his pocket and saw Palmer chewing thoughtfully, gazing intently at the silver-framed photograph on the sideboard. Abruptly, Palmer turned to him and said, "All things considered, I'd like to offer you a year's locum."

Sweat beaded on Sunny's forehead. He had not expected an offer so soon. There was still the New Government Hospital to check out. Wiping his brow he said, "It suits me, provided I have the option to purchase the practice also."

"One hundred pounds a month, with the furnished house."

It was twice as long as he'd dared to hope. *And* the house—furnished, thrown in. "Agreed." He looked at Palmer, who was cleaning up his plate.

"The balance of the income will be my goodwill up to the amount of £2000," said Palmer.

"Agreed."

"Let's keep the purchase confidential. It will make your breaking-in more acceptable than affronting the community with permanency before proven," he said as he pushed his plate aside and Leonard appeared.

"You're right. It will give me the opportunity to bow out without hard feelings if I am not satisfied also."

"Exactly."

Sunny put his knife and fork together on his unfinished plate. It was all too good to be true.

CHAPTER THREE

Securing a Contract

Leaving the house, Sunny and Palmer could hear the tennis balls popping at the bottom of the garden of the mine manager Frederick Doolittle's 'Big House' and Palmer spontaneously offered to introduce Sunny to him before embarking on his Sunday round of house calls. They watched as the Doolittles soon reached match point in mixed doubles with Pollock, the mine secretary, and his wife conceding. The players, in their tennis whites, walked off the court to join them in the thatched summer house smothered with a splendid show of Zimbabwe creeper: large clusters of trumpets of pink marked with pale yellow in their generous throats. Tea was laid out with cucumber sandwiches and split scones with a dot of lemon curd.

Sunny was introduced all round as they toweled down.

"Glad Palmer's finally found a replacement. How's your game?" asked Frederick Doolittle breaking the ice as they settled down to tea.

"Nobody would want me as their rugby forward," Sunny laughed self-deprecatingly, "but I'm good at ball games—cricket, squash, tennis, that sort of thing. I keep my eye on the ball. Think on my feet. Those are my strong points."

"Splendid. Palmer's bloody useless," said Doolittle. Everybody laughed except Palmer. "I warn you, my backhand's mean. I look forward to a game."

"I've still the New Government Hospital to see. Leaving on the 2.01. It's the only option out here it seems."

"You're right. You look so young. You'll be on your own out here, you know—in charge of the welfare of all my staff—over nine hundred Natives and over a hundred Europeans."

"I've had extensive experience—essentially in charge of a unit in the war at one stage."

"Tell us about your war experience?" asked Mrs. Doolittle.

Sunny held her gaze before he noticed her drop it to review the few pips on his shoulder. He did not have to justify himself to her. "It was a long five and a half years," he said.

"I must be going," interrupted Palmer. Turning to Sunny he said, "I'll come back after rounds and take you to look over the New Government Hospital."

The Pollocks took the opportunity to take their leave too.

Settling down again into the sling back canvas chair and extending his long bare legs out in front of him Doolittle said, "I've been running a tight ship, milling sixty-five thousand tons of ore a year on average, for a quarter of a century."

This didn't compare with South Africa's big Witwatersrand mines of course, but as Gelfand had said, for Rhodesia it was impressive. "What's the projected life of the Cheetah would you say?" Sunny asked.

"Well, it can't last forever, of course, but the company's doing damn well out of it. I'd say another twenty years or so."

Twenty years! Enough to get his son through university.

"Very good grades," Doolittle went on, relaxing into the comfortable curve of the canvas, "we're averaging over half an ounce of gold per ton, but before the Great War we had blocks of ore as rich as seven per ton."

"I believe that tops anything on the Rand?"

"We can't complain on today's yield and yes, perhaps we'll hit a mother lode again. We have about a hundred miles of drives, cross-cuts, raises and winzes in all."

"How deep are you then?"

"Down to the forty-third level. Close to five thousand feet."

"Hot down there with the humidity?"

"Yes, at that level, a hundred and ten degrees."

"No doubt you've got them on short shifts then?"

"To the contrary," said Doolittle. "We acclimate them topside beforehand to find out which ones can handle it." He tucked his legs under the chair, leaned forward and confided. "You know the Natives are lazy bastards—always looking for a way to slough off. That's your main job, you know, to weed out the loafers at Sick Parade."

"I expect I'll see a high number of lung diseases."

"We send the T.B.'s home to the reserve."

"It's a wicked practice, of course—needs changing."

"There's no cure."

"It's a question of responsibility. It's nice to see you have an X-ray machine on site. Your compound manager seems keen on the medical side. Perhaps we could document the lung cases—write a paper of our findings."

"Absolutely no need for that. We're a model for the country. Doing the best we can."

"I see the ablutions are communal in the compound."

Sunny saw Doolittle stiffen, stretching out his hand to carefully put down his Royal Doulton teacup as he replied, "This is not the Savoy. There are only three houses for the Europeans with indoor Elsan toilets, let alone the Natives. The honeysuckers do their rounds of the sanitary lanes in their mule carts. We haven't had any problems."

"I'd say you're pushing your luck, then," said Sunny leaning forward, his elbows supported on his knees, both hands cradling his delicate cup and saucer. He sipped his tea in an awkward silence as he watched the glint of sunbirds, exploiting the deep trumpets of the Zimbabwe creeper in the cool of the canopy of thatch.

"You're pushing yours," said Doolittle. "And you haven't even arrived yet, my boy. You see cutting corners makes all the difference to British shareholder returns. That's how you survive."

Sunny gazed out through the high wire fence that kept the fuzzy tennis balls within the confines of the tennis court. Thick impenetrable rubber hedge screened the hot bare glare of the tennis court from the mine workings. He drained his cup.

Rosalind Doolittle lifted the cozy off the hot water jug and topped up the teapot. "Another cup, dear?" she soothed. "Tennis is *such* thirsty work in this heat." Doolittle nodded and she poured. She extended the silver pot to Sunny and said, "More?"

"Yes, please," Sunny said, offering his cup. As she leaned forward he thought how pert she was in her whites, sweat-plastered hair framing her face. She had kept herself well in middle age though Africa's relentless sun had hardened her English complexion to coarse leather.

"Tell me, are you married?" she asked.

"My wife Mavourneen and a son Douglas. He's been ill, but I'm happy to say he's well on the mend. Another baby is on the way."

"Our two sons are both back home, married with lives of their own," volunteered Rosalind as she poured herself another cup too, set the teapot down and relaxed. "I'll be going back for the English summer. But living out here in the back of beyond does have some benefits after all. You know the Royal Family's coming out—a Victory Tour, traveling in a white train. Umzimtuti will be hosting a Royal Tea at the

Railway Park summerhouse. A Royal Retreat is going to be built for them at the bend in the river, just ten miles away. I'll have a *much* better chance of meeting them here than I *ever* would in England. I wouldn't miss it for *all* the world."

"I'm an admirer of Churchill myself," said Sunny. "My wife, though, is a Royalist. She'll be thrilled."

"How did you meet her?"

"In the operating theatre. She's a nurse. Of course Douglas now takes up much of her time. She very much enjoys the theatre, Girl Guides. She's..."

"Well, we don't have either of those...Girl Guides or the theater," she said as she crossed her legs and her right leg began to bounce off her other knee. "Opposite the doctor's house, as you've no doubt seen already, is The Club. Plenty of fun and games: sundowners every evening, billiards and cards. We've a library too. The Club's private, for the mine personnel and their families only, of course, but the film shown every Saturday night at our Chelmsford Hall is open to everyone, because there's *absolutely* nothing, besides the hotel bar, in the town down below. Of course, we've lots of children and we have a Saturday morning matinee as well."

Sunny, losing interest in the details, watched the metronome of her shapely calf swing below the short pleated skirt, down to slender ankles encircled in white turned down socks and clay white tennis shoes as she went on, "The town has a weekly local rag that comes out on Fridays—*frightful* editor, I might add. What can you expect, he's Irish Catholic via Tasmania. But there's no problem circulating gossip—it travels faster than the speed of light. Of course we do get the two daily national newspapers and the Johannesburg *Sunday Times* arrives on Tuesday. *The Illustrated London News*, *The Daily Mirror* and *The Daily Express* take six weeks or more."

"What chance of *The Financial Times*?"

"Oh, no," said Mr. Doolittle. "No point in subscribing to that. The financial news is way out of date by the time it reaches us. The BBC Overseas Service is what you want, although I admit there's a lot of atmospherics but you can usually get the gist of things. I know how expensive radios are but Palmer has rather a good one as I recall."

"Being from South Africa you'll find the government school here more than adequate. It's run on the British system. Oh, and I quite forgot," prattled on Mrs. Doolittle. "We have the odd dance now and then. The W.I. puts on a horticultural show every year. I'm very involved with that, but otherwise we don't have much to do with the town. There is everything here on the mine. Tennis for the ladies, mixed doubles too. Mind you, can you believe it tennis balls were rationed during the war, so the club was forced to close, but they've got it back up and running again. Golf, though of course it's all rather in the rough I'm afraid," she laughed. "Cricket in the summer and rugby in the winter. The mine hosts the semi-final and the final of the country's rugby tournament every year—The Cheetah Shield. The W.I. and the churches count for a lot. We're Church of England: Padre Huxley's very attentive."

"My wife's Church of England, though not an active member. I'm Jewish."

"Jewish. Well, there's no synagogue. Not even in Gatooma or Gwelo either, fifty miles north or south give or take a few. Still, you'll settle in. Wolfson, the baker, he's very good, very good indeed. Shapiro, the butcher and of course the Feldman brothers with the general store handling mining and machinery to agricultural supplies, cigarettes— even penny suckers. What a mess that store is, though I must say we couldn't do without it. They really do have everything, so long as you know where to find it. Shoe laces at the sweet counter, that sort of thing. Of course their children are away, at private school. And, I almost forgot, we have Jud Levine who owns the trading stores all around, even they have arrived and moved into town. He bought the Umzimtuti Hotel last year. I'm *sure* you'll fit in. Another scone?"

"No, thank you. Really, I must be going."

"What a summer we're having. The garden has never looked so good with all this rain—early this year. Much as the garden loves it we can't take much more. The rivers are full. Luckily, we've got the borehole to service the house and garden. Fred's greenhouse of begonias and fuchsias would never survive without it, would they, dear? Quite often the town's on water rations. Oh, how their gardens suffer, but not this year. My gladioli are prizewinners every year at the flower show. Would you like to look around the rose garden?"

"No, thank you. I must be going," said Sunny standing up, "still the New Government Hospital to see."

"Would you like a lift?" offered Doolittle.

"No thanks, it's all arranged with Dr. Palmer. I'll see you in the New Year." Sunny bowed slightly to Mrs. Doolittle, shook Mr. Doolittle's hand and turned into the long impressive driveway. His mind was churning as he stepped it out. He could feel Doolittle's eyes boring into the back of his head. He had blown it again—said too much. He could not help himself. Would Doolittle override Palmer and the offer be retracted?

Thankfully out of sight, he turned off mature tree-lined Jacaranda Avenue to peek behind the hedges of the modest red corrugated iron roofed homes of the mineworkers. There was a richness of color in the gardens: pride dwelt in the neat green manicure of the lawns and joy in the flush of flowers. Only a few blocks down the *kopje* the town indeed ended at the railway station. It really was, as Gelfand had said, merely an appendage to the mine. At first glance, it looked like a prospect limited by the fixed price of gold. What more could one make of it?

Sunny retraced his steps uphill. Palmer drove up. "Hop in," he said. He had indeed saved the best for last: the New Government Hospital way beyond the railway line. Jacaranda saplings with whitewashed trunks lined the driveway. Three big whitewashed stones marked the three doctors' parking spots at the entrance to Casualty. Here was civilization. "Inpatient and surgical facilities have white staff, mostly from England, but as I mentioned before, neither the GMO Maxwell, nor Dr. Eckhart are capable of much surgical practice. Essentially it's *all* yours," declared Palmer expansively. "I've been covering a narrow range of common general and traumatic operating, but you could easily expand it if that's your interest."

"What about a blood transfusion service?"

"Oh, no there's nothing like that. And the nearest consult is one hundred and fifty miles away. You'll have to be entirely self-reliant. Think you can handle it?"

"I'm confident. My non-European experience has run the gamut. In East Africa my field ambulance unit was faced with triage and evacuation of the onslaught of Italian POW's on their surrender at Gondar. My God, their forgotten army was a mess: malnourished, malaria, gangrene."

Palmer said, "There's one more thing. Eight miles out of town, near an old limeworks there's a big iron ore body. The government's purchased it. Rumor has it, it's going to be big. A new electric power station is being built as well. Surveys are under way," he said. "Not much to see right now."

"I presume you've secured the medical benefit society contracts for them both then?" said Sunny.

"No, no. I haven't sought that at all. Dr. Eckhart applied for them to supplement appointments he holds with the smaller adjacent gold mines. There weren't any other applicants as I understand."

"Secondary steel industries are bound to follow."

"I've got my hands full with the Cheetah practice," said Palmer as they drove along the muddy road.

"But Umzimtuti could become the heavy industrial center for the whole country?" He bit his tongue. Unbelievably, Palmer had let this once in a lifetime opportunity to get in on the ground floor pass.

"I don't see this paltry town amounting to anything beyond the Cheetah—nobody does. But don't get me wrong. There's plenty of work on the mine to provide a good living. You've only the Medical Benefit Society to satisfy."

Only the clinks and scrapes of cutlery on china and the slurps of Bundu beneath Palmer's feet punctuated the dinner, before they both retired. Sunny took off his shoes and slipped under the protective cover of the mosquito net, but couldn't sleep. He dropped the disappointment of the Lime and Iron Works prospect. This was truly 'just the job' for a start. The Cheetah offered stability, sunshine and the big expanse of house and garden, which Mavourneen and Douglas needed so badly. It offered him lots of scope in the operating theatre. Already he could see there were so many places he could make his mark: be his own man. The only question was whether Palmer's offer would stand, despite his blunders with Doolittle.

Sunny was sitting on a riempie stool beside the door of the verandah waiting for Palmer long before the 2.01 was due at the station. Bundu splayed out beside him and he stroked him. He'd never had a pet and to his surprise had rather taken to him. The garden shapes were silver in the moonlight: the swing, the spread of lawn, the trellis of vines, the Wendy house. Perhaps this baby would be a girl and they would have their pigeon pair. What more could a man want?

"There are no street lights or pavements in this town," said Sunny as the car rolled down the deserted avenue to the station.

"You have to make your own nightlife. The town shuts down pretty much after sundown. Only the Club up top and the bar at the Umzimtuti Hotel down below are lit up," said Palmer.

"There's no need to wait for the train," said Sunny.

Palmer insisted.

Sunny took it to be a positive sign that the contract still held.

The third and fourth class coaches were awash with Natives loading their families and handing up their meager possessions with loud conversation.

They watched the activity in silence, but with the time of departure drawing near Sunny felt the urge to confirm his appointment and said, "I'm glad we're so clearly in agreement on the terms."

"Yes, all the same, I'd like to get something in writing," replied Palmer. "But, well, you know a small town like this, it's liable to be nosey. Could you have it drawn up in Johannesburg?"

"Why, certainly if you prefer. I'd be happy to."

"I'll leave it to you then."

This was a surprise. Sunny had expected to receive an official letter of appointment from the mine in a week or so.

"If you elect to stay permanently, I'd like you to take over my furniture and household goods. I'm making a clean break. I'm sure you understand under the circumstances."

"I don't see why not. We haven't accumulated much ourselves yet. I don't suppose Mavourneen will have any objections."

"I'll have everything valued fairly before you arrive."

"Mid-February, then."

"Golf? Do you play? Comes in handy socially. I'm better at it than tennis."

"I've played, but can't afford a bag of clubs of my own."

"I'll leave my clubs then, too."

This really was the icing on the cake! Sunny shook his hand firmly before he mounted the steps of the carriage. The train started to pull out.

Palmer shouted out. "I wonder if you'd mind terribly collecting any outstanding debts on my behalf?"

"I'm no debt collector!" Sunny shot back. "I'll have my time cut out, you know, settling in, making my way, adapting, working at making a good impression. I tell you what—certainly, I'll collect anything that comes in on your behalf, but I can't go chasing after debts..." the Garratt was belching steam, the train gaining momentum. Sunny was out of earshot. The carriages snaked their way south for Bulawayo and on to South Africa and Mavourneen.

CHAPTER FOUR

New Life New Land

"It's only a year's locum with an option to buy," said Sunny as he enveloped Mavourneen and little Douglas in a triumphant hug on his return. He buried his face in the soft metal of Mavourneen's wholesome curls. There was a magnetism that radiated from her hair still which excited him just as it had when she had stuffed it all into her theatre cap as they gowned and scrubbed for their first morning roster of tonsillectomies together seven years ago.

"I know we will make a go of it," she exclaimed. "It will be lovely to get settled there before the baby comes."

"Yes," he said. He pulled away from her and viewed her from arm's length. She was in tip-top shape: there was a fullness to her face in pregnancy, the old sparkle in her blue-green eyes and a flush in her cheeks with the prospect and excitement of the move.

"I'm going to push the army for discharge. I've written a list of Umzimtuti's medical deficiencies on the back of my cigarette box already." He pulled the box out of his pocket and read:

1) Blood banking skills and equipment.

2) Dental extraction techniques and instruments.

3) Brush up on surgery—the more the better.

4) Bacteriology—a must.

5) Microscope—a good one."

"That's the Guiding spirit," she said as she returned the tight squeeze, "*Be Prepared.*"

"It's not the perfect set-up, medically," he admitted, "but I'll be my own man so I'll dictate on my terms. It's *perfect* for you and Douglas," he said. "A rambling big house—furnished, two fireplaces, and a huge garden with jacarandas—all sorts of flowers and a lovely big lawn for Douglas to rough and tumble on."

"Thank you, thank you. Finally a house and garden—perhaps permanently. I just know we're all going to love it there."

But as the days closed in with the turmoil of one more move, back to Johannesburg, before the great trek north, Mavourneen had her doubts. Would she fit in? Friends were so hard to make—you only made one or two real ones, if you were lucky, in a lifetime and she had Doris, her childhood friend, and her nursing friend Eve. Could she hope for more in her new land so far from home? She savored every minute of a going-away tea with Doris and Eve on the top floor of John Orr's and then another one, for good measure, long before departure day.

She had a strained visit to her lovely childhood home in Observatory. Her mother had had a heart attack on her wedding day, but, resigned with the fait accompli, wished her well. She had not seen her father since her marriage. He had attended the miserable courthouse ceremony—along with all the other criminals—to witness it, but declined the lunch reception at the Victoria Hotel: there was nothing to celebrate. Even the advent of a grandson had not softened him. She had seen her brother, Jack, only once since the war. She said her farewell to him. They were not close, but now with distance looming, she realized she would miss the physical closeness even if emotional closeness was a fantasy.

To keep these doubts in check she busied herself with all the practicalities. She was efficient, although there wasn't much. She crated her picture of The King and Queen, and Sunny's of Churchill and Smuts. His few mementoes and stack of photograph albums chronicling his war effort and a considerable assortment of papers she consolidated into one of his khaki-green army tin trunks along with a philosophy book or two for him. She tucked in an anthology of poetry for her and nursery rhymes for Douglas. The other trunk she packed with her fine linens, fancy clothes, crocheted beaded milk jug covers and fine tea showers she had embroidered on night duty when she wasn't knitting socks for the war effort: she had no illusions about the flies and heat, although Sunny enthused about a sub-tropical *Shangri-La*.

As the day drew near, she began to weed out her personal possessions. She still missed the purposefulness and companionship of her nursing days. She hated to give away the things from the happiest times of her life. Perhaps, there was still a future for her in nursing? She sighed as she reluctantly took down the uniforms hanging at the ready in the wardrobe, folded them into a cardboard box and gave them away. She vacillated on the hospital issue warm, navy blue cape with its bright red lining. It had served her so well on winter Highveld nights: sentiment won over practicality. She packed a few Girl Guide camping mementos: her knapsack, jaffle iron and billycan.

Douglas happily abandoned his toys in preference for the forts and tunnels they built out of packing boxes she collected from the grocer's as she packed the bulk of their clothing. She railed them ahead with the trunks, as well as her hat boxes—her one extravagance. They would make do in the interim.

She was ready long before Sunny's demobilization.

Sunny was hard-pressed for time. A priority was getting Ike Eidelman to formalize his agreement with Palmer. Riding the tram up sophisticated Eloff Street, as he passed John Orr's Department Store, he wondered how much Mavourneen would miss the swanky teas on the fifth floor with her friends. She rarely shared her news afterwards, he mused. A qualm passed through him, not for the first time.

He applied himself to the list of professional deficiencies he'd compiled on the train. The white colonnaded South African Institute for Medical Research supplied him with rudimentary laboratory equipment. He cajoled the Blood Transfusion Service into supplying him with porcelain tiles and Ortho antisera. The Witwatersrand Dental Clinic instructed him on dental extraction and temporary fillings. He spent time with surgeon Josh Lannon to brush up on the latest surgical skills. Honed, he took Mavourneen and Douglas down to Durban for a week's holiday by the sea while Surgeon Radford, the slickest surgeon in South Africa, broadened his spectrum further at Addington Hospital.

He was anxious and almost ready, but Gidney Palmer was slow to respond to the agreement. Now, he insisted Sunny collect his debts and manage his bookkeeping. Sunny apologized. He had an aversion to debt collection. Hadn't Palmer heard him as the train pulled out? Palmer now made it a demand.

Sunny vacillated momentarily. Should he risk the whole prospect by standing firm at this late stage? He telegraphed his refusal.

Promptly, Palmer withdrew his demand. Sunny was glad that Palmer had insisted not only on a written agreement but that he draw it up.

In five and a half years of army service he had accumulated £2000 savings. Ex-servicemen's entitlements were restricted to men settling in South Africa. But Sunny rode out of Voortrekkerhoogte Military Hospital on his last day of service in a battered old army Ford in camouflage green, a negotiated resettling allowance in kind. He triumphantly blew the hooter when he got home. Douglas ran out ready with his teddy bear and blanket to greet him, his cheeks ruddy in the flush of excitement—they were filling out nicely now—his spindly legs and arms too. He swooped Douglas up, threw him up in the air to great squeals of delight as teddy went flying.

They packed the car ready for a sunrise take off. The Zeiss microscope and laboratory equipment took up most of the boot along with Sunny's essential medical books that were so heavy.

The suspension hung low. Once Johannesburg and Pretoria were well and truly behind them, Sunny saw Mavourneen relax beside him and, with the heaviness of the new life within her and the upheaval of the move, saw her eyes close. Looking in the rear view mirror, Douglas, cornered between the picnic hamper and Mavourneen's preserving pot, was alert in the back drinking in everything with his enormous eyes but soon the rhythm of rubber on tar rocked him to sleep in his pillowed niche.

Topping forty mph eating up the miles of the Great North Road, hunched over the wheel, his calf and thigh taut, bearing down on the pedal, Sunny felt a weight lift too.

The road was long and dusk was falling as the Ford labored up the wooded Soutpansburg mountain range to overnight at the cool and beautiful *Mountain Inn* outside Louis Trichardt. They looked down in the evening light over the silent brooding blues and darkened shadows. They were leaving family antagonism and political intolerance behind.

Their spirits soared as they took off with the freshness of first light and rolled down the other side of the mountain into the hot bushy Lowveld after good rains. A new land and new life with opportunity and promise stretched ahead, north across the Limpopo River. Southern Rhodesia, open, yet secreting prehistoric and primitive life. The indomitable, thousand-year-old, gray baobab trees reminded Sunny of elephantiasis, one of the many mosquito borne parasitic diseases that were the scourge of Africa. Africa was alive with gray giants: elephant and rhino. But most of the animals were browns of every hue: tawny lion, dappled giraffe, golden impala, rump targeted waterbuck, spiral-horned kudu, stately sable, lowly warthog, relentless wild dog and scrounging hyena. They were all vectors of the microscopic trypanosomes of sleeping sickness and nagana that checked man and his domestic animals from intrusion. But Sunny visualized the potential for industry and growth in the Lowveld as soon as medicine conquered. It was imminent.

Mavourneen thrilled to the primeval world. How ironic that it was not size, ferocity, speed, agility or power that protected the animals from civilization and annihilation but little insects—tsetse flies and mosquitoes. The twitter of sweeps of swallows at the border post she recognized as a good omen as their passports were stamped and they crossed the coffee colored Limpopo River. Despite the heat, she wanted to stretch her legs, spread the blanket in the shade of a thorn tree, open the hamper and picnic on the riverbank in celebration and watch the birds—there were so many—but Sunny wanted to push on.

Those horrible monkeys would be a nuisance, she rationalized but couldn't they browse the roadside crafts? There were baskets to be bartered hanging from dusty thorn trees. Couldn't they linger over soapstone sculptures, bookends and ivory carvings displayed on hessian by barebacked and barefooted Natives balanced on their haunches, radiant with white smiles and so eager to negotiate and please? "What about a drum for Douglas?"

"Ask yourself," said Sunny, "do we really want that?"

"Look," she said, "at this truck made from mealie stalks and acacia thorns."

"You can see it won't last five minutes with Douglas' rough handling. There isn't room or money for non-essentials."

She didn't argue. He was right of course—*always* right. But she felt compassion for the hawkers. There was not much traffic and a small sale would make their day—go a long way to filling their *picannins'* tummies. She was unpleasantly aware these days of how Sunny's clinical analysis, coming to sensible logical conclusions annoyed her but up until recently she had clung to his every advice as indisputable. She didn't know how to disagree with him.

They filled up at the petrol station, freshened up and sped on. There were many more miles to go. They passed no cars in the long stretch of mopane veld on the strip road in the hot glare of the Lowveld. As they climbed out of it and into the hills, the fleeting blur of game from the window was superseded by the fascination of enormous gray whale-backed *dwalas*, their backs awash with brilliant orange and green lichens as they breached from froths of green bush. Out of seas of grass precariously balanced rocks secreted caves—lairs for leopards, retreats for baboons and shelters for early man. At a battered sign that promised Bushman paintings, Mavourneen exclaimed, "Oh, *do* let's take a look!"

Sunny retorted, "They have been there since the Late Stone Age. We can't stop now. Palmer's moved out and Umzimtuti's without a doctor. I've got to settle in as quickly as possible and get to work."

"Oh, do let's detour. I'm sure it's not far and we could all use a break."

"Aren't you keen to get on and see your new house, you've been wanting so badly?"

What could she say? High above the chaotic grandeur, an eagle soared. They made a quick roadside stop so she could 'go places'. This was a bad time for her to be traveling, pregnant, with all that pressure on the bladder and Sunny's impatience aggravating it. She was doing her bit: restricting her fluid intake as much as was prudent in this heat. She squatted behind a boulder. Here, where it reportedly hardly rained, a rainbow colored lizard scurried over the rock and was gone. She took it as another good omen, but what she wouldn't do now for a decent cup of tea.

An occasional car or lorry passed. Mavourneen waved, friends she didn't know yet. Vehicles advanced head-on relinquishing a strip at the last moment, as was the custom. They ate up the miles and miles of the grasslands of the Somabula Flats. Occasional stands of blue gums with splashes of color from bougainvillea or poinsettia surrounding the homes of isolated cattle farmers, small workers or a railway siding lured in the distance as exotic islands of civilization.

The sun had long set when they finally approached Umzimtuti, population 1300, elevation 4003 feet. A wide whitewashed boom announced *The Cheetah Gold Mine. Private Property.* The car lights lit up the whitewashed trunks of an avenue of old jacarandas that marked the way to 1 Jacaranda Avenue.

Mavourneen straightened up outside the car. Stiffly she unlatched the gate and approached the gravel path of the first real home in their marriage. A yellow dog jumped up to greet her and she patted him. She was too tired to do anything more than acknowledge happily the shadows of the garden layout.

"Down Bundu! Down!" said Sunny, "I guess he comes with the

house, too."

He pulled open the spring loaded screen door for Mavourneen and Douglas. They stepped in and it banged shut behind them. Mavourneen marveled at the long wide expanse of verandah. This alone was far bigger than their last flat.

"I can't wait to show you round the garden in the morning, I know you're going to be able to tell me all the names of the flowers," said Sunny giving her a big kiss and tight hug while Douglas made a beeline for the tricycle and sat down on it.

"It's time you learned to pedal for yourself," said Sunny releasing her, advancing on him and giving the tricycle a shove. Douglas squealed with delight as his feet whirled round and round while Bundu barked and slipped and slid alongside on the glossy floor.

Mavourneen was thrilled. This was what Douglas needed to flesh out his skinny little frame: freedom to explore the garden and beyond.

With all the noise, Leonard, the cook and houseboy, appeared to welcome his new employer, announcing with a flash of pearly white teeth, "Tea ready soon, Madam."

"Oh, that will be wonderful. Thank you," Mavourneen answered.

She and Sunny wandered through the rambling house, Douglas following behind on his tricycle with Bundu barking alongside as they banged around the big, airy rooms negotiating the furniture and corners. Finally they all retired to the sitting room. Mavourneen plopped into the Victorian recliner and spread her waistless form.

Douglas dismounted and Sunny said, "Douglas, my boy, we're home." He lifted him up and threw him up in the air.

Douglas screamed, "Do it again! Do it again!"

"That's enough," said Sunny finally. "Time to calm down."

Douglas, flushed with all the excitement, sprawled on the plush carpet, and sucked his thumb. Bundu splayed out next to him, head on his paws. They stared unblinkingly at each other.

Leonard entered with the tray and set it down in front of Mavourneen. The teapot had been warmed, the china cups also. Sunny said, "I know Bundu would love a saucer of milky tea with one lump of sugar. Palmer gives it to him while he waits for the pot to draw." Mavourneen was pleasantly surprised at Sunny's indulgence—but this was their new beginning after all. "Douglas," Sunny said handing him a saucer, "would you like to give it to him? Be sure and do it on the concrete. It would never do to spoil this fancy carpet."

To the sound of enthusiastic slurps, Mavourneen sank back and gazed up at the high ceilinged fan and took in the rich dark velvet curtains, as she waited for the tea to steep. It was worth waiting for—hot and strong. She closed her eyes as she savored each heavenly sip. They were draining the last of the pot when Leonard delivered a note on a brightly polished brass tray. It was an invitation to afternoon tea. Already! The small group of Jewish ladies wished to meet the new doctor's wife. Would she join them the following afternoon?

"Is the boy still waiting for an answer, Leonard?"

Not having anything handy, Mavourneen scribbled on the back of the invitation:

Thank you so much. Would love to meet you all but nothing to wear. Trunks due to arrive next week by rail. Sorry.

Exhausted, she was about to bathe Douglas when the phone gave three sharp trills on the party line. "That's us," said Sunny.

"This is Leah speaking. Leah Levine. *Do come* tomorrow afternoon. Everything is arranged. A simple tea. Nothing formal."

"Well..." said Mavourneen doubtfully.

"Most of the ladies work, but as tomorrow is Wednesday, they have the afternoon off. About three."

"It's very kind of you, but..."

"No buts, you can't be booked already, surely?"

Mavourneen hesitated.

"It's all settled then," assured Leah as she rattled off directions.

Replacing the receiver Mavourneen said to Sunny, "I'm not sure. I haven't really got the right clothes for afternoon tea...first impressions and all that."

"Oh, you want to make friends—fit in—don't you? Jump right in, they're not going to be concerned with appearances—they're not even skin deep after all."

"I suppose," she said, "I rather didn't get an option."

"Fancy that, we're off to a grand start." Turning from the telephone table in the passageway he suddenly exclaimed, "Palmer's as good as his word—he's left the bag of golf clubs for me."

Mavourneen longed for a bath and bed, but first it was Douglas' turn. The bathroom was commodious. She pulled up a chair, inserted the plug and reached to turn on the taps. Brown water spluttered into the tub. Suddenly a clot of dead fish fingerlings disgorged from the tap. Well, no place was perfect. Sunny, she knew, would tackle this right away as a matter of health and safety. She turned to Douglas and said, "Let's make-believe you've had a lovely hot bath and pop straight into your pajamas."

Douglas jumped into his big bed in his very own room. Bundu came to lie beneath the bed. Mavourneen stepped over him, lay back on the pillow herself, and began to tell Douglas a story. She had not got three sentences into it when they both fell fast asleep.

CHAPTER FIVE

Leah's Tea Party

Mavourneen's hair responded to the cold rainwater rinse from the bucket she hauled in from the tank outside. It shone chestnut, bobbing about her shoulders as she left the house wearing sensible shoes for the informal tea at Leah Levine's house. She knew she looked neat in a fresh cotton frock, chosen for travel, comfortable, anything but dressy. Little Douglas skipped alongside. Was it Sunny's bold intervention with the single Vitamin B1 and liver shot that had cured him overnight or her clean sweep into the rubbish bin of the battery of old wives' concoctions she had resorted to in her desperation over the years? Whatever it was, from that momentous day forward Douglas had never looked back.

What a surprise it was to have the Jewish community welcome her in contrast to the resounding rejection they had both received from their families on their marriage. When he'd married out of faith, his family had worn black in mourning for a year.

The sun was high and it was hot as Mavourneen and Douglas made their way under the shade of Jacaranda Avenue, through the big mine gate and into the glare of the treeless town streets below. She turned off into the small residential area and peeked over the garden hedges as they went along, ruminating as she went. She should never have succumbed to Leah's pressure and Sunny's encouragement to jump right in when she knew instinctively she was not ready. This was her new start. Her new life. She'd stand up for herself—challenge Sunny when she knew she was right.

These ladies' first impressions would be around the town before she got home, she thought harshly. She took Douglas by the hand and quickened the pace: she wanted to get this over with as quickly as possible. She let her naughty temper out, singing fiercely:

"And so if Mister Trouble finds me
He will never linger long
'Cause I've got a pocketful of sunshine
And a heart full of song."

She reached in and retrieved a slip of paper tucked into her bosom and checked the address as murmurs filtered through a fly-screened verandah beyond a garden gate. She walked up the path and tentatively pushed the screen door open. Ferns in sanitary pails stood on the red polished floor of the verandah. She called, "Hellooo, may I come in?"

In a flash, a young petite woman wearing cork platform sandals with crossover copper tone straps was at her side. Copper buttons on her fashionable indigo crepe dress flashed in the afternoon sun as she rushed to introduce herself, "Leah, Leah Levine. You *must* be Dr. Rubenstein's wife?"

"That's right, Mavourneen. And this is Douglas." She held his hand and smiled reassuringly at him.

"Mavourneen?" after a moment's pause Leah stepped aside and said, "Come in. *Do* come in." Copper embellishments glinted on a small indigo hat perched on her pretty little head as she led the way inside.

Mavourneen, still clutching Douglas' hand, paused on the threshold of the sitting room full of women. The party seemed subdued. She looked down briefly at her white nursing lace up shoes and out across the sea of peep-toe high heels, hats, gloves and jewelry up to the nines! All heads turned, taking in her bare arms, the fullness of her simple cotton maternity frock, the small boy beside her, another well on the way, and, she knew, they could see she was hardly Jewish.

Leah Levine smiled as she announced, "May I introduce Mrs. Rubenstein to Umzimtuti. You did say Mavourneen—is that right? And Douglas. We have all been looking forward so much to meeting you." Pausing, Leah cleared her throat and continued, "Her trunks are coming by train next week."

Mavourneen smiled ingratiatingly at the two-piece suits and classic afternoon frocks with the new fashion of gathered shoulder seams and contrasting sashes with bows tied at the waist. Presumably they had anticipated a sophisticated woman from Johannesburg, excited that a professional family was joining their tiny community. She must be a huge disappointment to them, but suddenly she realized the women's guarded expressions had softened.

Gesturing, Leah began her introductions: "Mrs. Kalderon, she's closed the store and come all the way in from the Lucky Star Trading Store just to be with us today."

Mavourneen was transfixed when Mrs. Kalderon turned her black eyes on her. Tall and olive skinned, ropes of jet black hair coiled like sleeping mambas over each ear. Shot metallic silk slid over her long form; dark sophistication from Madrid or Lisbon or perhaps even South America she guessed, collared by gold chains. But then her welcoming smile revealed ragged teeth. She must have fallen on hard times. Her face came alive and Mavourneen flushed, smiling back as she moved on into the room with Douglas. How could she have thought ill of her!

"Mrs. Wolfson, on your right, you will have to try her cheesecake, her bakery is famous for it. Mrs. Shapiro helps her husband in their butchery business. Actually all the ladies work with their husbands."

"Yes, yes, I used to work with my husband too," answered Mavourneen. She wished she had never surrendered. The assembled women looked pleased.

"The Feldmans, Mrs. Avigail and Mrs. Rivkah, well, everyone really *depends* on Feldmans to get you *anything* from a needle to an anchor. The town couldn't function without them. Avigail's son is off to Oxford, a Rhodes Scholarship."

Apparently Umzimtuti did not limit horizons. "Well done," she said.

Touching the arm of a small woman in a beautifully tailored suit, Leah said, "Mrs. Uziel is from the Greek Island of Rhodes and works in the haberdashery—slipped in just before all the restrictions on Jewish immigration in '20. Still no English." She added, "Her lovely twins here, Sarah and Esther, have just graduated from medical school. Soon they will be off to London and the Great Ormond Street Hospital. We are all so proud."

Mrs. Uziel nodded in acknowledgement.

Mavourneen sensed she understood a lot more than she let on but made a small wave, which was returned. She turned to the girls. They certainly were strikingly good looking and immaculately turned out. This community was certainly impressive. "What'll you do with your careers when you get married?"

"Husbands? We'll take care of them when the time comes, just like all the ladies here," said Sarah. Everyone laughed.

She wished she had never given away her nursing uniforms. Perhaps there was still a chance. "When are you leaving for London?"

"Oh, it will be a while," said Sarah. "We are helping our parents at the haberdashery."

"Haberdashery! Wouldn't you rather have clinical experience?"

"Any sort of posting is hard to find," said Esther.

"The boy, maybe he could use a little fattening. No?" interrupted Mrs. Rivkah Feldman.

"Quite," said Leah. "Tea's ready. It's easier if we go through to the dining room and help ourselves. We can finish the introductions there."

The ladies rose. The dining room table was covered by a tablecloth of cross-stitch panels with broad borders of heavy lace on which stood a silver tea-set and an array of good china cups and saucers. Dainty cucumber sandwiches, a chocolate cake, apple strudel, cheesecake, meringues, almond rugelach and more were spread before them.

It was anything but an informal tea party. But Mavourneen realized they all meant well.

Mrs. Rivkah Feldman moved to the head of the table, "Have we made this all for show? No, no. What is food but for eating. Help yourselves. Eat. Eat. Relax. Enjoy."

Taking a plate and handing it to Mavourneen, Mrs. Kalderon, as gracious as she was beautiful, said, "We far-far from town. From anyone. Your little one so good, amongst all the ladies."

"Of course, I should have thought. We must get you a nanny. I have *just* the one in mind. Mrs. Terreblanche next door just sacked her Beatrice and she's such a nice young thing. I'll see to it," effused Leah. "I must say Douglas is quiet."

"Actually, I prefer not, if you don't mind," said Mavourneen, standing her ground. "You see he was very sick for a long time and I got used to looking after him myself." She realized everyone must have a nanny. No one had brought a child.

"Who are we to tell the doctor and his wife how to look after the child?" said Rivkah Feldman.

"*Ja?* He *must* have big piece of chocolate cake, I make," said Mrs. Shapiro cutting a huge wedge out of it. She set Douglas down on the concrete floor away from the rug. Then, she tucked a serviette into the neck of his cotton rompers and put the plate in his lap. She was solidly built, boxed in with dour navy pleats and wasn't comfortable with tea parties. She ran the business side of the butchery. Turning back to Mavourneen she said, getting straight to the point, "We are nine. *Ja!* We need *one* more man for a minyan. Your husband, *Ja?* Would he be willing Friday nights?"

"Well, he doesn't bother much except for the High Holy Days. But

I'm sure if you need him..."

"Of course we need him!"

Mavourneen knew she was thinking her son would not count for the minyan. She would be an outsider, never truly one of them, but still there was a measure of acceptance that she could never expect in the exclusive societies of Johannesburg and she was enormously grateful for it.

"And what about you?" Mrs. Shapiro pressed on. "We are all working, *ja*, working hard for WIZO. Already we women we have raised two hundred sixty-three pound by cake sale and jumble sale for Palestine. A Jewish state one day. Soon. We make our contribution. We make *Aliyah* too one day. *Ja!*"

Leah said, "Let me finish the introductions of our WIZO members. Mrs. Fisher, her husband has a concession store out Gokwe way, sixty miles away. Mrs. Hershl, now she has been in Umzimtuti practically since the Pioneer Column raised the flag at Fort Salisbury." She was an old woman with a twisted back, probably scoliosis, thought Mavourneen. Her hair was blunt cut and slicked back with Brylcreem, she supposed, like her mother-in-law.

"Mrs. Hertzog is the wife of the newly appointed geologist on the Cheetah," Leah went on. "They're from South Africa of course. Mrs. Elazar, a lifetime with the concession on the Halliday Mine. Doing all right, mind you."

"Let me tell you, we will be dispossessed from all the fundraiser poker nights of the men," Mrs. Hertzog said dryly, smiling at Mavourneen.

"It's nothing. Only a pittance for the cause. Your Desmond always lose," retorted Mrs. Shapiro. "Can we count you in, once a month for poker? The stakes are high and WIZO takes ten percent of the winnings."

"Sounds like lots of fun," said Mavourneen. "Sunny made more out of poker than medicine in his early days." How she longed for a return to their fun-filled days and nights together. Perhaps they would come again.

"The Royal Family's coming next year. They're going to build a retreat for them just outside of our own Umzimtuti at a bend in the river," said Mrs. Hertzog, smiling even more broadly than before, baiting Mrs. Shapiro.

Mrs. Shapiro took it, "Such expense! For what?"

"Just a gesture, to thank the people for their contribution to the war," replied Mrs. Hertzog.

Mrs. Fisher, the lady stuck out Gokwe way, said, "Our people made a contribution too. My father walked into this country in '97 before the railway line was built," she said turning to Mavourneen. "We *wanted* British trusteeship for Palestine in '23 under the League of Nations."

"Here in '23 we had the referendum. Self-government under British protection," said Mrs. Hershl, as she twisted up and looked sideways to engage Mavourneen.

"British protection! And what happen in Palestine? Betrayal! Quotas on the survivors of the concentration camps going to Palestine," said Mrs. Wolfson.

Mavourneen poured another cup of tea for herself, and took another sliver of cheesecake. It lived up to the boast.

Mrs. Wolfson interrupted herself to say, "You like? You *must* take cheesecake to your good husband."

"*Ja!* Quotas here too in '38. The *Bulawayo Chronicle* headline: *This is Rhodesia Not Judesia! Let's keep it that way!*" said Mrs. Shapiro.

"They still have quotas here for Jews," Mrs. Wolfson pointed out.

"*Ja!* What a struggle to get my father here in '38 from Germany. Three hundred pound guarantee. We had ten shilling! The polony machines missing on the boat. My sister Ida and her husband—there's no news," Mrs. Shapiro protested.

Mavourneen said, "I'm terribly sorry. My father-in-law is also still making enquiries about his relatives. So far only the Norwegian branch survived—escaped to the forest and into neutral Sweden in the winter. No trace of any of the Lithuanians yet." She thought most of the women battled more or less to express themselves in English but all of them always fastened onto what they meant and not what they said. She could do no less herself. But otherwise they enjoyed seizing on each other's weaknesses.

"Where will you be going to have your baby?" asked Sarah.

"My husband will manage the delivery. He's the best," said Mavourneen between airy crumbles of crisp meringue, pure cane sugar melting in her mouth, making the most of the moment. Just as well Sunny was not here to monitor and admonish.

"Isn't that unusual?" Esther said, looking up sharply at Mavourneen.

"Since my husband had to redo Douglas' circumcision which was botched at the Voortrekkerhoogte Military Hospital by the number one surgeon there, we decided from then on to be self-sufficient."

"A man should doctor his own?" queried Mrs. Rivkah Feldman.

"It's a convention," said Mavourneen. "It's not against the law."

"There's nothing written, my dear?" queried Mrs. Hershl.

"Such courage! Such faith!" said Mrs. Feldman.

"That's the pioneering spirit," exclaimed Mrs. Fisher.

"We met in the operating theatre and worked a lot together and trust each other explicitly. How do you cope with the dirty water here? I've got dead fish bursting out of the bathroom taps."

"Oh, that," said Leah. "It comes and goes. There's no filtration of the reticulated water supply to the mine from the river five miles away. The town also depends on it."

"Oh, I see. Well, the rain water's lovely," said Mavourneen. "My hair really likes it."

"Oh goodness no! You can't afford to waste water from the rainwater tank on your hair. Strictly drinking only or you'll run out before the October rains come. The river can dry up as well," said Leah.

"Then, trouble," said Mrs. Hershl. "Three inches only for bath and everyone share."

Mavourneen realized she was being educated at a terrific rate.

"Mind you, your big house got more roof runoff than anybody—except the mine manager. Not to worry," pointed out Mrs. Wolfson.

"Fowls! I do love fowls," Mavourneen said, looking out the window in search of a neutral subject. "It does seem my garden is certainly big enough. I'd love to get a pair of bantams. You don't know anyone who has any do you?"

"Remember, Feldmans can get you anything you want," said Mrs. Hertzog.

"It just so happen," said Mrs. Rivkah Feldman, "Last week, we bought out old man Deary's place. Turkeys. Want turkey? I get some. Yes?"

"Why not? A bit more than I bargained for, but a pair would be marvelous. By Jove, they'll be ready for the pot—by Christmas." She laughed.

"Sooner, by Rosh Hashanah," countered Rivkah. They all laughed together.

"Your garden? Put in glads for horticultural show," enthused Mrs. Avigail Feldman.

"Well no, not just yet, thanks. I don't really know the garden. It does seem to be a shade one, all those lovely jacarandas, not really right for glads. I like the sorts of things that just keep coming up by themselves, no matter what."

"Avigail's gladiolus. She love them like children now hers are gone," said Mrs. Wolfson.

"She's been second to high and mighty Mrs. Doolittle up in the Big House for the last fifteen years at the W.I. Show. It's her life's ambition to take the blue," said Leah.

"What, a bit of ribbon? I can get at the shop anytime, as much as I want," said Mrs. Avigail Feldman facetiously.

Everyone laughed.

"Alright! Alright. Do I know it in my heart? Mine better."

"Perhaps you might part with some of the blood from the abattoir for the glads, Mrs. Shapiro?" said Mrs. Hertzog.

"No, bone meal for glads, blood for roses. Water. Early rain. Has Mrs. Doolittle got worry about that?" corrected Avigail. "She got bore-hole."

"Well, I'm sure yours are lovely," said Mavourneen. "Some other time perhaps..." She couldn't help feeling that her presence had made everyone sparkle.

"Vegetables. Now you must have fresh vegetables for the good doctor and your little one. I'll take you to market on Saturday. Show you the ropes. Sharp six thirty... Oh, I know it's early. Auction begins at seven and you must know what you are buying," said Leah, reclaiming Mavourneen.

"Ja! I boss-up cake stall. Bring cake. Buy cake. All funds for WIZO. Ja! German chocolate cake too messy in the sun." She looked at Douglas' chocolate and caramel smeared face. "I bring apple strudel, for sure," said Mrs. Shapiro. "You buy?"

"I'll be happy to," said Mavourneen, licking her handkerchief and stooping to wipe Douglas' face and hands. "It's been a wonderful party. I've so enjoyed it. Thanks so much. I think I must go now."

Leah packed Mavourneen a generous basket of goodies from the table to take home to the good doctor as Mavourneen took Douglas' hand.

"My car. A ride?" said Mrs. Rivkah Feldman.

Her own car? What a luxury. "No, No. Thank you so much, but we have been sitting in the car for two days. The walk'll do us good. We can look in on all the lovely gardens along the way."

Rivkah called after her, "Make *hok* ready. I ring. I bring turkey."

Mavourneen felt exhilarated as she hiked the hill with the basket in hand and Douglas at her side as the great ball of sun dipped low on the horizon.

By the time she reached her garden gate she realized the women had just been looking for an opportunity to tog up with no harm intended. She knew she would never be one of them really, but she longed to have a friend she could chat to quite often. They had all in their different ways been friendly and extended themselves to her: she looked forward to the promise of turkeys, gladioli, maybe some blood from the abattoir and an introduction to the market. She had come away with a very generous basket of goodies for Sunny to tuck into. She decided to accept them at face value. And this was just her first day in her new life.

CHAPTER SIX

Clearing the Air

Two days into his new job, Sunny could no longer contain himself. Gidney Palmer's conditions and routine at the European Surgery next door to the house were untenable and Sister Barbarus, the live-in nurse, unacceptable.

The last outpatient dispensed with, his fury rose as he jammed the patient's file into the file box. Palmer's records were just the accounts! Evidently clinical information was stored in his head. With no lead of past history, initial consulting depended on the patient's version of past diagnosis and treatment. This off-the-cuff symptomatic type of practice was not for him. He would have to set up a system. Suddenly he realized the wail of the hooter had not sounded. It was not yet five o'clock.

He walked quickly over to the mine management offices, a series of low-slung, whitewashed buildings fronted by verandahs along the road that led to the compound. He hoped Boss Jack, as Jack Napier Chelmsford, the mine's chief engineer and chairman of the Medical Benefit Society was affectionately called, was as fair-minded as his English fair head. He had a reputation as everybody's mentor and friend when needed, perhaps motivated by osteoarthritis, which confined him to a wheelchair.

Yesterday, on his introduction, he had seemed affable enough. Now Sunny knocked on his door and was motioned in. "I'm sorry to barge in on you but there's a problem that needs resolving right away." Without preamble he launched in, "To be able to practice medicine properly I must shut down the in-patient wards of the surgery and convert them into consulting rooms and an office so there's full privacy for consultations."

With his gnarled hands, Boss Jack rocked his wheelchair forward and back behind his big untidy desk. "Don't get me wrong. I do hear you. But you simply cannot turn the established order of things upside down just like that."

"I can't carry on this way."

"You've only been here—what—all of *two* days! Change takes time. You've got to bear in mind that the Mine Hospital saves money. Besides it's Mine and Benefit Society policy for non-surgical cases. It's especially convenient for single men not ill enough for the New Government Hospital but unable to prepare their own meals. Have you thought of that?"

"Yes," said Sunny, "but if we do away with in-patients there will be no need to have a live-in sister. That will save you the nurse's salary and free up her two living rooms at the back. These could be used for a proper Native clinic."

"Now, wait a minute! A full-blown private Native clinic? That's absurd! It would prejudice your whole standing in the town. The premises are European in the European residential area. All Cheetah Native mineworkers are treated in the Native Compound Clinic and Hospital. The general Native population is not our responsibility. They can get free care from the GMO at the Government Native Hospital. Natives, in any case, are uninterested in our medicine. They've got their *ngangas*. We only need to provide service where our interests are at stake."

"But our interests *are* at stake." Sunny looked at the bowed pant legs, which hung from the seat of the wheelchair and rested on the foot plates: his disability should have made him more sympathetic to the Natives' condition. "Our domestic servants expose the European population at large to TB, leprosy, typhoid, dysentery—the list goes on. Their general productivity too is influenced by their wellbeing, even if they're not infectious. We need to address their immediate needs and alleviate their suffering. Long term, we need to educate them to safe and clean practices—tackle the root cause of problems. Start with children in the schools."

With his back bent and his neck perpetually thrust forward, accentuated by a jutting chin, Boss Jack was in truth an ugly looking specimen: small-minded and selfish Sunny thought angrily. Of course, his disability meant he could not go for a walk or play a game of tennis, so timetables and routine filled his life and everyone catered to him. He was in a position of power. His anger rose as Boss Jack replied, "Take this advice from me as your Dutch uncle. I repeat myself: you've only been here *two* days! You've got to win the management and people's confidence over *first* before you attempt radical and controversial changes."

As though he had not heard, Sunny rushed on, "Sister Barbarus is very fixed in her ways, very admiring of Gidney Palmer and there're things I want to modernize. She won't change."

"I can't turn out the old dear who has given such long and loyal service. You should know her alcoholic husband deserted her and her two small daughters a long time ago. It's the only home they've ever known."

Well, thought Sunny, *she's so morose and contrary, I'm not surprised he was driven to drink—not to mention she's gone to seed, fat, as if a third infant's due.* But he checked himself. "She's *insisting* on segregating the Indians and Coloureds and making them wait till every *last* European patient is seen. It's just not fair."

"Indians and Coloureds! Surely you must know no European will tolerate sharing a bench with them, nor waiting while they're attended to. No, absolutely not. We can't have them all lounging about, that might lead to fraternizing. Everyone has been satisfied with the arrangements. I've never, in all my years as Chairman of the Society, received any objections. You *will* have to conform. In time you'll appreciate the importance of cost and the value of social norms." Boss Jack rolled forward in his chair to meet the desk. He shuffled his papers. The meeting was over.

Sunny paused on the verandah and took a deep breath. The hooter wailed. The sun was sinking, night would quickly descend and the air would cool. He stepped it out briskly. He would have to pocket his medical pride and bide his time. He realized that although he was alone with no one to fall back on he was *not* his own man.

Exercise always improved his mood. The screen door banged as he strode into the house, patted the dog, threw Douglas up in the air and gave Mavourneen a hug, before he stepped back and held her at arm's length and said, "That's it, I'm going to get my own consulting rooms so I can dictate my own terms."

CHAPTER SEVEN

Clearance

Sunny found plausible reasons not to admit any more cases into the old hospital. Sister Barbarus was apprehensive but probably pleased, he thought, with the reduced work and, especially, fewer meals to prepare. Tension mounted with each passing day.

An old man presented himself at the surgery one morning. Sunny ushered him into the dispensary and shut the hatch to the verandah.

"Doctor," the patient said, "Hardy's my name, Johnny Hardy. I'm the town undertaker and I'm also a member of the town council. I do a bit of joinery, too—make my own coffins. If there's any need remember me."

"Well as a matter of fact there might be. What's the trouble?"

"Dr. Palmer, you know, was a right fine doctor, yes sir, he was. I doubt we'll see the likes of him again. But the truth is he didn't do no dentist work and I got troubles."

"Let's have a look then. Please take a seat." When he opened his mouth Sunny took in the blast of tobacco, mint and putrefaction without flinching. Many of his teeth had been removed. Those that remained were yellow stubs set in an angry red mush.

He knew he should give up smoking himself. Here was a golden opportunity to put to use his recent week's instruction at the Dental School and the dental tray of instruments he'd bought out of his £2000 savings, which Cookie had already sterilized. He was all set.

"You're right, you've got troubles," he said. "If you don't do something pronto you may well get a fever and chills. Toxins can emanate from pyorrhea of infected gums to poison the system, leading to a whole gamut of general ailments. But I can take care of it today for you, right now in fact." He outlined the procedure to Hardy. It would all be over in an hour.

The old man shifted uncomfortably on his stool. His eyes searched around the closed cubbyhole.

In all likelihood Hardy had not expected such immediate and decisive action from the new man in town. It was understandable. To give him more time, Sunny riffled again through his file. Of course there was nothing clinical in it, just a list of invoices and receipts.

Finally, old man Hardy said, "Ag, Doc, I don't know, you look so young and you want to knock me out—just like that, man. You know I had this problem a long, long time. It can wait."

"No, no. I'm prepared. I just completed a course in dentistry at Witwatersrand University specially so I can take care of you," he smiled.

"Doc, maybe I won't wake up. I don't know, you see there's no one else can make my coffin. Embalm my body. I'm not ready, like."

"Of course you're not. I can see you've got a lot more life in you. It's only going to take an hour and you'll be a new man."

Suddenly Old Man Hardy opened his mouth and without moving his jaw shouted, "I...I'll ooh, ooh, ahhh...I'll take my chances."

"Good, I know you won't be sorry. We'll just be a few minutes while Sister sets up. If you'll just wait outside on the verandah bench, we'll be right with you."

Sunny went in to inform Sister Barbarus and prepare.

"I heard you," she said, "committing to a dental clearance. We just can't do it. I'm not comfortable with anesthetics."

"Well, why ever not? We'll just use a quick intravenous shot of Pentothal and switch over to gas and oxygen. We need to keep the anesthesia shallow, so we can keep the pharyngeal reflexes. That's important, so that he doesn't inhale the blood. There's really nothing to it. It's completely straight forward..."

"Dr. Palmer never did any surgery here nor Dr. Wade before him."

"Well, we are going to start now."

"We haven't any Pentothal or gas..."

Sunny picked up the phone and called P.Q. Oosterhuizen at the Native Hospital. "Dr. Rubenstein here," he said. "Could you crank your car right away and deliver some Pentothal and gas to the European surgery." He turned back to Sister Barbarus. "It's on its way," he said as he replaced the receiver in the cradle.

She stood her ground. "I'm, I'm just not accustomed to it."

"Mr. Hardy's waiting. Could we hurry, please. We'll need some pillows to support the neck but throw the head well back."

"I haven't managed anesthesia in all the twenty years I've been here."

"I see. I know how insecure you must be feeling. It's only natural.

Just follow my instruction."

"I, I can't."

"Look, I'll tell you what then. I'll call my wife over, we've worked in the theatre for years together. She's a fully trained theatre sister. She'll assist."

"Over my dead body! *I'm* in charge here."

"You're mistaken. I'm in charge. I must proceed."

"I won't have you come in here, temporary, and allow your wife to meddle in these affairs."

Sunny could fully appreciate why Jean Palmer was happy to have Sister Barbarus work with her husband. She was *hardly* a woman with whom one entertained less than honorable intentions and a foe to be reckoned with. Besides the full six inches over Sunny in height she had more than a yard in front, solid impenetrable adipose tissue, shielding her heart.

"I'm sorry you feel that way."

"I'll have Boss Jack put you in your place. It's you or me!" He heard the fly screen door bang. He watched her walk up towards the mine offices as he picked up the telephone and phoned home. The angel was on his shoulder. Mavourneen was in.

CHAPTER EIGHT

Brandied Marmalade

Mavourneen was determined to make use of the year she had spent at the Aberdeen School of Domestic Science, which she had loathed so much, now that they had this lovely house in which to build their new lives. With the house fully furnished, there was not much need for their meager household goods that had arrived by train. In the dining room, she took down the Palmer's pictures of English hunting scenes and replaced them with Sunny's portraits of Winston Churchill, South Africa's Field Marshall and Prime Minister Jan Smuts. On the opposing wall she hung her cherished portraits of King George VI and Queen Elizabeth.

It was time to put to good use her heavy preserving pot. She and Leah had bought a pocket of lemons at the Saturday market outside the Town House. Small as Leah was, Pat O'Connor, the auctioneer, had picked her out of the crowd and the hammer had gone down to her at one shilling and sixpence. It was a good buy. She and Mavourneen had split the bag.

Even so, Mavourneen had a lot of lemons on her hands. Thick skinned and juicy they were perfect for marmalade. Shredded, and steeped over the weekend, then simmering the fruit until tender, she added the warmed sugar, brought the marmalade to a roiling boil and skimmed off the scum. Then, she needed to pay close attention to get the right consistency. Ball jars from Feldman's, sterilized in boiling water, stood drying upside down in the oven ready to be filled.

Right at this crucial moment, as a cooled teardrop of marmalade hung off the wooden spoon, she heard those three damnable trills from the phone. She almost let it go. It was Sunny, wanting her at the surgery at once. She missed the days of their professional teamwork, gowned and masked: the challenges, the precision and the quick deftness of Sunny's gloved hands when he held the scalpel. She had anticipated his every need with just the right instrument to hand.

She turned the hot plate off. It was a pity she couldn't get the job done and fill those waiting jars. The consistency was perfect and the appearance bright and clear. For once, the Aberdeen School of Domestic Science would approve.

She washed her sticky hands. Quickly, she mopped her brow and took off her apron, calling from the kitchen back steps for Leonard to come in and watch over Douglas. In no time she was through the garden gate, hurried across the driveway and was over the threshold of the surgery door. With a nod and a smile she acknowledged the old man seated on the tube and wire mesh bench on the verandah, walked down the passageway and into the vacant four-bed male ward where Sunny was adjusting the portable screen.

"There's been an altercation and I'd like you to assist a dental clearance," he said glancing up at her.

"A dental clearance? Of course." Cheerfully and confidently she turned and went to usher the old man in.

"You're new here too?" Johnny Hardy said, lifting his bushy eyebrows and peering at her closely, moving his spectacles up and down over his rheumy eyes.

She caught the nervous quaver and shock of pain in his voice and reassured him with a steady gaze and comforting pat on his arm. "Actually I'm Dr. Rubenstein's wife and a qualified sister. We've worked together many years. He's the best."

"I was just expecting a script for the chemist to make the pain go away, like," he confided. "Sometimes Dr. Palmer mixes me something up himself, right here in the cubby while I wait. Can't the good doctor just do that? Like, I'm wondering if I'm doing the right thing..."

"I'm sure you'd rather a permanent solution."

"I'm afraid of that," he said, "you know the *new* doctor knocking me out, like—permanently."

"Oh, put that right out of your mind. Of course you're going to wake up!"

"I'm not really ready. The doctor, well, he does look *so* young, like."

"He's had an awful lot of experience. We'll have this over in a jiffy and you'll not remember a thing," she said, patting his arm reassuringly and giving it a squeeze. She picked up the scent of wood shavings mixed in with varnish on his splattered overalls mingled with cigarette smoke and bad breath and felt the coarseness of his hand as he clapped it over hers. She smiled, "This will all be over in no time. This way please..."

Sunny and Mavourneen scrubbed up side by side as Sunny clued her up on the procedure he planned. "I'm all set up, if you'll just check the instrument tray."

Looking the tray over, it was amazing how quickly everything flooded back to her, although some of the instruments were unfamiliar. She smiled. He'd be demanding *gimme this, gimme that*. She'd keep one step ahead, just like old times. Nursing was a part of her, which could never be erased. She remembered everything as though she'd never resigned herself to marriage. This was her chance, perhaps, to get back into it. Her professional pin, engraved on the back with her name and graduation date, was carefully stashed in the back of her jewelry box: she prized it above all else. She wished she had not given her uniforms away.

Sunny realized the risk he was taking upon himself with a procedure he had never actually performed before. He knew full well that he could not sustain any sort of a disaster the first year in practice in a town like Umzimtuti, where the bush telegraph operated faster than the speed of light, just as Mrs. Doolittle had told him. The old man had lived with his problem for so long he could easily justify referring him to Salisbury, one hundred and fifty miles away. He understood the first rule of medical practice was to get rid of the difficult cases—play it safe. But he thrilled to the challenge to see Hardy through himself. And drawing Mavourneen in, over Sister Barbarus' head, made it doubly risky. He was compelled by an inner drive to meet the challenge head on. He felt exhilarated. He believed the angel was on his shoulder and this gave him supreme self-confidence.

All went well and as his patient began to come round Sunny ripped off his gloves and gown and left him in Mavourneen's care. It had been a joy to have her at his side in the theatre again.

He let the screen door bang behind him as he hastily crossed over to the lean-to garage at the house, reversed the Ford quickly and swung into Jacaranda Avenue. The car bumper danged and dented against a whitewashed boulder in front of the verandah of Boss Jack's office.

"I'm sorry to barge in on you, again, but there's a problem." His tone was measured, belying his agitation.

"I was expecting you," said Boss Jack, wheeling back from his desk.

"I'm sorry, but I cannot be expected to function constantly directed and thwarted by a nurse, especially Sister Barbarus. It's a matter of her or me!"

"Not so fast," Boss Jack soothed. "I explained to you before, she's been here as long as I can remember."

"That's *just* the problem! I'd like to make full use of the surgery. Besides the personality problem she's limited in what she can handle. And, well, to be frank...incompetent!"

"She beat you to it over here."

"Well then, you must very well realize, we can't go on under the same roof. I have to point out again, there's no dignity or privacy in handling the outpatients. Examining patients perched on a wooden stool in the dispensary cubby! It's all preposterous and must change forthwith if I'm to continue."

"Didn't we discuss this already? What do you propose?"

"Scrap our in-patient service. The New Government Hospital is a godsend. It's stupid not to make full use of it. Besides the advantage of the services the Government puts at our disposal, it will free up our surgery's front rooms. One for a waiting room and the other for private consulting."

"I did give some thought to your ideas last week. I do concede that it might be a good idea to avail ourselves fully of the New Government Hospital. Why yes, it's a splendid idea. I'm sure I could get the Society to agree to that."

Seizing his advantage Sunny plunged on, "Then, we won't need a nursing sister in residence, so those back rooms could be brought into use also."

"I do declare, you have come with a very viable prospect. It will allow us to let Sister Barbarus go without any ugliness or loss of face."

"This will greatly reduce the Benefit Society's nursing costs," Sunny said. He studied Boss Jack in his wheelchair thinking incompetence should never be rewarded. He was bottom heavy, his backside filled the seat and overflowed the metal skirt of the wheelchair. He lifted his gaze to the thin lips and jutting jaw. He wondered at this man's reputation as everyone's much beloved Dutch uncle. He epitomized the mine: hard driving focus on the bottom line. With two world wars and a holocaust behind them now, the mine would have to step in line with the new thinking and recognize all men as human beings, not just cannon fodder.

Boss Jack wheeled forward to meet the desk. His face suddenly flushed and he said, "I tell you what, go ahead now. Make sure you keep the admissions to the New Government Hospital to a minimum. I'll handle the Society and see Sister Barbarus gets her pension and time to find new accommodation, that sort of thing."

"I'm grateful to you," said Sunny. He bowed slightly. He had won so unexpectedly, it was almost an anticlimax. So the Company could at least be counted on to take care of their own Europeans. Sister Barbarus would probably be as relieved as he was to part ways on such amenable terms. He felt no malice towards her.

Perhaps, after all, Mavourneen could get a nanny like everyone else, as Leah Levine had suggested, to free her up to come over now and then to assist, just to keep her hand in with the difficult cases. It had been such a joy to have her at his side again. There was so much else he wanted to push for, but taking a breath he checked himself.

The mine's heartbeat came through Boss Jack's small window loud and clear: the thunderous galloping sound of the thousand pound stamps relentlessly crushing the ore twenty-four hours a day, seven days a week. He looked out over the long red roof of the machine shop, the headgear towering above the top of the hill and the huge and growing anemic flat topped mine dumps. A slight breeze picked up their fine tailings, which carried in wisps above the Native compound. How much was cyanide, amongst other poisons from the processing plant, a factor in their health? And next to it was the receptor pit of neutralized acid seeping bright orange into the ground water. Here was an opportunity to study these things first hand and set a new standard for the industry in time. But this had all been in place for half a century. He'd only been here a little over a week and Boss Jack's concession was victory enough for one day.

There was a pause while Boss Jack swiveled his chair back and forth. "There's one more thing, though. We can't have your wife working there with you."

So he wasn't going to get around the standard thinking of the doctor's wife as an adornment and hostess. It was a pity. Mavourneen did have so much to offer the profession. He wanted her at his side, at the theatre, but her primary obligation now was to his young and growing family. No, this was not a battle to wage now. "Absolutely, it was an emergency measure. She's got her hands full at home. We have no intention of her working with another addition to the family on the way."

"Very good. We'll get on the grapevine for a temporary sister to fill in meanwhile."

Mavourneen was helping Johnny Hardy into a waiting hearse as Sunny swung into the driveway and parked in the lean-to garage between the surgery and the house. With Hardy settled in the passenger seat she shut the door firmly after him. With a reminder to him and his driver to phone if they were at all worried about anything, she gave them a friendly wave.

The papery pink peppercorns crunched underfoot as Sunny joined her and they watched the hearse recede down Jacaranda Avenue. Then they turned towards the house, arm in arm. "Victory!" he said, as he held the house gate open for her. "We've earned our lunch."

In the sitting room, Douglas was cuddled up to Bundu on the carpet, fast asleep and so they tiptoed into the dining room.

He pulled her chair out for her and once they were both seated, he said, "It's all arranged. Sister Barbarus is retiring. We should drink to it." He clinked his glass of water against hers.

"I'm so glad to hear it," she said. "Perhaps..."

"I'll have a free rein now," he interrupted, "to reorganize things just the way I want them—be my own man."

"Yes," she said, "wasn't it just like old times working together again—even if it was just a dental clearance."

"Don't go getting ideas now, Boss Jack specifically said, as I was leaving, that's out of the question."

"Oh, dear, I so want to be a part of your life," she said.

"Of course you are! What would I do without you? I did think to argue with Boss Jack but he had so completely conceded everything I thought it's a battle for another day. Maybe he's right, your place *is* in the home."

"All the Jewish women work with their husbands in Umzimtuti. I've simply got to get out of the house," she said as she ladled out a generous portion of thick stew from the tureen onto a bed of rice and passed it to him.

"What do you mean? I thought that's what you wanted. A house. A garden," he said as he tucked hungrily into the stew.

"Well," she said, "now that we are settled and Douglas is so well, he's such a grand little chappie—full of beans. I can hardly believe it's real, it's true, but I do need something to keep my brain alive." She picked at the meat on her plate, hardly taking a bite.

"I've so many battles ahead with the management I can't battle with you too. The baby's coming soon. It could be a difficult couple of years. Let's cross our bridges when we come to them."

She put her knife and fork down.

He mopped up the gravy with a hunk of brown bread. "I've got a full roster this afternoon." Her head was bowed but she felt his quick peck on the top of her head before she heard the door slam.

She sat for a long time with the cooling stew and congealing gravy before her. If he really intended to help her resume her career he would have said *it'll be different when I get my own consulting rooms*—but he hadn't. Tears welled up. She'd have to find other ways to live a full life.

Leonard appeared to clear the table. Quickly, she collected herself and followed him into the kitchen. The brightness had gone out of the marmalade. It was sullen with neglect: amber and thick. But too many lemons and too much work had gone into it to waste it. She bottled it anyway. After the jars cooled, as the Aberdeen School of Domestic Science decreed, she would label them. But what to call them? Brandied Marmalade was stacked in the pantry. The family would not know the difference.

CHAPTER NINE

Confronting the Matron

Getting rid of Sister Barbarus and removing the hospital beds from the Cheetah Mine's European Surgery was a great coup for Sunny. His next challenge was the New Government Hospital. Here too, Gidney Palmer had a reputation and a loyal following but, again, he had hardly used the hospital's potential. Sunny scanned through the past history of the surgical roster and realized that Palmer's prowess amounted almost exclusively to the uterine curette. No wonder he was headed for a career in gynecology.

Old Doc Maxwell, the silver haired gentlemanly GMO, was surgically incompetent and only too happy to refer patients. Dr. Eckhart, the ruddy-faced Anglicized Afrikaner, who reportedly had suffered every disease in the book himself—except pregnancy—had a special interest in leprosy. Sunny could see the theatre was ostensibly all his, just as Palmer promised. A review of the surgical instruments on hand came up short. He made a list of his needs and went directly to knock on Matron Griffin's open office door.

"Yes," she said.

The matron was a woman in middle age, slightly overweight, not unattractive, with intelligent brown eyes and pretty, tight curls mostly hidden under her well-secured veil. She said, "Dr. Rubenstein. Please close the door," and motioned to the chair in front of her desk. She removed her spectacles and put the document she had been reading in her drawer.

Sunny took the chair and bowed his head slightly, smiling. He took in the Matron's bright gaze. "Good morning Matron. May I come right to the point?"

"Of course."

"I believe there are some deficiencies in the equipment we have here. I've taken the liberty of drawing up a list."

The matron lifted one eyebrow and said, "Indeed?"

She put the list on her leather framed blotter on the bare desk and resumed her spectacles.

Sunny looked about the room. There was a photograph of her graduation class on the wall, and professional certificates. A watercolor of an English country house was the only decoration on the sidewall. On the other side, a window looked out through the convalescent verandah with its row of solid wooden Morris chairs to the scrubby savannah woodland beyond in its dusty yellows and browns. Two stuffed chairs and a small coffee table were arranged in front of the window.

She compressed her lips as she read down the list. She took off her spectacles and leaned back in her chair and cleared her throat. "Why do you want all this equipment? Dr. Palmer never indicated any such need."

"I'm going to do much more surgery than Dr. Palmer. I can only do it with a fully equipped theatre. We need to be fully prepared to cope with surgical eventualities."

"The theatre sisters will not be comfortable with your undertaking procedures that haven't been performed here," she said, her eyes narrowing.

"The sisters will be working under my instruction. It's not their decision to make."

"There's the question of anesthetics in cases at risk. Are you aware that Dr. Maxwell is only prepared to use chloroform or ethyl chloride spray and ether on an open gauze mask? Dr. Eckhart is not available. He always refers out."

"I'm only prepared to refer out in very select cases. Distances are great. Time is often of the essence. We are almost at the halfway mark of the twentieth century. This is the *New* Government Hospital, isn't it? We need to get up to date and put in for a Boyles anesthetic apparatus."

"We've got one," she said sharply. "I've put it in the storeroom, out of the way, since there's no one who knows how to use it." She put her elbows on the desk and rested her chin on her knuckles.

"I've just come from the Voortrekkerhoogte Military Hospital, I've worked directly with Jan Schulenburg—with the newest apparatus and latest techniques and physiological monitoring."

"Jan Schulenburg! I worked under him myself in my younger day—when I first came out to South Africa." She put her forearms on the chair, leaned back and smiled.

He held her eye and grinned. "Yes, I was fortunate to assist him.

Give me two competent sisters and I'll train them myself."

"Indeed. I'll give you Sister Elsie Fegan, married, she's good—but more than a fan of Palmers, one of his diversions you might say. You know I don't approve. Don't be fooled. She's an Afrikaner actually. Puts on airs. Her husband is an English police lieutenant with an Oxford accent—probably bogus too. But, no doubt you'll win her over. And Sister Alison Hoskins, fresh out from Home, young, and rather highly strung, but keen and conscientious."

"Alison Hoskins—highly-strung? Perhaps not the best choice, then. I need level heads in the event of a crisis. You know how quickly it can develop in theatre and obstetrics, in particular."

"They're the best we've got."

"Fair enough," he conceded, "I'll train them up." Suddenly he recollected Mrs. Doolittle's warning about gossip. A surgical failure would not be tolerated and he had just upped the stakes considerably. But he plowed on, "One other thing, I'd like to rig up a simple apparatus for inducing an artificial pneumothorax, if you haven't already got one. I have a tubercular patient in need of it."

The nursing pin at her throat lifted as she took a deep breath and her ample chest heaved before she exhaled audibly, "It would be easier to send him to a sanatorium."

"Separate him from his family for years? My preference is to keep him at home—he's getting all the fresh air he needs out on his farm. Only one lung is affected. He's a good chance of recovery, if we let it rest."

"Have it your way. I'll see what I can find for you," she said, as she adjusted the starched cuffs of her sleeves carefully, put the spectacles back on her nose and looked down at the list.

"I'm sorry," said Sunny to Mavourneen, "that I'm too late, again, to throw Douglas around." He bent down and gave Bundu a good rub behind the ears and pat on the back.

"Douglas does miss you," she said. "I've let Leonard go for the night. But the cottage pie's had a chance to get a nice crust on top in the warming drawer."

He gave her a peck on the cheek and put his arm around her as he pushed Bundu gently aside from under his feet and they made their way to the dining room. She doled out a generous portion of hot cottage pie from a Pyrex dish.

Tucking in, he said, "Would you believe it—the latest Boyles apparatus was mothballed! Matron's agreed to give it an airing and has given me two sisters to train. Not a bad day, hey?"

"Well done," she said putting her fork down and reaching out to caress his arm. "I know you're going to make a go of it here. I just *so* wish I could be a part of it all."

"You are, you are. You're doing a wonderful job with Douglas now that everything's sorted out—that's your job."

"It's not a job! It's work—for life," she said, retracting her hand and picking up her knife and fork again.

"Whatever you want to call it—it's the most wonderful and rewarding journey in the world."

"A journey's got a beginning and an end. 'Mothering' is without end—no promotions."

"You're queen of the house—on a pedestal—you can't get promoted higher than that."

"All the while my brain is atrophying. I was thinking..."

He cut her short, "Everything I do is for you. Let's each play our roles to the best of our ability. Umzimtuti offers so much opportunity to express ourselves—make a difference. If we can't make it here where are we going to make it? You're already fitting in with the Jewish community. Fancy that!"

"These Jewish women all work with their husbands."

Ignoring her argument, he said, "In the light of the showdown at the surgery, I don't think we should wait for year's end to exercise our option to take over Palmer's practice, do you? In fairness to him, I think I should write and advise him right away."

"If you're sure. You've a lifetime role to play here at home, too. I think you should get a partner, so we can be a family."

A match flared. He lit up a cigarette and it glowed. "I've thought of that. Denny Chapman's the man I have in mind, you know we've been pals since we shared a cadaver in our dissection days."

"His father's rather dictatorial as I recall."

"Nonsense. This is an opportunity of a lifetime—enough for two. His old man's not going to stand in his way. I'll write to both Palmer and Denny tonight. You know, Palmer's left us quite a well stocked bar. I think this calls for a whisky to celebrate."

CHAPTER TEN

A Day's Work

Sunny wasted no time in reorganizing the old surgery. There was, after all, plenty of space in this converted mine house. A proper waiting room, office and consulting complex quickly took shape. He now had two private European examining rooms as well as a plaster and dressing room. Its spaciousness involved much walking back and forth. The exercise was good for him he rationalized. It allowed for dealing with three European patients simultaneously: one disrobing, one dressing and one consulting in privacy, enabling streamlined proper clinical practice of history taking and examination.

He hadn't been successful in integrating the Indians and Coloureds but he had, at least, secured a separate proper examining room for them, although they would still have to wait out of sight on a metal bench on the side verandah.

A qualified nurse, Betty Forbush, a young attractive redhead, replaced Sister Barbarus. Homegrown and newly married to a mine artisan, she was an efficient and versatile nurse and drug dispenser.

The old bookkeeping was rudimentary, with Palmer's wife sending out the accounts. But now Sunny set about establishing a more functional system to allocate payments to the old and new practices and calculate the amount accumulating to offset the goodwill payout to Palmer, as agreed. To avoid contention, clear recording was imperative from the start.

But when would he find time? The days were long, beginning with the wail of the hooter at seven with Sick Parade, then theatre bookings at the Mine Native Hospital where native pathology and surgery were always challenging but, thank heavens, P.Q. was working out well as his anesthetist and theatre assistant. Returning home for a late and hurried breakfast was followed by a round at the New Government Hospital before he sped back to handle the European outpatient surgery. He crossed the driveway and returned home for a quick tickle and throw with Douglas, a pat on the back for Bundu, and a hasty lunch with Mavourneen as they went through the post together. In the afternoons he attended to his growing Native Clinic that gathered in the open air within the rubber hedge at the back of the surgery. Then it was on to evening rounds at both hospitals before house calls on the potholed roads until he found the lights out at the last house. So often he missed reading to Douglas at bedtime, missed the evening meal with Mavourneen. And when he did finally get home, he knew the night would be punctuated by the trill of the phone, followed possibly by night calls. It was a minimum sixteen hour day. Mavourneen was right, the sooner a partner joined him the better.

Sunny riffled through the pile of advertisements that came with the post. Amongst them was a letter from Mavourneen's friend Doris and he handed it to her.

Mavourneen tore it open and read it over mouthfuls of beef stew, "Oh, no," she said, "Doris' getting a divorce."

"I'm so sorry. Our *shadkhin*! She didn't do so well for herself," said Sunny, reaching over with his fork and stabbing at another slice of fresh tomato for himself.

"Yes," said Mavourneen, "we do have her to thank for bringing us back together again—making the match."

"I never did like that rich stockbroker husband of hers. She's better off without him, frankly."

"She's pretty shaky after three miscarriages and his indifference."

"You're not suggesting anything are you?" he said, squashing down a chunk of potato with the back of his fork to soak up the gravy. "We can't possibly have her here. Not now. We're hardly settled in ourselves. Douglas. A new baby coming soon," he said, suddenly aware how her pretty oval face had rounded out in pregnancy.

"I *am* suggesting we invite her. You know she's my very best school chum ever. I want to stand by her in her hour of need. A change of scene would do her the world of good. We've so much space. Four bedrooms—we're only using two."

"You know how much I depend on your support. Your attention." She was spoiling his favorite meal. He helped himself to another spoonful of stew.

"You selfish swine!" She scowled.

This was not the first time she had called him that. He did not want to let her get a rise out of him. He suddenly noticed a little fluid retention which was bloating her lovely slender hands. How could he have overlooked it? He needed to advise her to restrict her salt intake as she picked at the carrots in the thick gravy in the silence that followed, but he realized now was not the time. He said evenly, "We've got a history of your wanting to put your friends before me. I can assure you, once again, that they're not going to stand by you the way I will. Your loyalty is with me—first, last and always. Remember, we only have each other. On top of everything, I'm having a devil of a time with establishing an accounting system. Palmer's wife used to send out all his accounts, but it's much more complicated than that now. How'd you like to tackle it for me?"

"You know," she said, "sums are not my forte."

"You could make an effort, for me. Lighten my load. My days are sixteen hours long as it is."

"I thought you said I was queen of the house, which should fully occupy me," she shot back as Leonard brought in custard cups of gooey frogs eggs.

"Did I tell you, this is not my favorite pudding?" he said, reaching down and putting the custard cup under Bundu's nose. As he straightened up, and lit a cigarette instead, it dawned on him. "Wait a minute. Doris is a fine bookkeeper. I've got plenty to take her mind off her loss. You're right. We do have lots of space," he said, "I'll wire her this afternoon to catch the next train up." Bundu's enthusiastic slurps emanated from under the table as Sunny inhaled warm smoke deeply.

"I knew your better half would win through," she said, giving his arm a squeeze.

He blushed to his surprise.

CHAPTER ELEVEN

Temps

Sunny acquired the Railway contract. Umzimtuti was the midway switching station between Salisbury and Bulawayo and one day it could be big. He negotiated contracts with a few small profitable gold mining operations in the outlying Umzimtuti area in anticipation of Denny's arrival. He could not come soon enough.

He came home late, his corned beef all curled up in the warming draw, the mashed potatoes dry. Mavourneen got out of bed to join him in her dressing gown at the dining room table and cut him a big juicy red tomato to make up for it. She said, "I've had a brainwave. While we are waiting on a response from Denny why don't you hire those Uziel twins—Esther and Sarah, you know they are champing at the bit waiting for their acceptance to Great Ormond Street Hospital."

"Yes, I've talked to them, they seem as knowledgeable as they are darkly attractive. No doubt they're top of their class to be applying to Ormond Street. Still, I don't think the European community would accept them."

"Why ever not?"

"Well, a combination of things. One—young, fresh out of school. Two—Jewish, Sephardic at that. Three—perceived as fashion models rather than medical practitioners. So their use is limited."

"What about the backyard Native Clinic? Aren't you going to open up two new examining rooms for them now that Sister Barbarus has moved out?"

"No," he said. "I've pushed Boss Jack as far as I can—for now anyway. The surgery is in the European residential area. It's against the law. But good idea, passing on the outdoor clinic to the twins could certainly be a time-consuming burden off my shoulders and great medical experience for them."

Only a smattering of essential words for physical exams made up Sunny's *Fanagalo* vocabulary. The Native needed to learn English if he wanted to get ahead. "Cookie," he said, slipping into simple speech.

"You good with English, Shona, Ndebele, other ones. You went to school?"

"*Inkósi,* two years school on Mission."

"You in-charge. You get promotion."

"Promotion?"

"Yes. Two new young *Inkósikazi* doctors, Dr. Sarah and Dr. Esther, coming for work at Native Clinic. White uniform for you. Starch shirt and shorts—puttees and boots. Smart! I want you work here long, long time. I give raise."

"Raise?" asked Cookie quizzically as he pulled on both ends of the tourniquet dangling from around his neck.

"Yes. Raise. How much money you get paid every month?"

"Two pounds ten shillings. Five pound mealie-meal and sugar, two pound 'boys' meat a week."

"Now, I put one pound a month into Post Office savings account for you. We sign for pension."

"Pension?"

"When you *madala* this money look after you."

"Six children, from my number one wife. Four children my number two wife. Enough for *madala.*"

"Maybe. Maybe not. Maybe you sick. Maybe, need medicine. You put more in Post Office Savings Book I put same again."

"Same again?"

"If you put one shilling, I put one shilling also. If you put ten shillings more, I put ten shilling more." Sunny could see the distress on Cookie's lined face and wearied of the conversation, he said, "We talk again."

Finally, there was the much awaited letter from Denny. Sunny tore it open. "Mavourneen, you were right! Denny's obediently going to join his father's obstetrics and gynecology practice in Vereeniging. I'll say, this is a bitter disappointment."

"Everything happens for the best," consoled Mavourneen.

"He's taken the liberty of referring my offer to a Cecil Wolseley. Let me read it to you," he said.

"*He seems interested, and I get the impression he feels your offer of partnership sound and fair. I don't know him well, but he's very presentable. He reached the rank of major, trained in England, served in India, and may well meet your need. I expect him to be in touch with you soon.*"

Sunny rocked back on his dining room chair. "Well, I suppose I can't blame Denny, his father's practice is lucrative. Still, I have to admit this is a blow. We were such good pals."

"Have another helping of prunes and custard," soothed Mavourneen looking down at the bowl. "They so remind me of kidney dishes full of tonsils and pus. My, you were fast with their dissection and snare. You know Denny's main interest is in OB/GYN. Someone with a more general interest is going to turn up."

He ignored her, riffling on through the pile of post, mostly advertisements. Ah! He almost missed it. A letter from Palmer. The line: *I am prepared to offer to extend the locum for another year*...jumped out at him. He could not believe his eyes. "That blighter Palmer," he said, bending back the fold in the letter and smoothing it out, "is ignoring the agreement of *my* right to exercise *my* option of permanency. Just as well he asked me to have the agreement drawn up in Johannesburg. I'll write him back and remind him of it by return post."

CHAPTER TWELVE

First Successes

The Uziel twins were eager for work and started right away with Cookie, all decked out in his new white uniform, interpreting back and forth for both young doctors.

Only a few days passed before the twins approached Sunny. "You are charging *far* too much for a consultation. After all, there are no facilities out there in the back yard, examining the patients in the open. No privacy. No dignity," said Sarah.

"I'm only continuing to provide a service. There seems to be a need."

The twins were identical: foreheads broadened with their thick black hair brushed back, twisted and piled on top of their heads somehow. Sallow oval faces were dominated by long noses and luscious lip gloss lips. Always beautifully dressed, their shapely figures were concealed by the white coats they donned on the job. They wore their stethoscopes in lieu of jewelry around their necks. "One and sixpence for a consultation and half a crown if they get an injection. It's wicked!" said Esther, her black eyes flashing defiantly.

Now, that's youth and naivety for you, thought Sunny. He knew the twins from a young age had run the business end of their family haberdashery, before Mr. Uziel mastered English. He said, "The fee structure was set down by Palmer. I haven't given it any thought at all myself."

"We must reduce the consultation fees for them," pressed Esther.

"What do you suggest?"

"One shilling for a consultation, one and sixpence with an injection," said Sarah.

"They can always go to the GMO for free you know."

"Even the Natives know he's no good."

"Go ahead and charge whatever you think is fair."

"And..." went on Esther, "you know they should have the dignity of a private consultation, an examining room."

"I've asked to open up the back rooms to Natives like I've done quietly on the side for the Coloureds and Indians. It was turned down. In fact the mine management is against encouraging medical services for the Natives beyond the mine employees. This is a voluntary service I'm providing to meet the Native demand, against company policy. I'm not dependent on it for a living."

"Open up the back rooms," they pressed in unison.

"Do you want to get me fired? I agree, entirely, it's not right."

"We can't do our job properly," said Sarah.

"You know it's...wicked," said Esther.

"Tell you what, let's go ahead then, take a chance—on the quiet. Make sure Cookie keeps the waiting patients on the tree trunks, well back from the building. Make sure there is no loitering. I'll get my wife to supervise our gardenboy to thicken up the rubber hedge. In time, it will screen the backyard from the parkland beyond completely from public view."

It did not take much to seal off the back door clinic from the European and Non-European waiting and consulting rooms in front. There were beds and linen to spare, now that in-patients had been moved to the New Government Hospital. When Cookie was not translating, he was washing, ironing and sterilizing implements and trays. He could be relied upon, always cheerful and obliging. Sunny was heartened by patient response at the reorganized European mine surgery.

About to shut up shop on Friday afternoon, into the surgery came Mrs. Buchanan, the town's mayoress, with her pretty teenage daughter, Claire. "Doctor," said Mrs. Buchanan, "we need something, for my precious Claire. Gastroenteritis."

"Let's take a look," said Sunny, leading the way. "What's the trouble?"

"Dr. Palmer, he's always prescribed..."

"I am sure he had just the thing, but let's not jump to conclusions. Could be different this time."

"Doctor," said Mrs. Buchanan, "the pain is too much."

"Let's have Claire answer for herself." She was young, not yet sixteen, pretty, the picture of innocence, but could it be an ectopic pregnancy? He'd been bullied as a houseman by a rich overbearing mother, just like this one, into skipping a full examination—once. What an embarrassment it had been, being pulled up and rightfully discredited by the attending—never again."

"Well," said Claire, on the brink of tears, "Mama's right."

"What else?"

"I feel sick."

"Doctor, she's been vomiting. All the time. There's nothing left. She's not eating."

"It's very painful before I throw up," Claire said, "here, on the right side but I think it's settling…"

"How long has this been going on?"

"All day yesterday, all night. All day today. Still."

"Well," said Sunny, "let's take a look. I'll take some blood. Give me a urine specimen and stool too, if you can. There are jars in the bathroom. Then, I'll take a look, while Sister here helps you with this gown."

"Is that necessary, Doctor? We need a script, before the Chemist closes," said Mrs. Buchanan, looking at her watch.

"Yes, it's necessary," said Sunny. "Sick for thirty-six hours, coming in late on Friday afternoon, you can wait five minutes for a diagnosis, so we know what we're dealing with," he said tersely. He unwrapped the white cloth from around the stainless steel kidney dish, attached the needle to the glass syringe, quickly pumped up a vein and drew blood. He placed a drop on a glass slide and spread it neatly across with the edge of another, one cell thick.

While she changed, he fixed the slide and stained it. The white cell count was elevated. The differential revealed a neutrophilia with a marked shift to the left: a neutrophilia, too, in the urine. He was glad he had invested in the Zeiss.

He did a thorough physical. She winced as she coughed, he popped a thermometer into her mouth—a fever. He proceeded with auscultation: clipping his stethoscope to his ears he listened to her heart, her lungs and her bowel sounds.

Mindful of her sensitivity, he began palpation beginning at the belly button, noted the severe rebound tenderness on the lower right as well as the guarding reaction. Ah! The telltale Rovsing's sign: pain in the right iliac fossa on palpation of the left side of the abdomen.

Next he turned his attention to her hips: Rosenstein's and psoas signs positive. The obturator test positive too. "I'm afraid," he said, ushering in her mother, "there's no doubt in my mind, Claire has an acute pelvic appendicitis. We must proceed with surgery right away. I'll call the hospital now and alert them to your arrival. I'll be along shortly."

"Can't it wait?"

"No, not at all. Delay could spell all sorts of complications if it ruptures—peritonitis and sepsis."

"What do you mean?"

"Inflammation of the thin tissue lining the inner wall of the abdomen and infection. If we act quickly, we won't have any complications."

"But the gastroenteritis!"

"Not this time."

"I'll have to call my husband, he's the mayor of Umzimtuti you know."

"By all means call him from the hospital, while Claire is being prepped."

Matron Griffin had made Sister Alison Hoskins available to him as promised. She was tall and ungainly with a short upper lip exposing her gums and long teeth when she smiled. She tucked her large ears and mousy brown hair into her theatre cap before they scrubbed and gowned.

Her hands were large but surprisingly deft as she bent over the theatre table. She was good, not nearly as intuitive as Mavourneen, but attentive. The surgery went well. The appendix was acutely inflamed and distended. As he tied it off, cut and popped it in a jar of formalin, she exclaimed, "Just as well we did not delay!"

He was pleased she had adopted a sense of ownership. That was what teamwork was all about. They were off to a good start. She wheeled the patient out into the recovery room as he reassured the anxious parents.

Claire was up and discharged after the third day! The news spread. She was a wonder-girl.

On the weekend, Sunny drove out to check on Mr. Karel Ferreira. He was bedridden with pulmonary tuberculosis, which Palmer and a consultant physician had failed to arrest. A major landowner and the doyen of the Afrikaner community he had a lovely young second wife, Maudie, he had found in London. Sunny drove up to the crest of the kopje to the farmhouse that had a commanding view of the veld and parked beside his fancy Lincoln Continental.

"I wonder," said Sunny, as he listened to his chest, "there's nothing in your chart, but did Mr. Palmer ever mention the idea of inducing a pneumothorax?"

"A *what* Doc? No never! *Ja nee!* I'd have remembered if he'd mentioned anything like that."

"Well, it's simple. What I'll do is put air into the pleural space to collapse the bad lung."

"Collapse the lung! Doc, don't you see I'm having enough trouble breathing as it is?"

"The infected lobes collapse preferentially, so we can give them a rest to allow healing. The normal areas will stay inflated. You'll be coughing less, less blood too, so you'll be less infectious."

"This a new fangled idea? I don't want to be no experiment, man."

"No, it's not new at all. Dates back to the last century."

"Doc, you'se a barber surgeon then, man?"

"No, it's standard practice in T.B. sanatoriums."

"Doc, *yirra jong*! You, you, know, I mean, you'se young, man."

"Not really. I've just come from Voortrekkerhoogte Military Hospital. Five and a half years in the war, I've seen a lot."

"That so!"

"Yes, we can beat T.B. Don't you want to get up? Have some fun with Maudie?"

"You know I do, Doc, more than anything."

"Well then. I can arrange it."

"Doc, can't we beat it with some *muti*?"

"No, you know as well as I do there's no cure. Maybe one day—if you hang around long enough. There's no apparatus here, but I'll rig one up just for you, so we can accurately monitor the amount of air pressure."

"Rig something up! Doc, I dunno, man."

"Trust me. The matron wouldn't let me do anything experimental."

"Okay. I'm trusting you with my life, Doc, man."

CHAPTER THIRTEEN

Settling in the Turkeys

Mavourneen instructed Sugar, the young gardenboy, to prepare a *hok* at the bottom of the garden for the promised turkeys. He made an airy enclosure on the sloping ground with new chicken wire from Feldman's hardware. At the bottom end he built a roof with scraps of corrugated iron from a stack behind the garage. He laid a mat of elephant grass cut from the field beyond the rubber hedge and mine shunting track. They were ready for the turkeys.

They were handsome birds indeed. Mavourneen decided to name them Abu and Hassan. She and Mrs. Rivkah Feldman climbed into the fowl run to settle them. Hassan strutted around for some time before sitting on the grass mat with much aplomb. Suddenly, he took off with great clumsy wing beats. After a short flight he ran on his long capable legs, striding past Douglas on his tricycle, on the open path of the shaded garden. The gate was open. But Hassan chose the shelter of a squat date palm. Round and round Mavourneen and Mrs. Feldman circled but the low arched fronds with razor edges foiled them. Hassan kept close to the trunk. Sugar squatted on his haunches and reached. On the other side Mavourneen sat on her bottom, legs spread, arms outstretched, as she clucked encouragements to Hassan.

Mrs. Feldman hesitated, exclaiming repeatedly, "Oh, my goodness."

Hassan taunted them, inflating the air sacs in his bright red wattle lurking just out of reach. "Isn't he magnificent," said Mavourneen.

"Mrs. Rubenstein, remember, your condition," admonished Rivkah. "You all hot and dirty."

Mavourneen mopped the sweat from her brow. "Oh," she said, "a little sweat never hurt anyone. Don't you admire his spirit?"

"You so undignified—the servant!"

"Hassan's fighting to preserve his independence," said Mavourneen. "Don't we girls all know it, once we lose it, it's not easily regained."

Mrs. Feldman shook her head as Mavourneen and Sugar coaxed and prodded in vain. Finally, Mavourneen allowed Mrs. Feldman to help her up, and said, "His wings are not clipped. Even Sugar can't catch him. I think it makes more sense to turn the coop into a vegetable patch and give Hassan the run of the garden, what do you say?" Sugar grinned broadly. Mavourneen sensed he agreed that it was obviously easier to cage the pumpkins than the poultry.

"Oh no," said Mrs. Feldman, sadly. "What will happen my sister Avigail's gladioli? Remember, show quality from England." She helped Mavourneen up.

"I reckon," Mavourneen said, as she brushed her hair back and smoothed her skirt down, "they'll do fine. Abu and Hassan will fertilize, regularly. I say we've earned a good cup of tea."

As they relaxed on the verandah Mrs. Feldman laughed out loud telling Mavourneen, as they tucked into queen cakes and washed them down with copious cups of tea, that it was a long time since she had had so much fun.

Mavourneen walked her to her car. Just as she was about to drive off, Rivkah stuck her head out of the window and said, "Do call me Rivkah."

"Likewise, Mavourneen," said Mavourneen.

Rivkah, pressed on the pedal and the car shot off as she waved.

It wasn't until then that Mavourneen turned her attention to Douglas. There were still two queen cakes left on the plate for him.

It was a big garden, full of nooks and crannies and shaded hidey-holes. He loved to tuck himself under a clump of blue plumbago or tumble of canary creeper or hide behind the Wendy house. But call as she might he did not come out. Mavourneen was hot and tired and a bit irritable, exacerbated by the heaviness of the baby she carried, which gave way to annoyance. She was delighted that Douglas was growing stronger with every single day of exploration in this new world, but enough was enough.

Sunny came home as the afternoon wail of the mine hooter signaled the change of shift. He had had a hard Saturday, consisting of morning mundane ailments at the surgery followed by a frustrating afternoon of calls. Mrs. van Tonder had capped the day hysterically wrestling with her wedding ring embedded over a lifetime in a well-padded fourth finger. Was medicine in Umzimtuti reduced to marriage counseling and, when that failed, tin snips from the garage after a massage with slippery soap failed to budge the marriage band?

"It's been rather a busy afternoon," Mavourneen greeted him. "The gate at the bottom of the garden was left open and it looks as though Douglas has gone exploring. He can't have gone far. But we better get Sugar and Leonard and all fan out to find him."

"What on earth were you doing that he's gone unnoticed for a *whole* afternoon?"

CHAPTER FOURTEEN

An Incident at the Bar

Sunny, Mavourneen and the servants circled the garden calling Douglas, but there was no response. The gate at the bottom of the garden was indeed unlatched and hung open. The road curved gently to meet Second Avenue, and from there it was steeply downhill all the way to the dead end at the Railway Station. Beyond stretched the bundu. Sunny, Mavourneen and the servants fanned out to find him.

It was only a short mile on a brakeless blue tricycle on the dirt road. The town was deserted, as usual, on a sleepy Saturday afternoon. Douglas gravitated, like everyone else, to life at Umzimtuti Hotel. He sucked his thumb and, with his feet on the pedals, rocked back and forth on the smooth red verandah, taking in the men sitting in white wicker chairs at tables set behind the tall white colonial colonnades that held up the hotel and the bar within.

Since the war, things had changed. Returning ex-servicemen wanted to take advantage of the new entitlement scheme and get their own farms. Ex-RAF pilots who had trained here remembered the bird's eye view of virgin land wide open with possibilities. Englishmen generally, as they took stock of their country, and the years of austerity that loomed ahead, saw this backwater of Empire in a new light, not as an adventure, but a permanent place to raise a family.

The barefoot Black waiters, wearing white cotton pants and tunics, red fezzes and cummerbunds, stood to attention along the wall of the verandah, trays in hand to serve the White patrons *Lion* and *Castle* lager held down with handfuls of salted peanuts. Fans turned lazily below the pressed white ceiling of the darkened bar inside. There was a tight collection of bullet holes just below the ceiling, testimony to Umzimtuti's wild pioneer days.

These newcomers joined an assortment of the town's pioneer citizenry: regulars, outside the Cheetah Mine, who fraternized the bar. In a segregated society, they segregated themselves: British settlers sat apart from Afrikaners; hopeful prospectors with claims to exaggerate and disappointments to forget; small-workers who kept their stamp mills running twenty-four hours a day, seven days a week, while living on borrowed funds year after year. The tobacco, maize and cotton farmers came in on Saturdays, too. They were dictated by the relentless repetition of the two seasons, rain and waiting for the rain. It was always too much or too little, too soon or too late. The cattle ranchers, ever vigilant for plagues, rustlers, poachers and veld fires, were regarded by tobacco farmers as loafers who mostly relied on their herdboys. It was a gamble in or on the land. Affectionately recalled by the patrons were the absent losers. Some had gone broke or died young from alcoholism, malaria or silicosis; some had gone down South to anonymous, menial jobs, where coming down in the world would not be so hard to bear. The few government officials held aloof from the shopkeepers, who were governed by opening and closing, stocking and restocking, balancing accounts payable and accounts receivable. They knew who had good credit and who did not.

A motley lot, they all quenched themselves in a usually thirsty land, alcohol relaxing their tongues, dulling their aches and disappointments, buoying their hopes and dreams.

Jud Levine, serving from behind the bar, saw and listened to them all. He had slipped in from the island of Rhodes as a teenager, just before immigration got tight in 1920. He had achieved his dream, finally, with the purchase of the hotel just the year before, after years in isolation in a long string of trading store mining concessions. Married late, he was content with pretty Leah, a South African, and their two lovely children. He could hold his own in business and communal affairs. A councilman, he aspired to be mayor, if he could work out a way to unseat entrenched Angus Buchanan. Jud was friendly, but aggressive when crossed.

"So, The King and Queen are coming—Princesses too, next year, to stay in the bundu," boomed O'Connor, the editor and owner of the *Cleft Stick*, to the Town Clerk, Cameron Gordon Murray Paxton, who'd just walked in. "Who's going to get the contract to build the house—the retreat—for them out at Sycamore Bend? Aye, that's what the town would like to know."

"Anyone is welcome to put in a tender," declared Cameron Gordon Murray Paxton loudly, looking around, "it's closing soon. It's going to be big. It'll take priority on materials over the *pise de terre* temporary housing project. Lucky the firm that gets it. It's got to be a showpiece."

"My son Gerhardus has put in a tender. Man, he built the tobacco barn at van Wyk's place," said Verdoon to de la Rey. "He could use the money, hey."

"Fat chance, you know how they are. It's going to go to someone British," replied de la Rey.

"I bet it's going to go to Angus Buchanan's brother-in-law, Broderick Anderson. You know how that goes."

"*Yissis*, down on his luck, Broderick was, before the *pisé* housing project came along. Night shooting crocs for their skins on the Umzimtuti River to make ends meet," said de la Rey admiringly.

"*Ja!* Even dragging his wife and little daughters along with him. A tarpaulin on the ground and one between two mopane trees for shelter down by the river. What a picnic, hey," Verdoon sneered.

"All the same, he was making quite a packet—one quid per inch belly width—ladies handbags and shoes are all the rage, man. Besides, he was doing us a favor, getting rid of all that vermin," replied de la Rey.

Douglas was drinking them all in on the threshold of the verandah, with his large solemn eyes. He hopped off his tricycle and walked around the tables, looking at them all in turn while he sucked his thumb. O'Connor got him a cold bottle of *Sparletta* with a drinking straw. Bundu arrived at his side, wagging his tail, his tongue hanging out. Douglas emptied an ashtray and shared the first *Sparletta* of his life with him. Bundu lapped it up.

In walked Karel Ferreira, leaving his pre-war Lincoln Continental, with its long rounded bonnet and lots of chrome, parked at an angle right out front where everyone could see it. Nobody, it seemed, had seen him or the car for a year or two, maybe more. "Karel man! What you doing here? *Yirra jong!* We thought you were a gonner man," said de la Rey.

"Drinks on me," Ferreira said to Jud Levine behind the bar. "I tell you. That new doctor in town. He cured me!"

"Cured you? That little Jew doctor? I thought you had consumption?" said Verdoon, slapping him on the shoulder.

"Well, I do, but the Doc, he needled my bad lung. Collapsed it, man! It's resting. No cough. I'm getting around the farm. Bit slow, mind you, but every week he 'tops me up'. I'm nearly good as new, man—ask

Maudie."

"We wondered hey, he doesn't look like he can fill Dr. Palmer's shoes," laughed Verdoon.

"Well, you can laugh, I'm telling you, man. He's learned at Voortrekkerhoogte, not some fancy English outfit where they know nothing about our sicknesses."

"T.B.'s everywhere, hey. The whole wide world. Not just here," said de la Rey.

"*Ja nee*, I been to London, but what do I know about the rest of the world, man? I tell you this man's not afraid to try and improve your life. Take a chance."

"London, why waste your time with the *Engelse*? Have you forgotten what they did to *ons volk* in the camps?" said de la Rey.

"Sounds dangerous," said Verdoon, "needling the lung."

"You know what, it's not new," went on Ferreira. "Palmer was behind the times, *ek sê*. All that time I lay in bed, coughing blood, I could have had this—getting around, instead of missing out on life. Lucky for me he left."

"Maybe this Jewboy is letting you spread all your germs around so we can all get sick and he can make a quid or two!" said Verdoon.

"*Miskien*," said de la Rey, uncomfortably.

Five foot two but strong, Jud Levine had his back to the bar but could see Verdoon and de la Rey reflected in the big mahogany framed mirror. He turned around with beer glasses in hand and faced them. "We Jews get ahead because we work for it. I demand you apologize!" He put the glasses down carefully.

"Six million down, but you still want to take over the world. We better watch our farms," said Verdoon, turning to de la Rey.

"This is private property. Get out!" The conversation in the bar was dying down.

"*Yissis*, can't you take a joke, man?" said de la Rey uneasily, looking at Levine.

Levine leapt over the bar. Sharp punches to their beer paunches brought both big men's chins within reach. Uppercuts saw each man stretched out horizontal. It all happened so fast.

The patrons were incredulous. The frontier days were not over yet.

"I'll drive you to hospital so the good Jewish doctor can sew you up, or perhaps you prefer to bleed?" panted Levine, glancing down at his bloody knuckles.

The men were still milling around the verandah, watching the car recede, when Sunny rounded the corner. He saw the tricycle on the verandah. What had happened to Douglas?

"Daddy, Daddy!" he heard, triumphant and clear before he saw him and Bundu. Fear turned to fury. He grabbed Douglas' outstretched arms, bent him over his hip and smacked his bottom.

A stout florid man, with an Irish brogue, broke the sudden silence that Sunny realized surrounded him. "Ye be the new doc ain't you? Gidney Palmer's stand-in? Fine man. Aye, a fine man. I'm O'Connor editor of *The Cleft Stick*."

Douglas had not uttered a sound. Sunny dropped him from his hip. Bundu licked Douglas' face and Sunny lifted him up and hugged him.

"Doc, they'll be needing you at the hospital I believe," called out Ferreira. "Stitches and a broken hand, if I'm not mistaken."

"Mr. Ferreira! Nice to see you. What's this about?" asked Sunny as the crowd made space for him and Ferreira.

"It's nothing Doc," said Ferreira loudly. "I got to thank you again, I'm feeling so good. Just a few blokes letting off steam. I wouldn't worry about it, man. See you Tuesday for my 'top up.'" He smiled, picked up the tricycle and stepped off the verandah.

Sunny looked around at the men, bowed slightly before he bundled Douglas and the dog into the front seat of his army Ford, while Ferreira slung the tricycle into the boot. Sunny inclined his head to Ferreira and got into the car. He knew he'd made a fool of himself. In all the years of frustration and desperation with Douglas' illness he'd never raised his hand, nor had Mavourneen. He was very grateful to Ferreira. He was glad he had helped a good man. In the rear view mirror he could see he still stood in the road with an upraised hand.

Sunny soon dealt with Verdoon and de la Rey's superficial injuries and gave each a script for painkillers. He had no idea what the fracas was about. Doctors normally didn't enquire.

Then he walked to the fracture room where Levine was waiting. Carefully positioning the hand in the splint and wrapping the wet plaster of Paris bandage, he said, "Must have been quite a scrap. I hope it was worth it."

"An anti-Semitic remark. I won't tolerate it. If we learned anything from the war, it has to be to stand up for ourselves. We owe it to all those we lost."

"True, but don't stoop to their level. You're above them: proprietor of the hotel. You've made it, man. And look at them—they're down and out eking out a living on their marginal farms."

"Doc," he said, "I cannot allow myself to be a coward. We Jews have to change our tune—not lie down and take everything that's dished out to us. I'm not holding your marrying out of faith against you. In fact, Leah's taken quite a shine to your Mavourneen. We're counting on you, as one of us."

"Yes, I know, I appreciate your support and Mavourneen does even more. I'll be happy to make a minyan—not that I'm religious, mind you. But Mavourneen and I agreed to respect each other's faith."

"Doc, you should get her to convert. She's grand by all accounts, but your boy, well, he can't have a bar mitzvah if she doesn't."

"He'll choose for himself."

"You have to show him the way. That's what parenting is all about."

"Freedom of choice. That's what we believe in."

"Doc, it's a huge mistake. He won't know where he fits in."

"I think we're fitting in fine."

"Doc, you know I've got plans beyond the hotel. I want to get rid of that six term mayor of ours Buchanan—all the nepotism over tenders—they were just talking about it at the bar tonight. How'd you like to support me?"

"Emergency surgery on their daughter went well. I've got them eating out of my hand. What do you want from him? Aren't you on council already?"

"He's running the show just by himself. The council's a sham."

"I don't know what I can do for you. I'm advertising for a partner. Then I'll have time to think about other things. My little boy is in the car—and the dog. I've got to get home." He'd fixed Jud's hand up but he seemed oddly insistent that he owed him something. He turned his thinking to the fool he'd made of himself at the bar. Mavourneen had let him down over Douglas. He'd have to sort his mind out on the trip home.

CHAPTER FIFTEEN

Going Underground

The rhythm of the mine had quickly become a part of Sunny's everyday life, like the beating of his heart taken for granted, familiar and comfortable. Twenty-four hours a day, seven days a week, the U shaped cocopans whirred on the cable as their shadows passed over the contours of the garden, taking ore from the lower shaft to the mill that clacked away; the power plant hummed; the ordered rise and fall of the stamp batteries never ceased; and the wail of the hooter signaled changing shifts to the minute. There was an acceptance of the status quo and the risks and consequences of mining.

The family had moved their beds out onto the screened East verandah soon after their arrival to enjoy the early morning summer sunrise, the fresh air and chatter of the birds. Routinely, Sunny ran through his muscle control exercises: flexed his triceps, popped his biceps and played his hamstrings opposite his quads followed by squats, sit-ups and knee bends. Then he rang the bell for tea, tied up the mosquito nets and handed the tray Leonard had set to Mavourneen in bed. While he dressed she poured Douglas and Bundu their weak tea then handed Sunny a strong cup to start the day off right before he hurried over to Sick Parade.

He parked in front of the whitewashed stones lining the driveway to the Native Hospital and walked briskly over to the line of mineboys waiting beside the clump of gum trees that did not offer much shade. In a few hours the heat would envelope everyone and everything and the air rasp with cicadas.

He worked quickly through the queue sorting the sick from the malingerers.

Every day, before breakfast, there was a cross section of the nine hundred Native workers to deal with: under their skin was the fetid odor of tropical ulcer; the fungal, warty growths of mossy foot; the linear, nematode larval tracks of creeping eruption; the fungal gummatous nodules and ulcers of sporotrichosis or the flea borne ulcers of chiggers. They were plain to see and made the lives of the men miserable.

Craw-craw, indicated by small whitish burrows with a grayish spot at the end found between the webs of hands and feet, the creases of the wrists, armpits and the shaft of the penis, could spread quickly through the compound. It was intensely itchy, especially now on these warm summer nights. Scratching produced infection and the abraded skin oozed with pus. P.Q. had wasted no time in getting the infected miners' clothes boiled, while he supervised hot immersion baths, scrubbing with nailbrush and soap, followed by a full mop-down with a slurry of whitewash and sulphur. Their concrete beds in the barracks would be swabbed down too. The odor of rotten eggs overwhelmed the scent of wood smoke as P.Q.'s orderlies brought this concoction to a boil on open fires in four-gallon petrol tins behind the hospital. It roused Sunny's sensitive olfactory system and his nostrils flared as the smell wafted on the early morning breeze and overwhelmed the clean smell of the lance-shaped eucalyptus leaves and peels of bark that crunched underfoot. It was a five-day treatment to be effective.

The drawn-out "gowaaa-gowaaa," the go-away go-away alarm of the gray louries high up in the gums signaled his deeper concerns as he worked through the assortment of fevers and coughs as he briefly warmed the chestpiece of the stethoscope in his hand, lifted the earpiece into place, pressed the diaphragm to the bare chest and listened deep within them for the high pitched wheezes of bronchitis, the fine inspiratory crackles like cellophane being crumpled of pneumonia, the creaking and grating pleural rubs of tuberculosis or the diffuse bilateral crackles of silicosis. Selected cases would be followed up with a Siemens Global x-ray.

It was the sharpness of the early morning and chill after sundown contrasting with the intense heat and humidity underground that left them weakened and vulnerable to all these respiratory diseases. It was aggravated too, by the crowded living conditions in the compound and adherence to the Government's minimal legal feeding allowance—nothing more, nothing less—of five pounds of mealie meal and two pounds of meat a week. The Sun Mining Company's bottom line could well afford better. He'd have to tackle all these issues to make a difference.

Rounding out the line up were contusions to assess, a broken nose that had been bleeding for twenty-four hours before seeking help to be packed, lashes that had broken the skin to cleanup and dress. What were the roots of all these evils: the alien tongues of warring tribes, the compound policeman meting out his own justice or lawlessness in the underground world? No one was talking. After Sick Parade, Sunny took the short walk from the native hospital past the mine offices on his right, the machine shops on his left, the mill and the powerhouse to the shaft head on the hilltop. He had arranged with Jernigan, the mine manager to descend the mine. "We're on the forty-third level these days, pushing five thousand feet. Do you want to go down that far?" asked Jernigan.

"Yes, I do. I want to experience the work place."

"It's warm down there to say the least. You need to don these white one-piece overalls, gumboots, helmet and lamp. Attach the battery pack to your belt. Here's a bandana to absorb the sweat under the helmet. Lord, Doc, I'll have to fit you better. Here are extra small boots and an extra large helmet. It needs to fit well. We're lit as far as forty-two, then you'll be dependent on your headlamp entirely and the darkness may take some getting used to."

"Hop into the cage," said Jernigan. It clanged shut. The bell rang twice. The floor dropped away. Sunny's stomach slammed into his thorax and took his breath away momentarily as they plummeted into the pitch-black bowels of the earth, pungent with unfamiliar smells, entombed with clang and whirr as the increasing heat rose up to meet him. He hung onto the cage to steady himself against the jarring motion. He swallowed to adjust the pressure in his eardrums.

On the lower levels he glimpsed the adits lit-up extending from the central shaft stations towards the ore body as they hurtled down. Abruptly his knees flexed as the cage braked and then yo-yoed to a halt at forty-two. The door rattled open and Sunny stepped out into the brightly lit station. The air was clear here, the walls whitewashed. Several tunnels led from the station.

"We'll have to climb down the adjacent incline stope by ladder to forty-three. The adit follows a circuitous enveloping route, giving access to the skip station from both sides. You can get an idea of this from the curve of the roof lights," explained Jernigan

"That could provide an emergency exit then in the event of a rock fall?" Sunny could feel perspiration pop, wetting the bandana under his helmet, dampening his socks, soaking the underarms of his overalls.

"That's right."

"Are there other levels developed this way also?"

"Yes, there are quite a few."

"Good, good," said Sunny to reassure himself as they climbed down the sturdy ladder. The light was waning with each successive step. They were on a small landing, then as they cornered they found themselves plunged into complete darkness. Sunny's headlamp's narrow beam played havoc on the wandering dark shadows cast by the jutting rocks in the otherwise inky blackness. He felt puny and fragile in the threat of the tomb.

Jernigan saw Sunny's lamp sweeping around the cavernous stope as they stepped into it. "Doc," he said reassuringly, "You'll notice these pillars of ore are the vital supports. They're gold bearing. Loaded in fact! But they ensure the most solid of buttressing. It's the method used since the early prospecting days and is in place on all levels. We are as safe as we can be. Underground that is."

Everything is relative, thought Sunny. Suddenly, out of the eerie silence of the tomb, he recognized the bark of the rough, tough, unschooled rockbreaker, Simpson, as he shouted to his hammerboys. They armed themselves with their jackhammers, each steadied with its supporting leg, before steel drill bits supplied with water bore into the marked rock face. The small sounds of these waterjets wetting the surface, turning the silica dust to mud, was lost in this violent industrial war waged on this underworld. The noise of the drills hitting the rock struck like machine gunfire, ricocheted off the tunnel walls and bounced back off Sunny's tympanic membrane beating the hammer and anvil of his middle ear sending an onslaught of electrical signals to befuddle his brain. Could anyone think? No wonder those who worked here were pummeled to a relieving deafness.

Sunny's puny shouts to Jernigan were sucked into the bowels of the earth. The onslaught of the smell of crushed rock and mist from the jackhammers filled his nostrils and lungs. Sweat ran down his face. He swept his headlamp around, damp glistened from hanging wall to footwall. Water squelched beneath their gumboots.

At the end of each day a mineboy afforded himself a treat at the compound beer hall. By the end of his year's contract he'd earned enough to pay his hut tax. Perhaps he could wear a new suit home and bring his family in the reserve a *bonsella* of a bicycle, a blanket, or a few pots and pans. He would have to come back—even thank God for it—to keep alive, thought Sunny. The injustice was matched only by the senseless obsession with the useless inert metal, the barbaric relic symbolizing ultimate wealth and power.

This insane pursuit of gold had plagued man since the Akkadian Empire 4000 years ago. He wasn't going to be able to curb this lust but, perhaps, he could improve the workers' lot.

Climbing back up the ladder and tracing the circuitous loop on forty-two Jernigan pointed out escape options as they followed the tramlines of the side tipping cocopans filled with ore by the lashers to be pushed uphill by the trammers. It was backbreaking work without end. But the breathing was easier here, the light reassuring, it was dryer under foot, though the hanging walls still wept. Jernigan seemed at ease enough. Sunny paused to look back on the lashers slog. "How long are they assigned to this?"

"They're all illiterate, unskilled, and often can't even converse in *Fanagalo* when they come. If a native's assigned a lasher on day one he lashes until he finishes his contract."

"What about promotion?"

"Doc, we want to treat our workers well, but you know when tonnage falls it's all about holes, footage and fathomage and everything else. What the hell, the mine captain knows what his boots are for."

"I've been wondering about that—abuse. I've been seeing it, but I can't find out where it's coming from."

There was a pregnant pause. Jernigan wasn't talking either as he shifted uneasily.

Backtracking Sunny persisted, "What about positive incentives for the worker—I mean, advancement?"

"Incentives? There are very few bossboys in relation to the total workforce. Like I said, chances are a boy's going to stay a lasher for his contract. But he can excel in first aid or mine dancing. First aid is a necessity. Our teams are in tip-top form—P.Q.'s our instructor. You know they are separated in their barracks at the compound by tribe—else they fight—kill each other. We encourage the pride in tribal dancing as their only creative outlet besides the beerhall. It keeps them from forming unions."

"It would be so much healthier if they could play organized games—soccer, boxing, that sort of thing."

There was no response from Jernigan and Sunny welcomed their arrival at the skip station and their ascent. They emerged into the bright sunshine and walked over to change. He thanked Jernigan for the tour. "We'll need to do some monitoring of the dust and humidity levels periodically. Check the ventilation."

"Doc, don't worry about a thing. I come from generations of Welsh coal miners."

"Is your father still working, too, then?" asked Sunny.

"My old man?"

"Still in Wales?"

"Oh, no. Never had time to grow old. Pneumoconiosis is the fancy name they're giving it these days."

"I'm sorry to hear it."

"I started mining myself at age fifteen and believe me, conditions are much worse back home. We accept the risks. But don't get me wrong, we appreciate your work at the hospital."

"Oh don't thank me, hospital's not the answer. It's prevention we need to focus on," Sunny said as he disconnected the battery from his headlamp and lifted off his helmet. "I'd like to get the water pumped out, keep it as dry as possible from a medical standpoint. I'll be talking to the management about that." He peeled off the soaked bandana plastered to his head.

Jernigan handed Sunny a towel as they pulled off their gumboots. "Management's trying to keep costs down and the mine-issue gumboots do the trick you have to agree," Jernigan said.

"My socks, my feet are swimming in perspiration," replied Sunny. He undid his overall, and stepped into a shower stall.

"Nothing wrong with a little sweat, Doc," Jernigan called after him.

As they both emerged from the showers, Jernigan said as they rubbed down, "Look Doc, don't stir it up too much. You know we don't want heads rolling, the mine closing down. We know profits and shareholders' interests have to come first. We're so *much* better off here than in Wales. You know, the sunshine, the house, the garden. Huntin' an' fishin'. Not to mention my wife loves having servants, time for morning tennis and afternoon bridge. All the goings-on at the club."

Not to mention the booze, thought Sunny. The mine hooter howled and drowned out Sunny's response as he took his leave. The plaintive cry of the mourning doves in the heat of the day followed him as he departed.

CHAPTER SIXTEEN

Rejection

Sunny could see Cookie was agitated as he emerged from the sterilizing room, the smell of freshly ironed linen all about him. He'd been old for a long time, white springing around the temples in tight curls, his face etched with creases about his heavy lips, creases too around his eyes, ever ready to smile but he was not smiling now. He looked smart, took pride in his uniform. But pumping the rubber tourniquet around his neck up and down he said, "*Inkósi*, heart heavy, *makulu* heavy."

"Tell me what is it," asked Sunny impatient to get on with the day. "Are you ill?"

"It is not me, *Inkósi*."

"Well, what then?"

"My people."

"Family troubles? Your brother, one of your wives?"

"*Inkósi* it is my people."

"What's the problem?" said Sunny testily, looking at his watch. "You like new set-up and examining rooms?"

"Ah, ah! The rooms. *Mushie sterek*."

"What is it then?"

"The *medems*!"

"Cookie, I haven't got all day. Ah, yes," said Sunny. "The two madams, Dr. Sarah and Dr. Esther. What's the trouble?"

"*Inkósi*, my people not like one shilling visit."

"The madams, they make it *right* price for the people."

"*Cheap!* The *medems*, not like give injection. The people, they want it. They want the half-crown injection."

"Cookie, the madams, they want save people money. Good examination. Only give injection for *right* sickness: not for everyone. Fair price. Otherwise—same."

"Ah! *Ikona Inkósi! Ikona!* Not same."

"They clever. Their work good. *Very* good. They just come from big school for doctors in South Africa."

"*Inkósi*. See with two eyes," he said, as he pulled hard on the tourniquet, "my people not get well on one shilling. *Picannini Mfasi, ikona docotel!*"

"Cookie, they wear white coat, stethoscope. Doctor, for sure. For sure! I see their certificate."

"*Ikona! Picannini Mfasi* no good." He lost the grip of the stretched tourniquet and it shot across the room. He stood motionless.

Sunny retrieved it and handed it back. "You must tell them. Tell them the madams are good."

"My heart heavy."

"Cookie, tell them they are lucky. Soon the madams will be leaving for the big hospital near The King's castle in England."

Sunny left the surgery, crossed over to the house and sat down for lunch.

"I've been thinking," said Mavourneen, "let's have a family picnic this Sunday, before you lose the twins to Ormond Street. You've been promising us for so long."

"The Natives are suspicious of the girls."

"It's a disadvantage being so pretty."

"Cookie just told me *Picannini Mfasi, ikona docotel.*"

"Didn't you put the new, bargain fee structure into operation?"

"It's backfired completely. It compounded Cookie and the patients' lack of confidence in their professionalism—they think with the cheaper fee there's less professionalism."

"Hasn't moving from outdoors into the consulting rooms in the back made a big difference?"

"Oh the girls are competent and caring. *I* have every confidence in them—and we have a proper medical record system in place."

"Well, you'll *all* have to soldier on. The Natives will come to accept and value the girls with time."

"Unfortunately, by then they'll be off to Ormond Street."

"A picnic's a priority then."

They ate their dessert in silence.

CHAPTER SEVENTEEN

Showdown

Sunny wiped his lips, folded his serviette and slipped it into his serviette ring as Leonard removed his plate. He placed the pile of post in front of him and began to sift through it. "There's no letter yet from Wolseley or from any of my advertisements in the BMJ, the *Lancet or* the SAMJ. Despite the glut, no doctor wants to come here," he said to Mavourneen.

"*Someone's* bound to turn up soon. With the Railways contract and I don't know what else you've taken on, you're swamped."

"Oh, here's a letter from Palmer, I almost missed it," said Sunny, slitting the envelope with the bread knife. Words jumped up off the page as he opened up the letter:

How dare you quote agreements to me...

He read the letter in silence. His heart was pounding, He paled and looked at Mavourneen.

She said, "Whatever's the matter?"

The phone rang. He could hardly make out what Boss Jack was saying. He banged the receiver down and stuck his head back into the dining room. "I've been summoned to Boss Jack's office, it's about Palmer. Forgive me, I've got to sort it out." The screen door slammed behind him.

When Sunny entered Boss Jack's office, Boss Jack flushed, jerking his wheelchair this way and that, "I thought you were a decent chap, filling in well for Palmer—making improvements. Now I discover you're a mean little bastard."

"Mr. Chelmsford, explain yourself!"

"I've had a letter from Palmer saying that you're trying to blackmail him out of his practice because he will not have completed his studies by the end of the year. Worse still, knowing full well that he could not bring Jean back to the house so soon after the tragic loss of their little Samantha."

"Loss of Samantha? I had no idea."

"Some sort of rare kidney cancer. He must have told you."

"No," he said, holding up his letter, "I've just read his letter to me that's come in the same post. He doesn't mention it." A hypernephroma! So, he'd been spot on. "I'm terribly sorry to hear it." He wondered if he should tell Boss Jack he had diagnosed it off the cuff at breakfast with Palmer but the pounding in his chest was unbearable. "Sir, you are misinformed, I have the option to buy this practice at the end of the locum year. Dr. Palmer has *no* options..."

"Don't demean yourself any further by lying as well! As far as I am concerned your continuing here will *not* be welcome when your locum contract is over. We'll have to suffer you until then, unless Palmer manages to replace you before that."

"I don't lie and I don't blackmail. I will bring you proof, right now."

Sunny jumped into the old Ford. He realized he'd crush Palmer's claim and calmed down. He had full confidence in the agreement drawn up by Ike Eidelman. The screen door slammed. He brushed past Douglas' outstretched arms, and said, "My boy, I'm in a terrible rush. Look after Mommy." He pushed Bundu down and said, "There's a good dog." He flung open the French doors off the verandah to his office. Mavourneen appeared. "Everything will be fine but I have to rush back," he said. The wooden drawer of the filing cabinet needed waxing and he wrestled with it momentarily before it shot out onto the floor. He quickly found the agreement and rushed out.

Sunny watched Boss Jack's forehead crease into a deep frown. His pale skin flushed as he read the signed document. Slowly, he wheeled up to the desk and leaned forward across it to hand it back to Sunny. "I know you're young, but I didn't expect this level of naiveté from you. This document's not worth a damn!"

Sunny was astounded. He heart began to pound again. He'd drawn up the document and its conditions himself. Ike had formalized it with suitable legalese. What was wrong with it?

Boss Jack's voice was distant—he barely heard it—as he continued, "Don't you realize this appointment is not for sale, you fool?"

"What do you mean? It says there in black and white, I'm paying Palmer £2000 goodwill for this practice."

"Palmer has no right to sell the mine practice. If you are to be appointed to the post permanently you will have to earn it and be approved by mine management and the Medical Benefit Society. Palmer is contracted to the mine, nothing more and, of course, you will not be able to sell this practice either when your contract is terminated."

Leaning forward, knuckles supporting him on the desk, Sunny said, "So I'm paying Palmer for something I have to earn for myself?"

"Exactly. He has, of course, a small private practice in Umzimtuti itself, in competition with Dr. Eckhart, but it's very minor in comparison to the mine contract. Umzimtuti's a mere appendage to the mine, we all know that, so goodwill of £2000 for it is a king's ransom I'd say. Sit down."

Sunny took the chair in front of the desk and spoke slowly, looking Boss Jack in the eye. "No wonder Palmer wanted the document drawn up in Johannesburg. He asked me to keep it quiet to avoid gossip. But overturning it now might give him a chance to claim the practice back."

Boss Jack stroked his jutting jaw, raised his eyebrows and compressed his lips. "We wouldn't have him back, knowing what he's done. You've shown him up in other ways as well. I like the changes you've made here."

"Thank you, so far I've managed to make the changes by ignoring the accolades about Palmer and focusing on new ways of doing things."

Boss Jack put his elbow on the arm of his chair, rested his chin in his hand and said slowly, "You could sue. Plead the agreement was an act of fraud."

"If I sue, I'll have to rebut accusations from patients and staff that I want change to frame Palmer as a fraud generally. It's going to make my task much more difficult."

"Doolittle and I will back you all the way."

"I appreciate that very much." Sunny had calmed down, and was thinking clearly. "The facts are I entered this agreement thinking it was a bargain for Palmer to go to England to treat his desperately ill child and further his studies after the long interruption of the war. And for me, a post where I could give scope to my extensive surgical training and also afford comfortable living arrangements for my family who have been living in cramped quarters."

"Yes, but Palmer was too greedy. He sat out the war, and now he tried to sell something that didn't belong to him."

"Still, the benefits I expected from the agreement have largely met my expectations. It will be difficult in court to disentangle what is rightfully due to Palmer and what damages he should pay to whom for his fraudulent representation of the mine contract and bringing the mine into disrepute."

"You know this mine had an extremely costly and long-running dispute about mining claims during the Great War and after. It's true the directors would be vastly irritated by a new imbroglio even if it didn't last very long."

"Yes, the directors wouldn't take kindly to me for the rest of my career, not to mention the possible catastrophic effect on Palmer's career—he could be struck off the roll."

"Well you could try and come to a gentleman's agreement with Palmer to reduce the £2000."

"I refused a very promising partnership in Nairobi with the colonel of my ambulance unit in East Africa because he had just taken on an untrustworthy and arrogant young doctor that was in the same unit. As a matter of principle I never make agreements with people who have already shown they are dishonorable."

"Your principles appear to be very expensive to you and your family, but certainly Doolittle and I would appreciate the line you're suggesting after your initial blunder."

"Palmer introduced me to Doolittle that first day after I correctly diagnosed his child's illness at breakfast. It was Sunday afternoon and he was playing tennis instead of making clear what was what. He hoped I played a better game than Palmer and talked about tonnage."

"It was incumbent on you to clarify the position of the doctor on the mine. Perhaps you were intimidated by the Big House and grounds."

"No, you know perfectly well I am not easily intimidated. It definitely sounds like a court case could get really sticky. It's a tradition in my family to avoid legal entanglements like the plague. I'm not prepared to blackmail Palmer so that he might be struck off the roll. I don't want to embarrass the mine management either, and going to court would antagonize most of the white patients on the mine and in his legitimately owned practice who believe he is a fine man and a great doctor."

"A fine man and a good doctor is how he's going stay?"

"The average patient is unlikely to have the sophistication or the time to evaluate the merits of the case. It's all too likely that some sort of barroom consensus will emerge during the long legal proceedings that puts me in an undignified and contemptible light."

"Quite possibly."

"I also have the feelings of my wife to consider. In the circumstances, I believe you are entitled to know that marrying out of the faith caused considerable distress both to her family and mine. And a scandal like this would set us back with them as well as this small tight-knit community."

Boss Jack, rocking slightly said, "I certainly hope you don't make any medical blunders because your staying on will certainly have my support. I'll keep it confidential. You can still change your mind but it seems you have chosen the right course. I must come and see you about my arthritis." He rolled forward and leaning across the desk offered his gnarled hand to Sunny.

Sunny took it gently. He was pretty sure he wouldn't change his mind. "Thanks very much," he said. But being duped for £2000 was awful. How would he tell Mavourneen?

CHAPTER EIGHTEEN

Spinning Yarns

Sunny had a busy afternoon as usual. He lingered over hospital rounds, took his time over house calls. He did not return home for supper. Instead, he swung into the Umzimtuti Hotel. He needed a drink. Mayor Buchanan hailed him. He was sitting with the accountant Lucas Ramsey, a fellow councilor, and the Town Clerk Paxton. No doubt they were talking about municipal politics. Although he'd had a good innings with student politics, and Jud had alerted him to Buchanan's monopoly on the council, he had no intention of getting involved. Mavourneen would certainly object and he had enough to apologize for already. The £2000 was a dull ache in his chest.

Buchanan had had a few and for once Sunny decided to join him and his councilor cronies at the bar. Buchanan gestured to welcome him, "Doc, Claire's right as rain. Aye, we grateful, we are." Jud put down Sunny's whisky. "Aye, we've still got fisticuffs every now and then but it's nothing like the old days, '28 I think it was, soon after I'd been taken on as a hand at the Pegasus Garage. Fred Cartwright walked into the bar and asked, 'Big O'Reilly here?' Somebody said, 'At the end of the bar.' Quick as a wink, he pulled out his revolver, took aim and fired off six shots. Everyone took cover. I shouted 'Yer aff yer heid, yer bloody bastard!'"

Ramsey and Paxton laughed, looking at Sunny. He realized they had heard this story often enough. Obviously Jud had also heard it before and was not keen to hear it again and left them to it.

"Under the table, I found myself with a bloke I hadn't seen before. A bunch of men tackled Cartwright but he didn't resist. When we stood up, I saw the very fair-headed stranger was sunburned and untidily dressed in Bombay bloomers and a khaki shirt. He took off his spectacles and wiped them with a handkerchief. I asked, 'What brings ye here? There must be something wroong with ye?' He held his spectacles near and far as he looked at the wall, before replacing them slowly. He looked at me. The thick lenses made his blue eyes really big," said Buchanan holding his thumbs and forefingers around his eyes. "'No offence,' the fella said, 'technically, I'm blind and deaf.' I was embarrassed. To change the subject I asked him, 'Will Cartwright go to jail?' He said, 'Oh, I doubt it.' He pointed to those six bullet holes in a four inch cluster in the wall six inches below the ceiling you see over there," Buchanan said pointing. "He said, 'he's a pretty good shot. Obviously just showing off.' Aye friends, he was right enough! He could sum up a situation instantly. Amazing, the man could hardly see.

"Aye, aye, today he's Prime Minister Huggins right-hand man—Edgar Whitehead—coming here soon for a site inspection of the Lime and Iron *Werks* and the new power plant also. He told me his story back then in this very bar straight afterwards. Because of his bad sight and hearing he couldn't join the Civil Service in England. The British East India Company turned him down, even though his uncle was a big shot there. He joined the Rhodesian civil service but when he had his medical they fired him. A nod's as good as a wink tae a blind horse. So he paid a chicken farmer five quid a month for board, lodging and tuition. He told me, 'After twenty-two years of being educated at great expense I'm not prepared to be a vegetable.' He got his own farm soon after. Lang may yer lum reek, I say!" he clinked his glass with Sunny's and they downed their whiskies.

"That's a good story," Sunny said. But this reminder that Palmer had ignored the opportunity at the Lime Works Whitehead had urged him to take up before he even set foot in Umzimtuti only served to increase his agitation.

"Aye, he was in charge of a huge expenditure to equip the army in West Africa. He got Smuts himself to override the War Office and okay five million rounds of .303 ammo from South Africa."

Lucas Ramsey said, "Who manages the tenders?"

"Ah dinnae ken. Whitehead's straight as a die. I wouldn't try anything."

"How'd you know?" said Ramsey.

"I've told you, mon. He's a man that can hold his liquor. Tough as nails. Now the war's over he's promoting industry, though Umzimtuti's fortunes live and die with the Cheetah, we all know that."

"I don't know," said Sunny. "Doolittle told me himself the Cheetah's probably only got twenty years."

"Aye, that's long enough for me," said Buchanan. "All the same, like to join us when he comes for the site inspection of the *Werks*?"

"The future for Umzimtuti's there, but Eckhart's your man. He's got the medical contract already," said Sunny offhandedly. He ordered another drink, sliding his glass across the polished counter. "Finish your story. What happened to Cartwright?"

"Well," said Buchanan, "he was charged with attempted murder the next day, and of course he said he's the best revolver shot in the district and the charge was ridiculous. Sure enough, the case was reduced to 'discharging a firearm to the public danger,' with a thirty quid fine and confiscation of the gun. He declared on the steps of the courthouse, 'It's the best thirty quid I ever spent. I put the fear of God into the bastard.'"

They all laughed. Sunny said, "Goodnight, gentlemen."

With the verandah lights of the hotel behind him, Sunny stepped off onto the dark, unpaved road, climbed into the cocoon of the car and sat there.

Should he sue? £2000 would buy a good car and a down payment on their own house, or go a long way to building private consulting rooms to tack up his brass plaque.

Whitehead was a man who looked straight through adversity. All things considered, the £2000 had bought the goodwill of the mine management. He'd done well facing down the blunder when it had come to light today. Whitehead didn't put money first. But he'd chosen to stay single. He didn't have to face Mavourneen. He switched on the ignition, swung into the dirt road and the car climbed slowly up hill.

CHAPTER NINETEEN

Explanations

Mavourneen lay restless in bed, anxious to find out what had transpired between Sunny and Boss Jack. Sunny hadn't called all afternoon or evening. He was pushing himself too hard, acquiring all these smaller contracts to expand his practice, in preparation for a partner—but it was all too premature—the partner elusive—there was no word from Denny's referral Wolseley—or anyone else for that matter, despite the advertising.

Sunny was making good money, but most of it was going to Palmer's goodwill, as agreed, so she accepted money was tight—twenty pounds a month for housekeeping which covered the necessities. She was accountable for every penny she spent and still scrutinized the number of postage stamps she used a month, although she loved to pour her heart out to Doris in long letters and longed for hers in return.

The war years had been austere too, she hadn't had a new dress since the purchase of maternity wear when she'd been pregnant with Douglas. She didn't begrudge it. Her time would come—she was sure of it. She loved dressing up when the occasion called for it, hats—especially hats, with gloves and good shoes to match.

If she knew Sunny was going to be late she usually bathed Douglas, before he joined her in his pajamas and dressing gown at the dining table with his hair brushed and parted neatly down the side. Propped up on a couple of cushions with his feet resting on Bundu's back below to steady him, he looked so grown up and confident—he was a great companion. But tonight she fed and bathed him early, popped him into bed and read to him to be sure she'd be free for Sunny.

Waiting in vain, she dined alone. She felt acutely lonely but consoled herself that Doris would soon be here. She carved a good slice of chicken breast off the roast and doled out the roast potatoes, brown and crispy on the outside and fluffy on the inside, a wedge of golden pumpkin, green beans and then poured on the gravy. She was eating for two after all. Afterwards she stayed up awhile in the sitting room with coffee and darning and then she bathed and went to bed herself.

With the night still cooling, there was an occasional creak as the tin roof contracted. Finally, she heard the spring-loaded verandah screen door open and close. It was not the usual energetic bang but a controlled squeak: Sunny was home. She met him in the kitchen, retrieving his dinner from the warming drawer. She retied her dressing gown tightly and smoothed her tousled hair back. "I've been worried," she said, smelling the alcohol on his breath, "how did your meeting go with Boss Jack?"

"Well," he said, "it had its pros and cons."

Suddenly her concern turned to anger, "You know we've only got each other. Are you shutting me out? We should share everything—*for richer, for poorer, in sickness and in health.*" Roughly, she grabbed the tea kettle, filled it and put it on.

"You know," he said, "how much I appreciate your love and support. There's no way I can thank you enough for it. Where would I be without it? Don't think I take it for granted. Remember always, when I'm gone, everything I do is for you." He came to her and put his arms around her and pulled her close and kissed her. But she was stiff and unyielding.

Turning aside, she could see the plate of white chicken breast she had saved for him was tough and dry now and the roast potatoes leathery. A skin had developed on the gravy. With a single surgical movement he pushed it back, before deciding against gravy. He went to the refrigerator and pulled a leg and wing off the chicken carcass.

She felt sad the lovely dinner had spoiled—again. She was taken aback at his admission that she mattered. She warmed the teapot with hot water. The water boiled and she made the tea in silence before they went through to the dining room.

"I had a huge confrontation with Boss Jack," he said, picking up the chicken leg with his fingers and beginning to gnaw on it, "Palmer's a fraud. The mine practice wasn't his to sell."

"Good heavens! Where does *that* leave us then?"

"I won over Boss Jack and indirectly Doolittle and the directors pretty comprehensively."

"What about Palmer's £2000 for the practice that he doesn't own after all?"

"He was only *contracted* to the mine. So the question of my permanency is not assured, but rests with my performance. I can't afford a surgical loss if I'm to be approved by the Benefit Society at year's end." He licked his fingers, then wiped them on his serviette.

She softened, "I'm sure all will be well. You're the best." She got up from the table and leaned over the back of his chair and put her arms around his neck and kissed the top of his head. "I've every confidence you'll meet every challenge successfully."

"Thanks you," he said, sliding his hands down her arms and interlacing her fingers with his. She rested her head on his and they remained motionless for moment, before he released her and she returned to her seat.

"But," he said, resuming his meal, pointing the stripped down chicken leg at her. "When Boss Jack and I got down to brass tacks it seemed there were a lot of good reasons to go on with the goodwill payments to Palmer."

"*Whatever for?*" She frowned, "On the contrary, you *must* get back the money you've paid him *already*. Won't that be a bonus!" She brightened, "Think what we can do with it after all these years of frugality."

"Boss Jack initially said Doolittle would back me in court but when I talked it through with him very strong arguments emerged against it."

"*Why?* There's no question of your losing!"

"Of course not, but that's not the point," he said.

"He's such a scoundrel, you'd be unlikely to get a reimbursement for the payments you've already made. But to *continue* payments. Why, that's madness." Her fists were clenched, her knuckles white.

"It's true," he said, "in essence all we're buying is the small private practice he has in Umzimtuti with the townsfolk—but it could be big in time."

"Even though sums are not my forte," she said, "I know it's not worth £2000."

"The arrangements gave us this house and all his very nice furniture which he's priced reasonably, wouldn't you agree?"

"Used furniture doesn't fetch a price. He'd be hard-pressed to get rid of it and we're obliged to take it at his evaluation."

"He's even left the wireless and the golf clubs."

"You're easily bought," she said cuttingly. "Sunny," she went on, "forgive me saying so, but you're a working class boy from the Southern Suburbs and don't know a thing about refined living. With £2000 I could transform this place."

"It's very comfortable as it is. This is a fine dining room suite."

"It's not what I would choose."

"I'm not sure about the names of styles—these fancy feet," he said, bending down to give Bundu the bare bone, "but they're very English looking."

"He might choke," she said.

"If he was in the wild, he'd eat whatever he liked." But he retrieved it from Bundu's jaws before he stabbed the chicken breast with his fork and handed it down. Bundu snapped it up with one gulp. Saliva drooled from both sides of his mouth in anticipation of more to come.

"Ball and claw; Chinese originally, but these're Queen Anne. I would've chosen to support someone like Old Man Hardy. You know hardly anyone dies around here so the coffin business is pretty slow. We could've supported the local economy and commissioned him to design something simple with clean lines made with local woods— not putting money in that scoundrel's pocket back in England."

"You can still do that one day," he said. "But you must admit we needed something to get started on. You've been happy enough with it until now. We agreed to take it so it's not as though we aren't getting anything for the £2000."

"Sue!"

"No, the community would resent exposure of their hero as a crook. Let them judge me on the quality of the care I give them. Boss Jack's agreed to keep the information confidential."

"So you made a decision with him, without so much as a *single* thought for my opinion?"

"Believe me, it's in the family's best interests."

"What family? It takes two to parent and you aren't doing your part—not one iota. You're killing yourself, working like this to pay a fraud's *Goodwill*. Goodwill, my foot. The irony of it makes me sick. We never see you."

"We should hear from Wolseley any day, now. I'll give him all the small contracts I've solicited already which will lighten the load considerably and get him to do all the anesthesia for me."

"Wake up! Who do you think you're fooling? You haven't heard a single word from Wolseley. £2000," she ranted on, "That's as much as *all* your savings from *five and a half years* of army service. You've got to challenge Palmer. What a swindle!" The tea had steeped. She poured it. She was shaking, the tea slopped over the lip of the cup as she passed it to him. A stain began to grow on the linen tablecloth.

"You've forgotten to pour a cup for Bundu," he said, "but pass the sugar to me please. Look, suing's not the smart thing to do. Boss Jack assured me he and the management would support me in court, but don't you see, it would be so emotionally draining—not to mention the time it would take. We don't have time for that."

"You're a coward," she said.

He flinched. "We're happy here aren't we? Remember, we were expecting to pay the £2000 when we came so our hardship hasn't changed. Don't we want to make a go of it in Umzimtuti? There are so many possibilities to move forward with."

"For you," she said, "I'm happy you've wrapped Boss Jack and Doolittle and Matron Griffin around your little finger, but for me, Umzimtuti's horizon doesn't stretch beyond endless morning tennis and tea, and afternoon bridge with the women. It's so empty. I want to have something bigger to get out of bed for every morning."

"You'll find your way sooner or later."

Smiling for the first time that evening, she said, "I'll take that as a formal invitation to find a cause."

CHAPTER TWENTY

Doris Comes to Town

Mavourneen said, "Doris is arriving on the 1.01 tonight. Thank you again for agreeing to her coming up. I can hardly wait. Bundle up, it's unusually chilly tonight. I'll be ready and waiting with tea and sandwiches and think I'll light the fire just for fun so we can talk, talk, talk the whole night long—though I won't expect you to stay up."

"I'd quite forgotten tonight's the night, but yes, I'm looking forward to having her here too," replied Sunny.

Sunny immediately recognized Doris' long thin neck hanging out of the carriage window as the train shuddered to a stop. There was no mistaking her long angular face dominated by her *shnoz*. She ran a big hand through her wild shock of dark hair before she waved at him stepping out of the shadow of the baggage claim into the light. She handed down her suitcase, quickly moved down the carriage, swung open the door and stepped lightly down.

"*Ay-yay-yay!* It's grand to see you," Doris enthused, as she gave Sunny a warm hug and her heavy handbag thumped him in the back. "What's the matter with you? Couldn't you arrange a more civilized schedule?"

"*Shalom!* Give me time," he said. "I'm hardly settled myself but I've already acquired the local railway contract. Umzimtuti's a hub, halfway between the two main centers. It could be big in time."

"A hub?" she said letting her eyes rest on the single white bench on the single platform. "I'm doubly surprised you haven't got onto it, then."

"Gimme a break, Doris. Mavourneen's got sandwiches and tea all laid on for you."

"I could use a brandy to knock me out. I didn't sleep a wink the whole night, the train stopping off for half an hour, in God-knows-where, every five minutes. I'm covered in soot with fly ash and embers bombarding me every time I stuck my neck out. It's a wonder I didn't catch fire."

"Doris, Mavourneen'll be glad to see you haven't changed," said Sunny with a smile as he slung her suitcase into the back of the army Ford and sped up the hill.

Mavourneen's big embrace and Bundu's vigorous tail wags welcomed Doris at the front door. After hugs and kisses and great exclamations at Mavourneen's size, Doris settled into Mavourneen's favorite Victorian recliner, bent down and unstrapped her peep-toe tooled leather platform heels, tossed them aside and rested her feet on Bundu's fat backside as he plopped down in front of her. Mavourneen moved the tea trolley to the settee, lifted the tea cozy and poured.

"Darling," said Doris. "If you don't mind I'm *dying* for a brandy. You know there's no dining car past Bulawayo and I'm starving, too," she said. "I see you remembered my favorite chopped liver," she went on, not waiting to be offered the plate but stretching across the coffee table and tucking in.

Sunny went over to the liquor cabinet and poured a tot of Hennessy into a snifter and handed it to Doris.

"Thanks ever so, darling," she said, swilling the glass, breathing it in and downing it. "Fancy getting this even if you are a long way from anywhere."

"Savor it," said Sunny. "Courtesy of the previous occupant. He's left the house fully furnished...liquor and all."

"I'll take another, then," said Doris extending her glass to him.

"Doris, this bottle's it. Save some for later. I haven't got Palmer's resources. I'm five years behind in setting myself up."

"Drink your tea while it's still hot. It'll soothe that throat of yours," said Mavourneen.

"The brandy's smoother and stays warm all the way down into my tum-tum. Hennessy, I'd know it anywhere. Remember when my Dad took his life after the crash in '29?"

Mavourneen did. How sad Doris' life had been, she'd only been twelve years old. With her mother long gone, the fortune evaporated, her older brothers had brought her up.

"Darlings, you're so good to take me in. Could I go to anyone else? I'm falling apart you know."

"It's our pleasure," said Sunny. "Mavourneen's been counting the days—me too, actually, I've got a job for you to do."

"Don't you know I'm in the middle of a nervous breakdown?"

"I've got the cure for you," said Sunny, "a big bookkeeping job, starting tomorrow."

"For heaven's sake," said Mavourneen, slamming her teacup down. "I should have known you wouldn't waste a minute! Let her at least settle in first."

In the silence that followed Sunny got up, stoked the embers and fueled the fire before he refilled Doris' snifter.

Mavourneen, Doris, Douglas and Bundu had just finished breakfast when Sunny returned from Sick Parade and joined them.

As Sunny sat down, Doris said, "Your *boychick* is such a darling." Douglas climbed onto her lap and she bounced him on her knee. She was teaching Bundu to beg for the toast crusts on her plate. Bundu sat on his haunches with nose held high. She tossed a crust up and he snatched it without a fumble. Douglas squealed with delight.

"You're giving Bundu the best part," said Sunny.

"You've got the best—each other. You've got everything," she said, "is the house lovely, lovely? Have you done Mavourneen proud—all this furniture thrown in? And a new baby on the way. *Voilà!* After all the struggles are you suddenly part of the establishment? For all this should you thank me? I made a good match, you have to agree."

"Mmmm," said Mavourneen. "Look at you thin, free as a bird. All sorts of possibilities ahead of you."

"Me? I'm all washed up. You! Will you slim down again, just like you did after Douglas? Would I do anything to be in your position? Douglas—he's such a credit to you both. Such a credit."

Sunny said, "Doris, you've got to help me prevent a *shanda*. There's been a complication with the previous doctor's agreement and it's imperative that I get a proper accounting system in place. You're the one. There'll be plenty of time to chat with Mavourneen and go on walks with Douglas. Let me get you to work over at the surgery without another moment's delay. There's just time for me to orient you before my first surgery appointment."

"We've so much news to catch up on still," protested Mavourneen. "We've hardly got started."

"Can I sort out all your troubles in a jiffy? But, no worries, let me see what there is for me. I'll come back over for morning tea," Doris said, turning to Mavourneen and handing Douglas the last crust to throw to Bundu. "Still making those wonderful scones of yours? You know I was never much in the kitchen. Got to earn my keep."

"Nonsense," said Mavourneen. "Sunny has so much *chutzpah*, putting you to work. You're our guest."

"Come along" said Sunny. "Mavourneen, don't make a *tsimmes* out of this. You know Doris loves a challenge."

As they finished up supper, Mavourneen said, "Let's go into the sitting room for coffee and an after-dinner drink."

Doris said to Sunny, "Mavourneen is quite the *berryer*, she takes after her mother. She was so good to me after my father died."

"*Bobbemyseh*, almost as good as my mother," said Sunny.

"Heaven forbid," said Mavourneen. "I'm my own woman."

Sunny fixed drinks, a shot of Hennessy for Doris, a tot of sherry for Mavourneen and a whisky for himself and handed them around.

"Sunny," Doris said, "I need this shot...maybe two or three. I don't want to be a *kvetch*, but I'm appalled that you haven't billed so many patients. All those scraps of paper in a shoebox with addresses for house calls. Are you running a charity? Where are the invoices?" She downed the glass, flung out her arm with the empty glass.

Sunny had not even had a sip of his whisky yet, but he rose to fill her glass again.

"Should you work for nothing? And what about your poor wife and little child? Are people going to pay without an invoice? Should we wonder why there are precious few receipts? Are six out of ten surgery appointments billed?"

"That's why we got you up here."

"Not *we*," flashed Mavourneen. "I thought you'd enjoy the break. *I* had no ulterior motives."

"I'm enjoying myself. I accept the whole *sheemer* from you two. You're my best friends." She swilled her snifter and sniffed. "But can you afford another bottle of Hennessy for me if you don't make a bit of *gelt* along the way now and then? Is there shame in asking for fair remuneration for services rendered? Sunny you've got to pull up your socks."

If there was anyone in the world who could tackle Sunny it was Doris—her very best chum, she was worth her weight in gold. Mavourneen took a sip of sherry, picked up her darning and left them to it.

CHAPTER TWENTY-ONE

Doing the Conventional Thing

Sunny finally turned in and sat on his bed. He thought how beautiful Mavourneen was in the full ripeness of her pregnancy. She was sitting in her nightie at the bureau brushing her chestnut curls a hundred times with her grandmother's silver-backed brush. Their eyes met in the mirror.

"I'm so glad we got Doris up here. I never realized you weren't even sending out accounts!" she said.

"I knew we had to get an accountant urgently. That's why I appeared so crass about Doris." He let a shoe drop. "What's been bothering me is what on earth you were doing that day when Douglas escaped your notice all afternoon and cycled all the way down to the bar?"

"Well," she said as she put the brush down and turned to face him directly. "All's well that ends well."

"We could hardly say you set a good example of mothering. I think," he went on, "we'd better get a nanny: like everyone else."

"I'd rather not," she said. With that she turned and rose from the bureau.

"I can see," he said, "that the baby's dropped...any day now."

"Yes," she said. "I feel it myself."

"You should," he said, "be making maternity plans, easing up. Get a nanny."

"Doris. Let's ask her to stay on," she said, "Douglas loves her to bits."

"Who's taking advantage of Doris now?"

"She'd be happy to," she said.

"We'll run out of Hennessy."

"Sunny!" she said.

Why was it so easy to joke with Doris, and not Mavourneen, he wondered? He said, "She'll be busy doing my accounting every morning. Let's get a nanny."

"Perhaps. I've been thinking, it's not going down well in the community—us—you—doing the delivery, breaking with convention."

"Well, so long as we are happy and confident with each other, what does it matter?"

"Are we," she said, "confident and honest with each other? There's talk. You know the British are sticklers for rules. The idea of treating family's too advanced for this town. It could hurt your practice."

"I'd welcome less work. *They're* beating down my door. Isn't that why I've got an advert in the BMJ?"

"I wish you'd reserve Sundays for Douglas."

"You know I'm going to get landed with the Native clinic again."

"You were right about the Uziel twins. It's too bad, all that talent and education questioned but trust and respect are half the cure."

"I've got to find *someone*."

"Getting back to us," she said, "well, even the Jewish communi-ty...all of them disapprove. Some are shocked at the idea of you doing my delivery."

"Shocked? It's our personal decision: none of their business. They don't have to come to me if it comes to that. They can go fifty miles to Gwelo or Gatooma if they like."

"I know," she said. "But..."

"Didn't we think we were getting the best of the best to handle your mother's heart troubles and my sister's nose—*ever the nose*—after that ENT specialist in Jo'burg butchered her? My mother's gynecologi-cal troubles were mishandled. Douglas' circumcision was botched and the drainage of his middle ear was botched too. I'm confident I could have done better in every case."

"By all reports, Rosin at the Lady Chancellor in Salisbury..."

"You of all people! Have you forgotten your botched episiotomy with Douglas' birth by the best in Pretoria! Do we want to experience that again?"

"No, of course not," she said. "Things have never been quite the same down below since."

"I'm confident I can handle any complications with your delivery—another breech birth. I would have turned the fetus. The care I'll give won't be matched by anyone else, you know that." Why would she go against all the evidence when her and her baby's health were at stake? He let the other shoe drop.

"Of course," she said. "But what about the hospital?"

"I wouldn't be operating at the New Government Hospital if I didn't think it was at least adequate."

"What's Matron going to say about it?"

"Why do you worry about what she or anyone else thinks? It's only a convention. It's not against the law."

"I know you're the best—detached and unemotional and won't panic in a crisis. All the same, perhaps I should go up to Salisbury."

"Don't you believe in me?"

"Of course I do! I'm only thinking of your career."

"Have it your way." He began unbuttoning his shirt. "Make whatever arrangements you want. Ask Doris if she'll stay on. Get a nanny for Douglas so she doesn't feel completely tied down. She's quite a bridge player and she could play with the Jewish women. For the time being I'm still on my own and terribly busy." He pulled back the sheet and got into his bed.

Mavourneen knew she had no time to lose. Leah found her a nanny at short notice. Sunny pulled the car out of the lean-to garage and ran round to help Mavourneen in. Doris appeared in her dressing gown. She gave Mavourneen a big hug and said, "Darling, are you uncomfortable? Should I doubt everything's going to go well for you? Think always of the lovely baby you are going to come back with. Douglas is going to show me around town and I'll teach Bundu a few more tricks and keep the numbers straight for Sunny. Can a friend do more?"

"Whatever would I do without you," said Mavourneen, squeezing her hand.

Revving the car, Sunny said, "We must hurry."

Their parting was strained as Sunny deposited her small suitcase into her coupe. He kissed her lightly on the mouth and she responded. Alone on the dark station platform he seemed a lonely figure as he waved and she felt a huge ache in her heart that their marriage was not happier, because as Doris had said, besides each other, they had everything.

Hurt and sad, she enjoyed the comforting clickety-clack, clickety-clack of the carriage over the rails and the sway of her coupe as she tossed and turned trying to find a comfortable position to lie in. She couldn't wait to get the birthing over. She shuddered as she thought back to her desperate attempt to erase Sunny from her life, after her four years of nursing in Jo'burg, by fleeing to Cape Town and embarking on a year's midwifery course before Doris persuaded her to come back to Sunny and facilitated the match. How she had hated every single minute of midwifery.

At Groote Schuur Hospital, she had started off by collecting water flasks, cleaning lockers, dusting, emptying bedpans, swabbing women, bathing babies, swabbing breasts, changing nappies, changing more nappies, more bedpans, more nappies, more swabbings, more nappies, carting in and out food trays, folding nappies, changing nappies, more nappies. She had counted nappies in her dreams instead of sheep. Just as she got to the top of a terrific pile, they'd topple over and she would have to start again at the bottom. *Wotta* life it had been!

After what seemed like an eternity, she had risen in rank to labor ward nurse and was spared the chores in the mornings. In spite of herself, she rather liked babies from the deliveries she watched, and then later those she delivered herself, before duty saw her assigned to District Six to manage home deliveries alone. That work never ended: poor Cape Malay and Coloured women, locked in the eternal reproductive cycle, one baby a year from early teens to menopause. She'd never forget the fear and helplessness of the birthing mother, such a gory, messy process. The biology from start to finish gruesome and abhorrent.

She never wanted to give birth to a little girl herself. Girls had such a rotten deal given 'em in this world. A man as independent as he pleases; a woman never. She was just not safe anywhere. One unlucky break meant ruin for life, to be looked down on by one and all. The man who caused it could go through ten women in a night and never know or feel a thing. The woman, meanwhile, was stuck with nine months of discomfort and an agonizing birth. And that was only the beginning of her troubles! She could never see childbirth, as Sunny did, as a miracle: the gift of life to be marveled at on every occasion. She had stuck the year out. Now she herself was on the receiving end for the second time. She steeled herself for it. This thing called love that had got her into this pickle...

Sunny had been her platonic friend for years. She had only got 'involved' with him after Frank, her bomber pilot beau, told her to 'go to pot'. What had happened to him? She was sure he was flying high and seeing the world. There was no use wondering what might have been. She was alone, but the life within her was stirring. There was a commotion as the train came to a stop at yet another siding. Women, as always, burdened with babies strapped to their backs, bundles on their heads, small children and, very often, a *hok* of chickens by their sides, in the middle of nowhere, moved in the dark void beyond the brightness of her coupe. Isolated from all this overburdened, teeming, primitive life she raised up, plumped up the pillows and sank into them.

With a whistle, the train lurched forward to resume the comforting clickety-clack, clickety-clack and sway of the carriage, as it picked up speed again. She turned off the bunk light, grabbed the starched top sheet with both hands and pulled it up to her neck. How far she was from the carefree days holidaying at Durban with Frank and his pilot buddies, surfing in the sea. Playing catches with an orange washed up along the shore, javelin-throwing with bits of bamboo, long runs along the endless beach, cartwheels and head-stands on the soft sand. Cartwheels and headstands! Heavy, she struggled to turn over and reposition the pillows to overcome her discomfort. She'd never be able to do cartwheels again. After all the fun and games, they had ordered coffee and hot cream scones on the beach. How delicious they were on her sea salty lips. Frank! So dashing! What had become of him? Surely he'd survived. A civilian now, no doubt, doing all the things she dreamed of doing. They had strolled to Mitchell Park, under its umbrella of beautiful green trees. She had recited to him *Trees* by Kilmer, one of her favorites:

I think that I shall never see
A poem lovely as a tree.

A tree whose hungry mouth is prest
Against the earth's sweet flowing breast;

A tree that looks at God all day,
And lifts her leafy arms to pray;

A tree that may in summer wear
A nest of robins in her hair;

Upon whose bosom snow has lain;
Who intimately lives with rain.

Poems are made by fools like me,

But only God can make a tree.

With the kiss of the sun on her suntanned limbs and the cool wind in her hair, he had mounded her outstretched legs with sand right up to her waist. She loved the clean grit of sand on her scalp and salt in her hair, which sprang into tight curls in the damp sea air. She'd told him then she wanted a little house with miles and miles of lush grass on which to roll and roll, or stand on her head without it hurting, and lovely spreading trees, acres and acres of them all about, with the wind singing through the foliage, the chatter and songs of the birds in the branches above. Well, she had all that and more at 1 Jacaranda Avenue, as well as a swing and a Wendy house for Douglas. What she honestly wanted though, was *Frank's* life: the life of high flying adventure to lands unseen: the constant novelty of different trees and different people.

But she was well and truly rooted in Umzimtuti, as much as any of the jacarandas that shed their carpet of mauve flowers on the garden path in spring. The new baby would entrench her further. Her die was cast.

Suddenly, aware of her isolation in the coupe as the African night rushed by, she switched on the overhead light to cheer herself, folded down the table over the wash-hand basin and wrote a note:

Dearest Love,

Please do not worry or fret over me. Things will come right with time and a return to normal married life, of which we have known so little. Our little fella is a grand chappie and our big home and garden offer so much about which to be happy. You love your work. Things are improving so please have faith in our future together.

Give our little fella a great big hug and kiss from me. Take good care of each other and Doris and Bundu too.

All my love and longing,
Mavourneen.

The responsibility of Douglas, of the family, rested with her. She wanted her children to have a happy innocent childhood, like the one she had enjoyed exploring the wide-open kopjes of Observatory, protected from life's vulgarities by Edwardian sternness. The clickety-clack was slowing again and stopped. The murmur of humanity on the move again was comforting. She turned out the light and fell deeply asleep.

CHAPTER TWENTY-TWO

A New Addition to the Family

At the onset of labor Mavourneen caught a taxi from the Windsor Hotel to the Maternity Home; she had plenty of time to settle in as her labor progressed. When Dr. Rosin called to inform Sunny he had a daughter, six pounds even though a little jaundiced, he didn't mention he had delayed on the episiotomy and the tissues had been raggedly torn.

A faint, rain-laden breeze stirred the curtains in the ward, making Mavourneen feel good and clean inside, with the fragrance of flowers and milk all about her, as she lay in bed and her cuddly bundle suckled at her breast. It was Sunday.

Mavourneen was surprised and thrilled to see Sunny silhouetted through the window onto the convalescent verandah, the big assertive head on those broad shoulders and a bunch of flowers in hand. He came to her bedside and kissed her tenderly, squeezed her free hand and then kissed the baby nestled at her side. "These are fresh, Doris and Douglas picked them right before I left," he said. "The garden's looking grand." Then awkwardly, he pulled a small box from his pocket and handed it to her. He lifted the baby from her and cradled her to him as Mavourneen opened it—a bottle of Eau de Cologne.

Buying something frivolous was so unexpected, that tears began to well, but she checked them, unscrewed the bottle and put a sparing dab behind each ear. The citrus fragrance was revitalizing, the hints of lavender and rosemary calming: the garden distilled in a bottle. She took a deep breath before she screwed the cap tightly back on and set it on the bedside table. He passed the baby back to her. She said, "You know we've been so busy with the mine contract issue, Doris' arrival and so on that we haven't had a moment to talk about baby names. I favor Anne with an 'e', after *Anne of Green Gables*."

"I've never heard of it," Sunny said.

"It's a famous story about a girl who's obliged to leave the orphanage. An old couple has asked for a boy to help them with their farm on

Prince Edward Island. When she arrives instead they want to return her, but she wins their hearts and they live happily ever after."

"Well," he said, "I certainly don't want to return her, do you?"

"Oh, of course not Sunny, she's a darling! I love her so already. I know she's going to be an easy baby."

"We don't want to name our child after an orphan."

"Don't be silly," she said, "Anne was spunky with great imagination and spirit and red pigtails."

"Well, our baby hasn't got a lot of hair right now. There's nothing in either of our genes to suggest a redhead. The Annes that come to mind are Henry VIII's—one executed, one divorced."

"How about Elizabeth then?"

"The Virgin Queen?"

"One virgin in the family's enough."

"There is no need," he said, "to be mean about my sister. She's very dependable."

"I was thinking of King George VI's Queen Elizabeth and the Princess. Our Royals."

"I hardly feel a kinship."

"They mucked in with the common people during the war. The Victory Tour is coming up."

"They're human with all the common frailties. The biblical names have stood the test of time. Deborah, for instance, a prophet, a fighter: strong and independent."

"That's a surprise, you coming up with that, when you want me to be the Jewish mama—fully satisfied being the queen of the home."

"Perhaps Sarah," he said, "Abraham's wife begat Isaac at the age of ninety. You know, princess of the multitude. You like princesses."

She sank back in the pillows. Perish the thought—fecund at the age of ninety! She had her pigeon pair—all she wanted. Pain began to throb from her episiotomy down below. She shifted uncomfortably. She didn't want to mention it. Suddenly she felt very tired. "Let's both give it some more thought."

"The Jewish custom of not naming a baby until you can tell its character makes sense to me," he suggested. "Wait until she's two or so...at least."

"You know we have to register the baby within ten days. Homecoming too in ten," she said, "which reminds me, I don't want you to drive the three hundred miles there and back in a day. The night train really suits me fine—leaves at 8 pm, all you'll have to do is pick me up at the station at 2.01, although I expect you will have a full schedule of ops in the morning. I so want them to go well: for you to go ahead by leaps and bounds."

"I think I can arrange a lift for you."

"Oh, no! Not that! I hate the feeling of helplessness, asking favors of others. No, I am not, under any circumstances, prepared to accept lifts from other people, nor favors from Rosin. Don't ask," she said.

"You love to do little favors for other people. Why not let them respond when your own need arises?"

"I'm not in need," she said. "I'm happy with the train. I will," she conceded, reaching for a scrap of paper and a pencil on the bedside table, "need a few supplies between now and then," she said, scribbling away. "Be a dear, ask Doris to send rather too much than too little, will you?" Sunny took the list as she asked, "How's Doris doing with Douglas? I bet she'll have him spoiled rotten by the time I come home—incorrigible. And Bundu? I expect he's too busy learning new tricks from her to go out on the razz. He'll be incorrigible too."

"You're the one who invited her and they're all getting on famously. I'm enjoying Doris' update on the Jo'burg scene—all the friends we lost track of after we married. She's a sharp wit at the dinner table and I've enjoyed that—makes up for the meals. She's not much of a cook, I can tell you that, she's put Leonard clean off his stroke. It will be good to have you back. She's steadily getting the bookkeeping all sorted out. Trouble is I'll have to keep the system going after she's gone."

"You should hire someone before she leaves to learn the ropes. Take the load off your mind."

"With nanny taking care of Douglas in the morning you could be the one."

"No," she said, "I'm firm. Absolutely not. Perhaps a permanent nanny is a good idea, but I'm going to develop my own interests and sums is not anywhere on my list—not even close."

He bent and gave her a great big crushing kiss. She sent great big hugs and kisses home to Doris and Douglas and a pat on the back to Bundu.

Over the next four or five days the room filled out with flowers: pink carnations from Old Doc Maxwell and his wife, chrysanthemums and a wrapped box containing a Madeira embroidered frock between folds of tissue from Dr. and Mrs. Rosin. Bouquets arrived from Dr. and Mrs. Eckhart, the Feldman brothers and their wives, the Shapiros, the Wolfsons, Leah and Jud Levine and even the exotic Kalderons at Lucky Strike Trading Store. A telegram arrived from her parents in Jo'burg but there was no word from Sunny's family. How short a time she had been in Umzimtuti and yet she was surrounded by all these tokens of goodwill and welcome for her new baby. She was confident the baby would go steadily ahead and make up for Douglas' difficult years.

The fragrance of the flowers all around her intensified in the evenings. On the sixth day before her dinner tray arrived she grabbed a pencil from the bedside table and wrote a note on a scrap of paper to Sunny—she was so looking forward to going home and making a new start on her life:

Dearest Love,

I am up—on and off of course. I am sleeping like a top. I could sleep a lot more if allowed. I have a terrific appetite and the food is good and attractively served.

With three hourly feedings, my nipples have gone to glory. It is sheer agony to nurse our baby girl but she has put on five ounces in spite of jaundice and puny size.

I am sorry to hear about your mother's hysterectomy to add to your worries. No wonder we had no word of congratulations from her.

We will be back to the old days of spiritual and physical bliss very soon.

How is our big fella? How I long to hear his voice and see him peddling up and down the stoep on his tricycle while we have our early morning tea or walking dazed into the sitting room announcing he's 'had a nice sleep' after his afternoon snooze.

Try and relax as often as you can and enjoy Doris' company. Get Nanny to stay this Sunday afternoon. I hope she is managing the washing satisfactorily. I see now I should have hired her earlier. Cheerio!

Please remember that I love you with all my heart and soul and am longing to be home again. I hope we both 'understand' each other a little better now and that we will be back to our pre war days of spiritual and physical bliss very soon.

Kiss our little fella for me and give him a big hug. Pour Doris a generous glass of Hennessy to celebrate and a whisky for yourself.

Lots of little wet cuddly kisses from your baby girl.

Your loving,
Mavourneen.

CHAPTER TWENTY-THREE

Homecoming

The maternity sister-in-charge stuck her head around the corner of Mavourneen's private room at the Lady Chancellor Maternity Home and said, "Day ten tomorrow. Ready for discharge? Your husband's just called. He'll be here first thing to drive you home."

"It really isn't necessary. I do love the train, but I must say we seem to have accumulated rather a lovely lot of extra luggage haven't we?" she said, looking around at the vases of flowers and cards displayed on the windowsills and gift boxes stacked below.

Dr. Rosin said, "Your perineal tear is pretty extensive, but it couldn't be helped. It's on the mend—be sure and take your sitz bath with you and put it to good use three times a day."

"Don't worry," Mavourneen said, "I'll take care of it. Be a dear, please don't mention it to my husband."

"When we talk I'll focus on the baby. She's doing splendidly—a champion at putting on weight, keep up the good work."

Rosin had barely written up Mavourneen's discharge papers when Sunny arrived. It was lovely to see his familiar face, the bright all-seeing steel-gray eyes flashing behind the glass of the big round spectacles. "Here so early," she exclaimed.

"I took your advice and came up last night after evening rounds. Gelfand offered to put me up. Esther cooked a fine meal—almost as good as my mother. Mike's proving a real mentor and friend. Although it was late they waited for dinner and it gave me a chance to feel him out on organizing my Sick Parade pulmonary research project. It's long term of course, but I want to get it off on the right foot. He's such a font of knowledge and so generous with sharing it," he said. "You should see his office—it's just chaos—the walls, the floor and desk piled high with books, papers, journals. His handwriting is illegible so Esther types everything up for him. They make a marvelous team—they've three lovely daughters. They send their congratulations, by the way. Lucky we have Doris to hold the fort. I've cancelled all my appointments for today."

Mavourneen said, "We have so much to thank him for—recommending Umzimtuti to you. Urging you to take a look. I hope you weren't imposing."

"Of course not, he was only too happy to oblige. He wants to start Rhodesia's own medical journal and happy at the prospect of a contribution down the line."

"That's so smart, killing two birds with one stone. Thanks so much for giving up your day for us. We could have managed the train."

"Not at all. Here," he said, producing a wrapped box from behind his back and embracing her. She yielded to him. This brand new baby was a brand new promise in their marriage. She untied the bow and rolled the ribbon up. Carefully she unwrapped the paper and smoothed it out before she set it aside, opened up the box and pushed the tissue paper aside, careful not to wrinkle it. Beneath its folds were a tiny pink knitted matinee jacket, bloomers and matching cap and booties. "Oh!" she exclaimed, "It's *the* perfect homecoming outfit. Thank you, thank you!" She hugged him again, and said, "We've still the birth certificate to sign. I've decided it would be nice to name our baby girl Deborah Sarah: strong and independent, but a princess all the same."

"I thought Douglas cured you of fairytale fantasies. I hope she measures up."

"She's going to be an easy baby," she said.

"Glad you've chosen biblical names."

"I appreciated you letting me have Douglas from Ireland, after my father, for our big fella."

"Jews adopt the culture that they find themselves in. Even my parents realized that—but Deborah will make them happy."

"It's wonderful you came up after work last night—giving me the opportunity to shop this morning," she said, "before we head home."

"Shop! What for? Haven't we got everything a family could possibly need?"

"A few practical things." Oh how she resented the £2000 goodwill that made finances so tight, and resented, too, his tardiness to bill his patients. Thank God for Doris. She turned away.

He said, "I'm neglecting my practice. I'm sure Feldmans...."

"No, no!" she said, "Now that the baby is born I'd like to get a special dress for Deborah, a few new frocks for myself, too. I haven't had a new one since we got married."

"You did buy some maternity frocks as I recall."

"You're right," she said. "A necessity with Douglas and I've made good use of them again. I'm done with those now—I'll give them to WIZO for jumble."

"I wouldn't do that," he said, "you might need them again."

"No," she said, "I won't."

"I was thinking a big family would be good."

"We're done with that—we have the perfect pigeon pair. There are so many people in the world...too many," she said as she tossed her faded bed jacket into her suitcase.

"Your maternity clothes are hardly worn. If you were a true *berryer*, like my mother," he said, "you'd get your sewing machine out and re-fashion them. My mother made all my school clothes, Josie's too. Nothing wasted."

"I do need to move with the times, now that the war is over. Look respectable alongside you in the community."

"The old frocks will seem like new again as you slim down."

"I haven't made my mark on the community yet. First impressions. I was so embarrassed at Leah's welcome tea."

"They all understood your circumstances. Look at all the flowers in this room. It's forgotten. I can't afford excesses."

"A few things for the baby—for Deborah at least."

"Don't you like my gift?"

"Don't be silly," she said, "of course I do."

"There are lots of gifts waiting to be opened at home before you go buying stuff we don't need. In any case, Doris and Douglas are expecting us for lunch."

Of course he was right—she needed to slim down first. It would hardly be fun shopping with him hanging around the store champing at the bit. Perhaps if Doris stayed long enough they could put nanny to good use and come up together and shop, shop, shop—a taste of the old days—there was everything to look forward to. She turned and packed her things.

Mavourneen welcomed the familiar sound of the screen door slamming behind her. "Douglas, my big son," she said as Douglas careered his tricycle down the length of the verandah and bumped into the screen door and dismounted. She bent down and pushed the crochet shawl back from the tiny baby's face as Douglas peered at it and Bundu sniffed with the scent of mother's milk and perfume all around.

Mavourneen pushed his snout aside as he put his tongue out to lick the baby. "Can I hold her?" said Douglas.

"Yes of course," she said, carrying the baby through to the sitting room. Douglas flung himself down and arranged himself with crossed legs and outstretched arms to receive her.

Arms free, Mavourneen held her arms out to Doris. "What's the verdict?" she said, "How's everyone behaved?"

"Should I tell you?" Doris said, as the tea trolley arrived and Leonard exclaimed over the baby.

"It's good to see you, Leonard," Mavourneen said, "you make the very best tea in the whole wide world. I've missed it."

Sunny gulped down a cup of tea, grabbed a Marie biscuit and said, "I must be off." He gave Mavourneen a kiss on the top of her head. "It's lovely you are home, it truly is, but I must run," he said as he roughed up Douglas' hair.

"I thought you said you had the whole day off," said Mavourneen.

"I must just stay on top of things." The door slammed.

A silence fell, with only Bundu's slurp and the sound of the saucer sliding around the floor filling the room as Douglas, wrapped in wonder, held the baby.

"I invited you up for you to recover. I feel guilty that we have put you to such hard work...bookkeeping and babysitting," said Mavourneen. "I didn't plan to take advantage of my very best chum."

Doris got up and went to the window and looked out over the expanse of lawn bordered with all the flowers. She said, "I've been grateful to sink my teeth into something useful—take my mind off my ruin—no husband, no children. I didn't do well for myself. Maybe I wasn't so clever to bring you two back together again either."

"You meant well. We have only ourselves to blame for where we find ourselves. We can't change the past. We each have the future ahead of us," said Mavourneen.

"Should I tell you he loves you—very much? Should I be the one to tell you what the trouble is?"

Mavourneen poured another cup of tea. She was not so sure she wanted to hear.

"You have a *Goyisher* kop."

"That is nothing to be ashamed of. Remember, I was chosen to be the fairy on the top of the Christmas tree at our kindergarten concert at Barnato Park and my mother made your costume too with all that cellophane and crepe paper—you were a long lanky Christmas crack-er." Mavourneen giggled, spilling her tea into her saucer and surrendering a second saucer full to Bundu.

"Should I have agreed to that? But could I be pulled apart?"

"We have to be true to ourselves."

"But could you use a little *Yiddish* to brush off on you, maybe?"

"I think my father's stern Edwardian upbringing has served me well—although I resented it at the time."

"Is it too sad that your father wouldn't let you do the evening show because it was past your bedtime and that awful Larissa got to wear your fairy costume?"

"True, he could have made an exception once in a while. I want to give Douglas and Deborah the best of both worlds."

"All that reserve. Does it serve you well? I tell you talk, talk, *talk back!*"

"Talk back?"

"Sunny lives in that big head of his—he loves you very much in an intellectual way. We *Yids*, do we love a good argument? Spar with him. He is longing for it."

"I hardly think so. Marriage is all about duty, to husband, to family but to be the *berryer*, like his mother that he wants—it's too much."

"Okay, you need something outside the house? Of course you do. Get back into your uniform."

"He won't hear of it. He's completely at one with official attitude that a professional wife can't assist him. And the New Government Hospital is so small and he is the only one who does any serious oper-ating."

"Okay, what about your Girl Guide uniform?"

"There's a thought."

"Meantime I can teach you the bookkeeping. It's pretty straight forward."

"Doris, I always copied your homework sums. I'll find my own out-let—make a secret life he knows nothing about."

Deborah cried out.

Douglas said, "Mommy, take the baby, there's a bad smell."

CHAPTER TWENTY-FOUR

House Calls

Despite Mavourneen's misgivings, Sunny still scanned the post every day for word from Denny's referral, Major Wolseley, but there was nothing. There were no leads for a partner either from his advertisements. His practice was taking him far and wide across the bush, even as far as the *mealie* king, Japie van Hoepen. This family had settled long ago and pioneered farming vast acreages of maize with an ingenious irrigation system. They were a tough clan. Sunny knew that they would not summon him the forty miles to the farm without good reason. He drove out on the main strip road south towards Bulawayo, past the now familiar Ferreira Estates that separated the town from the new iron works, and turned onto the pot-holed muddy tracks which tested the suspension of his cumbersome army Ford. The going was slow.

Japie greeted him warmly and gratefully. His mother, known to everyone as Ouma, was disoriented, vomiting, sensitive to light and in severe pain with telltale neck stiffness: ominous signs of meningitis, perhaps.

"Japie, you need to bring her in to the hospital pronto," said Sunny matter-of-factly.

"Doc, is she going to be okay?"

"Japie, I can't make any promises at this stage. Get her in as soon as possible."

"Doc, you know Ouma's the driving force of the family."

"I understand. She's very dehydrated. I need to confirm my diagnosis with some tests," he said thoughtfully. He fitted his ophthalmoscope back into its black velvet lined case, gathered his things into his red and white lunch tin and snatched his stethoscope from around his neck, there was nothing more he could do here. Japie accompanied him out. But his bossboy appeared at the car door just as Sunny was about to drive off. "Baas," he said, "*M'fazi* bleed. Bad. Very bad. Come, come, please."

"Doc, his wife's pregnant. Would you mind? I'll take you to the compound in my Land Rover while my wife gets Ouma ready. Road's not too hot—a lot of dongas."

"Don't worry, I'll be okay. Hop in the back seat," he motioned to the bossboy.

As he slid in, Japie said, "Buchanan at the Pegasus Garage is importing his first new car since the war. Maybe you should take a look."

"Wouldn't hear of it. This old Ford's reliable—solid. Part of my army severance entitlement."

The back door slammed shut. Japie lifted his arms off Sunny's open window and raised a hand as Sunny took off. Sunny felt acutely aware of the bossboy behind him pressed against the door of the back seat. No words passed between them. He adjusted his rearview mirror and glimpsed the darting frightened whites of the man's eyes before he cornered.

The moon in the sky had not yet risen but the dual moons of his headlights shone on the ordered rows of young mealie lands: Japie's reputation well earned. A night jar sitting on the sand of the road, still warm from the day's heat, flew in front of the car lights, and called 'Good Lord deliver us'. Suddenly the steering wheel veered—a blowout. He kept his foot on the accelerator and followed the skid—a bush loomed up ahead as they began to leave the road. The bossboy sat forward gripped the back of the front seat with one hand and the armrest of the car door with the other. Sunny eased up on the accelerator, and gently corrected the steering. Momentarily they were off the grass, back in the gravel beside the *wag-n'-biejtiebos*.

"Ah, Ah, Baas!" said the bossboy. His door scratched against the thorns as he started to open his door. "Baas," he said, "*wag-n'-biejtie!*"

Sunny turned, pulled his torch out from under the passenger seat, played the light over the bossboy and the window. Thin zigzagged branches with long hooked thorns that burned skin like fire, he knew, pressed against it. He pulled the car forward, got out and surveyed the scratches along the length of his beloved car. He swept the light down to the right front tire. It was flat. "Damn!"

"Sorry Baas. Sorry," said the bossboy coming round to survey the damage too before he became preoccupied wrestling carefully with a twig caught in his shorts. Fear was back in his eyes.

Sunny chose to ignore it and turned his attention back to his car. He had worked up the mileage quickly since he had moved to Umzimtuti. He needed new tires, if not a new car soon. Japie was right, really. If only he did not have the £2000 goodwill to pay: how it niggled him. Perhaps he would talk to the flamboyant Scots mayor any-way. He wondered momentarily how pretty Claire Buchanan was doing these days. The evil laugh of a hyena carried over the air. "How far?" he asked turning back to the bossboy. He saw the twig had dis-turbed him greatly, probably some superstition of his, they were so full of it. "What's the matter?" he said irritably.

The bossboy lifted the branch. "Carry spirit of *m'fasi* to new resting place."

"Nonsense," said Sunny. "How far to your *kia*?"

"Baas, not far."

Natives always gave you the answer they thought you wanted to hear. It exasperated him so much. He opened the door and rummaged under the car seat again, extracted his medical paraphernalia and fol-lowed the bossboy hurriedly on foot.

The moon was rising. The air was cold and still. Descending into a valley, the wrenching sounds of African keening carried above the background night sounds. Had the patient died already? Soon Sunny made out the dark forms of the circular arrangement of round huts and kraal in the bare compound clearing. Incongruously the thought passed though him that Natives thought in circles not angular shapes: even the illiterate could draw a perfect circle in the sand.

The throng of blanketed Native women parted at his approach, though the keening continued unabated. The thatch of the roof of the bossboy's hut hung low and Sunny stooped at the open entrance, stepped in and straightened. His eyes smarted from the thick fog of smoke from the central fire burning inside. The scene swam before him as he played his torch light over the pole and dagga walls. He lifted his glasses and wiped his eyes momentarily with his handkerchief. Above, the thatch glistened black, like coal, from the thick accumula-tion of soot. From the rafters loomed the organic shapes of paraphernalia and calabashes of every shape and size. A gecko hung upside down searching for the odd mosquito braving the smoke. A mirror amongst a pile of things glinted off his light as it played off the shiny dung floor. On the right men's clothing hung from a nail, on the left women's things. At the back chickens stirred from their roost and clucked. The rooster crowed indignantly at his intrusion. A dog roused and began to mill about. Stacked beside the entrance was a *badza* and a few other gardening tools, a couple of baskets, and assortment of clay pots, an enamel basin and two pails.

An old midwife stood motionless. The flame from a single wax candle set in a chipped saucer on an upturned orange crate wavered with all the commotion and played over the anguished face of the grandmother who clutched at her throat but no sound came from it. Before him, a newborn baby wrapped tightly in a cotton cloth lay on a straw, blood-stained mat on the floor beside its collapsed mother. She was still bleeding steadily. He knew instinctively her placenta was retained and the hemorrhage would not stop until it was removed in toto. It had only taken a moment to take it all in. Time was of the essence.

There was no running water. He had only a rag and bottle chloroform anesthetic in his red-and-white striped lunch tin, no anesthetist, no intravenous line or oxygen, suction or blood supply. The single candle and his torchlight hardly substituted as theatre lamps. Could he justify intrauterine manipulation? He could not just let her bleed to death while he watched.

He stepped outside. He had to put paid to the cacophony of grief that was premature. Lifting up a clay jug, he said, "Make yourselves useful—*manzi, manzi.*" They were such fatalists, it hindered healing—even caused death: if a Native believed he'd die he usually did.

Briefly, with sign language, the bossboy and the midwife consented to his intervention. The infant cried out. Quickly he bent, and handed it to the old midwife. The grandmother began to keen. He sent her out.

Decisively he opened his red-and-white lunch tin and reached for the chloroform and a rectangle of gauze. By example he instructed the bossboy on the careful drip, drip application of chloroform to apply on his direction from time to time and how to keep the chin up and the airway open.

Satisfied the bossboy understood, he rolled his sleeves above his elbows. There was a small amount of water in a cracked enamel washbasin beside the fire. The bossboy handed him a bar of blue mottled soap from beside the mirror. He lathered up to his forearms. The bossboy responded with a calabash of water. Sunny cupped his hands as the bossboy dribbled water into them to rinse as was their custom. He flicked his hands over the warm fire briefly before he applied Dettol from the small bottle in his supplies and rubbed it into his hands and forearms. He hoped the angel was on his shoulder.

He was aware of the intense gaze of the midwife boring through him, the sound of the baby crying, the chickens clucking, before he blocked them out and focused on the woman's breathing. The bossboy shuffled into a comfortable crouch on his haunches ready to drip, drip, drip the chloroform on cue.

A pocket of burning white ants in the wood of the fire flared as Sunny knelt on the blood-stained straw mat between the woman's outstretched legs. He still did his morning routine of calisthenics including squats and knee bends but kneeling, a pose of supplication, was totally foreign to him. The coarse weave of the straw mat dug into his knees as he inched forward. His thigh muscles tensed as he leaned into the work before him.

He was calm. He recalled Professor Gordon Grant's lecture in his houseman year to carefully shave off the uterine wall with the side of his hand, resisting the temptation to pick it off with his fingertips. With the fire behind him, sweat began to bead on his back and run down his spine. He wiped his forehead on his shirt.

He groped carefully for the adherent placenta that was preventing the uterus from contracting down to end the bleeding. A thrill passed through him as the right layer became obvious and he separated it cleanly and delivered the placenta in toto. Deftly he reached for the tourniquet from the lunch tin and tied it around her arm. In her collapsed state he was momentarily stalled as he searched for a vein. He unwrapped the sterile kidney dish and assembled the glass syringe. The candle extinguished. The bossboy moved to play the light of the torch over Sunny's tin, but knocked over the basin. A rivulet of water dribbled into the fire and sizzled. Locating the vial of ergometrine Sunny tilted the vial momentarily into the torchlight to check the label before he snapped the head off, filled the syringe and injected it intravenously.

He had done all that he could. He straightened up. The baby, still clutched by the midwife, cried out once more and it moved him. He surveyed the chaotic scene: the upturned bowl, the splayed contents of his bloodied red-and-white striped medical tin in the eerie crackling light, the dark stain, sticky now, drying up beneath the woman. The rhythm of her shallow but even breathing was music to his ears.

The grandmother arrived at the hut entrance carrying a clay pot of water on her head, an enamel bucket in each hand. Gratefully, he filled the basin, washed and held his hands above the glow of the fire to dry. The old midwife opened up the cloth and offered the baby to him. A tiny hand closed around his index finger. He rocked it. In the winking firelight he gazed at the smooth chocolate skin topped by the frizzy black head of hair, splayed nostrils accentuated by a high broad forehead. He turned the baby over, checked the soft fontanelles. His hands passed over the baby's body checking the symmetry of the bones down to the small perfect feet. He laid the baby down and reached for his stethoscope. The dog came and sniffed. He pushed its snout roughly away. The baby had a powerful set of lungs, his heart was strong too: a perfect boy. He lifted the baby and handed it back to the midwife.

The cock suddenly spread his big white wings like an angel in the darkness and crowed. The mother stirred. She would come round.

Sunny looked down at his blood soaked trousers, the blood spattered shirt, the rolled up sleeves that had served as a bloody wick. The husband put his hands together and bowed back and forth. *"Mai-weh! Mai-weh! Dankie! Baie dankie, Baas!"* There was no doubt in his mind, the angel had been on his shoulder. The moment of intimacy with this family was over. He gathered his things and made for the hut's exit. "Now," he said matter-of-factly, "we fix flat tire, okay?"

He felt his stained trousers stiffen as they dried on the walk back to the car to the accompaniment of a choir of insect sounds: ticking, fizzing, humming as a background to the coo of insomniac doves. His adrenaline rush was over. He felt his knees were permanently imprinted with the pattern of the mat. His thighs ached, his forearms too. He was suddenly exhausted. In the darkness, fears welled up within him: the chances were the woman would die of puerperal sepsis. There was absolutely nothing he could do about it under the circumstances. He had done his best.

The night was cold. It took time to change the tire in the dark but finally, Sunny headed back to the farmhouse. Mrs. van Hoepen appeared at the doorway and waved him on. "Japie's on his way with Ouma already," she shouted. "I'm staying on here with the children."

"I'll catch him up," shot back Sunny.

The farm road required his full concentration until he turned onto the familiar strip road to town. The metallic smell of his blood soaked clothes filled the cocoon of his car. He lit up a cigarette to absorb it, and suppress his gnawing hunger.

Back in town, he detoured home. He let the door slam hastening to the phone. He was happy to hear Sister Hoskins was on duty and instructed her to prepare for a lumber puncture on Ouma. Mavourneen appeared in her dressing gown as he put the receiver down in the passageway.

"Whatever's happened?" she said.

"It's been a terrible night," he said. "I can't bath. I'm soiled—soot in my hair, all this blood. My knees will never be the same—irreparably bruised. I've got to have a shower like my Kikuyu batman used to do for me. Do you mind getting me a bucket from the kitchen?"

"Of course," she said.

He stripped and she poured hot water over him. He lathered up while she adjusted the hot and cold taps and filled the bucket again. "Thank goodness the water is clear tonight," she said. Water splashed way beyond the confines of the narrow six-foot bath tub. She grabbed a towel and spread it on the slippery floor.

"We must get a shower installed. It's so much cleaner than wallowing in dirty water."

"There's nothing more rewarding than a good soak after a day in the garden, but I can see there are occasions that warrant a stand up shower."

"I'm exhausted," he said, "I need a cold rinse to buck me up. The night's not nearly over yet."

"Whatever else?" she said, as she leaned over, turned on the cold-water tap and filled the bucket.

"I've got to pick up the microscope from the surgery right away, do a lab work-up and sort out Ouma van Hoepen. I'm fearing the worst there too."

"That's not like you," she said, "I'm sure you'll win through on both counts...but remember you can't win every case. You're human—after all. Don't take a loss personally and get into a black mood if you lose."

"That's the trouble," he said, "in Umzimtuti, they're not just cases. They're families I've come to care about deeply—even in this short time. The Natives, their lot is so desperate."

"They've been living like that for centuries—millennia. You're not going to change it in a hurry. You did the best you could. I'm sure they are grateful—whatever the inevitable outcome."

"I'm over my head with all this work and there's no one to consult with. I mean Maxwell's so far out of date. Eckhart's an undisputed expert on leprosy, but little else. I'd give anything to know what Gordon Grant would think of my performance tonight. What I could learn from it for next time."

"Of course, he'd have been proud of you, I'm sure of it," she said. "You can only do your best. I'll fix a glass of hot Ovaltine and throw together a sandwich for you to eat on the way to hospital while you dress," she said as he toweled down.

Sunny downed the glass of Ovaltine in one gulp. Mavourneen kissed him, gave his hand a squeeze. Her support meant so much to him, a catch welled up in his throat. He accepted a tin of thickly buttered sandwiches with slices of Sunday's roast beef and a smear of horseradish, gratefully. How comforting and thoughtful she was. What would he do without her?

The door slammed. He ran across to the surgery to pick up the black velvet lined portable case which held the microscope, the box of slides, a selection of stains and a counting chamber, all very compactly fixed in their respective places. This was the tool to give an immediate diagnosis, no posting samples and waiting a week or more for a report. As always, early detection was the key. He sped past the whitewashed trunks of the avenue of jacaranda saplings whose young skeletons arched over the New Government Hospital driveway. Coming to an abrupt halt outside Casualty their seed capsules exploded like gunfire. He parked and ran in with his equipment in hand.

Sister Hoskins, reliable and conscientious, had already admitted Ouma van Hoepen, set up the drip and prepared a lumber puncture tray. Ouma's pulse rate was slow and irregular. He scrubbed and gloved while she positioned Ouma for the procedure: curling her back into a fetal position. He injected the local anesthetic, and then inserted a needle between the vertebrae. The intracranial pressure was high. As he feared the cerebrospinal fluid was purulent. He placed a drop under the coverslip of the counting chamber and it filled by capillary action. Under the microscope he counted up the white cells, noted the bacteria. Just as he had expected, bacterial meningitis! Was it pneumococcal or meningococcal?

He clamped the hand-cranked centrifuge to the bench, spun the fluid down, smeared the deposit on a slide and fixed it by briefly heating it on top of the sterilizing unit. Meanwhile at the sink he extracted the dropper bottles from his microscope box. He applied the crystal violet to the fixed slide, followed up with iodine, quickly decolorized with alcohol and finally dropped on the basic fuchsin.

He dried the slide again on the lid of the sterilizing unit, dropped a blob of oil on it, topped it with a coverslip and slid it on the stage of his microscope. A field of purple diplococci crowded between a sea of polymorphonuclear leucocytes confirmed this was pneumococcal meningitis. It was usually fatal.

Damn! He wanted her to live with no permanent disability. Impulsively, he decided to try, in addition to the chloramphenicol intramuscular injection, a penicillin treatment of 5 cc's via lumber puncture. There was everything to gain and nothing to lose. As far as he knew, it had never been tried before.

Sister Hoskins assisted. As he was washing up afterwards she asked, "Dr. Rubenstein, is that a new treatment, intrathecal administration of penicillin?"

"Yes it is. We are going to administer it daily for least five days. Let's hope the angel's on my shoulder. The prognosis is bad without it."

"Yes, I agree it's—well, hopeless."

"No," he said, "We must never give in while there is still life."

"I'll keep a close eye on her and have a lumber puncture tray ready for you each evening. Mr. van Hoepen's in the waiting room wanting to talk to you."

"Thank you, Sister. Ring me if there's any change."

He'd always seen Japie with his battered bush hat jammed on, the smell of the earth embedded into the fiber of his khakis—at odds with the enveloping sterile smells. Hatless, Sunny was surprised to see how blonde Japie was in the glare of hospital lights. He offered Japie a cigarette, striking a match, holding the flame out to him. Japie drew on it and the cigarette flared, before he lit his own, extinguished the match and exhaled in long slow puffs. Finally he said, "Ouma has pneumococcal meningitis...a bacterial infection of the brain. The prognosis is not so hot but we are doing the best we can. We'll see what the morning brings."

"Isn't there anything we can do, Doc? I mean, man, she was fine, you know, *just* yesterday."

"Yes, I understand." The tips of their cigarettes glowed. "Life's a gift, not to be taken for granted. We really are doing the best we can, but I can't make any promises."

The sharp predawn chill took Sunny's breath away as he exited the hospital. The naked skeletons of the jacarandas shivered in the breeze as his car passed under them. He reminded himself that soon the oppressive spring heat of October—suicide month—would bring forth their glorious mauve splendor: despite their appearance there was still much life in them.

Two lives had been entrusted to him. The odds against winning in both these cases were enormous. It niggled him that Alison Hoskins, a good sister, had questioned his authority over his experimental treatment of Ouma. Didn't she see there was nothing to lose and everything to gain by it? There was no doubt in his mind the risk was worth it...and yet after all the years he longed for the support of the teaching hospital entourage of his student days and its collective wisdom. He took a last puff on his cigarette as his Ford lumbered up the hill. The car ashtray was overflowing as he ground out the stub of his cigarette and parked in the lean-to garage.

The cold had penetrated his very marrow. Bundu never failed to greet him and he took a minute to bend down and scratch him behind the ears, pat him on the back: what an unexpected joy Palmer had left him along with the furniture. He tiptoed into the children's rooms. They still slept: life was, indeed, a gift. There was still time for a quick warm-up and the solace of Mavourneen's embrace before the mine hooter mournfully summoned him to Sick Parade. He pulled off his shirt, dropped his pants and slid into bed with her.

But in the dark he agonized over every aspect of the procedures he had undertaken that night. Could he have done better, done differently, done more for either of these women? He knew there were others more skillful. He knew he should not allow himself to wallow in his limitations or the limitations of his circumstances—and his profession—and, he admitted to himself, sink into a 'black mood', as Mavourneen called it, which would adversely affected his work and his family for weeks. Medicine was a *practice*, the learning never stopped. All in all, the risks he'd taken were justified—whatever the outcome. He had done his best.

CHAPTER TWENTY-FIVE

Leah's Bid

Doris clued Sunny's new bookkeeper into the system she estab-lished, and had long since returned to the City of Gold. Mavourneen missed her best chum but had settled into a routine. Deborah was in-deed proving to be the easy baby she had wished for and the services of nanny certainly made life easier—freer. Leah Levine had first intro-duced her to the market as promised. Now she turned to her for companionship and it had become a standing date to attend the Satur-day market together.

The Municipal Market leaned against the sidewall of the Town House. Sheets of corrugated iron roofing supported by gum poles sloped down to a low entrance, the sides enclosed by chicken wire. At dawn each Saturday morning farm lorries backed up to unload their produce onto the rows of wooden trestle tables. It was always a color-ful scene, ripe with the smells of the earth, blue exhaust from the lorries and the sweat of Natives.

Live chickens were confined in coops made of laths wound with *tambu*. Blue eggs as well as brown were for sale by the dozen and by the crate, along with boxes of avocados, pockets of oranges, hands of bananas, pyramids of paw paws, boxes of guavas, bundles of red rhu-barb stalks. Bunches of leafy green lettuce, stacks of young dark baby marrows, white chou-chou fruits and purple eggplants colored the scene. Bottles of unpasteurized milk, their necks clotted with cream stood in zinc baths of ice, beside blocks of butter and mounds of homemade soft cheese. Jars of homemade watermelon *konfyt*, melon and ginger jam, orange marmalade, lemon curd and bottled guavas stood in rows. Rushdie's Rainbow Bazaar's curry mixes imported di-rectly from India mingled their aromas with cut flowers from Mrs. Cynthia Illbert's farm.

Mrs. Shapiro made a point to secure a trestle table at the entrance for WIZO's cake sale: it could not be missed, coming or going. Whole cakes, iced cupcakes by the dozen and assorted biscuits by the plateful, cellophane wrapped and tied with blue bows were priced and arranged on the table with German efficiency.

"Let's take a quick peek preview of what's for sale inside," said Leah to Mavourneen. "I never tire of the challenge to get a bargain. Rivkah and Abigail have arrived to help Sophie manage the till. We'll relieve them later."

Japie Van Hoepen had brought in crates of early gem squash and young ears of mealies, the silks still moist. Mavourneen had her eye on those. The cob was really the best part, Sunny loved to suck on it rolled in melted butter once he'd gnawed round and round and devoured every last tender juicy kernel. Dining separately in the children's alcove with furniture to suit beside the fireplace, Douglas did just the same—to her amused surprise.

Against the Town House wall was a platform and podium for the auctioneer. Colonel O'Connor, big and chubby with a melodious voice, musical laugh and charming Irish brogue, was a man who had occupied loftier roles amongst people of international stature in his heyday. He eased confidently behind the podium to take command of the chaotic auction proceedings, gavel in hand.

Mavourneen recognized her father's Irish brogue behind O'Connor's skilled rapid-fire singsong with which he quickly disposed of every single thing at the market. All these lovingly tended products took so long to grow, to nurture and to harvest yet in the final analysis were disposed of with such great haste.

Starting at one end, O'Connor's Native assistant would hold up an item and O'Connor would boom out, "What have I got? A crate of spinach or will it be by the bunch? By the crate it is then." That determined the words ran into each other in a singsong: "Do I have a shilling shilling it is one and thruppence I have one and thruppence any advance on one and thruppence yes, one and sixpence I have one and sixpence advances yes, one and nine—now two shillings I have two shillings. Must have more for a whole crate, ladies and gentleman yes, Mrs. van Vuren at the back half-a-crown. *Sold*."

Soon the Colonel indicated van Hoepen's stand and began with the mealies. His native assistant held up an ear. Mavourneen was ready with her bid. Yes, he recognized her.

"*Sold* to Mrs. Rubenstein."

She had six wonderful ears, six ears for a sixpence! O'Connor had hardly allowed for competitive bidding. At that price could van Hoepen make a living? Surely not? She knew van Hoepen made his money selling wholesale to Feldmans granary to be dried and ground into mealie meal and sold for a special price to the Cheetah Mine for the compound. This was really just a sideshow. Still, she felt he ought to get a fair price and was uncomfortable with the purchase. She liked a bargain just as much as anyone else but she didn't want to do anyone down.

Leah wanted a bunch of young carrots and was ready for O'Connor. She raised her hand high as the bidding proceeded but O'Connor missed her in the crowd. "Do I have sixpence?" She raised her hand again, but still he didn't see it. "No thruppence I have thruppence can we make it fourpence?"

Leah was jumping up and down now, waving.

"Fourpence no takers."

Leah was on tip-toe, frantic, but he was looking the other way. "It's thruppence then. Going once going twice *sold* to Mrs. Curtis. Next..."

Spittle sprang forth from Leah's lips. "That's not the first time he's passed over my bid. The *schmuck*! That Irish oaf has an inflated idea of himself and his silly little rag."

"Leah," Mavourneen said. "My dear, I think it's just a genuine oversight. There's a big crowd and his eyes are roaming the whole market. It's bedlam really. I don't know how he keeps track."

"No no! It's a *shanda fur die goy*. He deliberately overlooked me. *Ignored* me."

"Surely you don't think he intentionally wanted to embarrass you, do you?"

"Absolutely. He knows Jud is not going to support him in the Parliamentary by-election coming up."

"I'd give him the benefit of the doubt. You know it's fairly dark here under cover and he's got a lot to get through this morning."

"Benefit of the doubt! He's done this before! You know Jud has a lot of clout behind the bar chit-chatting to the patrons every night. He doesn't think O'Connor would make a good MP. He wasn't last time. His own party threw him out. O'Connor wants to undermine him—make us look small."

"Be bigger than him and ignore it. I do believe my carrots might be big enough for harvest at the bottom of my garden. I'll see what I can come up with for you although they might not be up to Cronje standards."

"No! It's a matter of principle. I'll ask Cronje to drop a bunch off at the hotel directly tomorrow. *This* week of all weeks. I was going to make a carrot cake for my Jud's birthday. His favorite."

"Carrot cake? I've never heard of that. Cake from a vegetable?"

"Yes, yes," she said testily, "it makes a very moist cake."

"You'll have to share the recipe. Make it for the cake sale next time. Mark it *sold*."

"If I ever get any carrots! You know with the hotel business we haven't time for a vegetable patch ourselves."

"Let's get back to the cake stand and forget it."

WIZO was wrapping up, having sold all their goodies.

"We made five pounds three shillings and sixpence today," said Rivkah.

"*Ja!* Should we make more? But it's enough, it's enough," said Sophie.

Just then Japie van Hoepen came up, arms laden with mealies, as well as a few gem squashes.

"Can I take them to your car?" he asked Mavourneen.

"No, no. You know I only bid for six mealies."

"We're so grateful. It's the least we can offer the good Doctor."

"You're very kind. I've got a basket on the front of my bike."

"Doc needs to get a new car for himself. One for you too?"

She felt suddenly self-conscious as his blue eyes beneath the bleached lashes roamed down her bare legs to her turned down socks and sensible shoes. "No, no, he's attached to his car. Part of his army entitlement, you know. I love my bike. Always have."

"What about a horse?"

"Every summer as a child I used to ride in the Drakensberg at Cathedral Peak."

"*Ja nie, die Berg.* Ouma and my late Oupa, God rest his soul, came from the Free State. Ouma's *baai gesond*. Doc saved her! *Ja*, saved her life with all that needles in the spine. She's back to bossing up everyone on the farm. The bossboy's wife, too, and her baby also, not that we need another *picannin* around the farm, but still, we're grateful. She was back on her feet after two days."

"Two days! I'm so glad to hear it."

"Maybe you'll all come ride the horses by the farm?"

"I'd love to but Douglas, my son, is not nearly old enough for lessons. He's not yet even ready for a bike—but he does so love to ride on the back of mine. We go everywhere together. He's such a lovely companion. I'm just longing for him to grow up."

"You want him to ride in the gymkhana, then?"

"No, no. I love the great outdoors, the animals, exploring the bush. That's what I want for him."

"What about Doc?"

"No, I don't think so. It's not something I've done since I met him. Nursing school. War. Babies. All that."

"You are *welkom*. Bring *die baba*. We'll have a braai—our very own meat—steaks and *boerewors*. *My vrou*, Marie, makes *lekker koeksisters*."

"*Baie dankie*. I'll talk to Sunny."

"My youngest, Stephanus, is six. He'll walk together with your *seuntjie* in the veld. He goes with me all the time. *Ons het die lekker lewe*. I can put your bike in the lorry and drive you home."

"No really. It's not hot yet and I love riding in the shade of the jacarandas. Reminds me of Pretoria. I've got to work up an appetite so we can tuck into the mealies tonight."

He held her gaze momentarily before he cocked his veld hat, nodded to Leah and turned and strode off in his veldskoens. No socks! His legs were long and strong. He walked deliberately with long strides. She put him in his forties. Mature and restrained, habitually formal and polite. The successful owner of vast acreage—the Mealie King. An Afrikaner! What was she thinking, watching him walk away? How many handsome Englishmen in uniform—Anglicans—had she met and dismissed in the war? Here she was, married! Out of faith! Two children! She checked herself: all the same, nice chap. It would be good to saddle up again. She hoped something would come of it.

"Such a nice fellow," said Mavourneen, turning to Leah.

"Mmmm," said Leah, "Besides O'Connor, did you notice how van Hoepen ignored me *standing right here*, too? Don't you know the Afrikaners hate us Jews?"

"I'm absolutely sure Japie doesn't think anything of the kind," said Mavourneen. "Good and bad types in every camp."

"Jud bust his hand defending Sunny's honor at the bar from a couple of *Jarps*."

"Surely not. What happened?"

"Well," she said, "I don't know the details myself, but that afternoon that little Douglas showed up at the bar, Verdoon and del la Rey accused Sunny of letting Ferreira out to spread TB around."

"Oh, how wicked!"

"I wouldn't tell Sunny, but watch out. Sunny never thanked Jud, you know."

"I am sure he's no idea."

"Did you know Sunny spanked Douglas down at the bar that evening? I gather it was quite embarrassing."

"Oh no, I didn't. He was very worried. These things are best forgotten," she squeezed Leah's hand.

"I can assure you Jud and I never forget."

"Let's get our cakes and get on with the day," said Mavourneen.

Mavourneen decided to let Douglas have a treat and join them for dinner that evening. She nursed Deborah early and put her to bed. She was such a joy. She thrived: fed, slept, put on weight. Others might take it for granted, but she had not forgotten her days of desperation with Douglas. What a relief—finally to be validated as a mother—*alles sal reg kom.*

At dinner, Douglas perched on a couple of pillows stacked on a dining room chair opposite her at the long dining room table. Scrubbed, with fresh pajamas under his dressing gown, hair brushed, eyes bright with anticipation as the mealies were served, butter, salt and pepper passed.

"These are mealies from the van Hoepen farm, fresh from the market today," said Mavourneen.

The butter dissolved into a lake as Sunny twirled his cob over a generous glob. "First rate," he said, as he tucked in and Douglas followed suit.

"We had a fine time at the cake sale today. Made over £5. I bought Sophie Shapiro's apple strudel."

"German," he said, "mixed up with the right cause."

"Japie van Hoepen's pretty impressed with the lumbar puncture treatment you did for Ouma's meningitis."

"Yes, the angel was on my shoulder that night. I wasn't sure she'd pull through but she's made a remarkable recovery—no disability whatsoever fortunately. Put it down to Afrikaner pioneer stock—tough. Sister Hoskins was attentive. That helped, too. Matron is impressed, that doesn't hurt either."

"I heard Sister Hoskins questioned your unconventional cure."

"Once I had the definitive diagnosis confirmed by the Gram stain, I knew the situation was desperate and called for desperate measures. You can't put a price on the value of the microscope. Where did you hear about the treatment?"

"Leah told me at the market."

"Must be all round the bar, then."

"I'd be careful."

"Of who? Ever since Matron heard I assisted Jan Schulenburg she's been very co-operative."

"No, careful of Sister Hoskins."

"No, no. Not her. She's reliable and conscientious. A bit highly strung—but good."

"I'd avoid her if I could—she doesn't respect patient confidentiality."

"She's not a patch on you in the theatre, but she's efficient enough."

Mavourneen let it drop, she didn't want to sound jealous of her position. "The van Hoepen bossboy's wife with the retained placenta was up on day two doing chores."

"Now that's truly a miracle! Her condition: the conditions in the hut. Amazing how the bossboy managed the anesthesia for me! Afterwards I doubted my sanity giving it a go, but I had to at least try in the face of such helplessness. I can see the Saturday market is the place to go for post-op reports."

"Leah got into a terrible state because Colonel O'Connor missed her sixpence bid for a bunch of carrots."

"Despite their age difference, she and Jud make a well matched couple. Both small, they're sensitive to being overlooked. Perhaps a bit over defensive about their Jewishness as well. It's such a small matter. So what?"

"Well, she said she isn't going to let it rest there."

"She isn't going to make a *tsimmes* out of it is she? There'll be more carrots next week, surely."

"I offered her ours—they might just be big enough to pull up. She wants to make a cake for Jud's birthday."

"Carrot cake? I'm not familiar with that. *Ingberlach* is a carrot sweetmeat tradition at Passover. But any time is the time for *taiglach* that marvelous plaited dough boiled in syrup. A Jewish version of *koeksisters* you might say, at a stretch. Was there any for sale? Douglas would love it."

"I promised I'd buy her carrot cake next time."

"No carrots needed for *taiglach*, and she's got an order already."

Turning to Douglas, Mavourneen wiped the butter smeared all over his face and hands with her serviette.

"My boy! You've been so good. What brings you to the table?" demanded Sunny.

"Dad," he said, "Mom got a book."

"A book? Tell me about it."

"It's a horsey book."

"What about it?"

"Mom's friend's got a horsey."

"Who's that?"

"Japie van Hoepen," cut in Mavourneen, "I think the van Hoepens are anxious to show their gratitude for Ouma's recovery and invited us out sometime. I dropped into Kingston's and couldn't resist this new illustrated version of *Black Beauty*. I haven't ridden myself for years. I think we should take them up on their offer. Apparently Ouma and Marie are good cooks. It'd be a break for you."

"Isn't Douglas way too young for *Black Beauty*?" Turning back to Douglas he said, "First you'll have to learn how to take care of a horse. You can't forget to feed him, brush him down, that sort of thing, not just when you feel like it but every single day. When did you last feed Bundu? Your mother's got to do it, or Leonard. The turkeys and the bantams, do you go down to the chicken *hok* with your mother every morning to feed them and collect the eggs? Ah, yes! And then you have to rake the muck out the *hok*, put fresh straw down and so on. A horse, same thing but just a lot more manure to clean up. When you start doing the bantams on a regular basis then we can start thinking of something bigger."

Douglas sucked thoughtfully on his mealie. "Dad, I hate chickens and I can't ride Bundu."

"Ride him? Now why would you want to do that? He's your pal. Your companion in the garden, beside your bed every night. He's not a beast of burden. He's your best friend."

"My friends are Marvin. Peter. Norman. Timmy."

"Come to think of it where is Bundu now?"

"We haven't seen him for a couple of days," said Mavourneen. "He's on the razz."

"Razz, razz? What's that?" asked Douglas.

"He's gone out to find himself a girl friend," said Mavourneen.

"There you are. If you paid more attention to him Douglas, he wouldn't mooch off."

"It's time for bed," said Mavourneen. "Choose two chocs from the Black Magic box and I'll come and read to you."

Sunny was nosing his whisky when she entered the sitting room with coffee and wide diagonal slices of Mrs. Shapiro's strudel.

The thin pastry layers were crisp, the dried fruit plump and juicy against the crisp slivers of tart apple sprinkled with cinnamon, just a hint of lemon and a toss of nuts. "Hmm," said Sunny, "This is good. How's the book?" he asked, as he leaned forward and tucked in.

"Oh, you're right, he still wants his favorites in *Mother Goose* but he'll grow into *Black Beauty* all in good time. I hope you don't mind. Kingston's had a banner outside saying *New Shipment Received* and I couldn't resist stepping in."

"Remember, the Cheetah Club Library, why, it's *right* next door. Probably a copy there when the time comes."

"I'm sure they do. But it's a classic. I think it's important to build up our own library for the children and this is a wonderful start. Remember, it's more than just a story of a horse from his perspective. Each chapter is a lesson in kindness for animals, people too. It's been a favorite of mine as long as I can remember."

"I didn't own my first book until high school. It was Benjamin Harrow's *Romance of the Atom*. I wanted physics for a career."

"I'll choose carefully. Lasting books read over and over again become a part of you."

"Don't go overboard—you haven't got notions to make the mink and manure set part of you, too, have you?"

"Of course not. Riding the trails at the Drakensberg was an important part of my growing up. The great outdoors: that's what I want to pass on to Douglas."

"Oh? You've never spoken about it."

"No, a past life before I met you. Took a back seat to the War. Marriage. Babies. Now that I'm done with all that, maybe I can get back to it?"

"You resent it. Marriage. Babies. You attend to these things out of duty—not love. No, not love. Douglas is way, way too young. I didn't get to ride a bicycle until university—first year medicine—out of necessity. Horse riding. It's pretentious. We can't afford that."

"It won't cost us anything. Japie van Hoepen made an open invitation.

"Even if we could we don't want it."

"He's hardly the mink and manure set. He doesn't even wear socks with his veldskoens! I bet his children would be a good influence on Douglas. He's so well now, he needs to toughen up. He's a new boy since we came to Umzimtuti. Talking nineteen to the dozen! How independent he's become riding all the way to the Umzimtuti Hotel on his tricycle. All he needs is the benefit of some older, outdoor boys with *bundu* experience."

"He's not *that* precocious at all, he's just caught up after all the troubles. You know in your heart he's just *normal.*"

"I should get a driver's license and a car and be independent like Rivkah. Then we could get out and leave you to your obsession with all work and no play," she said. "What about it?"

"What Douglas needs is an attentive mother who doesn't lose track of him for a whole afternoon."

"Well I understand you lost control of yourself when you found Douglas at the bar and embarrassed us all—but all these things are best forgotten."

CHAPTER TWENTY-SIX

A Lawsuit in Umzimtuti?

Sunny had a late night call, and afterwards, driving home he noticed there were still a lot of cars parked outside the Umzimtuti Hotel. He was pleased to see Ferreira's Lincoln Continental was there so he swung in for a nightcap and a word with him. As usual, late-nighters were propping up the bar. Teetotalers were shunned by all and had long since called it a night. Before Sunny could order a whisky Jud beckoned him aside and said, "Doc, I'm close to closing, can I have a word with you?"

"Why, yes of course. What is it? It's been quite a night. Past my bedtime. Mavourneen said she'd stay up for me."

"Please stay. Your whisky's on the house. Doc, did Leah tell you, O'Connor made a *shanda fur die goy* at the Municipal Market."

"Surely she is not making a *tsutcheppenish* out of a few carrots? Mavourneen's got a few for her from the garden."

"You see. It's such an embarrassment. He's done it before."

"Mavourneen thought it was a genuine oversight. Nothing personal. It's very busy there and he's just trying to get through the produce as quickly as he can."

"Nonsense. It may seem like a small thing to you, but it's the principle. Should I think of it—the insult in public? When she confronted him afterwards did he laugh in her face? Did he even go so far as to say how did she expect him to see her in that tall mob? The cheek of it! Did it make her the laughing stock of the town in front of everyone?"

"Jud, really. What was it? A tickey or a sixpence worth of carrots at most. There'll be more next week."

"I'm gonna knock the block off that big fat oaf as a birthday present to myself. He's got such an inflated idea of himself. All the colonel stuff with Field Marshall Allenby during the Great War doesn't frighten me. I'm sure he's phony."

"Remember what happened last time you lost your temper."

"Is it any wonder he was a Catholic priest who quit?"

"Really? Take a cue from his Christian teachings. Turn the other cheek."

"That'll be the day."

"I don't want to have to put your hand back in plaster and sew up a couple of individuals."

"Alright then, if I can't knock his block off, at least I'm going to write and demand he publish an apology in *that* rag of his."

"Look, the colonel's down on his luck pretty much. Everyone knows it. The rag doesn't really turn much of a profit and the auction-eering is pretty spasmodic besides the Saturday market. On top of that, it's no secret, he's got to contend with his alcoholic wife, who drains the till. Have some compassion. You're doing well in business—I mean from trading store out in the *gamadoelas* to owning the best hotel in town. The bar I'm sure is a money spinner. You've got a beautiful wife and a lovely pigeon pair. Let it go, man."

"Us Jews, centuries of taking things lying down. Not anymore."

He sympathized with Jud and admired his refusal to accept anti-Semitism but you had to know when to pick your fights. He'd ignored plenty of anti-Semitic remarks when the Nazis were popular with some of the Afrikaners at Wits University, but when Verwoerd's *Die Transvaler* newspaper was officially introduced into the medical students' common room it was an appropriate occasion to stand for election to have it removed. He'd won the election, but it had come at a price: he'd been under the threat of being beaten up for a few weeks and lost all his Afrikaner friends.

"Jud, I'm sure you'll think better of it after a good night's sleep. Colonel O'Connor just isn't worth it. Don't let Leah's *tsutcheppenish* drive you crazy. Ask your wife to put her energies into making some *taiglach* instead. We'll take an order for WIZO funds. Good cause. No carrots required."

CHAPTER TWENTY-SEVEN

A Tidbit

Pat O'Connor chuckled as he poured his wife Nancy another sundowner. "Look at this," he said, as he sat back with a drink at his side and letter in his hand. "That cheeky upstart Jew, Levine, is demanding a written apology in the paper for my overlooking his little wife's bid for a bunch of carrots at the municipal market. Can you believe it!"

"Ridiculous," she nodded as the whisky sloshed from her outstretched hand onto the carpet. "Ignore it," she slurred, as she slumped deeper into her lounge chair.

"No. I'm onto something. You know all the planning talk for the Royal Victory Tour coming up next year? It's been on the go forever. Of course the big contract for the Royal Retreat at Sycamore Bend went to Mayor Buchanan's brother-in-law, Broderick Anderson. No surprise there—nepotism as usual. No point in challenging that and alienating myself. You know how entrenched Buchanan is. But browsing the council's General Purpose Committee minutes for some tidbits for the paper, I saw the Royal Tea Party contract to supply the catering in the summerhouse at the Railway Park has gone to that Yid and his hotel. I'll have something to say about it at the next open Council meeting. But in the meantime, there's no harm in a brief report in the paper querying whether tenders were called for, and if so whether his was the lowest. That should get people reading."

"That's it, Pat! But don't lay it on too thick. Come to think of it, try to sort him out over a drink to show how fair you are," said Nancy, mellow.

"No, I'm certainly not going to appease him. He's a joke. I'm going to enjoy myself. And don't you interfere when you've had a few. The paper is such a powerful weapon, I'm going to really use it to get elected in the upcoming Parliamentary by-election."

"Wait until the New Year and all the festivities are over, that's when gossip travels faster than the speed of light around here..."

CHAPTER TWENTY-EIGHT

The Little Village that Could

After lunch, flopping down in the sitting room to read the latest *Cleft Stick* Mavourneen commented to Sunny, "Who would have thought this little community of 1300 could raise over £3,000 for the War effort last year from the Carnival and Fete. The target's £4,000 this year. Dr. Eckhart's the chairman. They say he's the driving force, determined the returning lads that need help are not forgotten."

"Whatever the trouble, he's always jovial. I imagine he can win anyone over to his cause," Sunny replied, "but everyone knows his real desire is to serve lepers."

"That's very noble—unexpected—he being an Afrikaner."

"He's been advertising to sell his practice for some time so he can devote himself full time to them, but as far as I know hasn't had any enquiries."

"You've got your plate *more* than full. Don't even think of doing anything rash like buying him out."

"It's a small practice but has possibilities, I have to admit it's crossed my mind. But I know I can't afford to lay out for another hefty goodwill. He'll demand it because he knows the Works is going to be big eventually. If only I could find a partner to share the load, we'd have a monopoly in town," he said thoughtfully.

He got up and walked to the window as the room darkened. Huge black cumulonimbus clouds billowed across the sky. He tapped his cigarette against the box before he lit up. The tip glowed red as he inhaled deeply and let the smoke out in measured puffs. She hated his smoking habit but tried to ignore it.

"This is quite a rainy season we're having here, where they say it hardly rains," she said. She got up to join him at the window, looked out over the rain washed garden. Sunshine and shadow played off the jacaranda trees that spread their canopy high above the lawn. These foreigners flourished with neglect—defying heat, disease and drought. Late spring bloomers, the gregarious bundles of glorious mauve trumpets clung on tenaciously well into summer. But the hint of new green signaled the inevitable: the blooms would surrender to royally carpet the earth before pop, pop, popping when they were squashed underfoot. Any more rain and they would be torn away prematurely, and rudely and unceremoniously swept away to memory: memories of those difficult times in Pretoria and wartime one-roomed flats welled up. It was all behind her. She turned in.

Sunny was saying, "Yes, it's adding up to a record year and the summer's barely begun. Farmers belly-aching. You know they're never happy."

"Any minute," she said, "it's going to bucket down again." Bundu was restless too, circling round the sitting room, his ears cocked, tail erect, whining. She pushed him down gently, patted him reassuringly, and fondled his ears.

"I heard the Umzimtuti River's really full—full to overflowing. Much more and the bridges will be underwater."

"How exciting!" she said. "Let's get the kids—take Bundu too, and drive out and take a look."

"My duty roster's full," he said. "Tomorrow—the weekend, after rounds—perhaps."

Disappointed she said, "The clouds are moving fast, by tomorrow it will all be back to normal, you know how quickly the rivers rise and fall—like the Transvaal, I expect. There'll be just enough rain to cut short the jacaranda bloom that I love so much."

"Well, this afternoon is out of the question." A fissure of lighting split the sky, thunder clapped and the screen door slammed.

Rain on the roof was music to Sunny's ears. He slept well. But at first light, before Sick Parade, the phone rang with those three damnable trills. "The bridges are down," said Sunny as Mavourneen turned over sleepily, "the 1.01 from Bulawayo's held up at the station. Don't wait on me for breakfast."

The muddy tree lined avenue was stained mauve. Sunny negotiated carefully through the mine property gates and slid on down to the Railway Station. No one had stirred yet in the first and second class carriages, the windows were still shuttered. There was a murmur of activity from third and fourth class, which, as usual, was crowded with Natives.

The Stationmaster had called Railway Headquarters in Bulawayo. An official along with an engineer had been dispatched. Meanwhile, the Mayor, Buchanan; a few councilors; the GMO, Maxwell; and the Mine Manager, Doolittle huddled out of the rain in the baggage room for a meeting. A decision was made to visit the bridge to assess the situation.

Sunny, the GMO and some of the councilors went in Sunny's army Ford. The tarmac strips shrugged off the rain, but still the going was slow. It was seven miles to the riverbank. Sunny reminisced about his army days when his convoy struck torrential rain in East Africa and mired in the mud, having to cut their own roads in stretches, sometimes only advancing three or four miles a day. Were the others listening or were they mesmerized by the sweep of the windscreen wipers?

The river boiled red, eating up the banks. Swift and undulating, it raced over both the road and the rail bridges. Tree trunks and bushes roiled on the surface as they rushed by. Sunny glimpsed the bloated carcass of a cow. The transformation from the winter trickle on the river bottom, with sporadic, stagnant-green rocky pools that were meccas for wild animals, was a marvel to Sunny. The bridges were constructed in a narrow gorge. Although low level, they were designed to withstand the short afternoon thunderstorms which broke the white formless heat of the October sky, as it took on shape and color with fast evolving cotton wool clouds casting moving shadows, before the downpour.

All this rain should be harnessed for the drought years, thought Sunny: no more dead fish fingerlings spewing from the lips of the bathroom taps. A dam would support a waterborne sewage system— flush disease down the toilet. It would put the farmers and ranchers out of their misery of insecurity and keep those lovingly tended mine gardens green all year. He joined Doolittle and Buchanan further up the bank and said, "All this water needs harnessing for the lean years."

"Aye," said Buchanan, "but yer aff yer heid, the toon's a wee bit short o' funds. Ye ken, we've not flooded like this in all my six terms as mayor."

"Everyone would benefit." I'm going to see to it, thought Sunny.

Doolittle said, "I guess it's going to take quite a while to build temporary structures after the river subsides."

Buchanan convened a meeting at the mayor's office at the Town House with councilors, headmaster Mr. Francis Asquith, Maxwell,

Doolittle and Sunny. Eckhart had left for his weekend leper clinic.

"We'll have to rely on a wee bit of mucking in by the toonsfolk to keep the travelers bellies full. We'll need some volunteers to help with that. We'll get the kirks to help as well. I'll inform you all when the railway engineer has made an assessment," said Buchanan.

Sunny mused that he still talked like a Scot and said 'toon' and 'toonsfolk' after all these years, unchanged, just like all the old time Jewish townsfolk and his own mother with their accents. "I'll get my wife onto the churches and you know the Jewish community will be happy to pitch in too," he said. "The station master's already alerted me to a family with measles. You know how infectious it is. I've isolated them in an empty carriage on the shunting track for now but I've got a local family with measles and I'll ask them if they'll accept this family. T.J. Llewellyn has agreed to extend his dispensary hours."

"We can put a roof over the Native passengers heads at our First Aid Pavilion," said Doolittle.

"Since they are on mine property, we can assume responsibility," offered Sunny. "I'll hold a clinic for those that need it."

"Thanks, I appreciate that," said Old Doc Maxwell. "Your turn, I've held many a fort in my younger day."

With a break in the rain, Mavourneen cycled down to the Railway Station. She was just in time to hear the Mayor addressing the first and second class passengers crowded into the Railway baggage room, while the Natives sat patiently on the wooden benches in their carriages. The Mayor announced, "We canna be sure about the amount of damage 'till the water goes down. 'Till then we'll arrange housing for you folk among the toonsfolk as fair as we can. We'll set up a center at the school dormitory for meals and beds."

Sunny offered, "Come to me with any medical needs you have and I'll see to them pro bono."

After questions and reassurances all would be well, the meeting closed and everyone dispersed. Mavourneen wheeled her bicycle up to Sunny and he said, "Surprised to see you here, but just as well. I've volunteered your services to get the churches involved, I hope you don't mind."

"Mind! Of course not," she said, looking at the low wet blotting paper clouds that began to rumble ominously again. "I better get going, while the going is good, and start the ball rolling," she said as he outlined the Mayor's plan to her.

She was panting with the uphill exertion as she wheeled the bike into the lean-to garage and the clouds let loose again. Warm and dry inside, she sharpened a few pencils from the jam jar and with a hot strong pot of tea Leonard had brewed, beside her, she pulled a chair up to the small telephone table in the hallway and got busy, shouting into the phone over the racket of the rain on the corrugated iron roof.

Mr. Asquith had already re-opened the school kitchen and dormitories. They formulated a plan of action. The churches agreed to rotate days of duty at the schools: Anglican, Presbyterian, Dutch Reformed and Roman Catholic. Vegetables courtesy of Cronje's simmered into a thick hot soup. Fruit from De Leon's made a large colorful fruit salad. Wolfson fired up the ovens at the bakery late in the day for an extra batch of fresh white bread. The small Indian community, Hindu and Muslim, wanted to show their solidarity and arrived at the school, unsolicited, with plates full of samosas and chapattis, bowls of dal and generous pots of curried stew and rice, which were a great hit.

Rivkah commandeered cars to transport the first and second-class passengers to the school and invited them to make use of the hot showers. Returning shuttles transported hot meals to the elderly in the train where W.I. members chitchatted and gave cheer as they distributed magazines and books.

Word spread and people phoned to volunteer a spare bed or a room to supplement the boys and girls wings of the small boarding school: a home away from home would be found for everyone. Mavourneen offered her house to families with young children. Why not give the children the run of the wrap-around veranda and the mothers the use of the kitchen to prepare bottles and baby food?

As the families arrived, Mavourneen explained to Douglas, "You must share you tricycle and toys. It's not going to be for long and we have so much after all. It will make everyone so happy."

"I don't want to," said Douglas as she slid his box of toys against the wall opposite the verandah door.

"It's going to be all *rather* fun. Put on your happy face now." The important thing, she noted was that all the travelers were in fine, if wet, spirits.

She pretended not to notice that Leonard too became increasing sulky and uncooperative as the invasion of his domain dragged on.

There were so many extra pots and pans to wash not to mention the endless blobs of pureed foods on the counters to wipe up and crusts of burned milk to scrub from the stove's wells.

Douglas reported in with one broken toy after another. She brushed his distress aside with a promise to make good on any damages after the flood was over. "I *do* see your dinky car has lost a wheel," she said as he persisted, "but, don't you see, it's served its purpose and spread so much joy."

Meanwhile, P.Q. Oosterhuizen had cranked up his car and gone into high gear on the Cheetah Mine. The Natives from third and fourth class were ferried by the lorry load to the first aid pavilion where mine emergency first aid blankets were handed out. Feldman's Hardware donated sacks of mealie meal for *sadza*, and oranges, to be dished out as well.

All the families had just been dispatched to the school dormitories or homes for the night when Sunny returned after a long and grueling day himself. He was dismayed to find the sanctity of his home violated. He righted Douglas' upturned tricycle, picked his way around the toys scattered about the verandah and made his way inside. The dining room table was far from set for supper. Strewn around were toys, baby bottles, the odd dummy or two which he wholeheartedly disapproved of as unsanitary, a baby blanket and soiled bibs, along with a stack of nappies and a pile of women's magazines. Douglas' dining alcove was scattered with coloring books, crayons and Plasticine—the rainbow of the colors that Douglas was meticulous about keeping separate wadded to a mottled brown. The tray on Deborah's highchair was a mess. Douglas hung on his leg and whined, "I'm hungry." Deborah cried out from her crib. Where was Mavourneen? "Where's Bundu?" he said, realizing he'd even missed a welcome wag.

"Oh," said Douglas, "he's locked away in my room. Mom said *not* to let him out."

"Fetch him!" said Sunny.

Mavourneen hadn't heard the screen door slam signaling Sunny's homecoming. She didn't realize it was so late. She was busy helping Leonard clean up, her hair plastered to her forehead, her apron splattered with baby food. The kitchen reeked of burnt milk. Oh, the memories it brought back of Douglas' illness after Sunny had insisted Douglas' weight gain was too much and instructed she take him off the breast, started him on solids early and feed him barley water. What disastrous years of worry had ensued as he failed to thrive.

Suddenly Sunny was upon her. Bundu bounded in, tail swishing, he barked as he leapt up to greet Sunny. Douglas brought up the rear, stopped beside Sunny at the kitchen table, grabbed hold of it and peered over the tabletop. "What's happened?" demanded Sunny.

"Oh, everything is under control," she said, smiling through happy but tired eyes. "I just offered to host the young stranded families with babies and toddlers during the day..."

"How dare you!"

Mavourneen took in his tight jawbone, the sudden flush on his cheeks, his steel-gray eyes boring through her as the light glinted off his glasses. She drew back as he leaned across the kitchen table and hissed, "How dare you allow the privacy of *my* home to be invaded!"

Leonard exited the back door. Bundu, ears erect, tail up, the hair on his back bristling, circled around the kitchen and snarled. Douglas' eyes widened, before he blinked. He stood motionless. "Let your naughty temper out," she said, standing her ground. "We're *so* well equipped for young mothers—the kitchen's *so* big. The verandah's *so* wide, perfect, for the little ones to let off steam...we're *all* cooped up with the rain."

"Aren't I doing enough!"

"I want to do my part, too."

"You didn't *even* think to consult me, did you?"

"I thought I was Queen of the home. *You* asked me..."

"*All* I asked, was for you to contact the churches. *Just* a few phone calls."

"I needed to set a good example. Lots of people are opening their homes. We're not the only ones."

"You've gone way, way, way, overboard—*as usual.*"

"*You* even imposed on a family with measles to take in a traveling family that you confirmed had measles too, to isolate them," she said. "It was the right thing to do and I'm doing the right thing too. I'm sorry, you'll have to bear the burden graciously. I've made a commitment." She bent to give Bundu a pat to settle him down and said, "I'll try and have your supper ready tomorrow. They'll all move on soon—they all want that as much as we do. How're the bridge repairs?"

He turned abruptly. And was gone.

She lifted Douglas onto the kitchen table and handed him a carrot stick to gnaw on, out of the fridge she fetched the beef bone from the Sunday roast that she normally used to make a soup stock and passed it down to Bundu. He wagged his tail approvingly. She heard Sunny's tuneless whistle, before the wireless crackled in the sitting room. She knew the family would suffer one of his silent brooding black moods for a week or more. The best way to handle it was to ignore it. She called Leonard to come in and start supper before she went to retrieve Deborah from the cot.

A daily bulletin was posted on the station notice board, as well as a progress report of the damaged bridge. Bets were laid. The cheerfulness was infectious, and an air of festivity persisted.

The sun came out. The rain had washed every living thing and cooled the earth. What a welcome sight it was to be back to the familiarity of blue sky with not so much as a wisp of a promise of rain in it. Everyone and everything sang—the rasp of cicadas building to a pitch, the throaty frogs and the liquid babble of the rainbird relishing the rejoicing frogs and, as the sun set, bats feasting on whining mosquitoes.

"We'll have something rigged in no-time," said the railway engineer. "Feldman's Hardware is providing the lumber for the temporary bridge. Luckily the Garratt, with its engine separated by the boiler to spread its weight, can run over bridges that might not be able to support other types of locomotives."

Food and hot tea in thermoses were sent to the engineers and their gangs.

Christmas was just around the corner. The air throbbed with heat. Mavourneen gave Fredrick Doolittle a ring and got right to the point. "Mr. Doolittle, the swimming bath's dense as pea soup."

"It's not a week since we emptied, cleaned and refilled it."

"Any chance of a scrub up, and refill—and opening it up to the whole town and the stranded passengers? It would *so* help to cool tempers."

"We are doing our bit here in the Native compound. I hope this doesn't go on too much longer."

"Yes, quite, I know, it's generous of the mine management. But opening the bath up to everyone wouldn't cost the company anything."

"It's a privilege for club members only, as you know."

"But under the special circumstances, all the children would so love it."

"We have to conserve water."

"I know it is *so* precious, but our rain water tanks are overflowing and the water table is saturated. These are unusual times."

"I suppose in the interests of public relations."

"Oh, I so appreciate it."

"I'll get right onto it."

All you have to do is ask. It's that easy, thought Mavourneen.

Doolittle was as good as his word: the bath was siphoned out. Mavourneen heard the mineboys singing in harmony as they scrubbed down the walls to the rhythm. She got Feldman's Hardware to deliver a few beach balls and swimming towels. Mayor Buchanan's Pegasus Garage patched, blew up and delivered a stack of used inner tubes. Mavourneen got onto the telephone exchange and asked them to ring around with a request for outgrown ladies' and children's swimming costumes to be delivered to the bath. The response was marvelous. The rusty corrugated iron gate to the bath was opened wide. It was six blocks uphill to the bath from the station. Everyone was invited and had a whale of a time. The men stripped to their undershorts. Ladies rummaged around for a suitable fit, wool costumes being pretty forgiving. The corrugated iron changing rooms were like ovens in the noonday sun but the plunge into the bath soon dispelled that discomfort.

Soccer balls appeared and a tournament was played on the station platform. La Tea Da Tearoom provided cool drinks, packets of biscuits, sweets and chips along with cigarettes and matches, too, for the team supporters. Wolfson's Bakery did a roaring trade with trays of meat pies and sausage rolls, along with sticky buns.

By the time Friday came around, it was reported that the bridge was close to completion. The great iron horse would soon load up to resume the trek North. Mavourneen decided to celebrate with a swimming gala: all fun and games. There were egg and spoon races, diving for pennies, a watermelon seed spitting contest and, for the men, a contest for the Knobbliest Knees in Umzimtuti, with a bottle of whisky donated by Umzimtuti Hotel for first prize. For the ladies, there was a contest for the most beautiful legs with a pair of rayon stockings from Feldmans Ladies Wear Department for the winner. Mr. Doolittle and Mayor Buchanan were the judges. For the ladies fresh out from England who'd been reduced to eye brow pencil or gravy browning drawn down the back of the leg, this was luxury they hadn't enjoyed since the war and rationing began.

The Garratt was uncoupled for a trial run over the new bridge to make sure it would hold. She was stoked carrying a full load of water, two thousand two hundred and fifty gallons forward, five thousand four hundred and fifty gallons aft and fourteen tons of coal loaded from Feldmans coal yard. With smoke belching from the smoke stack and steam billowing from the pistons below, it slowly pulled out of the station and down the track.

Children put their ears to the line. Yes! Yes! They heard the hum, then a far off engine toot, toot—a whistle of success. Cheers and cat-calls broke out as the chug of the pistons grew louder and louder before the Garratt came into view. Coupling and completion of the journey north was assured. Mayor Buchanan donned his red robe and gold chain. He strode onto the platform to officially speed the passengers on their way. "This was no wee accomplishment. I want to thank all you laddies 'n lassies for your sterling efforts. The Umzimtuti School motto *not for ourselves, but for all* has been upheld this week by the whole toon: a good example for our youth."

Everyone cheered. "Umzimtuti," he concluded "is the wee toon with the golden heart, the wee toon that can."

The excitement of these hectic days over, Mavourneen felt happily exhausted as she turned to leave. But Pat O'Connor was at her side. "I took some photographs at the nonsense gala," he said, "and I'd like to do a feature article on your fine efforts."

"By all means," she said, "report on the fun and games, but leave me out of it. The ones you need to mention are Mr. Doolittle and the Cheetah Mine's generosity in making it possible by cleaning up and opening the baths and of course all the suppliers in town, *very* generous they were, every one of them. I'll send you a list, so no one is missed."

Finally, she had really got past the superficial veneer of the community. It had come at a price for her—her marriage would never be the same, she knew. But there was no doubt about it, the community had come up trumps. They had offered their talent, how diverse it was; their resources, how plentiful they were; their time, how generous they had been with it to bring joy to strangers. It was true altruism, though she doubted anyone would use such a pretentious word. Sunny had not spoken a word to her since their confrontation. She hurried home to their shell-shocked house. It would all be put back to normal in the morning and he would see the light. It was early to bed for everyone.

Mavourneen did not hear the mine hooter wail in the morning. Heading out for Sick Parade, Sunny left a note on her pillow:

Dear Mavourneen,

Though I've known it a very long time, I've not wanted to really believe it—beyond hope. But I do acknowledge it now. You do not truly love me. I know you say you do and tell yourself, no doubt, you do; but in fact you don't. It is revealed in many ways.

I'm not your first loyalty, nor in the ultimate choosing, your first choice. You choose to serve the needs of passengers passing through, inviting them to invade the kitchen, wreck our children's toys and disrupt our home rather than tend to your own children and my needs after a harrowing day, day after day. I am not your final joy.

You did not even do me the courtesy of asking for my approval before opening our doors so unconditionally.

You've not responded to love or kindness or consideration but your attentions are reawakened or promoted, rather, by offhandedness, unkindness, thoughtlessness and the like.

I seriously do wonder whether we should not call it a day in some way or other. Perhaps I will find a way to more lasting peace of spirit and you as well.

As ever,
Sunny.

In the cool early morning breeze on the verandah she sipped her early morning tea thoughtfully and read the letter again. It was out of the question for either of them to admit defeat and dissolve the marriage. In any case, she was pregnant again and would not be able to conceal it from him much longer.

To delay would just inflame him further. She picked up a pen and replied on scratch paper:

Dearest Sunny,

I am truly sad that things have gone so awry with us.

It did not occur to me that you would not want to open our home to our community in need. But I see now the greater need is for you to refuel yourself after the stresses of your very long days, and I apologize for my unthoughtfulness.

I feel an utter failure as a wife, and marriage partner. I did think I was making headway. I have given up my career, my family, my friends. The home and children are all that occupy my life. I have tried very hard to submerge myself into you and efface my independence and feelings and all that. I will try harder.

When you are in a black mood it is senseless to ask you to see my point of view. I am sure that things will smooth out with time.

Your loving,
Mavourneen.

At lunchtime, ten days later, the front door of the verandah slammed, followed by Sunny's tuneless black mood whistle. Bundu's tail drooped. Douglas' outstretched arms dropped. Without a word Sunny strode to the dining room. He sat down at the table and put down the folded newspaper and post beside him.

Mavourneen said, "Douglas and Bundu do not deserve this treatment and neither do I, for that matter. It's high time you pulled yourself together. I'm doing the best I can."

"So am I," he said. "All I want is for you to be Queen of our house. Is that so much to ask? I know 1 Jacaranda Avenue is not Buckingham Palace, but it is a long way from the series of dingy wartime flats we occupied in Pretoria. This is a good country that's being good to us— but remember, we only have each other."

"Yes, I know," she said, "a lot has changed. Except me."

"Accept you! Everything I do is for you."

A long silence followed before Leonard entered balancing two tall conical glasses of knickerbocker glory on a tray.

"Everything's coming up peaches and cream," Mavourneen said sardonically. "Aren't we lucky, De Leon's Fruitiers got in a fresh shipment from the Cape."

He wasn't going to share this with Bundu whose snout would get stuck in the flute anyway. He picked up his long silver spoon, tucked in and on the side opened out *The Cleft Stick*. The front-page headline read *DOCTOR'S WIFE MASTERMINDS A NONSENSE GALA*. "What's all this about?" he said. "Do I have to read the paper to find out what my wife is up to?"

"Oh heavens," she said, leaning over to take a look. "It was just a bit of fun— you wouldn't understand it. It's not front page—or any page— material for that matter at all. O'Connor's blown it all out of proportion. Leah's right, he's a *schmuck*. He's gone and made a *tsimmes* of it. There's nothing to report. The subject's closed."

CHAPTER TWENTY-NINE

Paying Homage

A piercing whistle shot through the verandah mosquito gauze, ricocheted off the walls and pierced the ears of the Rubenstein family, jolting everyone awake just as the sun rose over the horizon on Christmas morning. It was followed by an explosion of drumbeats. The concrete floors pulsed with the rhythm of foot stamping.

Bundu leapt from beneath Douglas' bed and shot to the front verandah, barking all the way. Hindquarters extended, his front paws gripped the lintel, his nose pressed against the wire gauze. He bared his teeth and snarled.

Douglas rushed into his mother's bed on the east verandah. Deborah cried out from her cot. Hastily, Sunny and Mavourneen pulled on their dressing gowns. Sunny grasped Douglas by the hand as they stepped out barefoot onto the cold verandah floor.

Mavourneen ran to retrieve Deborah from her cot, slung a blanket over her, clutched her to her chest and joined them at the screen door.

A rotund hessian clad figure swayed before them on the front lawn. A whitewashed, giraffe-patterned bodice and skirt were held wide by a wire frame onto which a long supple grass fringe hung down to brown Oxford brogues. Beyond baggy sleeves, each hand held a black fly whisk made of cattle tails. The giraffe pattern was repeated on the mask that accentuated the chin, nose, cheeks, eyeholes and forehead with white, prominent wood strips. Crowning the forehead was a stiff conglomeration of upright bird feathers. At the flick of his whisk, chanting broke out from the helmeted mineboys behind him with their trousers tucked into their gumboots, torsos bare, despite the chill of the early morning. Another flick and the chanting changed to song united in a pounding symmetry of movement pulverizing the front lawn. They advanced and retreated between the spreading jacaranda trees and the stately silver oaks. It was Christmas Day. The family stared, befuddled.

"Down!" said Sunny, pulling Bundu by the collar. "Down, down, down. There's a good dog," he said reassuringly, patting the dog on the back before he straightened up. He jammed his hands into the pockets of his dressing gown but there was only a handkerchief there. This was the one time in the year the workers could expect a *bonsella*. He was uncomfortable with ceremony and emotional display and anxious to end it. What should he do to acknowledge it?

"Douglas," he said, "there's a good boy, take Bundu to your bedroom and close the door. On your way back, fetch my loose change from my trousers, you know, they're hanging over the white wicker chair in my bedroom." He never carried much cash, but however much he had it would have to do. Bundu resisted missing all the fun, but Sunny gave him a shove in the right direction and his paws slid over the polished floor.

Douglas returned with three tickeys, four shillings, one half crown and a few copper pennies. "That's my boy! Excellent," said Sunny. The family stepped outside and the door slammed behind them. "Go ahead, throw the coins one by one."

Douglas took a step forward. The pitch heightened.

Mavourneen whispered to Sunny. "Your carton of cigarette packs arrived yesterday. They are waiting for a *real bonsella*."

"*Premium Gold Leaf*. That will be the day!"

"You swore you'd give up smoking after Johnny Hardy's dental clearance. Now's your chance to go cold turkey."

"They smoke *Star* with the red circle, you know."

"These will do."

"They won't appreciate the filters."

"Where's your Christmas spirit?"

"Me! What about the pocket of oranges from Mrs. Biancardi's backyard, rather? Preventative medicine for all the scurvy that I've been seeing."

"That's it! Something you can easily implement long term—start right now."

"Okay, but the cigarettes are bad. I wish I could quit myself."

"Now's not the time to theorize. At least you can rationalize—these have filters. This is your opportunity. Go on. The lawn's getting destroyed!"

"Douglas! Hurry and tell Leonard to bring the pocket of oranges from the pantry and the case of cigarettes from my study."

"*Kunjani, Inkósi*," Leonard bowed as he deposited the unopened case of cigarettes and draped the pocket of oranges on top of it.

"I bet P.Q has put the boys up to this," said Sunny. "His idea of a joke, and the boys are enjoying it too. Hurry, open the case, Leonard."

"*Mai-weh! Inkósi, maningi* good!"

"Mavourneen, Umzimtuti is going to buzz. *Gold Leaf* is much too fancy."

"We've nothing else. You can defend it: Christmas generosity."

With a pack and an orange in hand, each Native took his leave. The dancing, stamping, drumming waned with distance.

With their going an eerie silence descended. The shadow of a coco-pan on the lawn hung motionless from the cable overhead. There was no clack from the mill, or hum from the power plant. Absent, too, was the heartbeat of the mine, the ordered rise and fall of the stamp batteries. "Douglas, my boy, your turn," said Sunny. "Father Christmas, I bet, has spoilt you if your mother's had a word with him. Run along and see if he's left a stocking at the end of your bed...check Deborah's cot too, while we settle down and Leonard brings out our early morning tea. We've all earned it."

CHAPTER THIRTY

The Hospital Christmas Tea

Mavourneen looked forward to attending the New Government Hospital morning Christmas Tea. Acting decisively during the railway washout had given her a boost and Deborah was blossoming to a lovely, fat, cuddly baby, so different from Douglas when she'd lost confidence in herself as a mother. Those days had been unbearable in a succession of pokey little flats with Sunny gone most of the time. She laced her corset up tight. She wouldn't be able to hide her pregnancy very much longer. She wasn't ready for another child, but there was no denying it. She'd have to accept the inevitable soon. Sunny would be delighted. It was Christmas. She should share the promise of the greatest gift she could give, but a busy day lay ahead.

She stepped into the fitted skirt of the three-piece suit she had bought at Feldmans as a present to herself after Deborah's arrival. The chiffon blouse with lace collar and cuffs was soft and over it she buttoned up the fifteen covered buttons of the fitted jacket. She wondered if she would be able to get into the evening dress she planned to wear on New Year's Eve, as she adjusted the handsome, large-brimmed, matching hat, bordered with a tiny fringe of lace which she'd commissioned from her Great Aunt Henny, the very best milliner in Jo'burg. She arranged its fine net over her eyes. The green lights of the large black opal pendant at her throat and matching earrings matched her eyes.

"You look stunning," assured Sunny as she looked at herself critically in the mirror and smoothed her skirt over her tummy.

"Thanks," she said, blushing. "Even if I say it myself, we make a handsome family." Busily, she checked Douglas in his white cotton shorts, buttoned front and back to a cool white shirt, cotton socks and buckle-up leather shoes. She swooped up Deborah in her embroidered muslin dress before she could mar it with red polish from the verandah floor. Deborah had inherited the best of both sides of the family: her father's fine dark hair, and her curls. But most importantly she was ever so friendly. The hospital staff would take Deborah under their wing once they got there.

The Hospital Christmas Day Tea was a *must*. Anyone who was anyone came to join the jollification: Buchanan, accompanied by the mayoress of course; the Chief of Police and his wife; the old GMO, Dr. Maxwell; the mine manager, Mr. and Mrs. Doolittle, and other Cheetah Mine officials; and chubby Dr. Eckhart and his wife. Included too were the hospital staff's husbands, and of course the patients' families.

The Casualty entrance was gaily festooned in plaits of red and green crepe paper streamers caught in the center with a concertinaed crepe bell. Great big tableaus made of plaster of Paris from the fracture room stood in strategic corners. Tall, steepled ceramic churches nestled in solid snowy fields, set apart from rows of miniature brick houses.

A mopane sapling stood implanted in a shiny stainless steel sterilizing drum at the far end of the convalescent verandah. Its big butterfly leaves had closed but its branches and twigs were dotted with tufts of cotton wool snowflakes and tied with Christmas crackers that held plastic charms and paper hats. The Sunshine Sisters, white veiled, long sleeved with shoes laced, served tea in government issue heavy ceramic cups.

They offered cucumber and Marmite-and-egg finger sandwiches sprinkled with shredded lettuce. Hot scones with a dollop of lemon curd or marula jam, a substitute for strawberry and accompanied by whipped cream were in big demand. Matron's special Scottish shortbread wasn't to be missed. The centerpiece was a heavy fruitcake entombed in marzipan topped by an unmelting snow of rock-hard royal icing. Cemented in the snow was a ceramic Father Christmas and his sleigh beside a bristly fir tree.

Everyone helped themselves. With plates full, they spread out along the length of the highly polished concrete floor in the hope of catching a bit of a breeze. Mavourneen's winning smile and genuine interest in people lit up happy responses in the patients as she did the rounds dutifully while the sisters took charge of Deborah.

When Mavourneen turned around to replenish her tea, she found herself facing Mayor Buchanan. The veil of her hat screened the intensity of her blue green eyes as she asked, "What would it take to get a swimming bath built for the town?"

"Aah me lassie, the mine's got a pool," he managed between hunks of fruitcake.

"Yes, but it's exclusive, and besides, within less than a week it turns to pea soup. The children all get ear infections."

"We haven't got the funds for luxuries."

"Oh, it's not a luxury, far from it. It's important for public health," she said. "We need to break the life cycle of bilharzia in the rivers somehow—by stopping people using them for ablutions or by eradicating the snails or stopping people swimming."

"Aye, you don't say?" he said indulgently.

"My husband's seeing so many cases. Think of lost work because of sick days, poor work because of low energy levels, and then there's secondary complications and the cost to benefit societies to consider too. Bilharzia shortens lives."

"This is the smallest municipality in the world you know," he said as he pulled a monogrammed handkerchief from his pocket and wiped his lips. "We canna hope to change the world. What's it got to do with a swimming bath?"

"Haven't you made the connection, Mr. Mayor? It'd keep people out of the rivers with safe family fun."

"Aye, I reckon people will still swim in the rivers."

"You're wrong. The mine swimming bath during the floods was very popular. If there's a safe, convenient alternative to cool down they'll use it, so if we could come up with a plan and capital, would the council support it?"

"Aye, you organized the mine bath when we had the floods. You did right weel," he popped a whole piece of shortbread into his mouth and looked around. "Aye, if you could come up with a specific plan and the capital to fund it that would be all fine and dandy, now wouldn't it. Aye, we're always looking to improve and attract new folk such as yourself to toon."

She'd nailed him. "What a brick you are! I take it I can go ahead and count on you then?"

"Aye! As people say, you can always count on Buchanan for a worthy cause."

"Why, Mrs. Rubenstein," cut in Matron Griffin, "how is the little one then? Where is she?"

"Doing the rounds with Sister Hoskins, I think," said Mavourneen, "She's no beauty but ever so friendly and healthy, thank goodness."

"Mayor Buchanan," said Matron, "how's your beautiful Claire?"

"Aye," said Buchanan, "my wife an' I've been wanting to thank you for all the good care you took of Claire—out and about in three days."

"It was the good doctor you need to thank," she said, "taking action in the nick of time..."

It had been surprisingly easy to nail Buchanan. Mavourneen moved off to cheer up two patients without family on the verandah.

Sunny found himself facing Dr. Eckhart, ruddy faced in the heat, normally so affable, but uncharacteristically disconsolate.

"I've been offered the appointment as head of the Ngomahuru Leper Hospital run by my Dutch Reformed Church Mission," he said. "I cannot refuse. This is my calling."

Congratulations were definitely in order. Sunny set down his cup and saucer and shook his hand.

"But you see," Dr. Eckhart continued, "The trouble is, I can't find a replacement for my practice here. I feel a loyalty to my patients, I can't just leave. I've tried and tried—advertised everywhere. Won't you take it over from me?"

"I'm hardly settled in myself," answered Sunny.

"I'm desperate. It's not a large practice."

"I'm overwhelmed myself, as it is. In fact I've been advertising too: BMJ, *The Lancet*, SAMJ, besides speaking to colleagues but so far, no takers."

"What I've got are the Acacia, Leighfield, Edifice, the Penga—and a few other medical service contracts. You know they are all small gold mining outfits pegged on ancient workings. It's really not a big practice."

"But they do keep you busy."

"I also have the Lime and Iron Works contract."

"Now, that could be big!"

"Yes, the survey team and clearing gangs are already on the job and in my care. The practice will grow. Now, *that's* a gold mine of a different sort!" Eckhart chuckled. "You'll have time to find a partner."

"I'd love to help you out, but I'm still *so* much in debt with Palmer's goodwill." Oh how the fraud still niggled him.

"Oh heavens no! No goodwill necessary. God *wants* me at Ngomahuru. If you'd pay for my equipment I'd be grateful. It's not much mind you."

What a gift! But he said, "I'll have to think about it. My wife's complaining she never sees me as it is."

"I don't know, with your family growing so quickly...well the equipment's not worth much and you can pay for it gradually. I'll be all found at the mission."

Growing so quickly? Douglas was four already, Deborah crawling and cruising. Whatever did he mean—*so* quickly? But his mind raced on—Eckhart was right. The Iron Works was in its infancy right now, not that much work immediately. He'd still have time to find someone. This loomed big for the future: the opportunity that Whitehead had endorsed but Palmer had not even bid on. It was not just more work, it offered the opportunity to dictate his own destiny independent of the Cheetah—truly be his own man. The chance would not come again. But Mavourneen's objections would be loud and clear. When could he make time for family of which he knew so little? "I...don't think I can at this time," he faltered.

He studied Eckhart's downcast eyes focused on consolidating crumbles of shortbread on his plate before he looked up and met his gaze and pleaded, "*Please.* I'd be forever grateful."

Sunny looked out beyond the verandah to the wild bush. It held so much promise. He took a deep breath and sighed, weighing the dilemma that career and family posed. Whitehead's assessment that one could not be completely loyal to both career and family and had made the choice and sacrificed popped suddenly into his head. Could he have his cake and eat it too? He reached down to nibble on a piece of fruitcake, that delicious heterogeneous and rich concoction.

The Matron stepped up to stand on a chair next to the Christmas tree. The room fell silent. "Please welcome Major and Mrs. Wolseley," she gestured. All eyes turned to the double doors. "Doctor Wolseley will soon be discharged from the Indian Army Medical Service." A tall man in the uniform of an officer of the Indian army, with a redhead on his arm, dressed in Christmas red with hat to match stepped forward. "He'll be joining us quite soon," went on Matron Griffin, "tacking up his brass plaque in the Mutual Insurance offices next door to the Umzimtuti Hotel."

She stepped down and moved forward, smiling benignly.

"Very pleased to see you again Matron," said Wolseley, as he moved amongst the guests and patients, with his beauty at his side.

Sunny blanched—*Dr. Wolseley*—his buddy Denny's referral! Doolittle had suggested he was too inexperienced to handle civvy street and here he was proving his naivety again. He had to admit to himself,

Palmer's fraud and now this double-cross had never entered his mind. All these months of waiting and hoping every time the post arrived. Wolseley had not even had the decency to acknowledge the introduction. Now he was setting up in opposition! Such bad manners! He turned back to Dr. Eckhart and said quickly, "Alright, I'll take over your practice and buy your equipment. Let's shake on it."

Doctor Eckhart was still staring at the glamorous newcomers. Beaming, back to his affable self, he turned to clasp Sunny's hand firmly in both of his. "The Lord works in mysterious ways. You're the *very* best Christmas present I've ever received. *Baie, baie dankie!* You've built up a fine reputation in the short time you've been here and it's a great comfort to leave the community in such competent hands."

Sunny replied, "I'm very grateful to you." He picked up his full plate of Christmas goodies, and took a nibble of his fruitcake thoughtfully. Already, his days were sixteen hours long. Had he bitten off more than he could chew?

Mavourneen watched Buchanan rapidly make his way to the new couple. "Setting up here—in Umzimtuti," queried Buchanan, stepping forward to shake Wolseley's hand.

"Dr. Wolseley, please meet our Mayor, Mr. Buchanan," said Matron.

"Aye! It's about time we had another doctor. What do you say, Mrs. Rubenstein?" he said.

Wolseley! What a blighter! fumed Mavourneen. "Dr. Rubenstein," she said slowly, "has been advertising, and corresponding in hopes of a partner for months now. His work load is very heavy." She held Wolseley's gaze.

"Aye. There's plenty of work for you doctor," said Buchanan.

"Yes, indeed."

Mavourneen stepped back. "I'll be in touch with council on the new pool in due course. If you'll excuse me."

"Aye." Turning to face the major, he said, "Now tell me more about yourself, Major, or should I call you Doctor?"

"Delighted to have met you, Mrs. Rubenstein," said Cecil Wolseley as he stepped forward and bent to kiss her hand.

A whiff of the verandah breeze brought his scent to her. She recoiled, noticing he was wearing brilliantine. She turned away from his dark and warm but shrewd eyes. She felt uncomfortably that he had undressed her in his mind.

Propped up in bed, Sunny watched Mavourneen as she sat in front of the dressing table brushing her hair a hundred times. "What a nerve that chap's got," she said.

"Who? You mean Wolseley, Denny's referral?"

"Of course," she said, "who else?"

"A *pukka sahib.*"

"Well, aren't you worried?"

"Do you think I should be?"

"Well, he's pretty impressive looking."

"I agree. But someone who barges in here without reference to his introduction and sets up in opposition makes him suspect. He's far from his stamping grounds."

"It really struck me today how very English the hospital crowd are. The townspeople too. He'll obviously fit in with the sundowner set."

"But in the long term, service and efficiency count. I expect he's had too much non-military diversion in the Punjab. I saw him looking at you."

"Matron informed me after their formal introduction that Vanessa's his third wife so she's hopeful he's sown his wild oats, though Vanessa looks as though she might be quite a handful herself."

"A leopard doesn't change its spots. There's no question, she's pretty and vivacious. I gather she's mad about horses which will go down well too."

"Eckhart offered me his practice today—a Christmas present. Can you believe it—*no* goodwill!"

The brush was stilled in mid-air. Her hair, charged, lifted to meet the brush. "What do you mean?" she said staring past the little red Christmas tree in the mirror to meet his reflected gaze from the bed.

"He's got an offer to head up Ngomahuru."

"The leper hospital?"

"His calling. How could I refuse?"

"So Wolseley's shut out. Well done."

"He could have had it if he'd joined me."

"He's got what he deserves. However, you promised me you'd try and see more of the children. We've another one well on the way. You haven't had time to notice."

He saw it now, through the sheer nightie. Of course! She'd hidden it well. Must be five months gone. "Early April," he said.

"Yes, I think so."

"I'm sorry," he said. "There's so much on the go."

"What about that Indian applicant you had? Sounded qualified. University of London, Royal Free housemanship and all that, if I remember correctly. Extensive experience in tropical diseases in India afterwards."

"I didn't even submit his application to the Benefit Society."

"Really! You're such a Gandhi admirer. Why ever not?"

"Remember the performance to get benches on the surgery verandah for Coloureds and Indians?"

"We ought to set an example."

"Boss Jack's afraid of them 'lounging about leading to fraternizing'. The best I could do was get them accommodated on the side verandah."

"You should do what's right. He's well qualified. Let the Benefit Society have the benefit of making a decision."

"The Government isn't even hiring Jewish GMO's let alone Indians. There's absolutely no sense in creating a ruckus with the Benefit Society and alienating myself further, pointlessly. Boss Jack, for a start, won't support me on that. In your heart you know it. I've got a lot of feelers out. Gelfand's looking for me. He knows everyone."

"You promised me you'd try to find time for the children on Sundays."

"How about you finding time for me tonight? No interruptions."

She went back to hair brushing. "I talked to Angus Buchanan about building a swimming bath for the town," she said. "He said council would agree to it if I raised the capital for it."

"Everyone's sleeping off Christmas excesses. There won't be any calls tonight, with any luck. Let's not waste time while the going's good."

"First, I'll have to come up with a specific plan and costs. Met any architects at the surgery?"

"With our own Christmas excesses, I'll be losing interest if you don't hurry up." Sunny watched the electricity fly from her hair.

"I bet it's going to cost a packet. It's going to take a lot more than Saturday cake sales to do it. Who could come up with the kind of capital we'd need?"

"Funding for a new swimming bath? State Lotteries, is as good a gamble as any." It was like lightning the way the wire bristles of the brush conducted the energy away from the sheen of her chestnut hair. It crackled with the speed of the quick repetitive flick of her wrist.

"What a good idea!"

"I was only joking." Her hair was fully charged now, chasing the silver backed brush, refusing to lie down. "You can't be serious about all this. You've got your hands full with Deborah and Douglas. And then there's the one on the way." God! She was beautiful, but exasperating. If she went on much longer she might spark that red wire Christmas tree of hers and set it on fire.

"There's a need for it. We just saw how much the whole community enjoyed the primitive mine baths during the flood. It really was so much fun."

They'd had a major row over it. Didn't she remember that? "Actually I've advised the mine management to have the bath scrapped on medical grounds."

"Oh, surely not!" she said.

"Our garden's plenty big enough: we could have Sugar dig a paddling pool for the children and have friends over. That's one hundred strokes I'm sure."

From the symmetrically angled branches of the tree hung laced angels on invisible threads, wax faced and flaxen haired amongst plaster of Paris snowmen, Father Christmases, Chinese parchment sunshades, Japanese foil fans, gaily-colored clowns and a black golliwog. An unfamiliar tree with alien figures, flocked with never-experienced snow.

"That's a selfish solution and you know it. What about all the *other* families? They get just as hot as our children."

"Since I can't be home as often as I'd like, I don't want you distracted from the family. They need you, you're the undisputed Queen— this's no castle I'll admit, but, at least, this rambling tin-roofed house and garden at 1 Jacaranda Avenue is more than we dared hope for. You have to admit we're comfortable. Lucky! The turkeys at least appreciate it. Take a cue from them. They wouldn't be anywhere else, they have it too good here. You promised me you'd try harder..."

"Of course I appreciate the house, the garden, the children," she said. "It's just that the Queen needs a consort—especially on Sundays. A public bath with a proper filtration plant would lighten your load. It's in your best interest too."

"I concede," he said.

She looked at him through the mirror as she put the brush down. His big brainy head was propped up by the feather pillows and his broad shoulders were relaxed in his striped pajamas. For all Cecil Wolseley's good looks and English charm, his well-oiled hair gave him away. She was confident Sunny would prevail. He opened the ironed cotton sheet. She slid into his bed and drew him to her.

CHAPTER THIRTY-ONE

New Year

Boss Jack and his wife Sheila had invited Sunny and Mavourneen to sit at their table for the New Year's Eve dance at Chelmsford Hall, a St. Arthur's Anglican Church tradition. The parishioners would provide a buffet supper and the whole town was invited.

Mavourneen dressed carefully after she read to Douglas and Deborah and handed them over to nanny for the evening. She brooded once again that she had never quite overcome the first impression she had made at Leah's tea party before her trunks had arrived. Her long sheath dress dating back to those weekend forays to Knysna, dancing the night away with her beau Frank at the Air Force base, was still as good as new. An overlying peplum skirt hid any hint of her pregnancy. Around her open neck she wore her Great Aunt Henny's delicate sapphire and diamond necklace. She brushed her hair a hundred times. It shone. She clipped matching sapphire teardrops to her ears.

By nine o'clock Sunny had still not returned home to change. On the bed, she laid out his navy suit, tie and matching socks, white shirt and cuff links. His dress shoes shone. She knew that he ought to wear a tuxedo. He had dismissed the suggestion out of hand. How many occasions would he have to justify purchasing something as fancy and expensive as that?

She wrote a note on a scrap of paper and left it on the telephone table. She put on her sensible shoes, gathered up the drawstring bag with her high heels and clutch bag and the basket with the *melktert* she had made and closed the back door.

It was only a short walk over the mine spur shunting tracks, across the open field that bordered the swimming pool and onto the lane that lead to Chelmsford Hall. The Southern Cross pointed the way. The crickets chirped. When she passed the mine swimming pool an army of happy frogs accompanied her in her favorite song:

"Ac-Cent-Tchu-Ate the Positive
Eliminate the negative
Latch on to the affirmative

Don't mess with Mister In-Between."

By Jove! She could count her blessings. Douglas was truly well. Deborah, was easy. She loved the rambling mine house, especially sleeping out on the verandah and waking to watch the birds over early morning tea in bed. The coral creeper was in full summer bloom, entangled in the wire gauze threatening to obscure the view of the garden: the paths lined with lupine and larkspur which had flourished with all the rain. Douglas loved to pump the swing hanging from a spreading jacaranda tree while she pottered in the garden. She was making new friends. But she was not ready for another baby. Sunny was more and more distant. She still pined over living in the surgical moment with him in the theatre: family duty stretched endlessly ahead.

She could hear the strict tempo of Victor Silvester's *You're Dancing on My Heart*, slow, slow, quick-quick-slow. She paused at the back door to change her shoes. She walked around to the front and paused, looking for Boss Jack in his wheelchair. She took in the swirl of ball gowns in soft shades, some with an asymmetrical bouffant of taffeta or lace, others were tight sheaths. But some of the new English immigrants wore gowns made with industrial blackout cloth or parachute silk or even the harsher new parachute nylon, made gay with a dash of color, wrapped or tied, cut from a bolt at Kasim & Son. She had the utmost respect for the sacrifice these English folk had endured in the world's darkest hours. Cecil Wolseley wore a white tuxedo and Vanessa was glamorous in a strapless boned top with a full skirt of red Indian silk, the very latest in fashion.

The hall was festooned with plaits of green and red crepe streamers strung from the four corners of the hall, caught up in the center by a collection of balloons. A handsome Christmas tree in one corner was decorated liberally with tinsel, glass balls and cotton wool snow.

Chairs and tables decked with starched red tablecloths ringed the hall. At every place setting sat intact bright paper and foil crackers. Dinner hadn't started. She could pick out the Jewish tables, divided further into Ashkenazi and Sephardic: the Wolfsons, Feldmans, and Fishers and Greenbergs sitting separate from the Levines, Uziels, Kalderons and Elazars. The Afrikaners, mostly farmers and ranchers, clustered at the far end, the newly emigrated British separating themselves from the old-time colonials, who sat separate from the English South Africans.

The music stopped. Suddenly, she felt all eyes turn to her standing on the threshold. She was flushed by the walk, her hair tousled. There was a hush, a moment of hesitation, before Boss Jack realized she was unaccompanied and motioned her to his table. The band struck up again.

"He's caught up, he'll be here shortly," she said by way of introduction as she reached Boss Jack's table, grasped his gnarled hand and returned his welcoming squeeze.

"You must risk a glass of Padre Huxley's punch," he said.

"First I need to deliver a tart before the feasting starts."

"Be sure to pick up a glass on the way back," he called after her.

A grand centerpiece of red amaryllis and white arum lilies cut short graced the center of the buffet table. Asparagus fern intertwined plates of Swiss roll sandwiches filled with rich savories of cream cheese and tomato sauce, chutney and chicken, egg and Marmite. Bowls of stuffed olives and pickled onions, deviled eggs and plates of cheese boats with walnut sails, sardine fingers, pyramids of sausage rolls, devils and angels on horseback and salami canapés filled out the table.

She placed the *melktert* on the table of confections. It was as inviting as the savories: a pyramid of mince pies, plates of lemon meringue tarts and fudge, an iced fruit cake, two gingerbread loaves, a tipsy cake and a chocolate Yule log. A glass pudding bowl of sherried trifle and a wobbly jellied fruit mold stood beside a pile of whipped cream. Surveying it all she thought, England and Europe are bombed out and heavily rationed, how spoilt we are!

"We'll be eating soon, one more round of dances I expect," welcomed Sheila Chelmsford as Mavourneen sat down next to her. She had barely taken one sip of Padre Huxley's traditional concoction of white wine, tea and Angostura bitters when Dr. Cecil Wolseley was at her side. "May I have the pleasure of this waltz?" He bowed and extended a hand. It was hard for her to say no. She excused herself from Boss Jack and Sheila. She was in Wolseley's arms. He held her close, fully in control as he led effortlessly.

"Mrs. Rubenstein. May I call you Mavourneen? Irish of course."

"South African."

"Jewish?"

"Anglican. My father came out from County Cork for the Boer War."

"The apple of his eye, no doubt."

"Disappointed I was a not a boy."

"You're the belle of the ball."

"Your wife?"

"She's not well, sitting it out right now. Your husband?"

"Caught up. He'll be here shortly."

"I understand from Mayor Buchanan you have ambitions."

"And you?"

Dr. Wolseley pulled her closer, her whole body pressed against him in rhythm as she rose and fell in step with him. "This doesn't quite have the richness of India, but that's in the past already. Time is ripe now to exploit the much forgotten scramble for Africa."

"*Exploit* isn't the word I'd use. Africa offers an *opportunity* to make a difference—a positive one, I might add."

"I can't say I apologize for enjoying good malt whisky, the good life...the refinements of civilization. Do you ride?" he asked.

"Over mountains," she said, "not the steeplechase. And you?"

"I enjoy jumping fences and ditches."

"I might have known," she said.

"I'm sure," he said, "there's room for more than one horse in this town."

"I've placed my bet already and I can tell you, in no uncertain terms, that I'm not going to switch jockeys now," she said, glancing down between the starched pleats of his shirt at the black bead of a button—like a third eye watching her.

Abruptly the music changed. His hand slid from her shoulder blade down her back to her waist. She never flinched, looked past the impeccable white bow tie propped between the wing collar at that neck she'd love to slit and over his shoulder. Without hesitation he switched to the quickstep—slow-quick-quick, slow-quick-quick. He led expertly, light in his patent leather shoes, they promenaded and counter-promenaded in double-time. It seemed they barely touched the floor: soon they had it all to themselves. She was breathless.

Sunny was crooning Bing's *Don't Fence Me In* as he pulled up the car in front of Chelmsford Hall, slammed the door and hurried in to join the party.

"Oh, give me land, lots of land under starry skies above
Don't fence me in
Let me ride through the wide open country that I love

Don't fence me in."

He was hungry and hoped he was not too late for the meal but most of all he loved to dance and smiled as he remembered how he and his sister, Josie, as teenagers, used to slink in to the neighborhood Masonic Hall whenever a dance was on, study the latest steps and rush home to try them out together to the jazz rhythms from His Master's Voice.

At the door he saw *that pukka sahib* holding the floor alone with Mavourneen in his clutches—all eyes mesmerized by them. No wonder: how beautiful his wife was. What a performance they were putting on! Was Matron Griffin wrong—Wolseley tired of his third wife already? Was Wolseley about to presume to take not only his practice from him, but also his wife? Was there no limit to his *chutzpah*? He had not revealed to anyone Wolseley's introduction to Umzimtuti. Let his actions speak for themselves over time: it would be more powerful that way.

The music ended and he saw them break apart. Mavourneen waved to him as he leant against the doorway.

"You're too late to rescue me from the clutches of *that pukka sahib*," she greeted him.

"Caught up at Casualty, I'm sorry to have let you down—again. But you seem to be enjoying yourself—immensely."

"Should I have made a scene?" she challenged. "I had to show him I also know how to dance. Your Dutch Uncle has rescued us again," she said, "saved a seat for you." He felt her wince as she touched his threadbare jacket elbow and lead him to their table.

Dinner was being announced and they joined the buffet queue.

With plates filled everyone sat down at the candlelit tables, crossed their arms with their neighbors and pulled the crackers apart with bangs and exclamations. They donned their paper crowns, traded the spilt charms, and ridiculed the riddles printed on little rolls of paper. After dinner, couples popped out to their cars with increasing frequency as the night wore on for a nip at the bottle, a long established tradition.

Mavourneen caught a glimpse of Wolseley and Vanessa leaving the party right after the meal and relaxed. She danced and danced the whole night long with young and old. Perhaps she was, after all, fitting in. Waltzing around the floor with Mr. Lawley, the Club Secretary of the Cheetah Mine, after all the wonderful food, she was not sure if she was floating on his portly stomach or he on hers. Happily she noted that Sunny too seemed to be fitting in, his opinion much in demand, called to this table and then that—it seemed everyone excused his disregard for the evening's dress code.

As the witching hour approached the band began to belt out Nat King Cole's *Christmas Song* and the crowd began to sing along: *There will always be an England*, *The White Cliffs of Dover*, *We'll Meet Again* and *Lili Marlene*. Then came Sunny's favorites—Bing Crosby's *I'll Be Seeing You*, and *In the Mood*. Mavourneen wished she could have just one dance with Sunny as the singing got louder and more rowdy but he was still caught up in conversation. The clock ticked down the final minutes to midnight. Everyone joined hands for *Auld Lang Syne* and suddenly he was at her side drawing her to him kissing her and she yielded. She raised her glass and wished him a prosperous New Year and a new partner. Everyone cheered, threw streamers and confetti, blew on paper horns and clinked their glasses of punch.

But the party was far from over yet. Everyone prepared to make their way down to the railway station, bottles in hand, to greet the Bulawayo northbound and Salisbury southbound passenger trains at 1.01 and 2.01. Mavourneen cursed herself that she had forgotten to bring Sunny's *Johnny Walker*. He tied a balloon to her wrist. They wended their way arm in arm with the crowd past the cemetery under the tall dark silver oaks through the park, over the War's civil defense trench, crossed Third Street, then on down to Main to dead-end at the station just beyond it. The moon hadn't set. A bottle of whisky and a fruitcake was presented to the Station Master. Someone plugged a gramophone into his office and put on some jitterbug. A happily inebriated partygoer climbed onto the Dutch gabled roof and waved a Union Jack. Sunny and Mavourneen joined the throng in singing Irving Berlin's *Blue Skies*:
"Blue skies smiling at me
Nothing but blue skies do I see.
Bluebirds singing a song
Nothing but bluebirds all day long.

Never saw the sun shining so bright,
Never saw things going so right.
Noticing the days hurrying by
When you're in love, my how they fly!
Blue days, all of them gone

Nothing but blue skies from now on."

The northbound train rounded the corner, with a plaintive *whoa, whoa*, brakes on hard, steam blowing, pistons slowing, coming to a stop with the engine beneath the water tower. A horde of Natives alighted, as always. Windows slid open and heads popped out of the first and second class passenger coaches. Everyone waved and cheered. Streamers were thrown into the open windows.

Generous hampers of leftovers from the party were thrust fore and aft for the engine driver, the fireman, the guardsman and the conductor and bedding stewards. A pocket of oranges for the Native stokers was slung aboard. It only took a few minutes. The train was stoked again, rolling forward, picking up speed, clickety-clack over the narrow gauge tracks, rounding the bend north, one last toot. It was gone. Another hour of revelry ensued before the southbound 2.01 arrived. It was a little over a year since Sunny had first arrived in a rainstorm. Now, in a clear sky, 1947 loomed full steam ahead for the Royal Victory Tour.

CHAPTER THIRTY-TWO

A Special Delivery at the Railway Station

Umzimtuti Railway Station was abuzz. The very first Cadillac to be imported into the country ordered direct from America by Mr. and Mrs. Elazar had arrived and car buffs from far and wide came to see it.

"By Jove, it's gorgeous." Mavourneen reported to Sunny over lunch. "Douglas and I went down to the station to see it. It's a hardtop convertible in Burbank Green. Mr. Elazar was on hand to point out the tail-fin styling and explain about the power it's got—an overhead-valve V-8 engine. Mrs. Elazar told everyone it has slipper pistons. Do you know it can clock 0 to 60 mph in thirteen seconds and easily top 100 mph."

"Maybe on the open road in America. Not here in Umzimtuti with only dirt roads. Isn't the sump very low slung?"

"Sump? I don't remember if they said anything about that. Goodness me, it's such a beauty I tell you."

"All you have to do is look underneath to see how much clearance it has. How practical is it? Come to think of it," said Sunny, "I thought the Elazars couldn't drive."

"You're right," she said, "they haven't learned yet, but he and his Missus somehow got licenses already, without doing a test. Mr. Elazar's shop assistant did the honors of driving them home in it."

"You know I'm against Jewish ostentation. It only does us harm. This takes the cake."

"They've both worked hard for it—a lifetime running their concession store at Halliday Mine—you could hardly call that glamorous—everything from men's shirts, socks, blankets—the usual, but also Scotch carts and wagons, grain and livestock. She runs the butchery. That's where I'm getting the smoked kippers you like."

"Scottish. What I'd really like are some kosher pickled herrings. My mother..."

"There are only *ten* Jewish families—hardly enough to support a business in pickled herrings. They deserve this. Nobody begrudges them. They've plenty of time to learn to drive before the big day."

"What big day?"

"Boy oh boy, how could you forget, The Royal Tour of course. They've generously offered to chauffeur the Royals to their retreat at Sycamore Bend when they come."

"I'm against building a house for the Royals to occupy for just a few days on the prettiest spot on the river. It's all so extravagant and wasteful when we're in the throes of a housing shortage with immigrants flooding in."

"I think Whitehead's jolly clever to determine the Retreat be built *pise de terre*, so that the Royals lend glamor to a low-cost local material, given the shortage of bricks."

"Agreed, the Royals liked to show they mucked in during the war and shared the hardships, though it was all token, of course."

"It did wonders for morale. They could have holed up in Canada, out of harm's way—but they didn't."

"The Retreat might be something to see. Broderick Anderson is building it. He's coming in every other day for his bilharzia shot, much as he hates it. Used to hunt crocodiles before this post-war housing boom started."

"I heard he once bagged himself an eighteen footer. That must have fetched a packet. It made front page news in O'Connor's rag I heard."

"How many people would you say get killed by crocs each year?"

"Oh, I don't know, quite a few African women and children fetching water from the river, I suppose. Imagine being grabbed by those jaws, pulled under, drowned. Can you think of anything worse?"

"Bilharzia's the third biggest tropical disease in Africa. *Millions die every year*. But you don't see that hitting the headlines of his rag do you?"

"You must admit it lacks the daring of crocodile hunting."

"There you go with your Captain Hook and Peter Pan fairy-tale stuff, again."

"Adventure. Sensation. That's what people want to read about."

"Bilharzia's severity is seriously underestimated. If only the people knew that those fork-tailed devil cercaria burrowing through the skin could lodge and mature into adult worms anywhere—not just the bowel or bladder—but the brain, the spinal cord, the kidneys, the liver, the lungs: like syphilis or T.B. to pull them down agonizingly slowly. If only the institutions—the mines, the farms, the factories knew the financial loss they suffered in compromised manpower they'd apply themselves. It's all a matter of education," he said.

"Who's doing the fantasizing now?" she said. "Bilharzia's been around since the time of the Pharaohs. I've got as far as roping in Headmaster Asquith to support the swimming bath project and he's got the PTA backing us too."

"At least, we've got past the bleeding and purging stage, but medicine's all so primitive still," continued Sunny.

"Think of the smallpox vaccination."

"Over a century ago. Nothing since. We should have a vaccine against bilharzia— diphtheria, measles, malaria and T.B. too. We've nothing!"

"Well," she said, "we've got penicillin for bacterial infection, aspirin for a fever, digoxin for the heart, insulin for diabetes. Vitamins—we've B1 to thank for Douglas' recovery. Meanwhile you've just got to be realistic. We *can* help the European population with bilharzia prevention, but you're not going to change centuries of tribal custom for the Natives overnight. The Government gave up their 1923 cinderblock latrine pilot scheme in the Reserves for lack of use, you know."

"There's a cause," he said, "for you to take up. Education. Start with the women."

"Is that a challenge," she asked, "to get stuck in with women's rights?"

"You've got the right to vote."

"I'm a slave to the home. When the war was on, women's services were welcome."

"It was a necessity then. Now, we're getting back to normal. Home's a sacred time-honored place of power and influence in the background."

"Are you trying to flatter me?" she smiled ruefully.

"It's true—where would I be without you? Look at Wolseley: how successful do you think he can hope to be with that tart at his side?"

She put her knife and fork together.

"Our servants," he said, "are learning in the kitchen: simple hygiene. They take it back to the Reserves when they go. It's a matter of time."

Leonard entered and Mavourneen leaned back as he took her plate. She wondered momentarily what he heard and thought of all their conversations. "*You* could make a start," she said to Sunny, "you've got the clout. Get the NC's onto education, prioritize hygiene and nutrition over everything else in the Reserves."

"I'm not the GMO and Maxwell's past it."

"Don't shortchange him before you ask. He's a member of the Sons of England and Grand Master of the Freemasons: both huge forces for good."

Leonard returned carrying two plates of wobbly blancmanges struggling to keep their shape. Sunny took one look and said, "I'm not sure I'll ever get used to these English puddings of yours—but Bundu seems to have quite a sweet tooth for a dog, so it's not going to waste."

Before he could lower his plate down to Bundu waiting beneath his feet, she said, "It's a dainty food of the aristocrats. It's a favorite of Douglas and Deborah's, I'll save it for their supper. Leonard's tried so hard, I don't want to discourage him although talking about educating in the kitchen, it's hardly something he can take back to the Reserve where there's no refrigeration."

"That technology will get there all in good time," he said seriously, "but getting back to the subject, medicine's lagged every other avenue of science. The connection between mosquitoes and malaria was only proved less than 50 years ago. But the Greeks discovered the tides are caused by the moon in the 2nd century BC. The Germans taking the mystery out of rainbows in the 13th century."

"That was one mystery best left unsolved. I like the idea of a pot of gold at the end of a rainbow."

"A Dane," he went on ignoring her frivolity, "first measured the speed of light in the 17th century."

"I thought it was Einstein," she said. "Anyway, what we do all know for sure is that news travels faster than the speed of light here in Umzimtuti."

"That Dane also introduced the first street lights in Copenhagen in the 17th century. We still haven't got a single street light in Umzimtuti!"

"Well, all the better to see the stars," she said.

"Seriously," he said. "Medicine needs a revolutionary invention—you know the way the steam engine revolutionized industry."

"All in good time," she said. "We won the war and for now we're going to enjoy the Victory Tour."

"I've got to run. Anderson's given me an open invitation to take a look see how the Royal Retreat is coming along...would you like that?"

asked Sunny. "It's almost done, he says."

"Oh, I'd love to."

"He tells me he did his apprenticeship in the ship building yards in Glasgow decorating the interiors of passenger liners."

"Who'd have thought we'd get such talent out here in the back of beyond."

"People say being Buchanan's brother-in-law got him the job, but I reckon he's quite capable. The Government panjandrums probably decreed a Rhodesian style."

"I'd love to see it."

Sunny mused, as he drove up to the hospital for rounds, The Royal Tour was overshadowing the development of the Lime and Iron Works, the biggest thing since the Cheetah Mine's 40-stamp mill started at the turn of the century—and he had the medical contract for it now. The Works could become the industrial hub of the country in its own right and outstrip Umzimtuti if it did not play its cards right.

As he bumped over the railway line he saw Broderick Anderson's car parked on site at the new temporary *pise de terre* housing and decided to take a look.

One by one, the one hundred and twenty-five modest two bed-roomed houses on three quarter acre plots were taking shape. Broderick strode over in his khaki shorts and long socks, open necked shirt and bush hat. "Doc, let me show you round," he shouted above the native workers singing in unison, and then in harmony as they tamped the red earth into twelve inch wide forms with their bare feet. "You see," he said, "I'm building these to last, like the Burgalimar Castle in Spain built by the Moors a thousand years ago. I've seen it myself. Bloody marvelous. Still intact. What we have here are solid, twelve inch thick walls. Our red clay is especially suited to this type of construction, add a little lime—you know we have plenty of that on hand from the Works. Our 'secret' ingredient is pulverized anthill. No shortage of that either. Something about ant spit makes it stronger than concrete, I tell you.

"Mind you there's an art to it. Mustn't be too wet or it shrinks and cracks. Compact to the right moisture content...no further. Right amount of drying—mustn't be too hasty removing the formwork. Surprisingly, erosion occurs from the top down rather than the bottom up so it's very important to have a good roof—no shortage of thatch around these parts. Experience and patience is the name of the game, otherwise not much to it."

"Well, Broderick, if it's the wonder building technique you say it is, why isn't everyone using it?"

"Doc, high labor costs. That's the luxury of Africa, an endlessly cheap supply and along with all the right local materials: we absolutely can't lose. Imagine, these walls could last for a thousand years. Oh, and I forgot to mention the bonus—these small houses being thermally massive will be cool in the day and warm at night."

"We won't always have cheap labor. Just as well you take advantage of it now."

"Yes, it's too bad these are slated for demolition in five years. I'll be very sorry to see them go."

Just then the dear old town foreman, short, squat Bertie Carlisle, ex-garage mechanic, climbed down the electric power pole and joined them. "Just connected up the first three houses," he declared proudly.

Sunny felt a chill, "You're *not* connecting those bits of wire to the already overloaded overhead lines from the Cheetah are you?"

"Why yes," he said, "council hasn't the money for a fancy electricity distribution network, I just have to make do, string a new line, one by one, to each new house as it's added."

This setup would obviously never support street lighting. Outdoor bucket latrines and the honey sucker service would be extended to these houses too. The Industrial Revolution was coming with the Lime and Iron Works, and yet Umzimtuti, with its fortress suburban construction that could stand for a thousand years married to this primitive set up would fall short of moving into the twentieth century. It just didn't make sense. It was all so shortsighted.

It needed a comprehensive plan if it was going to amount to anything. Mavourneen was right, the swimming bath was just the start of something big.

The women were already planning their get-ups: a whole ensemble for the Royal visit. Storeowners were planning their shop window displays and ordering bunting and flags. There were prizes at school for patriotic songs and poems. Neglected old timers were suddenly in the limelight for interviews with Pat O'Connor to recount 'the good old pioneer days' for a new column in *The Cleft Stick*. It was not so long ago that the Anglican priest cycled forty miles each way between towns. Umzimtuti's last lion had been tricked into falling down a mineshaft and a brave soul had been lowered down with insufficient ammunition to finish him off. Seven tons of dynamite had once exploded near the slimes dam shattering all the bottles of hooch at the Club and Umzimtuti Hotel. Everyone thought the end of the world had come.

The Cleft Stick circulation was up and Pat O'Connor was in his element as he featured the protocol and formalities expected on the arrival of the new Governor.

But then the town was rocked by quite another explosion.

CHAPTER THIRTY-THREE

Hitting the Headlines

It was high noon on Friday and the bar was already stocked in anticipation for an evening of sundowners and long night to follow. A waiter brought Jud and Leah a pot of tea on the verandah and they watched the occasional car pass north or south. Fresh off the press, the newspaper boy rounded the corner, leaned his bike against the white column of the hotel and hauled out a stack of *The Cleft Stick* from the bike's front basket. He bowed, handed one to Jud and moved to deposit the rest in the lobby.

Jud opened the paper out and stared at the headlines: DID COUNCILMAN USE CIVIC POSITION FOR PERSONAL GAIN?

"*It's outrageous! Take a look*, talk about a *shanda fur die goy*," he said to Leah, downing his cup of tea with one gulp, passing the paper to her. "I'm no lawyer but this is *blatantly* libelous—O'Connor's suggesting the catering for the Royal Tea at the Railway Park didn't go out for tender. I was the lowest bidder. He hasn't done his homework. All he had to do was look up Miss Hutchinson's minutes from the council meeting. It's all in black and white."

"Better check," said Leah.

"No need, Miss Hutchinson never misses anything. Doc's right: no more of this punch in the gut and a bloody nose to sort someone out. Not only does this nail O'Connor, I'm going to see to it to crucify his political career and ruin him financially into the bargain. It's too wonderful, the means of his destruction is his very own newspaper—all his own doing."

"I knew if we waited around long enough that big fat oaf would trip himself up. Still this could tarnish your own ambitions for the mayoral office one day."

"Of course. All the more reason why I have to take him to book on it. I won the tender fair and square."

"Better get William Pringle, he's the best attorney-at-law in town, before you do anything rash. But keep the visit short, you know how costly lawyers are."

"I'm willing to mortgage the hotel if necessary—stake everything I have against him—to avenge your honor over the bunch of carrots and now mine as well and uphold the honor of our Jewish community."

Jud moved inside the dark cool lobby of the hotel and into his office to make an appointment with Pringle.

Neat and brisk Pringle sat behind his big oak desk. "I agree the reader cannot but conclude that you have used your civic position for personal gain in securing the contract for The Royal Tea at the Railway Park summerhouse. The allegation is untrue. Of course, I'll get confirmation from Counsel."

Jud sat forward on the edge of his seat facing him. "I'm a businessman. Normally I avoid lawyers because usually they are the only winners. But this bloke is making my wife very unhappy, he's questioning my integrity in front of the whole town and putting at risk my whole future if I don't take care of it. On top of it he's an anti-Semite. I'm not really interested in the amount of damages but it must be enough to take him to High Court. I want a knockout."

"Five thousand pounds will be enough to do that..."

"Go ahead as fast as you can. I'd like it heard before O'Connor's parliamentary by-election."

"Right, I'll brief Counsel as soon as possible and file the action straight away."

CHAPTER THIRTY-FOUR

An Official Visitor

Sunny, as the contracted doctor who'd recently taken over from Dr. Eckhart, was invited to join the town delegation to the site visit of the Lime and Iron Works with Huggins' right-hand man, the new Minister of Finance, Edgar Whitehead.

Sunny looked forward to meeting Whitehead again. He had often recollected his conversation with him on the train and come to realize how privileged he'd been to have such an introduction to the country.

Several officials and engineers accompanied Whitehead as they toured the extensive foundations of the smelter and the steel mills sprawled across the valley ten miles from Umzimtuti. Only towards the end of the inspection did the town party have an opportunity to express their views.

"The government's already acquired all the blast furnaces, converters, rolling mills and other equipment for steel production. We're fully committed," Whitehead said to Buchanan.

"Aye, that's very good to hear," said Buchanan. "All the makings of a fine *new toon*, hereabouts."

"Wouldn't it be to Umzimtuti's advantage, Mr. Buchanan, to have the municipal services keep pace to ensure its role as supply center, lest it lose out to the competition from the neighboring towns?" said Sunny.

"We can hardly keep up with our own expansion. Nay, nay, our *toon* would hardly want to merge with the *Werks* and take on its financial burdens now would it? Aye, we might lose control, too. Have you given a wee thought to that now?"

"It would give all our local businessmen a terrific boost. After all, we do have basic structures in place: we could anticipate the needs and meet them. We have such an advantage. There's nothing here."

"Aye, and raise the taxes? I'd like to ken if you thought of that? Doctor, methinks you ought to stick to doctoring and let the councilors deal with the counseling," admonished the Mayor.

Whitehead interrupted, pointing up hill, and said, "I'd like to get a bird's eye view of the Works. Anyone game?"

It was rather late in the afternoon and the ironstone hills all around were rather high but Sunny joined the small party.

Whitehead's appearance belied his fitness. Underneath his red and peeling skin, which refused to acclimate to the harsh African sun after twenty years, he was tough as nails. He climbed with collar turned up, sleeves rolled up, and his trousers stuffed into his long turned down socks, setting the pace in long strides in rugged shoes. In his earlier days on his own farm, Witchwood, in the Vumba, having the whole work of the farm entirely in his own hands, where no part of his property was less steep than one in nine, the top boundary nearly two thousand feet higher than the bottom, he had travelled up and down three or four times a day, between a labor gang working near the bottom of the farm, and another working near the top. But the routine had changed with his new role as Minister of Finance, relying much more on his farm manager and acquiring a callow heavyset secretary, Vincent. He was fresh out of high school so Whitehead would not have to 'untrain' bad habits, and Vincent had taken up residence in his newly acquired Salisbury house, so he could be ever at his beck and call.

Whitehead relished this opportunity to get out and explore the untouched deciduous forest of mountain acacia trees in full leaf. The path was steep and narrow on the red, heavy mineralized ground. At the summit, he searched for a good vantage point to see through the trees before he worked on getting his pipe evenly lit waiting for the stragglers, including the sweat soaked and breathless Vincent, to join him.

He adjusted his thick glasses, looking out across the serene broken countryside of woodlands and vleis stretching back to Umzimtuti. Three fault-lines afforded access through the hills for the road to the Works, the growing Native location that was servicing its development and a railway spur from the main line. "There's not much land in the bowl below but the extensive countryside beyond, which is very picturesque, could be used for the major secondary industries. There are various options open to the Government," Whitehead said. He exchanged glances with Sunny. "It'll soon be time for sundowners. Anyone got a firearm or a torch?"

Nobody did.

"There hangs a tale, I'll be happy to relate it in the bar if anyone cares to hear it at the Umzimtuti Hotel after supper. We better get moving."

When Sunny entered the bar, Whitehead and Vincent were settled on bar stools with beers in hand. He took up a stool beside Whitehead and ordered a whisky.

Sunny always dressed neatly and economically himself and clinically appraised appearances. Whitehead's thick head of hair, bleached almost white by the sun, was neatly combed and parted down the side, as he remembered it on the train. Below that everything was somewhat disheveled, which he too remembered. Though he was hardly a qualified judge of fashion he thought Whitehead's jacket was of good quality and yet it hung awkwardly off his frame. The buttons on his shirt beneath were misaligned, his trousers rumpled. But Whitehead seemed oblivious to any deficiency in this regard. He had a reputation as a man who could hold his liquor: down a dozen beers in an evening, never once take leave to find the p.k., be the only man standing at the close and make sure everyone got home safely.

"Ah," said Whitehead, "I'm very glad you've settled here and have the contract for the Works. Bowled any googlies lately?"

"I haven't had a moment for cricket since I arrived."

Jud slid Sunny his shot of whisky.

"I'd like you to elaborate on the comments you made," said Whitehead.

"Umzimtuti's businessmen are keen," said Sunny earnestly, "to provide all the supplies and services for the Works as well as to the secondary industries that are bound to follow. They've served the goldmines and farms for decades."

"Umzimtuti as a supply center is proving useful, but ultimately we are planning to create the Works as Rhodesia's model community—doing it right—starting from scratch."

"Servicing the adjacent countryside will be fairly difficult. I'm seeing a big increase in malaria in the rainy season—including the malignant tertian parasite. Government will have to drain the marshes."

"I had quinine poisoning during my first bout of malaria in the Sabi Valley back in '39. In West Africa during the war I took Atabrin tablets. It suppressed my malaria but gradually turned me yellower and yellower as time went by."

"Bad for your liver. I avoided malaria in my service in East Africa by religious adherence to prevention: long sleeves from sundown to sunup, never slept without a net."

"I got so used to malaria that I came to regard it as nothing worse than a bad go of the flu."

"The Natives, I'll grant you, do have an immunity to a certain extent. I'd like to make a study of it."

"Back from the war I was very depressed over the ruin of my farm in my absence and suffered a bad recurrence of malaria. I was laid very low," said Whitehead, pulling out his pipe and tobacco pouch, filling the chamber, packing it in batches, before he lit it. "But attending a really good bullfight across the border in PEA in the midst of it has, I believe, cured me forever!"

"That'll be the day! Seriously, we don't want an epidemic on our hands."

"I negotiated a row between the army and the RAF and the civil power over the financial responsibility for draining the Takoradi Swamps in the Gold Coast."

"You didn't see it but I'm operating the Native Clinic at the Works out of a pole and dagga hut," said Sunny, "but I'll soon have a room attached to the Native concession store, although it'll just be a sorting office, admitting warranted cases to Umzimtuti's New Government Hospital. I'm not—and the hospital's not—equipped for an epidemic."

"Concentrate on expanding out there. The Government's already well into negotiating to buy the farm adjacent to the Works for the residential settlement."

"I wish I could persuade you to keep Umzimtuti as the main center. There's everything here especially with the proximity of the new power plant going up..."

"Ah," said Whitehead interrupting, repositioning himself on the stool and clenching his pipe firmly between his teeth, "It's useless being in politics unless you have a definite object in mind. But don't allow anyone else to find out what it is. Your mayor's in the way: not exactly forward thinking."

Jud cleared his throat from behind the counter. Sunny glanced at him, but he remained silent.

"Perhaps he could be persuaded."

"I doubt it," said Whitehead. "Your town needs leadership."

"Strange, I'm having difficulty attracting a partner when there's so much opportunity here. 'Till then, unfortunately, I'm too busy to enter politics myself."

"Pity," said Whitehead, "I reached the highest pitch of efficiency during the war. My mind was so fertile for solving seemingly insolvable problems then, averaging eighty-four hours a week at the desk in the Gold Coast at Achimota. Maybe it only happens once in your life."

"I operated at quite a pitch at the fall of Gondar when my advance Field Ambulance and Casualty Clearing Station was flooded with wounded, ill and malnourished surrendered Italians but I hope my best is yet to come."

"You'd be a good man to have onside," said Whitehead.

Just then, Buchanan made a noisy entry into the bar with some of the town councilors. Striding up to the bar he introduced Umzimtuti's patrons, scattered around the room at round tables, to Whitehead recounting the story of Cartwright's famous shots in the wall when Whitehead and he had sheltered under the table together.

Whitehead slid his dimpled beer mug across the counter to Jud, as excess links of his metal wristwatch band dragged across the counter. "Being a good shot certainly helps one's reputation. On the day I installed the first livestock on my farm and got ready to corral them for the night I found a leopard between me and my hut and rifle. He showed no sign of getting out of my way, so I rounded up my staff and he made off up the hill. My beaters drove uphill while I detoured up the road to pick up my rifle and then intercept him. In due course he appeared near the skyline running fairly fast in front of the beaters. I fired a shot at about seventy yards. Missed! He came bounding from rock to rock down the hill straight towards me. I don't think ever before or after have I aimed so carefully. I fired the second shot when he was about thirty yards from me. The bullet went right through his chest killing him almost instantaneously. The skin was superb. I had it very carefully dressed and sent it back as my first present from the farm to my sister Frances."

"There's big money in croc skins," said Broderick Anderson. "No limits: vermin you know."

"It didn't make me think of hunting commercially. What it did was raise my standing amongst my Natives and gave them confidence that I would protect them and their animals."

"Protect them! I was in the Rusape hotel last week, man, and a bloke there said, 'I hang every kaffir that comes my way,'" said Verdoon.

Whitehead put his hand to the side of his face, elbow propped up on the bar counter, and set his alarmingly large blue eyes on Verdoon. There was a pause and the room fell silent. "Rusape. Oh yes, back in '41, I was there on army leave and the same individual said the same thing to me. He's the hangman at the Rusape Prison. I suppose he's been punting the same line to every stranger who's walked into the bar since then. Some individuals get stuck in a shithole of fear and pulling them out is as hard as picking up a turd by the clean end. Mind you it can be done. One of my laborers was so constipated that he thought his grandmother had bewitched him and he'd die soon. I gave him half a bottle of undiluted castor oil with instruction to drink the lot and he came back the next day very relieved and said the White man's *muti* was very strong." Still glaring at Verdoon, he straightened, grasped his mug and roared:

"Behold the Lord High Executioner
A person of noble rank and title-
A dignified and potent officer,
Whose functions are particularly vital!
Defer, defer,
To the Lord High Executioner!"

He turned and gestured the crowd to join in the chorus. Vincent's high falsetto voice led:

"Defer, defer,
To the Lord High Executioner!"

Everyone looked at Verdoon. He scowled, shrugged his shoulders and left the bar.

Whitehead's watch clasp was undone. He tightened up the strap links, took his glasses off and wiped them clean. He downed his mug and slid the glass across the counter again.

"How'd you learn to be such a good shot?" questioned de la Rey doubtfully, as he stared at Whitehead's unmagnified eyes.

"Being from an English country estate, I was used to shooting for sport in the New Forest. It was new to me out here to shoot only for the pot—or the destruction of vermin. Rats in the hut I was living in, while I was building my house, and before that snakes—banded cobras mainly in the fowl run on the chicken farm I was apprenticed to near here—gave me plenty of practice."

"I thought you were a Major-General in the war?" said Paxton.

"Of course they did ask me to be a Major-General in West Africa, but I turned them down."

They all laughed.

Once again he drew breathe and sang loudly:

"I am the very model of a modern Major-General,
I've information vegetable, animal and mineral,
I know the kings of England, and I quote the fights historical
From Marathon to Waterloo, in order categorical;

I'm very well acquainted, too with matters mathematical,
I understand equations, both the simple and quadratical,
About binomial theorem I'm teeming with a lot o' news,
With many cheerful facts about the square of the hypotenuse.

Vincent gestured once again waving both hands up and down palms up for everyone to sing:

With many cheerful facts about the square of the hypotenuse
With many cheerful facts about the square of the hypotenuse
With many cheerful facts about the square of the hypotenuse

Whitehead resumed:

I'm very good at integral and differential calculus;
I know the scientific names of being animalculous:
In short, in matters vegetable, animal, and mineral,
I am the very model of a modern Major-General.

Vincent led the bar again:

In short, in matters vegetable, animal, and mineral,
I am the very model of a modern Major-General."

Whitehead got off his stool and bowed very elaborately. The bar erupted in cheers and whistles.

His fast, tongue-twisting gabble was flawless and his diction plumily-perfect, Sunny thought. He hated Gilbert and Sullivan but he remembered Whitehead telling him of his six months of rainy solitude on the farm, reading economics and singing aloud to himself, just to hear the English language.

"Tell us another one,
Just like the other one,
Tell us another one do," chorused the bar.

Sunny was about to pay his tab and leave, but O'Connor shouted out, "How many times have you been arrested for singing Gilbert and Sullivan?"

Whitehead looked solemn. "Once, my neighbors did try."

The bar groaned.

"In the middle of the night I had to rush down the mountain to help one of my workers who'd taken ill. Fearing a poisoning, I grabbed only my first-aid box. I stayed with him for a couple of hours until he recovered somewhat by which time the moon had set. So with a *picannin* carrying a hurricane lamp to guide me home, we set off back up the mountain. I suddenly smelt a powerful smell like half a dozen foxes, and then I heard the coughing grunt of a leopard. The *picannin* promptly tried to run away but as he had the only light I grabbed him by the back of his collar. I'd forgotten to bring my rifle. I therefore sang Gilbert and Sullivan fortissimo while the leopard continued to follow us at a respectful distance. When I got into the house I proceeded to take two of the stiffest whiskies that I ever had in my life. About ten days later I received a letter from the local secretary of the SPCA threatening me with prosecution for cruelty to one leopard."

Everyone cheered and clapped.

"Tell us a crocodile story," said Whitehead gesturing to Broderick Anderson.

Sunny slipped away, bowled over by this tour de force of English obstreperousness.

CHAPTER THIRTY-FIVE

The New Governor

A stickler for protocol, Southern Rhodesia's new Governor, Sir John Kennedy, alighted from the train at Salisbury Railway Station in full dress. His black hat with white silk cockade accentuated his great height. The rows of medals spread out across his broad chest showed to full advantage against his red, single-breasted coatee sporting nine gilt buttons down the front. His standup collar, epaulets, cuffs and pocket flaps were stiff with gold embroidered trim. His black trousers with a single red stripe along the side seams down to his patent leather shoes further accentuated his height. A sword in a black scabbard with gilt mountings hung from his side.

The ADC too was in full dress kilted uniform with bearskin and sporran. Prime Minister Huggins and his wife Blanche, along with the ministers, including Edgar Whitehead, and his sister Frances visiting from England, had gone down to the station to officially welcome them to the colony. The Boy Scouts and Girl Guides of all colors were there too, along with the Native BSAP Band which played *God Save The King*.

Frances was highly amused at all the fanfare, until Lady Kennedy shook her hand and hissed in her ear, "I've been reading all your letters."

A formal dinner party followed. Frances and Edgar were met at the door to Government House, and along with everyone else, were lined up in the hall according to the Comptroller and the ADC's liking. The Governor and Lady Catherine Kennedy, whom Edgar was soon to rudely refer to as 'the Governess', suddenly emerged from the adjoining room. Solemnly, they walked down the line and spoke to each guest in turn before the guests were marched into the dining room arm-in-arm in order of precedence, just as she and Edgar remembered as children at their manor house, Efford Park.

The Presbyterian Minister said grace. The dinner was excellent. Then His Excellency retired to one room with the men, while Her Excellency sat in the drawing room with the women. At five-minute intervals little Miss Dawson got up and brought each lady for an audience with Lady Catherine on the sofa. Later still, each lady was introduced to the Governor by the ADC. All this formality was quite a switch from the relaxed style of Sir Robert Hudson. Every detail of The Royal Tour was now going to be scrutinized.

It was only a few weeks later that Frances cemented her friendship with Lady Catherine when she found herself in Bulawayo to welcome another batch of children into the Fairbridge Child Migrant Program at Induna for which she and Edgar had worked so hard. The Kennedys happened to be in Bulawayo too and invited her to join them in an afternoon picnic to explore the Matopos, Rhodes' burial site. Frances had visited before with Edgar, and thought this particularly rocky and barren part of the country much overestimated, but nevertheless, she jumped at the chance to get to know the Kennedys.

Sir John was being shown around by an old man from the Archives Department and Lady Catherine, Frances, the Dawson girl and the ADC followed in their wake, trying, *not* very hard, *not* to be frivolous.

Frances looked out over the hills at all the big, bald rocks thrown up from the bowels of the earth, worn down over the eons by all sorts of weather, blotched and scabbed over with alarming colored lichens and said, "It's all rather grotesque, don't you think?"

"Very solemn and grand, enormous scale," replied Lady Catherine.

"Only a man could think this was beautiful and want to be buried here all alone." They were trudging up the almost black dwala, a colossal boulder, to Rhodes' World View.

"Rhodes loved the colossal. They called him a colossus. Isn't this colossal?" said Frances. Rhodes' grave was a simple slab of stone bearing a large brass plaque at the top of the dwala. Big boulders were precariously piled one on top of another as far as the eye could see.

"We have to think of them as the prehistoric castles of Africa," said Lady Catherine.

"Rather unsettling, don't you think? The boulders are poised, it seems, to crash down the hillside into moats of yellow grass," replied Frances.

"The sunshine is so bright, one can't be gloomy."

"It's rather an odd spot for a final resting place, looking out on all this vast nothingness with not a sign of civilization as far as the eye can see."

"The clouds are incandescent."

"Quite the most impressive thing about the place, in my opinion, is this very ancient Native attendant keeping watch all day over Rhodes' spirit."

"Well, that square block over there, though not a triumphal arch, does have a Roman brass frieze; quite a good compromise of ideas don't you think?" Lady Catherine inclined her beautiful head under her large straw hat. "Let's have a closer look."

"Imagine all the hidey-holes for hordes of impis with their assagais poised."

"Rhodes did come unarmed to parley with the Matabele warriors; his finest hour by all accounts."

"It's amazing there haven't been any impis since then. Edgar has decided to devote his life to the colony's economic development. He's as immovable about it as this huge solid rock. But, as you can see, nothing's happened yet."

A snake, the color of the dark granite, slid past them and into a crevice of the whaleback dwala. It was not the first they had seen. They exchanged glances. "I thought," said Lady Catherine, "we were supposed to see all sorts of splendid big wild animals here, but I haven't seen a one, have you?"

"Hmm," volunteered the ADC, "actually there are thirty-nine species of snakes around these parts. Lots are poisonous: mambas, gray, long and thin. Egyptian cobras with big hoods have wandered down all the way from the pyramids. But the puff adders are the ones to watch out for, short and fat. They are rather lazy blighters and won't get out of your way. Don't step on one."

"This whole place reminds me, come to think of it, of Medusa, with her hair full of snakes, turning everyone's head into a granite boulder," said Frances.

"If you'd rather have a big squeeze, there are rock pythons twenty feet long. Too bad we have left the picnic basket in the car," he went on, "we could feed crumbs of bread to these gangs of rainbow colored lizards."

"Actually, I was invited to a picnic!" said Frances.

"Are you volunteering, by any chance, to get the basket?" said Lady Catherine.

"I have to stay close to Sir John," said the ADC.

"Sir John seems to have distanced himself," said Frances.

They arrived at the Jameson Memorial and slowly walked around it.

"Ah! There's a lizard," said Lady Catherine. "The butterflies are also lovely."

Frances said, "Edgar sent wonderful specimens he collected himself to add to Hugh's collection."

"I'm so sorry you lost him during the war. And Arthur too." She put her hand on Frances' forearm. Frances put hers on top briefly before they fell away.

"Yes, despite his polio Arthur got into the RAFVR and was shot down over Rotterdam."

There was a silence. "What sort of eagle is that?" said Frances.

"I'm not sure, it's hard to see, it's probably a black eagle," said the ADC.

"Let's go back to the shady side of the Jameson Memorial," said Lady Catherine. "I'm not that keen on the boulders." They leaned against the granite below the frieze.

"Edgar just couldn't bear the thought of being left out, so when the Rhodesian Army turned him down on the day war was declared, he resigned his Parliamentary seat in Umtali and made his way back home."

"No doubt they turned him down, too."

"Yes, but despite his eyes and ears, he got in somehow. He moved up the ladder quickly to Lieutenant Colonel in West Africa, offered Colonel if he stayed on but he wanted to get back to Britain for the invasion of Europe."

"Typical. Where's Sir John got to? You're supposed to keep an eye on him."

"I have. Follow me, Lady Catherine," said the ADC.

Miss Dawson said, "No. They're beyond those boulders."

Frances said, "These rocks do get rather hot."

Once Sir John and the curator came into view, Lady Catherine paused and turned to Frances and said, "What happened to Edgar after West Africa?"

"Well, Huggins eventually claimed him back for a short temporary stint at Rhodesia House and he returned to Witchwood the very day the Americans dropped their atom bomb. The farm was in ruins. He dug out and burned the remains of the three thousand cherry trees he had planted and nurtured for ten years."

"Oh dear!"

Sir John and the curator approached.

Frances said, "He's had to start all over again. He's switched to dairy. There's a milk shortage."

"And he got his Parliamentary seat back," said Lady Catherine.

"None of the old soldiers were re-elected. He had to stand for a by-election in a safe seat. Huggins was determined to have him for his Minister of Finance."

"What a slog."

"Reading his letters I decided to come out and check up on him. But as you can see, he's got everything in hand and is in fine fettle. Also, I wanted to see for myself the Child Migrant Program is on a firm footing. The Government has bought a new chance on life for each one of those children. Do come to Witchwood after The Royal Tour."

"It sounds marvelous."

The party began the walk back to the car park.

The ladies fell back. "I don't want to mislead you," Frances confided. "Edgar camped in a tent for a year while he saw to the construction of the house. It's rather primitive and of course it got rather run down in his absence. Fixing it's not a priority for him. His priorities are the Ex-serviceman's Resettlement Scheme and development of the Sabi Valley for citrus. Still, whatever its shortcomings, the view from Witchwood all the way to P.E.A. can't be beat."

"We must find a lady for him, she'll put his house in order."

"Don't waste your time on that. He's not one to be married, at all."

"Okay, a visit just for fun. But first things first. I've got to get the pomp and ceremony right for The Royals. I think you ought to pitch in."

CHAPTER THIRTY-SIX

Fate and a Fete

Abu and Hassan's necks had escaped the chopping block on the Jewish New Year and again at Christmas. Life was just so busy. They had become a part of the family. Rulers of the backyard, they roosted in the low, spreading branches of the guava tree. This allowed a clear view of the back door. When Douglas appeared each morning to feed them they would make the short flight down and strut importantly up to the back steps.

Mavourneen hadn't made much of an effort in the back yard. The kitchen courtyard was dry and dusty, thirsting for the Monday and Thursday wash to be hung on the line to lend it color. Leonard polished the household silver and brass at the bottom of the kitchen steps on Sunday mornings. Both he and Douglas would sit on their haunches and talk over the chalky polish and blackened polishing rags and observe the birds as they scratched and pooped their trail through life with the free choice of worms, grubs, caterpillars and perhaps the special treat of a black shiny *chongololo* with its hundreds of red legs in the back garden after a good rain. What more could a pair of turkeys want?

The front garden was different. Mavourneen more than kept up appearances, even surprising herself. Abigail Feldman's original misgivings gave way to admiration.

The secret, if any, was the application of a carefully steeped manure tea of Abu and Hassan's droppings procured by Sugar, the gardenboy, and applied to the garden gems judiciously from time to time.

The precious imported gladiolus bulbs thrived on it. "I do declare, Mavourneen, these are even better than mine. What do you do?" queried Avigail.

"I'm not sure really. I'm rather surprised myself," admitted Mavourneen. *If only she knew how I had just bunged them in any old how,* she mused.

"The W.I.'s horticultural show is coming up and it looks as though this *Mauve Delight* of yours is going to be perfectly timed to bloom just then. I've got some entry forms in the car. You simply must enter. Together we might beat Mrs. Doolittle...into third!"

Over supper that night Sunny shared the highlights of his day as usual with Mavourneen. The monotony of his battle against the excesses of alcohol, smoking and eating of the Europeans had its lighter side.

"Mrs. Parker came in today," he began over hot vegetable soup, "and I needed to weigh her."

"Oh, the scale isn't broken is it?"

"No, it wasn't and I didn't want her to wreck it. Three hundred and fifty pounds is the limit."

"Oh, how sickening!"

"It was rather awkward. I had this bright idea. I got Cookie to move the native scale from the back so we could use one scale for each leg."

"How could you!"

"No, no, she was puzzled but acquiesced to the idea."

"What was the problem then?"

"It was quite a job getting the two scales together, but it was only after we summed up the readings on both scales to four hundred and thirty-eight pounds that she became furious. She said that even on the cattle scale on the farm she didn't weigh that much."

"How cruel of you."

"To the contrary, I was only doing my job but she thought I was conning her into a boosted reading as a therapeutic inducement."

"You're not going to win friends and influence people that way."

"Actually, she's quite a handful to manage medically, mind you. Diabetic."

"I'm not surprised."

"Still, we parted good friends."

Mavourneen looked at him skeptically.

"There's a cake in the kitchen to prove it. She makes them to order."

Leonard brought in the cake. Fruitcake lay entombed in marzipan and white royal icing on which clusters of rose buds and blooms in pale pastels nestled in green leaves. Candied violets popped their heads from the shell-patterned perimeter. Delicate and balanced, it really was a work of art.

"She could win a prize," exclaimed Mavourneen.

"She claims she has. There's a horticultural show coming up."

"Funnily enough, Avigail and I talked about it this morning."

"Why don't you enter that marmalade of yours?"

"You mean the stuff I burnt the day of old man Hardy's dental clearance?"

"It's very good."

"Like burnt toast."

"Carbon's good roughage. But, you do yourself an injustice."

"We should eat our failures in solitude like your Mrs. Parker obviously does."

"Heaven forbid you should have so many failures."

"James Barrie said *we are all failures—at least the best of us are.*"

"I don't consider myself a failure. And neither are you. Who's he?"

"The author of *Peter Pan and Wendy.*"

"I might have known. Your fairytale stuff again."

"Well, nobody's perfect. James Barrie believed in fairies and did a lot of good. He donated all the rights to *Peter Pan* to Great Ormond Street Hospital."

"I do wonder how the twins are settling in, if they'll ever come back? I think the country's lost two much needed talents."

"Well, in the end, Wendy did decide to come back from *Neverland* and take her place at home."

"Now, there's a fairytale ending you should take heart from." Not a day passed without this patient or that complimenting him on the Nonsense Gala Mavourneen had pulled off without him even knowing—already it was drifting into the folklore of Umzimtuti. It wouldn't happen again. He said, "I do so want you to fit in but you've rejected tennis, bridge, the W.I., the church—all the things the other mothers are doing."

"Bridge," she said. "I'm not interested in tricks and trumps, it all seems a waste of time. Tennis—you know I've no eye for ball games. I know it's good exercise, but I prefer a good ride on the bike with Douglas on the back or a brisk walk with Deborah in the pram. I did appeal to all the churches during the flood and they all rallied to the cause admirably—every one of them, but you know I could never be a regular. The W.I. is arts and crafts and women's campaigns. You know I'm not in the least bit crafty." Her bowl was empty. She wiped her lips with her serviette.

"For now," he said, "won't you make a token effort for the show from the home front?"

"Okay, just for you—for fun. I'll enter my *Brandied Marmalade*. I do still have a jar or two left. I won't enter the glads. They have done extraordinarily well and I'm afraid they might overshadow Avigail's and that would never do. The Feldmans have been so generous and the ribbon means so much to her."

Accepting seconds from the tureen that she doled out generously, Sunny shook his head, "I give up. Where's your competitive spirit?"

The day of the horticultural show and fete had barely dawned when Mavourneen heard the phone ring those three confounded trills. Sunny groped for the phone and picked up the receiver.

"I say, what a damnable underhand thing to do!"

"I beg your pardon?" said Sunny, instantly awake.

"*You*, sabotaging my glads!"

Sunny turned over onto his stomach, his elbows pressed into the pillow and cradled the phone. "This is Dr. Rubenstein. Can I help you?"

"Rosalind Doolittle. My glads! My glads!" came over loud and shrill.

"Glads? I don't follow you."

"The show, today! Your *bloody* birds. I've a mind to get my Fred to shoot the bloody things."

"I haven't the faintest idea what you are talking about."

"Your turkeys have ruined my gladioli. Don't tell me it was an accident!"

"Of course it was."

"Your wife plotted with Avigail Feldman. She's always wanted the blue."

"Don't be absurd."

"You damn Jews are trying to take over this town." The line went dead.

"What an infernal woman. You won't believe what Mrs. Doolittle has just said." Sunny turned to Mavourneen.

She was already up, sliding her legs over the side of her bed and pulling on her dressing gown. "I heard," she said. "I'm sorry, I didn't think they could—or would fly long distances. They have it so good here. I'll make her a batch of scones and send Leonard over with them and a pot of marmalade as an apology."

"You what! The woman has accused us of a Jewish plot and you want to send her a pot of marmalade! Where's your self-respect? I just don't understand you. Your upbringing is completely incomprehensible. Six million Jews have just been murdered in the last few years. You're unbelievable!"

Tears welled up. She looked down at her dressing gown and fiddled with the cord.

"I'm sorry. Let's just take a moment to think about things." He was up, out of bed, rounded it and reached for her hands. He put his around both of hers before he dropped them and hitched up his pajama pants. Then he lifted his hands to his head and began to pace. "Look, these turkeys caused us a lot of worry the very day you got them and on top of it I embarrassed myself in front of all the men at the bar on that Saturday afternoon. Now they have caused the mine manager's wife to abuse me in the worst possible way. What is it about these turkeys?"

She met his gaze. He was looking at her intently. He smoothed down his hair. She blushed. She remembered very clearly that she had decided to allow the turkeys freedom as a gesture against her own confinement. How could she possibly tell him? "I'll get rid of them."

"Yes, I'm afraid you should. I'm sorry, I know you are very fond of them. But you are right, a batch of scones and a pot of marmalade is the best way to rise above the mine manager's wife's base inferiority." He opened his arms and embraced her. "It's going to be alright, I love you and we're going to be a happy family together."

She nodded. They clung to each other, then their arms dropped and they held hands momentarily, before he gave hers a squeeze and she turned and said, "I'd better get started." She tightened the cord of her dressing gown, slipped into her slippers and headed for the kitchen.

Chelmsford Hall was laid out for the show. White-clothed trestle tables in closely fitted rows filled the hall, one for every category imaginable. In the horticulture section individual blooms of gladiolus, dahlias, roses and many others were stood singly in long-stemmed vases for close scrutiny. Mavourneen walked down the rows, looking for Avigail and her glads. She felt loyal to Avigail, but she couldn't help thinking, *why scrutinize a flower and have a judge grade it on a chart?* There was room in the world for imperfection—a petal here or there to be nibbled by a caterpillar so a butterfly could emerge and a bird sing.

Tortured bonsai were sited next to the flower arranging which was segregated into subsections for posies and arrangements in formal and free-form categories. The rules were strict. She passed on.

There was Avigail. Avigail, smiled at her, and said, "My dear, Mavourneen so nice to see you. What do you think of my specimen glad?"

"It's lovely, it really is. It deserves first prize. And I know you're going to get first prize."

"First prize? The blue? Of course not. But Mrs. Doolittle—have I seen her? Not yet."

"I have to tell you something. Let's go and look at all the entries."

Seeing Avigail, glad to see her and proud of her flower entries brought back the afternoon when Rivkah had brought Abu and Hassan to the backyard. She knew her admiration for freedom had won Rivkah over in spite of herself. She felt sad.

"My dear, what is wrong?"

"Mrs. Doolittle is not going to enter glads this year. The turkeys escaped and ate them."

"What! You pull my leg? It's not right."

"No, it really happened."

"Oh my goodness!"

They had reached the home industries section. "I did a lot of knitting for the war effort. I didn't enjoy it much really," said Mavourneen.

"I did it when I was younger, but I prefer to read a book or write to the children. But do they write back?"

They looked at the crochet tablecloths, blankets and babies dresses. Smocking, sewing and knitting were each to be scrutinized in their respective places, Mavourneen thought dolefully to herself. Complicated cable knit sweaters sat segregated from baby matinee jacket and bootie sets, which in turn were set apart from the intricacies of four-needle knitting of men's socks where precisely turned heels counted.

Avigail said, "My dear these embroidered linen table cloths are very good don't you think?"

"Yes, but you have to count all the threads."

"Well what else can the Scandinavians do with all those long cold nights?"

"Not my cup of tea, I'm afraid."

"Mrs. Doolittle upset you. She's not my cup of tea."

"No, not really, Sunny got terribly angry with me."

They moved on to admire counted cross stitch and Greek embroidery and then there were tea showers and milk jug covers weighted with intricate bead or shell work alongside fancy tea and egg cozies: knitted, crocheted or sewn. Hundreds and hundreds of hours of busyness. Her own embroidery and sewing were mediocre. She was practical: hadn't the patience for attention to detail that perfection demanded.

Avigail said, "It's always lovely to look at food, no?" She put her arm around Mavourneen and steered her towards the aromas in the domestic science section. Loaves of quick and yeast breads lay in profusion. There were regiments of queen cakes. Reluctantly she remembered from the Aberdeen Domestic Science School all the rules that would be used to judge the heaviness of loaves of fruitcake wrapped in marzipan and royal icing. Sponge cakes would be evaluated for their lightness and chocolate cakes for moisture. Biscuits and scones would be judged outwardly by size, shape and uniformity and inwardly for texture and taste. She turned to Avigail and said, "It all goes down the same little red lane after all doesn't it?"

"Mavourneen tell me what happen. So Sunny blame you for turkeys eating Mrs. Doolittle's gladioli?"

"Yes, he answered the phone and Mrs. Doolittle insulted him and straight away I suggested I make scones and send a pot of marmalade to her."

"So he thought you make light of an insult?"

"Yes. And somehow he knew that my allowing the turkeys so much freedom was to blame."

"Oh my dear. Rivkah told me she worried about you with the turkeys that afternoon."

"Yes, I made a mistake didn't I?"

"Yes, you made a mistake, but freedom the most important thing. Jews remember they were slaves in Egypt."

Vegetables of every type were on display for external and internal examination: avocado, gem squashes, chou-chou fruits, green beans and new potatoes. Fruits: guava and mango for blush and blemish. Row upon row of pickles in Ball jars proudly took their place. Watermelon *konfyt*, melon and ginger jams and marmalades had specific criteria to be met: clarity, consistency, color and flavor counted. Mavourneen sat her jar of *Brandied Marmalade* down. She realized that Avigail did not want to say more but she believed in her. She said, "You see you are going to win the blue ribbon, but I know you won't be happy because Mrs. Doolittle was sabotaged by Feldman turkeys."

"Of course we plotted it. Isn't that what she said?"

Mavourneen said, "Yes, she said 'The Jews want to take over this town.'"

"And straight away you offered to bake some scones?"

They both laughed.

Mavourneen said, "I have to tell you why my glads looked so good. It was the manure from the turkeys."

"But you have to get rid of them?"

"Yes, but you can take them and beat Mrs. Doolittle fair and square next year."

They laughed and laughed.

"God willing, I'll be in Jerusalem next year," Avigail said. "Don't tell anyone anything about this."

Many of the women had been up at four or before in order to set up in time. The hall was abuzz as the entry deadline of 10 o'clock approached and judging commenced. Bulawayo and Salisbury judges, experts each in their chosen field, had been met at the station on the 1.01 and 2.01 respectively and put up in Umzimtuti homes. They deliberated up and down in analytical brooding.

Everyone was there at two in the afternoon when the doors opened and the town flooded in. Names were clearly displayed on the ribbon winners. Men came to proclaim their wives' and daughters' industry. As the speeches and tributes were made, Mavourneen mused there was so much still to be done in Africa, weren't there more meaningful things than obsession with minutiae to occupy all the free time afforded by the luxury of so many servants? Some of these women wouldn't even share their recipes! How she despised this smallness of mind. It was such a joy to share the good things in life. But she knew many of these women lived in isolation in the bush on farms and small workings and were starved of recognition. Their infrequent trips to Umzimtuti for supplies were made especially to coincide with special days like this.

In the year 1947, Mavourneen could see trouble looming ahead for Sunny as Mrs. Parker, fatter than ever, hovered over her iced wedding cake, which had taken the blue of course. It was a magnificent five tiers, enough to treat the whole of Umzimtuti, but soon to be shipped intact to the capital to fill an order.

Mrs. Kalderon from Lucky Strike Trading store at Leighfield Siding, fairly swept the sewing table with her smocked child's frock and baby's bonnet, as well as embroidered tea cloth with eight matching serviettes, a tea cozy and tray cloth. It didn't seem fair that she had no children of her own and lived so far from company that she couldn't invite anyone for tea.

Avigail Feldman won Best of Show for her blood red *Gladiolus grandiflorus*. The florets were round, face forward, ruffled, with an upward thrust, throats visible, with no hooding, cupping or reflexing, the color vivid, the markings uniform. The stem was straight and strong. The scent was heady.

Caroline Creswicke of the Mighty Melville Mine won Best of Show for the black rose, the *Star of Africa*, she was developing. Sixty miles from Umzimtuti and civilization, she aspired to membership in the Royal Rose Society of London and this new hybrid brought her one step closer to qualification and acceptance.

Mavourneen won an orange ribbon 'Highly Commended' for her *Brandied Marmalade* with the judge's comment: *Somewhat off color. Clarity and consistency could be improved but can't be beat for original flavor.* Would Mavourneen share the recipe?

Was honesty the best policy or would this seem to mock the seriousness of the affair?

She decided to compete with the men next year and go for the blue for the largest pumpkin: no subjectivity.

CHAPTER THIRTY-SEVEN

The Warning

"Colonel O'Connor," warned Ian McDougall, attorney at law, "you have no more than a fifty-fifty chance of dismissal of the libel action at best, on the plea of public interest and that you acted in good faith: that you had sufficient reason to believe that what you wrote at the time was factual. We could make a big issue of the duty of the press to be a public watchdog. If we drag it out there is a better than even chance that he will call it a day sooner rather than later. It can't do him any good and he may well fear disclosures coming out of court. You realize such a strategy escalates costs."

"What's involved if I capitulate? I have to consider the impact on the election. That's the important thing. I haven't got five thousand half crowns let alone pounds. That demand is a lot of baloney. As you explained, it's to move the case to the High Court."

"He can insist on the £5,000, a full public apology in your paper and perhaps the national press. The court, of course may only award him nominal damages, but you will be liable for costs. I don't think you have any option but to fight it in the circumstances. Would you like me to take Counsel's opinion?"

"What will that cost?"

"You will have to put down £250."

Pat felt optimism and strength drain from him in a vision of disaster once more. He forced a brave face. "This isn't going to be funny. But I suppose in for a penny in for a pound. I can't see any other way out either."

CHAPTER THIRTY-EIGHT

Consultations

A surgical case following Sick Parade set Sunny behind schedule. Once again he wished he had a partner. The consulting roster was full.

So much of European general practice was repetitive, mundane, routine, trivial and symptomatic. He would always have a soft spot for some patients like Old Man Hardy, and Ouma van Hoepen and the doyen of the Afrikaner farmers, Ferreira. But dealing with Miriam Kalderon's neurosis was a trial. Now Jud Levine was in his consulting room.

Once he sat down with Jud, he said, "Let me guess, you've got a bad dose of O'Connor? Normally you get my professional expertise for the price of a whisky." He swiveled impatiently in his chair as he heard Jud out, thinking *this is serious—it isn't about a bunch of carrots anymore—it's about Jud's reputation.*

O'Connor had unquestionably gone too far. He reminded him of drunken Major Coghlan, head of his ambulance unit in East Africa. The officers had covered for his alcoholism but after the fall of Gondar their loyalty looked decidedly misplaced when the unit was swamped with Italian prisoners in tatters: wounded, diseased, malnourished, filthy. Subsequently Major Coghlan had shot himself. He wasn't going to see Colonel O'Connor disgraced and dead on his watch. He stopped swiveling, drew a deep breath and said, "Don't go on with it."

"Just watch me. He'll be taught a bloody lesson he won't forget."

"Hold it, hear me out. What will be the impact with a councilman suing the prospective Member of Parliament for libel, especially if O'Connor wins the election? What do you hope to achieve by it? Personal satisfaction? I'm sure you are not after his money. You know very well he hasn't any.

"Remember he had humble beginnings in Tasmania but got on the staff of Field Marshall Allenby before he was discharged on medical grounds. You know he's gone into farming without knowing what he's doing and he's broke. He got elected to Parliament by sheer luck but his blarney and digging for scandal got him expelled from the party.

He's his own worst enemy. His new small working is only digging himself into another hole. He's used to army admin. where it's all expenditure. You know his wife, Nancy, has her hand constantly in the till to buy liquor. Taking on *The Cleft Stick* and the auctioneering business suits him better, but the rag's not a business success despite the advertising income. I know he's dependent on his meager Australian pension.

"But you've risen from refugee to owning the Umzimtuti Hotel. You're lucky."

"Lucky?"

"Lucky, to make the refugee quota into this country before 1920. Think of all the Jews in Rhodes taken by the Nazis. Only a handful survived and now they can't find a place in the world. You found a beautiful young wife and have two lovely children. Yes, you're lucky..."

"Luck Doc? We make our own luck. Fend for ourselves. I should have defended my wife's honor over the bid for the carrots and pressed my demand for a public apology. If he thinks he can walk all over me, he has another think coming.

"You can't go round knocking people and expect everyone to suffer it lying down. Isn't that what we should have learned from two thousand years of history? The concentration camps! Your family escaped the pogroms in Lithuania but you yourself never experienced anything, so it's easy to be generous," said Jud.

"Easy to be generous? Even now, my father is still trying to trace his family. Nothing. Only the Norwegian family who hid in the forest during the Occupation and escaped to neutral Sweden survived." He knew his father's continued dogged pursuit would be fruitless and he would never get to know the cherished faces of his Lithuanian family in the photograph albums his mother prized and brought out at every celebration.

"We mustn't forget. I won't be walked over. What's O'Connor think he's doing telling everybody how to run the country when he can't bloody well run his own affairs? He needs to be taught the lesson the party tried to teach him. It's too late anyway. It's in the hands of the legal boys. You know they won't let up because their costs have to be met. No, it has to run its course."

"Jud, you know you can stop it if you want to."

"You needn't be worried about the town, because he won't win the election this time, and that's a damn good thing."

"I thought you were bigger than wanting to destroy a man who is down: Queensbury rules. Like I said, he has enough trouble with his wife and his business problems."

"Now, you want to make me feel a schmuck, working your psychology stuff on me, damn you! Sorry, Doctor. I understand your concern for the so-and-so. I appreciate your good intentions but the answer is *No!*"

"What about your year on council? Drop it. It can only benefit the legal sharks." Sunny rose and opened the consulting room door. "Jud, do think about what I've said. Too bad I can only charge you seven and sixpence for a standard consultation."

Sunny collected Sister Forbush. They popped back to the other consulting room to do an abdominal and pelvic exam on Mrs. Kalderon. She wanted a child so badly. He had done a sperm count on her husband's semen himself: twice. Confirmed azoospermia. But she was always coming in, claiming missed periods, insisting on a pelvic. She had all the signs and symptoms of pregnancy—morning sickness, breast tenderness and changes in the nipples. Her cervix was indeed softened, her uterus enlarged which was putting pressure on the bladder causing frequency but tragically there was no fetus: a classic hysterical pregnancy. Her disappointment was profound. He looked at his watch, scanned the appointment list again. He sighed as he met her tearful gaze and explained, again.

As noon approached, Sunny looked forward to the wail of the mine hooter signaling lunch, when who should drop into the consulting room unscheduled but Colonel O'Connor. Instantly, he took in his bulging belly against his ill-fitting shirt and his pale face.

"Colonel," Sunny said as he rolled his chair back and stepped forward to greet the patient. "What brings you in today?"

"Doc, I'm restless, can't sit still. I feel tight-chested on and off, but it's got so I can't ignore it. You've got to help me."

"Let's take a look then, check a few things." He rolled back the Colonel's short sleeve, the skin cool as he strapped on the blood pressure cuff and pumped: systolic 220 mmHg over 130 mmHg diastolic! Pressed his fingers to his wrist: pulse irregular.

"You're living too well! You got to cut back on the drinking, eating and smoking—literally, the good life's killing you. Your heart's overtaxed. Let's listen." Momentarily he warmed the chest piece of the stethoscope in his hand before pressing it to the Colonel's chest. In place of the normal lub-dub, lub-dub there was a galloping and whooshing.

"Doc, life's not that great. It's all the stress, you know, the court case..."

"Pat, pocket your pride. Apologize. Settle. Costs are mounting which you know you can't afford. Your election, your business and your health, everything is at stake."

"I know, I know. I don't feel up to the fight."

"You came to me for help and I have come to two conclusions. As your doctor I must tell you that your health is seriously jeopardized, and as your bush lawyer that you will lose the case."

"Doc, I wish I could get out of it, but the lawyers have taken over. Their fees are the issue now. I haven't the money to pay both sides or possibly even my own. If you can help clear up this mess, I'd appreciate it. In any case I'll lose the election, my heart's not in it anymore."

O'Connor was worth saving. When he was young he'd been ambitious and hardworking and had gone far as a priest in the army in the Great War. After it he'd left the army and the priesthood which couldn't have been easy. He still had a lot of Irish charm and a pleasing Irish brogue. He was a good man going to ruin. His wife wasn't helping. His bad judgment had made him unpopular with his own party and lost him his parliamentary standing. Anti-Semitism was the creed of failures who feared they were inferior.

"First off, we have to get you over to the hospital and do some tests. Get you over your immediate medical distress. I don't want to alarm you but we need to do some ECG tracings, keep you under observation for a while. I'll make arrangements. Is Nancy with you?"

"No Doc, I'm on my own, if you know what I mean—she's a little under the weather right now."

The hooter wailed. Sunny rose, "It's lunchtime and you're my last patient of the morning. I'll drive you up to the hospital. We'll get started to sort you out right away."

"Doc, I'm so grateful. If you would intervene, you know, in the lawsuit on my behalf, I know I could get back on track."

"Relax for now. Put it out of your mind. I'll do my utmost: tackle the lawyers and if necessary their Counsels. Let me help you to my car."

CHAPTER THIRTY-NINE

Anticipation

The next day, Sunny had blocked out all his afternoon surgery appointments to take Mavourneen out alone, which he hadn't done since they'd moved to Umzimtuti. He found himself looking forward to it but last minute he was having second thoughts, with O'Connor still unstable and so much else on his plate. But he'd promised Anderson he'd save him the trip in and give him his bilharzia shot at Sycamore Bend, so doubly committed he grabbed his red-and-white striped tin of supplies and let the screen door of the surgery bang behind him. The wail of the hooter sounded the noon hour and he quickly crossed the driveway to the house, before any drop-in could forestall him.

Mavourneen was ready with a lunch box of sandwiches and a thermos of tea as Sunny reversed out of the lean-to garage. He put the car in neutral and hopped out, opened the door for her and helped her in. She was getting heavy. He tucked in the flair of her skirt behind her and patted her knee affectionately before he slammed the door shut. They were off. They rolled down the hill to the railway station, turned right onto Main Street and bumped over the railway tracks. Before the New European Hospital receded in the rear view mirror, virgin bush loomed ahead.

Mavourneen said, "Life was awfully hard for the few pioneer farmer settlers around here."

"Ferreira told me, before he went into tobacco, during one terrible drought he hauled dead cattle out of the veld to be boiled up and fed to the pigs. This district has always been considered a mining area. Big companies like Lonrho have sat on vast acreages waiting for others to make investments so they can enjoy windfall gains in land appreciation."

"I love it like this, untamed. I bet there are leopards in the granite outcrops."

They did see game adept at concealment or flight: solitary small duiker dived into thickets. Herds of gold and tan impala made running leaps through savanna. Small gray-brown herds of kudu, the big bull with long spiral horns, drifted in the intricate gray-brown patterns of bushveld like half thoughts. Mavourneen said, "Let's keep a look out for zebra and maybe even giraffe. What do you think the chance is we'll see sable? Wouldn't that be a treat?"

"It's possible we might see them all at Sycamore Bend."

Birds of every description abounded: flocks of spotted guinea fowl foraged in the red earth, crested gray louries flitted in the deciduous woodland, flocks of doves flew up as they bumped over the corrugations of the gravel road.

Sunny said, "I wouldn't be surprised if this will be made into the first full tar road around here before this Royal Tour is over."

"A coup for us in Umzimtuti," said Mavourneen brightly.

"We could definitely use it as far as the hospital of course but beyond that, don't you see, there are so many *other* roads that deserve the attention."

Stones and dust spewed up and clunked on the underside of the car as he fumbled with his cigarette box. "Oh, don't," she said staying his hand, "I know you're hungry." She leaned over, spread a tea towel across his knees, and passed him half an egg-and-Marmite sandwich. "Slow up," she said, "tea's coming up when you're ready. Steaming hot."

Settled into the seat that had molded to cup his shape, munching away, he began to relax to the hum of the engine and rhythm of the corrugations. He loved the car and it was a treat to have Mavourneen's company.

"I've only just put two and two together," she said, as she spread a towel over the bump of her tummy and tucked in herself, before pouring her own tea into the inner lid of the thermos. "The baby's due *right* at the time of the Royal Victory Tour. I don't want to miss it."

"Well," he said, dismissing the concern, "you're luckier, getting a preview of the Retreat instead. I can't imagine why they're coming out—the *whole* Royal family with Britain rationed and broke now that the battle to save the world is won."

"They want to personally thank the seventy-five thousand people of this country for their contribution to the war. You know, Rupert Brooke: *God be thanked who has matched us with this hour.*"

"Actually it was those left behind, including thousands of Natives, supplying strategic minerals, canvas and beef who made the biggest contribution—and the Empire Air Training Scheme, of course."

"O'Connor's rag says *our* boys suffered the biggest losses and were awarded the most medals."

"I'm glad to see," he said, "you've taken to heart *our* new country, *our* new land and brushed Frank Winthrop out of your hair. But you're talking about a very small contingent."

"They first earned their reputation in the Great War. A telegram to the British Government said, *All Rhodesians ready for duty* the moment war was declared. Nearly half volunteered. Lots paid their own passage to England. A third became commissioned officers. All in all, we do deserve Royal recognition."

"On the strength of it, the British Government granted self-government to Southern Rhodesia in '23, although strings remain for foreign and Native affairs. Huggins has cajoled them into relaxing some of those restrictions. We should amalgamate with Northern Rhodesia, though they've very little experience with self-government. Then we should go for full independence."

"I don't think people spend much time thinking about constitutions and that sort of thing. They just want to see The King and Queen."

"You're mistaken. Whether to join the Union of South Africa or ask for self-government was a tremendous controversy in '23. But you are right about The King and Queen. Such a pantomime: a wave here, a handshake there."

"Pantomime my foot. It means everything to the people. They've been talking about it practically since we got here and the litigation over the tea tender has only heightened anticipation. Boy oh boy, Jud Levine is going to have to put on a *mighty* good spread or face a lot of music."

"I'll take another cup if it's still going," he said, passing the empty lid back to her. "All this energy on a *tea*. What could be more simple? And as for building *this* house *just* for the Royals, *just* for a few days, on the prettiest bend in the river, the money would be so much better spent on education, industry, roads that lead to somewhere...so many *real* needs that would make a *real* impact on people's lives. It's such an extravagance."

"We haven't seen it yet," she said. "Let's not get our hopes up too much. Those *pise* houses Broderick's putting up on the other side of the tracks look pretty modest to me."

"Have you forgotten our succession of miserable little flats in Pretoria? I'm sure all these ex-servicemen, Air Force types who trained here and bombed out Poms are going to think Broderick's two bedroom houses are luxurious."

"I'll admit," she said, "the big plots have garden potential. Mind you, rental property usually suffers from neglect once the novelty wears off. People don't want to put their hearts and souls into something that belongs to the government."

"The Housing Board has them slated for demolition in five years, but Broderick says this *pise* construction will stand for a thousand years, you know. I've been mulling it over, if he's right there's potential to turn those government rentals into long term homeownership."

"How's that?"

"You see the government is going to have to pay for demolition as it stands, but if the municipality buys them at cost and turns around and sells them at a reasonable price, it would make home ownership attainable for those who can't afford a conventional dwelling—dreams come true."

"A house to call their own—we don't even have that ourselves."

"A victory for government, municipality and the people."

"Buchanan told me at the Hospital Christmas Tea Umzimtuti municipality's coffers are empty. Remember, I'm having to find the funds for one swimming bath. I'm not complaining—I'm so enjoying working on it, but I doubt council's got money to buy a hundred and twenty-five houses from the government."

"Buchanan's so short-sighted. He could ask government for, say, a ten-year interest free loan. I'm sure Whitehead would agree to it. The Council would redeem its land and service costs and an eventual handsome capital profit. There'd be additional income from rates and the interest on the mortgages. Think of the possibilities with the capital: a dam and a proper filtration plant for starters. No more fish fingerlings in the bathwater! Waterborne sewage: no more honey suckers! Streetlights! Paved Roads! Pavements!"

Sunny slowed at a weir over a spruit and as they climbed up the other side, Mavourneen spotted a pair of reedbuck. "We must be close, start looking out for gates. Broderick said you can't miss them," he said. "Any more sandwiches?"

"Yes," she said reaching into the tin. "Last one."

"This road is rough on tires," he said, as she offered it to him. "The faster we go the less we'll feel the corrugations." He ran over a long thin road alligator, a sliver of tire retread, stretched across the road and pressed on the accelerator.

"Why don't you run for council? Wake the town up. It's like a *Sleeping Beauty*."

"I've just got to find a partner to share the work before I commit myself to anything outside medicine, although these issues all arise out of public health, really. Your swimming pool, reducing bilharzia, should be just the start."

"Don't lose heart, someone's got to come to light soon. I can't wait to see what a masterpiece Broderick has come up with," she said, as she offered him a guava and packed away the picnic things.

They dropped into an easy silence. Lunch had gone down well. She spotted another herd of impala browsing in dappled sunlight. Glancing left and right, Sunny said, "Now's the time to enjoy all this. It's all so wide open with possibilities. It's going to change—earmarked to be carved up into three thousand acre farms and ten thousand acre ranchland for ex-serviceman. Edgar Whitehead's encouraging these farmers-in-the-making by offering tuition and Government financial backing lest we lose out to Australia, New Zealand or Canada. He's moving fast to try to avoid the unemployment he saw in England as a lad after the Great War."

"It'll all be fenced then, I suppose. Pity," she said. "I expect hunting will be on the rise, too."

"Yes, cattle are what you'll see on the ranches, of course. Game in the game reserves, there's lots of land set aside for that."

"It won't be nearly the same."

"Well, we can't have it both ways," said Sunny as he braked for a sounder of warthogs in the road ahead. Startled, they took off with tufted tails in the air.

"Oh," said Mavourneen. "Those're such wonderfully ugly creatures, they're beautiful. You know, with all this talk of immigration, the Jewish community has been complaining. No loosening up on the Jewish immigration quota or even the restrictions for refugees. They, of all people, should get a break."

"You're absolutely right. Huggins is clinging to keeping the country exclusively upper class British, not even letting up to admit working class Englishmen, let alone the Czechs for instance."

"What's special about the Czechs?"

"Well, when Chamberlain let Hitler grab the Sudetenland, displaced Czech farmers offered to bring their own equipment in lieu of money.

All they needed was land but only a token of fifty were admitted, with all this wide-open space crying out for development. Even the offer of whole Czech industries, to keep them out of the hands of the Nazis, was turned down. Only Bata's thirty-three artisans were grudgingly admitted to start the country's first shoe factory. Think of Italian engineering—I saw the roads they built in the Highlands of Abyssinia—masterpieces," he said as he swerved to miss a *donga*. "The short sightedness is staggering.

"Huggins' pride in Britishness, overlooking the long-term benefits from the diversity and talents of foreigners—Europeans, Jews, Mediterraneans too—will be this country's downfall."

CHAPTER FORTY

Fifty-One Steps from Wildest Africa

Rounding a corner, in a clearing of the indigenous masasa, mufuti, and mongongo trees, an imposing stone arch declared *For King & Empire* in iron lettering. The enormous iron gate itself hung open. A uniformed guard waved them on.

"I say," said Sunny. "There's really no need for a guard out here in the back of beyond. There's nobody around to steal anything."

"Yes," she said, "It's so nice, after South Africa, to be able to leave the house unlocked in the care of the servants and never worry about it. The guard just serves as a reminder of the far reaches of Empire." A long track through the woodland led to a circular driveway and the residence. A heavy thatch hung low over the whitewashed walls of the house which was wrapped in a gauzed verandah, under the shade of an enormous tree. It arched over fifty-one steps that descended to a deep pool in the bend of the river. On the far side of the pool was a crash of hippos very sensibly wallowing in the heat of the day. She looked down onto the blue-black backs of these obese animals with bristly square snouts. One lolled on the far bank in an orangey red blood sweat, groomed by yellow-eyed and red-beaked oxpeckers. In the shimmer further upstream, a saddle-billed stork poised motionless on its spindly knobbly-kneed legs. Masked weaver birds' pendulous nests hung from twigs over the river. The diving of a brilliant malachite kingfisher and fluttering as he returned to his perch were the only movements in the languid scene.

Sunny came to a stop, turned the key and opened his car door, but Mavourneen had set aside his red-and-white tin and he rummaged under the car seat for it. She opened her door. Her tummy was slowing her up these days, starting to get in the way of everything.

Broderick hailed them from the verandah steps and then suddenly shouted, "Freeze! Freeze!"

Sunny looked up. Mavourneen was about to swing her legs over and step out, eager to explore. Momentarily from beneath her car door a long thin rippling ribbon shot to the riverbank, flung itself over the brink and was gone.

"My goodness Mavourneen!" shouted Broderick, striding to the car, taking her hand and helping her out. "That was close," he said. "Doc, what do you mean letting a black mamba hitch a ride with you?"

"A mamba?" said Sunny, momentarily rounding the car and coming to Mavourneen's side.

"Surely not," said Mavourneen.

"No mistaking it. The coffin shaped head. Greased lightning. Maybe nine feet long, I'd say. I could see it unraveling under the car. Is that sandwiches or antivenin in that lunch tin of yours?"

"It's your bilharzia shot. In all my calls to houses, farms, clinics, I've never come across any snakes. Not one," said Sunny.

"Well," Broderick said. "Your luck just ran out. You ought to be prepared. Twenty minutes to an hour is all you've got after a mamba strike."

"The SAIMR does have a polyvalent antivenin, I'll get some."

"Hope nobody saw it but us. My workers will all desert. We're pretty much done on the retreat, but have the finishing touches on the outbuildings to do. They are superstitious as hell about all snakes—bad luck—but in the case of mambas it's justified. It could easily have been tickets for Mavourneen! Let's go in and have a drink to celebrate life, before I show you round."

"How could this have happened?" asked Sunny, circling his arms around Mavourneen and pulling her close to him.

"Doc, you didn't happen to run over any road alligators on the way out did you?"

"Actually we did, after we crossed the weir," said Mavourneen.

"They're not making retreads like they used to and the road's bad," said Sunny.

"That's it! Crocodile hunting at night is one thing, road alligators in the day are quite another. If you run over one you've got to check the rubber's in the rear view mirror. A mamba likes to bask in the heat of the open road. Faster than the speed of light it can wrap itself around the axle as you pass, make his way around the underbelly of your car. Easy as that. But I expect the engine warmed him up a bit too much for comfort and lucky for you—for Mavourneen—he skedaddled. Normally, they're very aggressive.

"Let's have a drink. I've got a bottle of whisky," said Broderick as he led the way in.

Safely inside, the gauzed in verandah had a sweeping view of the river. Sunny put a protective arm around Mavourneen and they stood side by side to drink in the grandeur of it in silence and collect themselves. Broderick produced the bottle of *Johnnie Walker* and three shot glasses. "I know it's a bit early for sundowners," he said, motioning them to take up the riempie chairs, "but here's to life! And your new addition too."

"To life!" said Mavourneen.

"*L'chaim!*" said Sunny as glasses clinked, and they all sat back and admired the mahogany coffee table and fell silent.

"I do hope the Royals will be amused watching the hippos tiptoe in the shallows here, keeping cool until sundown before they head inland, single file, to graze. That's when the bush parade begins as the animals come down to take their turn at the water's edge."

"I must hand it to you. This's a perfect setting for a Royal Retreat," said Sunny.

"Must be about twenty or so hippo down there with their young," said Mavourneen.

"Yes," said Broderick, "One territorial lord and master over his harem."

"Isn't all this rather close—risky—for The Royals?"

"No, no, the hippo keep to the gradual slope of the far bank of the bend. This side's awfully steep."

"Well, they've staked their territory alright. Good thing. It will keep the Royals safely out of any temptation for a dip—and bilharzia—the real and present danger. Let me give you your shot before we forget," said Sunny, opening the tin, getting out the tourniquet, the syringe, a swab and checking the label on the vial of sodium antimony tartrate, before drawing it up.

"Give me a moment to fortify myself," said Broderick. "You know how I hate that shot. Counting the days 'till I'm done. Let's not boast about the mamba. We should keep it to ourselves. Luckily, the boys are still on lunch break. Come to think of it, no sense either in getting the officials and so on, let alone the Royals, nervous."

"The tree," said Mavourneen, "It's really magnificent. What is it?"

"It's a sycamore fig. I'm guessing it's four hundred years old or so, planted by the Portuguese explorers as prospecting markers. They also visited the Cheetah quartz reef and there's a huge fig near the headgear there but there was too much malaria and nobody came back until Thomas Baines a hundred years ago. He camped right here at the bend. Despite all the prospecting that's gone on in this country, there's only been one new discovery—the Anzac. Apart from that, the ancients worked them all."

Broderick looked away as Sunny searched for a good vein to slowly infuse the toxic metalloid, careful to avoid any leakage to the tissues. "I've scoured the country for the best Africana," said Broderick wincing. "This is my chance to get on the map as the top contractor and decorator in the country."

Sunny pressed a wad of cotton wool to the site and strapped a strip of Elastoplast over it. Broderick waved his arm, sighed, cleared his throat, before he rose and they followed him inside. "First off, feel how cool the *pise de terre* makes the interior," he pointed out. The focus of the ground floor was the granite fireplace. Above it, black glass eyes stared out from beneath thick eyelashes in a distinctive sleek black face with white markings of a mounted head of a sable antelope. Three-foot-long ringed horns arched back to touch the rock. A ridge of stiff mane bristled behind long pointed ears. Framing the fireplace were a huge pair of elephant tusks. A large zebra skin lay over a Rhodesia teak parquet floor glowing with reds and browns. Beneath each of the finely upholstered wingback chairs lay softly tanned leopard skins. Gleaming brass trays from India topped campaign side tables. Hung on the back wall were Thomas Baines' original paintings on Parliamentary loan.

Broderick paused as they passed the mahogany bar backed by shelves up to the ceiling. "It will be fully stocked last minute, of course, but that's not my responsibility." A long dining room table and chairs and buffet of brownish-yellow mukwa were handsomely accommodated in the airy room with a view of the river.

"I do hope they're going to feature our Rhodesian beef," said Mavourneen. "You know at war's end, Rhodesian farmers' farewell gift to Britain was one hundred tons of our first-class beef."

"Well, no actually, so far as I know, with all the refrigeration they've asked for, I understand they are planning on importing Dover soles—that sort of thing."

"What's the bet," said Sunny sardonically, "if we were to offer one hundred tons of beef in ten years time they would accuse us of dumping."

"Doc, everything in life is a matter of timing."

"What a pity," Mavourneen said, "not to embrace our local bounty and expertise."

"No expenses spared to carry England out to Africa along with them: fifteen carriages and a pilot train besides. I understand the Chef, the Senior Bar Steward and, well, all The White Train staff are to be on hand here. Makes sense. They'll have to be housed somewhere and we need the world-class service down to the last detail: make sure the beds are made with envelope corners, sheets turned down just right each night and so on."

"Oh well, they *are* Royalty after all," excused Mavourneen.

"I hope," said Sunny "when the English staff turn down the beds every night they don't forget to go around the entire house and spray with the Flit Gun. It wouldn't do for them to take malaria home with them as a parting gift."

"Doc, no worries, man—see windows and doors gauzed in. Mosquito nets over the beds."

"Can't be too careful. Always ensure the three layered approach is in place: gauze the windows, spray the walls and nets over the beds. And don't forget long sleeves after sundown too. Saw the very best of them go down in the War. It doesn't discriminate between classes or cultures—Royalty's no exception."

"We've got a big generator to fuel refrigeration, the ovens, hot water for the bathrooms and so on. I'll show you the separate kitchen. Here's the library, to be stocked with books on loan from the Parliamentary library."

Mavourneen stroked the sable newel post finials of the staircase to the bedrooms.

"See," said Broderick, "how the added height gives such a different perspective of the bend in the river through the mid-story of the fig."

Mavourneen was drawn to the bird song filtering through the gauze of the windows, the bend in the river below, the granite strewn kopjes stretching to the blue horizon, cotton wool cumulus clouds fixed above in the still air.

"The Queen of the River Bank I call this tree: it's home, hunting and feeding grounds to plenty of animals, birds and insects. It's quintessential Africa—so undisciplined—drops its leaves whenever it pleases and fruits copiously several times a year. Elephants, baboons and monkeys boozing it up on carpets of fermented fruit."

"Oh dear!" said Mavourneen, "I hope all the animals are going to be on their *best* behavior for the Royals."

"I hate to spoil the party, but all the fruit will be raked up before they come. Everything spick and span."

"What's that huge untidy nest in the fork of that branch," asked Mavourneen. "It must be three feet across."

"Hammerkop. The nest is made of sticks and mud...their own particular *pise de terre*. Would you believe, it's strong enough to support my weight. The entrance is at the bottom and tunnels in about two feet to the nesting chamber. The birds have gone fishing, no doubt. But the tree's also alive with lizards, chameleons, snakes. At night it's awake with fruit bats, pookies and owls on the prowl."

"The Royals will never want to come downstairs," said Mavourneen.

"There's a pair of binoculars and Roberts *Birds of Southern Africa* in each room. Notice, again, *pise de terre* even keeps the upstairs cool and comfortable."

She turned reluctantly away from the windows as he began to describe the different woods used in the different rooms for the handmade wardrobes, dressing tables and writing desks, the canopied four poster beds enshrouded in mosquito netting bordered by heavy Belgian lace. The chaise lounges covered in rich tapestries and linens. It was all luxurious but uncluttered and airy beneath the bitumen ribs supporting the sweet smell of new thatch.

A distance away, of course, the kitchen and laundry *rondavels* were screened from the house. Beyond was the extensive compound: European domestic quarters distanced from the Native servants and groomsmen for the stables in case the Royals wished to ride. "The farmers from all around are clamoring to put their best horses at their disposal. The final pick hasn't been made yet."

Absorbed in the beauty and serenity they wended their way back to the front verandah in silence. Sunny said, "I have to hand it to you, it's all *very* impressive. I'm confident you've come up with the world's most luxurious game hide. Let's drink to your success."

"Fit for The King and Queen," agreed Mavourneen, "Just fifty-one steps away from wildest Africa."

"Why thank you," said Broderick pouring another round from the bottle of *Johnnie Walker* and tearing open a bag of salted peanuts.

"Your opinions mean a lot to me."

"Cheers," said Mavourneen, "here's to a royal launch to your career."

"Another pip!" said Sunny, clinking glasses again and downing his tot. "But I'm afraid, we must be going."

As Broderick closed Mavourneen's car door firmly after her, she reached down and handed up a jar of *Brandied Marmalade* to him. They departed reluctantly.

"That old fig tree draws an omnium-gatherum of life of gigantic proportions to it," exclaimed Mavourneen as they settled down in the car, "For all the fanfare over the tea, I'm sure it's the tree that will be the highlight of The Royal Tour. What do you think is going to happen to the house after it's over?"

"I've no idea," said Sunny. "I expect it will be incorporated into one of the farms in the resettlement scheme."

"Your talk of the *pise* housing's got me thinking about having our own house."

"1 Jacaranda Avenue is a valuable mine perk for us."

"All the same," she said, "just as you'd like to get your own surgery, it would be nice to own our own home too, independent of the mine. Be in control. You never know."

"This is way too far from the hospital: the back of beyond. It's far too big. Too fancy. All those outbuildings, stables. We've absolutely no need of any of it."

"Perhaps we could look for a plot, design our own dream house once life settles down."

"Actually, I've got my eye on a stand on the corner of 4th Avenue and 3rd Street."

"Oh no. Let's find something in the *bundu* away from the surgery and the hospital. A retreat for you and a wonderful experience for the children."

"This would be for my own surgery." He was wondering whether word of mouth with Gelfand's extraordinary outreach from Salisbury or the advertisement in BMJ written on flimsy paper for worldwide distribution would deliver the partner he so desperately needed. His thoughts drifted to O'Connor. He knew what it would take to cure him. It wasn't any medicine he could administer.

She fell silent. She watched the yellow orb of the sun turn the sky orange and red. The bushes lost their shapes as it rapidly grew dark.

He put on the headlights and began to sing:

"And so if Mister Trouble finds us
He will never linger long
'Cause we've got a pocketful of sunshine
And a heart full of song."

She joined him in all the verses, before she said, "That was rather a close shave with the mamba, today. It reminded me of your questioning how low the sump is on the Elazar's Cadillac. It's much lower than the Army Ford. Perhaps you're right, as always: it's not suitable for The Royals."

"Oh, I wouldn't worry about that. That incident today was a complete fluke."

"Broderick says it happens."

"It's much more likely the Cadillac will get gravel rash between the ruts in the road and bleed out all the oil. They'll all be stranded."

"Imagine how upset Elazar would be."

"I know, he treats it with kid gloves and only drives it around town."

"You might order up an extra snakebite kit and give it to Elazar, with a bit of instruction. You know, *Be Prepared*."

"He's a highly excitable fellow—not really medical assistant material. Even the thought of the possibility would unnerve him."

"Well," she said, "somebody ought to be prepared."

"The mamba's out at Sycamore Bend now, happy on the river bank."

"I'm sure it's not the only one."

"Are you suggesting a kit out there too, then? We could have a mamba in our own back yard. Where do you want me to draw the line?"

Mavourneen chuckled at the thought of Elazar giving The King a snakebite injection. "I do so hope we can make the day. Did you see the gilt-edged invitation? We've been formally invited by *His Worship* the Mayor to the Royal Tea. Buchanan appreciates the effort we both made during the flood. Grateful for Claire's appendectomy too, I'm sure."

"Well that's personal. It shouldn't enter into it."

"You're right, but it doesn't hurt. At any rate, it looks as though we're fitting in. We'll be able to size up Jud Levine's efforts for ourselves." They sat in companionable silence as the car rumbled on. "I'm going to put my Girl Guide motto to the fore myself and *Be Prepared*. What do you think? Get a pair of long white gloves—above the elbow they have to be—from Feldmans before they sell out. Commission my Aunt Henny for a hat. My maternity frocks have seen better days. Perhaps the baby will come early and I'll be slim again? I do feel so self-conscious with this big tummy."

"You should be proud. Even now you don't accept the consequences of *happily ever after*."

"I do. You're the one who's never home."

"You'll always be the belle of the ball," he said leaning over and patting her knee reassuringly.

"I'm such a size already! Feldmans is going to be all picked over. What about my asking Miriam Kalderon, designer par excellence, to make me something that she can nip in at the waist if necessary?"

"Seamstresses are going to be a thing of the past pretty soon. But good idea. It'll keep her mind off babies and out of my consulting room."

"Some Lucky Strike. She must be so lonely out there in the back of beyond with no one to talk to."

"She's got Isaac. They've the trading store in common."

"She's mysterious. I'm sure that O'Connor is a phony, but I'm positive she really did have something to do with Paris fashion."

"You know what I think of the French."

"I'm sure she's not French herself, but they can't be beat for fashion."

"There's not much place for it here."

Mavourneen laughed, "Don't be silly."

CHAPTER FORTY-ONE

On a Wing and a Prayer

The afternoon had been a very happy one for Sunny and Mavourneen—one they would long remember. As they approached town, Sunny turned off to the hospital to check on O'Connor while Mavourneen dozed in the car. But there was an urgent message waiting there for Sunny to call on Mrs. Biancardi.

Leonard had cottage pie in the oven waiting at home. Mavourneen went through to the children while he ate his supper quickly before he hopped back into the car and drove past the dark form of the Native Commissioner's office and on down First Avenue, the border between the European community and the Coloureds and Indians. The Indian families lived behind their concertinaed storefronts: the Bombay Trader, Rushdie's Rainbow Bazaar, Despande's the Shoemaker and Mehta's Butchery. He turned at Santos' Cycle and General Dealership and parked on the gravel road in front of Mrs. Biancardi's.

She was one of his favorites, often rocking her three hundred pounds with laughter. Coloured, but easily passing for White, she was married to a taciturn Italian. They had a brood of five children who all adored her. She had undergone upper abdominal operations for her biliary problem, leaving her with a very scarred abdomen and a ventral hernia. But nothing dampened her spirits.

Lately, she had become acutely ill with recurrent high fever and jaundice. After a few episodes Sunny diagnosed acute infection of the common bile duct, with or without gallstones, with enough swelling to obstruct the flow of bile. Her swarthy husband met Sunny at the door. Her five children, stair-step young heads, boy, girl, boy, girl, boy, anxiously gathered around the bed.

"Ag, Doctor," she said, "I'm so sorry to call you at night time, but I'm very sick again."

He met her gaze. "It's acute cholangitis," he said calmly.

"Doctor! Is it serious again?" asked Mr. Biancardi, alarmed.

The family's eyes begged for good news, or at least reassuring news that he was not able to give.

"I'm afraid it's back to hospital," he said. "Right away. We can look after her properly there."

He got her through the night.

He wanted the best for her. She needed the best. In the morning, he picked up the phone and dialed the best surgeon in Bulawayo, Dr. Parker-Knowles, who had previously operated on her. Her chart indicated he had removed her gall bladder.

"Parker-Knowles."

"Rubenstein, Umzimtuti. Recall Mrs. Katie Biancardi? Dr. Gidney Palmer referred her originally a few years ago."

"Can't say I do. Remind me."

"Obese. Acute inflammation superimposed on a chronic infection of the common bile duct causing enough swelling to obstruct it. You removed her gall bladder."

"Biancardi? Gall bladder? Yes, yes! My God! I *do* remember her." The pitch of Parker-Knowles' voice rose. He spoke rapidly, "No, no! There's nothing I can do for her. She's a difficult case. You know the first rule of medical practice—get the difficult cases off your hands. Put her on a plane I tell you. Send her off to the Jo'burg Gen. Get Lannon."

"She's not in any condition for transport. Barely made it to our hospital. I need a consult. Would it be too much to ask you to come up to Umzimtuti? Including the surgery, you could do it in a long day, there and back. I'll assist. The position is, well, dire, in my opinion. No time to lose."

"Heavens, no. Remember the first rule. It's out of the question! As I say put her on a plane. Lannon. Get Lannon!"

His voice was shrill with alarm Sunny realized but he persisted, "You're welcome to stay overnight if you prefer. My wife would be only too happy..."

"You're young—you'll learn. Save yourself and your reputation. Get rid of her."

The dial tone buzzed in Sunny's ear. He stared at the receiver. Drive? It was six hundred miles to Jo'burg. She'd never survive the rough ride on the strip road. Fly? Umzimtuti's airport was a bumpy stretch of grass with a windsock to welcome a Tiger Moth. Would she even fit in a small plane, assuming he could drum one up?

He couldn't imagine what could be done surgically to relieve the biliary obstruction unless she had a silent stone in the ampulla, where the duct enters the duodenum, or adhesions were a major factor. Coping with bleeding in a jaundiced patient was an additional challenge.

He walked slowly back to the waiting room and invited Mr. Biancardi into the doctor's duty room. "Mr. Biancardi," he said apologetically, "there's nothing I can do. Mr. Parker-Knowles recommends Lannon in Jo'burg but your wife is far too frail for a long journey. Surgery is very risky at this point in any case."

"Doctor!"

"I'm afraid that's the situation."

"But she must have an operation, yes?"

"Parker-Knowles won't operate on her."

"But you know she needs an operation, isn't that so, Doctor?"

"Well..."

"Are you going to *just sit around* and let her die?"

Surgery was her only hope—though a slim one. He wanted to see her through. "I could take her to surgery myself to see what's there." What was he saying! The first anniversary of his mine appointment was almost up, with review for permanency by the Mine Benefit Society looming. He couldn't afford a death on the table, regardless of circumstances. Parker-Knowles words on the phone echoed *save yourself and your reputation.* But he went on, "I'm not sure what can be done 'till I open her up. And I can't be sure she will survive the trauma of surgery in any case."

"Doctor! Please do it. We have faith in you. We will pray."

"I can't promise I'll succeed. It's very, very risky, you understand."

"Yes, I understand."

What had he just taken on? Was he crazy?

He ordered a number of bleeds and did the cross matching himself so that an ample supply of blood was on hand. Sister Hoskins and Sister Fegan gowned and scrubbed alongside him. He established an intravenous line, an achievement in itself, with Mrs. Biancardi's buried veins all but obliterated by previous surgical sessions. He stepped to the head of the table and leaning close to her said, "You'll be fine. Just fine. I'm going to put you to the best sleep you've ever had. The family's already waiting outside for you to wake up."

"Doctor, I'm grateful, I can't let my hubby and my kids down..." She faded as he induced the anesthesia and handed over to Sister Fegan. He was confident he had the best team Umzimtuti could muster.

Now the clock was running and time was of the essence. He made a neat, firm incision. The mass of dense adhesions took almost an hour to dissect through. "Adhesions following abdominal surgery are the rule rather than the exception," he commented. The density and severity of these adhesions indicated that, during a previous operation, there must have been a major bile spill, severely irritating the peritoneum.

The common bile duct was a hard, fibrosed cord and obviously obstructed with the inflammatory swelling of the infection. It was difficult to visualize any patency, and certainly obstruction would be total on any future inflammatory flare-up. But there were no apparent gallstones. And to Sunny's complete surprise and relief the gallbladder was intact. "Parker-Knowles only drained it!"

"Well, that explains all the bile spill and massive adhesions then," Sister Fegan observed.

"He must have balked at removal and too ashamed to admit it. No wonder he didn't want her back on his table!"

"Maybe he's got a point. The best thing you can do is sew her up," said Sister Hoskins firmly.

"I've got an inspiration!"

"You don't want to chalk up your first table death," insisted Sister Hoskins.

"No. No! Parker-Knowles didn't know it, but he did us a favor. Surely, the gall bladder can be used as an alternative bile duct? I think we can anastomose it to the duodenum!" He looked at Sister Fegan.

"Join it to the duodenum? No, I've never heard of that," Sister Hoskins protested.

"I know you can mobilize the second part of the duodenum without blood vessel problems, but I've never done the procedure or even seen it done."

The two Sisters exchanged glances above the surgical masks.

"I wonder if the duodenum will mobilize sufficiently to reach the gall bladder without tension?"

"Are you asking my advice?" said Sister Hoskins acerbically.

"No, I'm just thinking it through. Sister Fegan, check the vitals, please."

"I wonder how the junction should be done?" he said, still talking to himself.

"Sew her up quickly!" Sister Hoskins said.

"The die has been cast," he said as he glanced at the instrumentation. "There's no going back," he said calmly, looking her in the eye.

"Why did you take this on? It's beyond us," said Sister Fegan.

"We're committed now," he said. "It's vital we all stay focused on the job at hand."

A sense of relief came over him. He wasn't over the hump by a long shot, but he knew what to do.

Sister Hoskins, still agitated said, "We don't have all the answers. Your reputation is at stake. The hospital's too..."

"We're going to anastomose the gall bladder to the duodenum. She's counting on us. Her family's counting on us."

"They don't understand," said Sister Hoskins.

"They're going to think differently, later, if she goes on the table," said Sister Fegan.

"They won't. I've counseled them. They understand the situation. Clamps, please, Sister Hoskins. Sister Fegan, how are the vitals?" His hair stood up on the back of his neck. Under the lights, he felt beads of sweat prick on his forehead under the surgical cap. The angel was on his shoulder. He wished there was a way to relax the abdomen; as it was, the work was painstaking and exacting.

Eventually, with the operation complete, he pulled off his gloves, elated. "Thank you," he said to the two Sisters. "Success. I couldn't have done without both of you."

But he knew it was far from over. After his afternoon clinic and quick rounds, he checked on O'Connor's condition, which was unchanged. Then, he pulled up a chair for the long night ahead. Mrs. Biancardi was now more dear to him than he ever could have imagined. She fought on, brave and uncomplaining, through all the pain. The family silently prayed in the waiting room.

Chain-smoking suppressed Sunny's appetite as he thumbed through the current edition of *Gray's Anatomy* as he kept vigil. A biliary bypass-cholecystoduodenostomy was quite a mouthful for anyone to pronounce and a sophisticated surgical achievement for the hospital. His mother would provide an excuse to go down South at regular intervals so he could stay in touch, stay current with Lannon. Yes, Lannon, that surgeon with the delicate touch with the tissues was the man to emulate, indeed.

Finally, in the pre-dawn cold Mrs. Biancardi rallied. It looked hopeful. He took his leave and went home for a quick warm up in

Mavourneen's embrace before the daily routine started afresh with his early morning calisthenics and muscle control exercises, a bath and shave and a hot plate of *Maltabella* before the wail of the mine hooter sounded. The next seventy-two hours would be critical.

CHAPTER FORTY-TWO

A Proposal and a Recovery

Mavourneen found growing pumpkins and making marmalade very easy but what really engaged her was settling on the design and then getting estimates for the swimming bath. She made marmalade in the kitchen and telephone calls in the passageway.

She had a way with people. Perseverance paid off. For the price of a jar of marmalade and a batch of scones Mavourneen enjoined the town's architect, Charles Greene to draw up detailed plans on the proposed plot of land they had in mind on the far side of the railway tracks. Refining the plan with the school committee took time. She knew what she wanted: generous changing rooms for the children, private cubicles for the women and men, showers and a disinfectant foot bath before entering the pool. She wanted a paddling pool for toddlers near a kiosk for tea and snacks, which would be privately run. Copious grounds dotted with shade trees punctuating a wide perimeter of lawn were stenciled onto the drawings. The bath itself would be Olympic size, thirty-three and a third yards long; white tiled with eight racing lanes marked in black; and at the ten-foot deep end, one meter and three meter diving boards. The entrance and office would overlook the bath and, on the street side, bicycle racks and ample car parking bordered by flowers and an expanse of lawn. Umzimtuti had never dreamed of anything so sophisticated in its half-century history.

But once Mavourneen got everyone involved, everyone had an opinion on everything, from what were the preferred shade trees for the extensive grounds to what should be permitted at the kiosk.

Finally everything was agreed on. She could not delay further. After Sunny had tucked into cottage pie, a favorite, for supper she announced, "Francis Asquith and I have been invited to present our proposal to the State Lotteries Allocation Committee in Salisbury tomorrow."

"Proposal?"

"The swimming bath plans for our loan application."

"Of course, my apologies, I quite forgot. I've been so wrapped up with work."

"That's quite alright."

"I'll start now to document the number of European cases of bilharzia and see if there's a statistical drop once the bath is up and running. I need a sizable sample set to make it meaningful. There's time. It's not going to get built overnight."

"Nanny was a good idea of yours after all. Have you noticed the kids are doing fine?"

"I'm sorry," he said. "You know my difficult days will pass."

"I hope the kids will not be all grown up before you get a chance to know them."

"Would you like to hear the details of my surgical case: a real challenge. She's survived the table but we are not out of the woods yet by a long shot."

"Can it wait?" She was surprised at how detached she felt from his surgical world. "I really do have to go over my presentation tomorrow. You know the cliché *no second chance to make a first impression* and this is so important not only to me but to everyone in Umzimtuti. Everybody has had their input and feels a part of it. I mustn't let them down."

"This patient's more to me than just a case."

"Who is it?"

"Mrs. Biancardi."

"Oh, one of your regulars."

"The situation's dire. If I lose her I could lose the confidence of the Benefit Society. Review for the permanent post is coming up. I came home to be with you but as you're busy, and don't need my help, I think I'll swing back up to the hospital. The sisters are good, but too much hinges on this to leave the responsibility with anyone but myself. Her family's counting on me. O'Connor's also still a worry—heart's really dickey, and I've had to hospitalize Nancy too, in accelerated inebriation. I hope you understand. Good luck tomorrow. I haven't time for pudding—treat Bundu." He folded his serviette, rose and gave her a peck. Bundu got up, followed him and the door slammed.

Mavourneen and Headmaster Asquith returned from their meeting with State Lotteries in Salisbury in time for supper. "Guess what!" she said as they sat down at the table.

"You've got me. Bundu's gone on the razz again?"

"No, it's me this time. Remember, Asquith and I went up to Salisbury this morning. Back already and you didn't even miss me." There was actually more freedom in her life than she realized.

"Of course. How did it go?"

"We got the grant to cover the capital cost of the swimming bath!"

"Congratulations are in order." He reached over and gave her hand a squeeze. "I never doubted your ability to persuade—I wish I had it."

"Mind you, it's come on the one condition that the municipality assumes the responsibility and running costs thereafter. We'll have to submit the documents to the Town Clerk tomorrow and request inclusion on the next council meeting's agenda."

"Oh, that'll just be a formality. Jolly well done."

That was a compliment indeed coming from him.

Mrs. Biancardi was holding her own. Surely the angel on his shoulder wouldn't desert him after all the effort he and his patient had put in. What was making the difference: Catholic prayers, her great spirit and determination not to let the family down, the hospital team effort or the saving surgical factors? Still he could not take anything for granted. She would need daily monitoring in the weeks ahead.

Entering Pat O'Connor's room, Sunny was relieved to see the rise and fall of his corpulent form under the starched hospital regulation sheet pulled tight over it: he was at least alive. His color was bad. He knew what it would take to see recovery. It did not lie in the latest medical tomes or surgical techniques.

"How are you today?"

"Doc," he said rousing, trying to sit up, "Can't you see, I'm poorly?"

As Sunny ran through his vitals he said, "You should be feeling better, blood pressure is still high, but down from that frightening level when I admitted you. Ticker's running a little smoother. The diet I prescribed for you, I do declare the chart says you've lost a few! All good signs. You need to lose a whole lot more. You're not out of the woods yet, I'll agree."

"Doc, you know how weak my heart is. And the food— jelly's not enough."

"Come on now, it's not a surgical diet I prescribed." Sunny pulled up a chair beside his bed. "The good news is Nancy's all dried out again, discharged. She should be in to see you."

"Doc, you know she'll be back in again probably before I'm discharged."

"I should blacklist her, but now is not the time to worry about that."

"Doc, I wouldn't go to the trouble. You know my *cailín* is always going to get her poteen one way or another. I've got to get back to *The Cleft Stick*, there's so much to report with The Royal Tour coming up. Subscriptions are up. The auctioneering. I'm gonna lose the election. I can hardly make it to the lavatory let alone get out and canvas the constituency that's so spread out. I'm bankrupt don't you see. Washed up."

"Look I said I'd help you." He was the epitome of a man in ruin. Could one feel anything but compassion for him? Jud should see him now and take pity on him.

"Doc, how you gonna do that? You know how tough that mean little bastard Levine is. He's kiboshed everything for me."

"Remember, you started it. I told you to apologize and settle, before the costs escalated. Yes, it's got way out of hand. Let me ring a few people."

Days turned into weeks as Sunny guided Mrs. Biancardi's stormy recovery. But then, one morning, on routine rounds Sunny found Mrs. Biancardi's bed empty. Surely the angel on his shoulder had not deserted him after all this effort. The sisters had not reported anything, but a chill ran through him. Had she had a reversal? Frantically he sought her out.

He found her sitting on the ward verandah admiring the birds. She turned to him with her infectious smile and said, "Doctor, you needn't worry now. I'm so sorry I gave you so much trouble."

"Why so confident?"

She smiled with a glint in her eye, "You made such a good operation Doctor, but I got better faster because of Sister Hoskins and Sister Fegan."

Sunny's smile waned.

"No Doctor, it's not what you think. Coming out of the anesthetic I heard Sister Hoskins and Sister Fegan reporting to Matron Griffin that I didn't stand a hope. What could you expect with Dr. Rubenstein doing operations that Dr. Gidney Palmer never did. That made me mad. I was determined we had to teach them all a lesson. Seriously Doctor, I couldn't let you down quite apart from my hubby and my kids."

She reached out and touched his arm. Uncharacteristically overwhelmed, his eyes moistened. He turned away and looked out through the verandah gauze to the wild bush beyond. Her recovery was a miracle.

But Pat O'Connor in the male ward was another matter.

"Pat," said Sunny, "how are you this morning?"

"Doc, I got Nancy to come in with some real food."

"You disappoint me. You've got to follow orders."

"Doc, I'm a long time out of the army. Can't you have a little compassion?"

"Pat, you've got to lose some weight. Ease the strain on the constitution. Let the heart rest."

"I've got to have some simple joys in life."

"How can I help you if you don't follow my advice?"

"Levine's out to destroy me."

"I've talked to him. It's a question of his honor. I know he is not after your money."

"He's going to take me all the way to the High Court."

It was pathetic to witness a man in such ruin. "I'll ask him to drop the charges if I settle the lawyers costs on both sides. That should make everyone happy." Even as he said it he knew this was going to be difficult for Mavourneen to accept. She was drawn to O'Connor's Irish brogue but he knew she felt he was manipulative and didn't trust him. She wanted a house in the bush and though she never asked, he knew, a car—her key to independence.

"Doc, settle all the costs? I can't even afford a ticket in the lottery and unless I win it I'll never be able to repay you, you know that."

"Of course, I understand."

"Doc, you'd do that for me? I'll be eternally grateful to you. If you ever need anything..."

"I wish you'd taken my bush-lawyer advice for seven shillings and sixpence in my consulting room. Take my medical advice now. Put your troubles out of your mind. Hospital's full. You've been here long enough. We need that bed of yours."

He knew Pat's progress from then on would be slow but steady. Financially this would make Palmer's goodwill swindle pale in comparison. It would considerably set back his development plans for his own private surgery on the 4th Avenue property he had his eye on.

His father had always advised him, *when you help a man, ask him first how hard he is going to kick you afterwards.* A qualm passed through him.

CHAPTER FORTY-THREE

Just What the Doctor Ordered

As usual, the wail of the mine hooter summoned Sunny to Sick Parade followed by rounds at the Native Hospital. But this was not an ordinary day. For some weeks the mine had been spruced up. The Native Hospital was a well-constructed red brick building with an ample *stoep*: male and female wards with six beds each, separated by a common orderly station with operating room and recovery room behind it. Its red corrugated iron roof had been repainted and the wards whitewashed. The rocks marking the circular driveway were newly whitewashed, and the Union Jack hoisted. Everything was as spick and span as it could be for the London registered Sun Gold Mining Company Chairman and Directors' walk-through inspection.

Sunny reflected, as he finished up Sick Parade and strode over to the hospital, that the range of operations that could be handled were limited by the primitive conditions and absence of trained nursing sisters. But P.Q. was indispensable as anesthetist and radiographer and the Native orderlies had basic training. The purpose was served, but it was hard to dickey the hospital up beyond what it was: rudimentary.

He had promised Doolittle he would be on hand for a walk-through with the visitors but he and P.Q. were engrossed in the delivery of twins by Caesarian section when they arrived. Full term, unblemished by the mauling of vaginal delivery, they were beautiful babies, rich-chocolate, with pink heels and palms. Sunny never got over the thrill of delivery and the mystery and beauty of new life. P.Q. and the orderlies were delighted. There was approval from the female ward as well as the male patients but unfortunately the all-important visitors had moved on.

Mavourneen and Sunny had been invited to join the visitors at the Big House for a dinner party that evening. Miriam Kalderon had made her a blue shot satin bodice, which hung smoothly over an expandable matching long skirt. She had tamed her chestnut hair with her grandmother's silver pins, accentuating her naked shoulders. Her clavicles framed her neck and plum center beneath the sternal head rested her Aunt Henny's black opal. She felt confident she looked her best as she stood back from the mirror. Sunny changed into his one dark suit and wore a bow tie, and arm in arm they headed across Jacaranda Avenue and up the long silver oak lined driveway.

On either side expanses of manicured lawn were bordered by clumps of midnight blue Lily of the Nile, daisies, coral-bells and coreopsis—absent of course were gladioli. The sunny rose garden and grove of indigenous aloes were out of sight beyond the tennis court.

The house itself, on top of the hill, was beautifully situated facing north. The headgear, the dumps and the slimes dam, even the overhead cable of the cocopans and the machine shops, smelting works, office, the Native compound and the European settlement, although nearby, were completely obscured. They climbed the shallow steps to the deep veranda framed in a huge tangle of bougainvillea in full summer splendor. Doolittle introduced them to the chairman, Sir Harvey Pittman and his wife Shirley and the directors, Sandringham and Earle and their wives. The mine secretary, Pollock and his wife, and the South African geologist Desmond Hertzog and Rebecca were there too. After a while, they settled into comfy wicker chairs as drinks and canapés were served on the verandah, whisky or brandy for the men; gin or Bristol cream sherry for the ladies.

The house was not ostentatiously furnished, but was comfortable. The African mahogany dining room table easily accommodated the party. A straightforward menu of chilled grapefruit appetizer in crystal goblets was followed by roast beef on fine china. Yorkshire pudding, puffed up just right, roast potatoes and gravy, rich golden wedges of pumpkin, long green beans and a casserole of cauliflower and carrots were served by a white-uniformed servant wearing a red fez. It was all impeccably presented as Cape wine flowed along with reminiscences of the mine and the pioneering days.

"The Matabele Rebellion and the rinderpest delayed the start-up of the mine but we finally started milling in 1900. We've pulled out three million ounces from under five million tons of ore," said Doolittle.

"Forty million pounds," Sandringham added.

"Yes, shareholders received very good dividends, around fifty percent of revenue, eighty percent when the British went off the gold standard after 1931," confirmed Earle.

"It's a very rich vein," Hertzog agreed.

Hertzog was young and lean in a well-fitting tuxedo, his face and hands tanned from his fieldwork. Seated next to Mavourneen he noticed the black opal at her throat. It had to be Australian, sedimentary opal from Lightning Ridge, no doubt. The play of color was magnificent. He'd love to take a closer look. *Like quicksilver gaily colored, passed through the shades of night,* he thought. Amazing how carbon and iron traces in the stacked regular array of silica spheres and the tiny spaces between them fractured light. This opal was exceptional, matching the blue with green lights of her eyes as she turned to engage him. Rebecca, he remembered, had commented on her spunk on meeting her at Leah Levine's tea party when she'd first arrived, but he hadn't realized 'till now how beautiful she was. A goy, she was an unlikely match for the egg-headed doctor—but despite it, undoubtedly, by far his best asset. His professional association with him was distant, but they had swayed together in the Shapiros sitting room reciting the Friday sundown ritual prayers mixed in with town gossip when they could scrape together a minyan which had spawned a mutual respect and familiarity over time. He pulled his attention back to the conversation.

"Costs have risen in the last few years," Sir Harvey was saying.

"Well, we are pushing five thousand feet from surface. Production costs increase with depth," Doolittle replied, "The mine's not inexhaustible."

Hertzog said, "I've been thinking we could acquire the mining claims on our northeastern boundary."

"Make the presumption anything we find is part of our reef?" asked Sir Harvey.

"What if it's a different strike that doesn't extend to the surface and won't be included in the extra-lateral rights of our reef?" asked Earle.

"Then legally we wouldn't be able to lay claim to it."

"What if there's nothing?" asked Sandringham.

"It's a risk. Unlikely. The Cheetah is really a lucky strike: in the past, some of the richest ore in the world. The quartz is solid. No breaks, so far. As it stands it does look as though your luck is running out, though, going deeper. You can afford to take a chance. It could extend the life of the mine another twenty years."

"You a gambling man?" queried Sir Harvey.

"It's a risk, not a gamble. I've taken some samples already. I'm confident, but it's not a certainty."

"What would that cost?" enquired Sandringham.

"Well, I expect you could purchase the rights quite cheaply on the basis that the vendor companies retain an individual one half share in any minerals found."

"Give them a share in what we bring up?" queried Earle.

"Yes that seems fair, an inducement," confirmed Hertzog.

"What will it cost, Mr. Doolittle, to put down a few vertical shafts on these properties? See what we find?" asked Sir Harvey.

"I'll have to work with the underground manager for an estimate."

"If we don't do this how long have we got?" asked Sandringham.

"There are a lot of factors involved," said Hertzog. "I'll need to study the mine a lot more."

"Umzimtuti has only arisen as an appendage to the mine. Without it the town will die too," said Doolittle.

"There's precious little town," observed Sir Harvey's wife, Lady Shirley.

"We're not concerned with that really. Just the shareholder interests," cut in Sir Harvey.

"The town is developing, actually. Government purchase of a Lime and Iron Works eight miles away could spawn a huge heavy industrial complex here—for the whole of Rhodesia," offered Sunny.

"That sounds ambitious," said Lady Shirley turning to him. "We'd love to visit the Works, if there's time."

"It's still very much in the development stage, right now. There's not a lot to see, yet."

"By the way," Lady Shirley said, "you may not be aware of it, but I couldn't resist a return visit to the Native Hospital this afternoon to see those twins you delivered." Turning to Mavourneen she said, "Everyone there was very happy with the babies. What wonderful work your husband is doing with so little." Turning to her husband she said, "regardless of the mine's longevity, you can't expect the doctor to struggle on under these conditions. The very least we can do is provide him with whatever he needs to do his job properly. What do you say gentlemen?"

"I think he's managing quite well, as it is," said Sir Harvey.

"I'm sure you could use a thing or two?" she pressed, looking directly at Sunny.

"A new modern theatre table and Boyle's anesthetic apparatus there would greatly extend the range of surgery we could tackle. I've had extensive experience with it under Schulenburg, the best in Pretoria, introduced it to the New Government Hospital here and could train up the Cheetah Native Hospital staff too even though they're not qualified."

"Admirable," she said. "Can we drink to it then, gentlemen, ladies?" Lady Shirley said raising her glass. "Here's to a theatre table and anesthesia equipment."

"A theatre table and anesthesia!" they echoed. Glasses clinked.

It's true, thought Sunny, behind every successful man is a woman. He shot a glance at Mavourneen across the table from him. Her eyes smiled back. They were losing touch in the rush of everyday work, but at moments like this he was reminded, fleetingly, that she was his greatest asset.

Sunny ventured. "Lady Shirley, did you know, it's estimated that ninety percent of disease in southern Africa is preventable?"

"How so?"

"The focus on palliation instead of eradication perpetuates the treadmill we're on."

"What could we do differently?" said Lady Shirley obviously genuinely interested.

"Improve housing for the natives, improve their food, teach them hygiene, educate the mothers, improve underground conditions, even their leisure hours." Sunny felt a kick under the table from Mavourneen—a sign he should cork-up. He ignored it and rattled on, "Better health would greatly improve attitude, performance, and general well-being with fewer on Sick Parade." His mine position was still temporary, he didn't want to alienate Doolittle but this was his one chance to alert the board to the real situation at the mine below the gratuitous veneer and get real improvement. On the other hand, persistence could jeopardize his permanent appointment—his review by the Benefit Society was coming up soon. They'd already been forced into a concession on his behalf by Lady Shirley. Perhaps Mavourneen's signal should be heeded. It was a big enough victory for now. Heaven forbid that they should renege on it if he pushed too far.

"Doctor, you've got carried away. Remember, we are running a mining operation for profit not a welfare institution," cut in Sir Harvey.

Sunny couldn't help himself, persisting "That's just it. I'm talking profits. Medical bills could be drastically cut if public health measures were undertaken: prevention being the operative word. For instance, the marshes beyond the Native compound provide a breeding ground for mosquitoes and the workers a reservoir to perpetuate the disease in the rainy season. If we drained the marsh the cycle of malaria would be broken. The Cheetah could be a model for the country."

"We are already. Remember, the National First Aid Competition is next weekend," asserted Doolittle.

"That's different—readiness in the event of a mine disaster. I'm talking about improving everyday life," Sunny replied.

"There is fierce competition amongst the different mine teams. The Cheetah does have a winning reputation under our Compound Manager, P.Q. Oosterhuizen's direction. Why don't you all join us for the judging?" said Doolittle. "It's followed afterwards by tribal dancing and it's very impressive. The ladies especially will enjoy it."

The company unanimously agreed.

So they wanted to dance around the real issues thought Sunny resentfully. Doolittle indicated there would be places made for them at the grandstand. Mavourneen reminded them to wear sun hats against the African sun. It was all arranged.

Dessert was served, trifle topped with whipped cream in crystal goblets. It was a geological concoction of layers of jelly and fruits and, digging deep, a thick golden custard above a bed of ladyfingers soaked in sherry. They retired to the library for liqueurs and assorted cheeses and biscuits.

Doolittle outlined the safari which he had laid on for the directors and their wives. They would return in time for the First Aid Competitions and Tribal Dancing that the English ladies were so very keen to see. Hertzog said he'd get to work on the feasibility study straight away.

CHAPTER FORTY-FOUR

Railroaded

Mavourneen, neatly dressed with white gloves and securely fastened hat, popped the cardboard cylinder of swimming bath plans and the packet with the agreement from the State Lotteries into the front basket of her bike and freewheeled down the hill to arrive cool and collected at the Town House.

Mr. Asquith joined her as she parked her bike against one of the white columns of the portal. They were directed to the double doors of the Mayoral Chamber. Although she was well prepared and Sunny had assured her approval would be a mere formality a sudden qualm came over her but she took strength from the large portrait of King George VI that graced one wall of the small room.

Mayor Buchanan stepped down off the rostrum and greeted them warmly, shaking hands and offering them each a seat behind the Councilors. "You're just in time," he said, "aye, we were about to start proceedings."

All the councilmen were in attendance and after a few formalities Buchanan announced, "I move that the municipality reject the offer Headmaster Asquith and Mrs. Rubenstein have received from the State Lottery to fund a swimming bath. Aye, it's all very well entertaining fancy ideas, but this toon simply can't afford the running costs nor the staff to maintain it. I'm sure we're all agreed, Councilmen, we certainly can't raise the rates for something that the toon doesn't need. Aye, there are far more pressing things to discuss. I move to dismiss the proposal."

"Do we have a seconder to the motion?" asked the Town Clerk Cameron Gordon Murray Paxton.

Mavourneen could only see the backs of the Councilmen's heads as she faced the po-faced Buchanan. The blighter! After a moment's hesitation, she rose, her pregnant tummy pressed up against the table in front of her as she leaned forward and blood rushed into her cheeks. "I have the plans here," she said, reaching for them and holding them up. "We'd like to put our case forward before there's a vote."

"Mrs. Rubenstein, you're out of order. You may only speak when invited," said the Town Clerk, looking uncertainly at the Mayor.

"Aye, in the interests of time, I've been through the agenda me-self already, madam," replied the Mayor. "I'm sure council wants to vote on the motion immediately." Turning to Paxton at his side he said, "Git on with it will ye."

"Do we have a seconder to move the motion before us that the State Lotteries offer to fund a swimming bath be rejected?"

Mavourneen looked at the limp Southern Rhodesian and Union Jack flags flanking The King and wondered what had become of the red, white and blue sense of fair play that they stood for? A shaft of late afternoon light from the single small window fell on the mayor's rostrum. Was Buchanan God incarnate she wondered sarcastically?

She knew all the Councilmen quite well. Old Man Hardy had done some woodwork for her—there was precious little undertaking in this young community to occupy his time. T.J. Lewellyn, the chemist, was so accommodating over the counter—but didn't he now have an opinion? She expected Timmy Curtis, a fitter and turner to go along and Lucas Ramsey, the accountant, was a close friend of Buchanan, but Jud Levine, surely, he would support her? She had never thought to canvas any of them directly, individually. She believed the swimming bath would be voted on its merits after the proposal was presented.

"Seconded," said Old Man Hardy.

"Mr. Hardy seconds the motion," said Paxton. "Accordingly, the council must now vote on the proposal. All those in favor of the motion raise their hands and say 'aye'."

All the Councilors raised their hands and uttered the word without any show of reluctance.

"Thank you for coming. Mr. Paxton will see you out," said Mayor Buchanan.

Mavourneen stood with Mr. Asquith next to her bicycle and held his gaze, "He can't get away with it surely?" All the meetings and detailed planning with the PTA, negotiations with the Lotteries and juggling the numbers—how she hated those—had all been for naught. She was trembling with anger, frustration and disappointment. She'd been made to look a fool: a housewife who didn't know her place: how she hated being a woman.

She hardly heard Asquith as he said, "Remember, with the funding for the facility already secured, we're more than halfway there. Unfortunately as a government employee I can't stand for election to council myself, but we'll find a way to release Umzimtuti from Buchanan's stranglehold." He clasped her hand in both of his. They were large and warm and clean and suddenly, she was close to tears. Only a woman would dissolve. Quickly she grabbed a hold of the handlebars, mounted the bike and rode off.

Getting back home was an uphill slog, pushing the bike most of the way. By the time she parked the bike and opened the screen door she was hot and sweaty, her tummy weighing on her. She called to Leonard to make her a pot of tea. Though defeated, she felt she'd more than earned it. She threw the plans onto the sitting room floor before she plopped down in her favorite chair. Fortunately nanny had taken the children for a walk. She kicked off her high heels, carefully removed the hat and laid her head back against the antimacassar. She stroked Bundu with the soles of her feet while she waited. The ritual was comforting and the hot tea soothing. She drained the pot and fell soundly asleep.

She awoke to find Bundu gnawing on the cardboard cylinder of the swimming bath plans. The Axminster carpet was strewn with a slobbery mush. The plans had holes in them.

The Mine Manager's Paper House was the first prefabricated building imported into the country, erected before the turn of the century. It had been manufactured in Britain and brought north by ox wagon from Port Elizabeth, about the time of the Matabele Rebellion and the rinderpest epidemic. Besides being practical, it had style: Cecil John Rhodes had slept here. Built on stilts to protect against white ants and damp made the house sit daintily on the landscape. It was all set about with exotic trees planted by the mine half a century ago, the grasses beneath them yellowing under the white hot glare of the African sky. The galvanized zinc roof shimmered in the heat, its steep pitch made to deflect the deluge of rain from afternoon summer thunderstorms. Sunny stepped up onto the house's wrap-around verandah and turned around to squint for any sign of clouds, but saw none. The joy of Mrs. Biancardi's full recovery against all odds was still with him.

He was surprised to be summoned here last minute instead of Boss Jack's office to sign his permanent appointment to the Mine Benefit Society following his year as a locum for Dr. Palmer. He was still paying off the £2000 goodwill to him, but it meant this would be a mere formality, as agreed with Boss Jack at the showdown over Palmer's fraud. Still, he needed to read the fine print before he signed the contract that would serve him for his lifetime. Accordingly, he'd dressed for the occasion. He adjusted the knot of his tie, before he ventured inside.

Boss Jack Chelmsford, in his capacity as chairman of the Medical Benefit Society, flanked the Mine Manager Doolittle on his right and on his left Mr. Pollock the Mine Secretary. Though the silver haired Pollack kept a low profile Sunny knew he was influential and had the ear and confidence of the London Office and in particular the Chairman Sir Harvey Pittman.

The floorboards creaked as Boss Jack's wheelchair rolled over them. All three men turned to face Sunny standing on the threshold. Immediately he sensed the atmosphere was strained.

Boss Jack cleared his throat and addressed him formally. "Dr. Rubenstein welcome please be seated. Let me get right to the point. We expected the Medical Benefit Society to unanimously approve your permanent appointment today, however objections have been lodged which have caused me to bring the matter to the attention of the Manager and Secretary."

"Indeed, what objections?" Sunny could not conceal his surprise.

"Serious opposition has been canvassed by Mrs. Jernigan."

The Underground Manager Herb Jernigan's wife Jean? Surely not? Besides getting along professionally with Herb he'd been called out, often enough, at all hours of the night to referee the Jernigan marital fights when they were both plastered. He maintained patient confidentiality, of course, but the problem was common knowledge. "On what grounds?" he said.

"She's been saying you are ambitious—'Jewish ambitious'—to populate the town with Jews."

Rage welled up within him before he checked himself. Much was at stake here: not only his livelihood, but also the spacious house and sprawling garden for Mavourneen and his growing family. The houses in Umzimtuti weren't half as commodious and with the housing shortage he'd be hard-pressed to find anything at all. He could not have something built overnight. He'd have to find office space too and hire staff for consulting rooms: pay rent on both properties without the security of the fixed income from the Cheetah contract. He certainly wouldn't be able to justify—or afford—a partner in that event to share his unrelenting night duty. He had just promised O'Connor he would pay off both lawyers to shut down the case if Levine agreed, which was no small obligation. He didn't want to over dramatize it, but O'Connor's well-being, if not his life, depended on it—he was sure of it. He took a moment to loosen the throttle of his tie's Oxford knot. His head buzzed with the incessant, deafening drone of cicadas blasting through the gauze of the open window.

He looked at Fred Doolittle and remembered the gladioli. Doolittle shook his head imperceptibly. Sunny realized he'd disowned his wife's allegation at the time and would do the same with Mrs. Jernigan. "Why is Mrs. Jernigan's prejudice of any account?"

"I'm afraid it's gone beyond just Mrs. Jernigan. She's canvassed quite a lot of support amongst the mine workers," said Pollock.

"On what grounds?" asked Sunny.

Boss Jack looked at Pollock. Pollock nodded slightly. Boss Jack said, "The mine Management is turning a blind eye to the upgraded facilities you created for the Native outpatients at the back of the European surgery which is against the law—in a designated *Europeans Only* area, but she's not. Then there's the upgraded section for the Coloureds and Indians on the verandah which she contends—as I warned you—could lead to fraternizing, and most of all, the employment of the Uziel twins."

"I took in hand and made arrangements from what was present and available. To give credence to a Jewish conspiracy by picking out elements of my reorganization is too contemptible for me to answer. Haven't you been satisfied with my performance?" replied Sunny.

"Absolutely, we have never questioned your competence. Your reorganization of the European surgery saving the Benefit Society on nursing services and the functioning of our Native hospital are great improvements," said Boss Jack, rolling his chair back and forth.

Mr. Pollock lifted his hand from the desk, "We know you would fill the permanent position admirably. We're just unsure of how to handle her accusation that you plan to introduce into the practice—and elsewhere in the town—Jewish personnel and Jewish liberal ideas which would upset the status quo."

"The criterion for the selection of a partner will always be on availability and competence—not race or religion. I can't let their prejudices dictate my actions." But he couldn't suppress the uneasiness he felt remembering the applications of two very well qualified Indian doctors that he had rejected despite not finding any suitable English or South African candidates, Jewish or Gentile. But he temporized, *if I can't get acceptance as a Jew myself, this confirms the belief that acceptance of an Indian in this day and age is ludicrous and would only alienate me further*. It would be pointless—suicidal—to stand on principle as Mavourneen suggested and 'do the right thing'. "You're not suggesting," he went on, "I canvas the mining community to rebut her accusation are you?"

"No, no! We do not expect you to respond to Mrs. Jernigan's campaign," said Mr. Pollock. "It's all quite outrageous and most embarrassing for us to have to address it to you confidentially. We should also not have to dignify her accusations with a public response." His chair rasped as he pushed it back.

Sunny said, "Soon after I came here, it emerged that my agreement with Dr. Palmer was made under false pretenses. When it was discovered, I insisted, in an interview with Mr. Chelmsford, that I should make a considerable financial sacrifice in order to avoid controversy. We agreed that the matter should not emerge in public and so it has been 'till now. If this still leaves you in any doubt as to my integrity then I am honor-bound to withdraw my application for permanency." His heart sank as he realized he had lost another year in his bid for a place on civvy street. But there could be no question of groveling. "I hereby submit one month's notice as stipulated in the locum contract."

"Steady on!" Mr. Doolittle said, "We appreciate your very intelligent sacrifice. We can't have you throw away the investment you've made in the community. Mrs. Jernigan's asseverations have no doubt been stimulated by the news from Palestine on the BBC. I shall have to persuade the Medical Benefit Society committee to take the large view. If necessary we can pull in Sir Harvey Pittman." He glanced at Mr. Pollock. "I earnestly enjoin you to accept the appointment."

Pollock nodded, "Please go over the agreement of the appointment in detail with Mr. Chelmsford, as Benefit Society Chair."

"We look forward to a long association," said Doolittle, reaching across the table to shake Sunny's hand. "My office is at your disposal for the afternoon."

Sunny swung into the driveway and parked. He leaned on the garden gate and paused. Beneath her straw sunhat Mavourneen was on her hands and knees with a pile of weeds at her side. Under the shade of a spreading jacaranda Deborah, wearing one of Mrs. Kalderon's sunbonnets, was caged in the playpen to keep her out of mischief. Douglas pumped the swing hanging from the spreading branch of the jacaranda tree that shaded her. When had he grown so tall, and sturdy? Had the time passed when he could throw him around? He hurried over to pick up the rhythm of the swing and give Douglas a good boost before he gathered Deborah in his arms. She was growing up too fast as well. Her first word had been 'dada': he hadn't earned the honor. He hugged her tight as she clasped her hands around his neck. This garden had been his family's salvation. He couldn't put a price on it.

Mavourneen had put down her hand trowel, straightened up and waved a soiled hand up to him. "It's a lovely surprise to have you home early," she said coming to his side. "Give me a minute, I'll wash up and get Leonard to make tea."

"Grand, I've earned it," said Sunny.

When she rejoined him he said, "Did you know I finally discharged Mrs. Biancardi?"

"Well done! Let's take a moment to enjoy the garden to celebrate life," she said, steering him off the lawn and onto the path.

"I'm in awe of her indomitable spirit—and the family's faith. That's what won the day."

"She really was the ultimate test. Congratulations again," she said, "not a single loss this year so far." The borders of flowers overflowed their beds and all but smothered the whitewashed stones that marked the way.

"Actually," he said, "it's the anniversary of our arrival and I was due for review by the Benefit Society for approval of permanency. You were out when I popped over to suit up for the occasion."

"I quite forgot. Stew is simmering but we should be celebrating with a roast," she said. "I'll make it up to you tomorrow."

"No, down to earth and hearty is perfect." In the cool of the pergola where pendulous bunches of green grapes protruded he went on, "Truth is, I never doubted my approval for a moment. But would you believe it—that boozer Herb Jernigan's wife raised a complaint about me to the Society objecting to my job being confirmed because I'm ambitious—'Jewish ambitious'—to expand the practice and fill the town with Jew doctors."

"What a cheek Jean's got! On what grounds?"

"The temporary employment of the Uziel twins servicing the illegal backyard Native clinic." Sunny reached up. The grapes were hard.

She said, "You were right then. Be patient they'll ripen soon."

"Herb Jernigan apologized for his wife but it's forced me to realize I simply must have my own surgery, and build our own house. It's the only way to true independence and security. This town's going to go ahead. I know it."

Back in the glare of the sun they reached the gate to the Club across the street. Soon the mine hooter would wail and the workers begin to fill its colonnaded verandah for their proverbial sundowners. Who, she wondered had sided with Jean Jernigan? She turned her back on the Club and caught sight of Leonard carrying the tea tray into the summerhouse.

"Tea's ready," she said, giving Sunny an unexpected peck and taking his arm.

As she poured, she said "I doubt Umzimtuti'll go ahead with this *toon* management."

"What makes you say that?"

"Well, Francis Asquith and I went to the council meeting this afternoon. I had the plans all ready to roll out and the details of the maintenance costs council would incur after the bath was built."

"My apologies, I quite forgot. Good girl! Always pays to do your homework. Another reason to celebrate." Back in her playpen he handed Deborah a rusk to gnaw on and dunked one for himself in his tea.

"Would you believe it—*His Worship* Angus Buchanan dismissed the proposal out of hand and the other council members concurred, even Jud, before we had a chance to say *one* word. That wimp, Cameron Gordon Murray Paxton, called me *out of order* when I tried to interject. I'm afraid, we've established ourselves in a one-horse town. Tea!" She said, "What we both really could do with is a stiff drink." Her rusk was saturated and collapsed into her tea. She fished for it with her teaspoon.

"That's preposterous."

"I was stupid to think I could pull it off."

"You've done well, getting the capital committed."

"It was silly of me, a school girl's fairytale dream to think I could do it. I should grow up, as you say," she said.

"To the contrary, I'm with you all the way," he said. "We can't have the Mayor running roughshod over you in such a perfunctory manner. Aren't the municipal elections coming up soon?"

"Run for council? Me—enter politics? I never thought of it." That was where she could make a real difference. But it was a man's world. She couldn't even take care of paper plans. Douglas was doing cartwheels on the lawn.

"No, no, you've a young and growing family to take care of. I'll protect your interests. You know Gandhi says, *the best way to find yourself is to lose yourself in the service of others.*"

"You've too much on your plate already. I'll try again in six months."

"The Lotteries offer might have a time limitation on it. We can't afford to wait six months to bring it before council again."

"Limitations?" she said.

"Always read the fine print."

"Already, we never see you." She wanted to succeed with this swimming bath proposal herself. Once he got beyond the portal of the Town House he'd have an agenda that was endless.

"I'm bound to find the right partner sooner or later," he went on.

"Those Indians were so qualified. Perhaps one of them is still available?"

"You're way ahead of the times. The community won't be ready for a multiracial society for decades—maybe a century."

"This has been quite an eye-opener for both of us today."

"At least Jud backed you, I'm sure," he said.

"He never said a word. Old Man Hardy seconded the motion to dismiss our request."

"That settles it. I'm going to break Buchanan's deadlock on council and then oust him from the Mayoral office."

"Leah tells me Jud's got plans to don the mayoral robe himself. Leave it to him. He's not nearly as busy as you."

"For all his fisticuffs and fighting spirit, it doesn't look as though he can stand up to the Scotsman."

Mavourneen was silent. She hadn't expected Sunny to make more than a passing consolatory remark on her project. She was torn. She knew he would win the day for her but when would the family see him then?

"I've got a following through the surgery door."

"You're not that interested in the swimming bath."

"That's not the point. It's the principle. But you know it's more than that: the bath is just the beginning of bringing Umzimtuti into the twentieth century."

"I'll fight my own battles."

"I love a challenge, you know that."

Not another one she thought. "Did you hear the British are preparing to occupy sectors of Jerusalem? The Irgun will fight them. The British know it and are evacuating all their women and children from Palestine. Looks bad."

"That's over there—the Middle East. A world away."

"All the same, there's that loyalty and devotion to King and Country. It's so strong."

"Surely you don't think they'll associate terrorism there with me here?"

"Anti-Semitism is latent in most British folk. You just sampled it today."

"Look at Boss Jack, the management and all the people who have befriended us. Basically they're good people. They'll support me if they think I can give the town a boost. Jean Jernigan is the exception not the rule."

"I hope you're right. They have accepted Jud on the council and the Jewish folk have made a huge contribution to the town with their businesses."

"Jews have only to arrive to succeed. It's settled then. I'm running."

"I don't know when you are going to find the time," she said.

"Actually," he said, "I'm sitting on an enquiry from a George Hyde-Clarendon. English, sounds stable, married, two children. The rather posh name puts me off. But Navy type so a good counter to Cecil Wolseley."

"Hyde-Clarendon? Perfect. What are you waiting for?"

"After a short housemanship, he joined the Navy and saw action in the North Atlantic so his experience has been isolated from broad medical practice and professional contact—absolutely nothing in tropical medicine—nothing like the credentials of the Indian applicants."

"Never mind. Who knows when we will get another candidate? You're never going to find the perfect partner. Look on the bright side: he won't be set in his clinical habits. He'll learn fast. Perhaps we can start to enjoy a family life at last."

"You've tipped the scales for me. It's settled then, I'll cable him in the morning and offer him a six month locum with an option of partnership if mutually agreeable thereafter."

"Let's hope to heaven he takes it."

"Where's Bundu?" he said, giving a sharp whistle.

"He's in disgrace. I put him in solitary confinement," she said.

"Nothing serious I hope."

After Sick Parade and hospital rounds in the morning, Sunny ran up the wide shallow steps and through the portico of the whitewashed Dutch gabled Town House to register for the upcoming council election. Whitewash: slaked lime and chalk was the white man's token bactericidal for all that ailed Africa. The Town House was much more in need of a whitewash job than the train station and its jacaranda tree trunks and stones marking the parking places. But not being on the royal route, it would be ignored, he was sure. It was symptomatic of council, of Umzimtuti's cobbled solutions, with no plan for the future. He couldn't wait to get into action.

After registering, he walked a block over to the Umzimtuti Hotel. Jud was busy at the bar, stocking up before the thirsty lunchtime regulars drifted in. "Don't tell me," said Jud. "Let me guess why you're here. Whisky?"

Sunny hopped on a bar stool, "No, thanks, it's a little early," he said, "I'll take a cold tonic water." Jud reached into the refrigerator to retrieve one, and poured. Sunny continued, "Let your lawsuit with O'Connor drop. You know the confidentiality of my patient must be respected, but really, Pat's been knocked for a six and he's at the point of no return. Can't you find it in your heart to put this *tsutcheppenish* behind you and settle?"

Jud got back to concentrating on shining up a glass beer mug with a tea towel. "Doc, you know how it is, as I keep telling you, it's out of my hands. It's up to the lawyers now."

"Costs are mounting exponentially with every exchange and you know he can't pay his own costs let alone yours, which he'll be obliged to do if he loses."

"Exactly, he'll have to declare bankruptcy when all is said and done."

"*Forgiveness is the hallmark of the strong.*"

"Doc, you preaching Hindu stuff to me? Trust in our faith: *an eye for an eye.*"

"That only results in *making the whole world blind*. Will you drop it now if I guarantee the costs?"

"Guarantee the costs! It's a generous offer. I don't see how you can afford it. You're still trying to establish yourself. What's Mavourneen got to say about it? What's O'Connor to you that you should make such a huge sacrifice?"

"Look, I didn't do the right thing by an alcoholic officer during the war and he ended up shooting himself. Pat O'Connor won't live long the way things are going."

There was a silence.

"And there's another point, Pat O'Connor owns the only newspaper in this little town. Everybody reads it. I can't see a competing newspaper setting up for years. If O'Connor lives he'll be your enemy for life and he will probably manage to at least continue to edit *The Cleft Stick*. It's not going to do your political career any good. If he dies people might well say you hounded him to his death."

"So all the public will know is we settled out of court?"

"Yes."

Jud said, "I could pay both costs, but O'Connor or especially his wife would probably spill the beans sooner or later. It would look as if I was afraid of him or that I didn't have a case. But if you paid, they'd keep quiet to avoid embarrassment. So I'm afraid, sorry, if I drop the case it *does* have to be *you* that picks up all the costs."

"Quite."

"But remember he's an anti-Semite. Leah's not going to be happy if I back down."

"You have to pick your fights. Think strategically, man. Convince Leah that ruining him will ruin you in the long run. Even in the short run, the sweetness of your revenge will sour. "

"You still don't know I broke my hand on Verdoon and de la Rey to avenge an insult against you."

"Why didn't you tell me? Why don't we play open cards with each other? I can stand up for myself. You should have stood up for Mavourneen."

"I thought you'd come in about Mavourneen's proposal."

"You made a big mistake not even giving it a hearing."

"There's no fighting Buchanan: he's entrenched—six terms. Runs it like Frank Buckland before him—probably to the grave like him too."

"Buchanan can't see further than the railway station that he sees from his garage. I just registered at the Town House. I'll be running in the upcoming council election. Once on council I'll unseat him."

Jud threw down the towel and held up the beer mug. Sunny saw a confused pattern of Jud's face multiplied in the dimples of the mug.

"You'll need more than a tonic water to carry O'Connor."

"If you agree, it's a deal."

Jud poured two whiskies and slid one over to Sunny. "Okay."

Sunny lifted up the glass and said, "Good man." He clinked his glass against Jud's. They both knocked the whisky back. Sunny gasped and said, "May the best man win."

CHAPTER FORTY-FIVE

Heartbreak

Monday and Wednesday afternoons, Sunny headed south along the Salisbury-Bulawayo Road past Ferreira's tobacco estates before turning west, crossing the railway line to the clinics, European and Native, at the Lime and Iron Works he had acquired from Eckhart. But on Thursdays he headed north from town and then a few miles west out on the rutted road to the power station under construction to do the rounds at the clinic there—another of Eckhart's budding new contracts.

He enjoyed the ride, the feel of the car beneath the seat of his pants. Cocooned from the demands of the surgery, the hospital and the clinics, free from the eternal trill of the telephone that summoned him hither and yon, he could sing to his heart's content, think clearly and incubate his ideas.

His private practice was growing all the time. He thought back to the opportunity his CO had offered to join his well-established practice in Kenya and the profound disappointment he had felt on arrival to realize a new partner had been taken on—his wartime *bête noire*. He had turned the offer down on the strength of it. Here he was his own man, with opportunity at every turn to make a difference in the lives of the people with whom he came in contact. He belted out:

"And so if Mister Trouble finds me
He will never linger long
'Cause I've got a pocketful of sunshine
And a heart full of song..."

The bush was covered with red dust churned up by the car as it bounced over the rutted road. The windows were open wide to allow a cooling through-breeze, dust seeped through every seam of the bodywork and settled on the car's interior: it was all part of the journey as Africa rushed by, before a stand of blue gums signaled the clinic was close at hand. A rash of red geraniums threatened by a smother of honeysuckle, which seemed to thrive on neglect and poor soil, framed the outside of the small, whitewashed clinic. A throng of Natives was lined up to see him. As he got out, his nostrils dilated with the mix of the camphor-like smell of eucalyptus mingled with the sweet fragrance of honeysuckle and the pungency of the bodily odors of Africa rising with the heat.

It would be a full afternoon he could see, forty patients at least. Sister Nel and the male nurse assistant, Jeremiah, always gave him a cheerful greeting. Tea, poured into thick ceramic cups, slaked his thirst. A last draw on a cigarette suppressed his appetite but he accepted a *Marie* biscuit. There would be no break in the work until nightfall. He donned his white coat and stethoscope.

There wasn't anyone in the European Clinic to be seen today but there was a message from Isaac Kalderon at the Lucky Strike Trading Store near Leighfield Siding asking if the good doctor would come out this evening to see his wife.

Sunny settled into the routine of the Native clinic. The Natives were much sicker than the Europeans and there were so many of them. He recalled Whitehead saying how administering first aid to his workers helped him get to know them. But he couldn't see it happening in his situation. He moved methodically down the queue.

In a single afternoon he could expect to see the usual run-of-the-mill maladies of the Natives. Bilharzia, the flat worm harbored by the snails in the reeds along the river banks, typhoid and amoebiasis from rivers contaminated with human waste, malaria from stagnant pools, hookworm from walking barefoot on the well-worn paths, epidemic and murine typhus from their flea infested huts as well as tuberculosis and leprosy, paradoxically from overcrowding in such vast and open bush—one and a half million in one hundred and fifty-thousand square miles.

The list of nutritional disorders was long, including pellagra, scurvy, the gamut of vitamin deficiencies, and anemias. It was a marathon trying to cover each and every one, ever open to the unusual, and not turn anyone away at the end of the day.

They came reluctantly really, fearing that by coming to the white doctor they were provoking the wrath of the *nganga* or the spirits of their ancestors or the wizard. So the job was harder on him, harder on them, because the disease state was usually far advanced before they lined up to see him. They lacked confidence in his treatment, afraid that even if cured, something worse would happen to them. He was sure this pessimism affected outcomes. It so contrasted with the psychology of European practice, exemplified by the Catholic faith of the Biancardi family.

Natives never volunteered past history or current symptoms unless specific questions were asked. With the press of time Sunny found it excruciatingly annoying. With Jeremiah at his side to interpret he would ask, "What's the matter?"

"Who me?"

Rudely he would retort, "Who do you think?" He knew Jeremiah tempered responses on both sides: he was a moderator, like Cookie.

As the afternoon wore on, Sunny would get more and more testy with the slowness of the responses, extracting symptoms one at a time to puzzle together a history and figure out what the priorities were in the combination of diseases presenting in each patient.

There was no hope of getting ahead of the workload. He could always count on a burn case or two: a baby left unattended in the hut crawling too close to the fire and then the parents waiting days before seeking help by which time the burns were seriously infected. Cleaning and dressing the wounds was time consuming. The tragedy was most of the pain and suffering was avoidable.

He'd explained to Lady Shirley, education was the key, but Government schools for the natives were few and far between, and the church-run schools not enough. Personal hygiene and a balanced diet should be priorities. If industry had to come first, as Whitehead insisted, then they should set the example. Lady Shirley had given him the confidence to press for change.

The sun lay low on the horizon when he and Jeremiah finished the queue. Sister Nel offered him another cup of tea for the road but he declined, reminding her that he was headed further north for Leighfield Siding and beyond to the Lucky Strike Trading Store. He would probably be offered a sundowner there. He tried to ring Mavourneen from the paraffin phone system party line but it was engaged.

Back on the Salisbury Road he was getting into cotton country. The Umsweswe Cotton Mills had mushroomed during the war to meet the demand for canvas and absorbent cotton wool. The mills would only get bigger: another contract in the offering. He had never considered it before but it was not too far afield. When would he get a partner to share the opportunities that stretched in every direction?

He turned off onto another gravel road and sped on. How did Miriam get to be out here with only the one roomed, corrugated-iron, un-manned shack of Leighfield Siding within walking distance for company? Tall and slender, she was beautiful, with sallow skin, big dark eyes and black coils framing her unforgettable oval face.

He rounded the store. An advertisement for *Sunlight* soap was bleaching on the blistering wall. He looked up at the rusting corrugated iron roof and wondered how profitable a store out here could be serving the Natives from the surrounding cotton, maize and tobacco farms, ranches and small workings who earned perhaps a pound a month. Miriam was the persuasive partner who encouraged down payment on that first suit or three-legged pot. Farmers and ranchers owning vast acreages had little disposable income and the small workers lived on hope that always stretched ahead. European accounts were often delinquent by several months. What could Isaac do but offer extended credit?

Sunny parked in front of the Kalderons' ramshackle house. He passed the huge rainwater tanks, propped on bricks with air spaces between them that flanked the building. The guttering that fed them, at least, was well maintained.

The verandah was cool, shaded by a thick vine with pendulous white fruits dripping from it. Mr. Kalderon short, portly and middle aged, emerged on the verandah and greeted him. "Thank you. I begin t'ink you forgot."

"No, no, how could I forget your beautiful Miriam! Just caught up at the clinic. What's the problem?"

"She sick already one month. A disappointment. She stay in the bed. What will happen? The house? The store?" He waved his arms. "What will happen to business? Does she talk to me?" He motioned Sunny into the bedroom.

Sunny adjusted to the darkness. "Can we have some light here, Mrs. Kalderon?"

She turned over. He drew the curtains apart letting in the waning light of the day. The patina of a suit on a mannequin before the window lit up, which even Sunny, unconcerned with fashion, recognized as special. A matching hat with a feather springing from the headband was cocked at a jaunty angle on the faceless white head. Spanish leather shoes and handbag to match sat on the chair beside it. The dressed mannequin seemed incongruous here, holding this position of pride against the collection of cotton dresses, housecoats, slippers and dusty flat-heeled shoes that lay strewn about.

The adjacent wall was stacked with shelves weighed down with bolts of fine fabrics, not the cheap, colorful, muslin sheeting she sold to Natives in the store next door. Dress patterns filed in shoe boxes stood stiffly in their packets. Once she had lovingly catalogued all these. A riempie chair faced a Singer sewing machine with a collection of bobbins and spools of cotton of every color and hue surrounding it. Pinking shears and scissors of all sizes stood in a stout glass jar. The floor was scattered with fashion magazines: *Elle, L'Officiel, Vogue, Votre Beaute, Pelliana* and *Verve*. Sunny picked his way to the bed.

Her face was tear stained, her beautiful eyes were red and swollen and her hair lay in a disheveled, black tangle on the pillow. "Doctor," she said, "Isaac say you come. Too tired."

"Let's take a look. What's the trouble?"

"Trouble! No friends! No life! See." Her lips quivered. She was going to cry, again. "Lucky Strike nothing! Nothing! Nothing!"

"Come now," he said, "your husband needs you to make the sales at the store. Counting on you. Only together can you make a go of it."

Sunny did a thorough physical before going through to the sitting room to join Mr. Kalderon, "Do you mind if I take a moment to sit down?" Sunny asked. "Your wife is going to join us."

"Doctor. What? News bad?"

"There is nothing physically wrong, though she's lost weight. She's depressed. Does she have good reason?"

"Doctor. Do I do my best? She, not interested, if you know what I mean—not interested in anyt'ing."

"Yes, well, that's part of the depression."

"She lost this friend—everyt'ing fall apart. Are there many women out here to make a friend? Pick and choose? Is my fault?"

"No, I agree, it's a long way from town. Perhaps you should come in once a month? Something to look forward to from the routine of the store."

"Doctor. Is life hard? Is there someone else run the store while we go? Is there another petrol pump for thirty miles? Punctures. Repairs. The store—mealie meal. Lots of t'ings. Many t'ings. Does everyone count on us?"

"Shut up shop early once a month. Come in for poker night for WIZO. Stakes are high but know your limits, you can always fold. It's for fun, for the cause—ten percent of the winnings for the creation of the State of Israel. Next time it's at our house, last Saturday of the month. Why don't you both join us? See if that doesn't improve things. Also, the women on Wednesdays, I think, work for WIZO, sew, knit together—talk. You know all this already. The cure I dispense for your wife is company."

Mr. Kalderon sighed with a doubtful nod.

Mrs. Kalderon entered the sitting room. She had dressed, scraped her hair back in a ponytail accentuating the drawn cheeks. She needed counseling. It took time and patience. Sunny knew he should play his part by popping in every Thursday after the clinic.

"Miriam!" exclaimed Isaac, "*My* Love!" He took her arm and guided her to the rocking chair. She rocked herself slowly.

"A drink, Doctor?" he asked.

"A whisky would be nice." He lit up a cigarette. Took a long draw on it. Exhaled slowly as Mr. Kalderon poured.

"Mind we listen? Six o'clock BBC News Overseas Service? We never miss."

The wireless crackled with thunderstorm atmospherics. They caught the gist of the headlines *Irgun members... carrying firearms...Sir Evelyn Barker...British Commander in Palestine confirmed death sentences by hanging...*

"What our people to do?" said Miriam despondently.

"Why they promise with the Balfour Declaration, the Mandate?" said Mr. Kalderon.

"Let's sing *Hatikva*," said Sunny, as he put down his cigarette, got up and raised his glass. "I haven't forgotten my Hebrew from *cheder*. I've quite a voice."

Isaac helped his wife up out of her rocking chair. Full-voiced they sang the heartwarming anthem of hope:

"Od lo avdah tikvateinu,

Hatikvah hannoshanah

Lashuv le'eretz avoteinu

La'ir bah david k'hanah."

"*L'chaim!*" exclaimed Sunny.

"*L'chaim!*" said the Kalderones in unison as glasses clinked.

"The sages remind us always that there is no royal road to possession of Eretz Israel. It's paved with suffering. Here we are living in this pocket full of sunshine," said Sunny as they settled down again. "Everyone—well almost everyone—here is open-minded, accepting all faiths." But through his mind flashed white ponies and the Boer Republic flags held high at the Voortrekker Monument on his return from the war. It had influenced him to look beyond South Africa's borders for a job but had his move been a wise one after all? The ugliness of his and Mavourneen's own personal experiences of anti-Semitism cut deep and on the national level Rhodesia's Aliens Act had recently been introduced requiring £1500 capital or an assured job of £500 per annum to qualify for immigration. For the most part, only professionals and entrepreneurs from South Africa and England could meet those criteria. In all this vast emptiness, crying out for development, there was no reaching out to the desperate Holocaust survivors searching for a place anywhere in the world to fit in. What a crime it was against humanity: what a tragic lost opportunity for Rhodesia.

He was one of the fortunate few, staking everything he had on Umzimtuti and Rhodesia: the land wide open for Mavourneen and the children. Was it too idealistic, too naïve, to think that Jews here in this remote place would escape from a two thousand year history? Indeed if it wasn't safe here then where to next? A State of Israel would be the only safeguard. How paradoxical that Britain stood in the way of it: hostilities there were escalating every day.

Miriam interrupted his reverie as she put her glass down, "I work for fashion houses in Paris. But then they start refuse. Was I beautiful enough? But not French! You call this Lucky Strike? Where friends I ask you?"

"I tell you," explained Isaac, "she make dress, the best. The very best for Mrs. Caulfield at the Chancer Mine to wear at her sister's wedding. She not come final fitting. Off to Salisbury in Tiger Moth to buy Barbours store. Readymade, I tell you! No word. Not one word, I say! No sorry. Is not here anti-Semitism at Lucky Strike?"

"I am sure it was unintentional," said Sunny "Mr. Caulfield was an RAF fighter pilot. He took a lot of chances in the war. He's lucky to be alive. I'm sure he never intended to slight you."

"Doctor, maybe him, but his wife, she never apologize."

"He loves any excuse to get into the plane and fly away from the Chancer, perhaps he insisted Mrs. Caulfield join him. Last I heard he had lost the reef. You know what a tight ship he has to run, tributing to Lonrho. But, come now, this is not about the Caulfields, it's about you and Miriam. WIZO is working hard for the State of Israel as you know. Come for poker. Last Saturday of every month. Doctor's orders."

The thunder rumbled and silenced the conversation under the drum of the rain on the corrugated iron roof. "Stay for supper 'till storm finish? Not long. We lucky no?" Isaac shouted above the din, "Miriam teach Joseph cook foods of home. You like chicken liver stew, Spanish rice, stuffed chou-chou fruits? We pick a bag of chou-chou for you to take home to your good wife."

"Thank you." Chou-chou fruit? What was that? He was suddenly homesick for his mother's Ashkenazi chopped chicken liver, but he was hungry. He was going to be home very late tonight. There was no way to contact Mavourneen now. His dinner, all dried up in the warming drawer, would go to Bundu.

CHAPTER FORTY-SIX

Waiting Up

Mavourneen stayed up for Sunny, listening to the sound of rain on the roof as she made herself useful darning the socks she had knitted during the war on night duty. She had posted them to him in Abyssinia before they were married. Back then she had volunteered for work at the Fever Hospital in Johannesburg. The only defense against disease was a healthy diet. It meant extra delicious meals: fresh fruit daily and pudding with cream at least twice a week. Who wouldn't sign up?

But night duty in the diphtheria ward had seemed endless and nerve-wracking. The only sounds to keep her company were the creaking of the floorboards, the uneven breathing of each child and the occasional roar of a lion carrying over the air from the Johannesburg Zoo as her four knitting needles clicked away.

Diphtheria forms a tough false membrane in the air passages that suffocates the child. At regular intervals she tiptoed from bed to bed to log each child's chart in the beam of her torch. A locker at each bedside had everything on it she needed. The most important instrument was a goose quill. If thc child was pallid and breathing labored she feathered their tracheotomy, a tube inserted into the windpipe as an alternate breathing passage, to keep it open. Constant feathering was vital to remove the deadly membrane.

How purposeful and important every minute of her life had seemed back then.

She reached down into her sewing basket and retrieved the big glossy cowrie shell, a treasured memento from their wartime honeymoon in Durban, which had been cut short when Sunny was recalled unexpectedly to duty. She popped the cowrie into one of Sunny's socks stretched the worn heel over it and began to weave the thread back and forth leading with the heavy darning needle. Durban was where they had encountered their first brush with anti-Semitism, being turned away from the city's premier hotel, the Lonsdale, with *we don't accept Jews here*, despite his being in uniform.

Finally, she heard the car on the gravel, the creak of the lean-to garage and then the bang of the screen door.

"It's good to be home after sliding around on muddy roads. Did you listen to the BBC tonight?" he asked.

"Yes, I heard. Deplorable! Violence is sure to escalate. It could affect your upcoming municipal election."

"You think so? I was just at the Kalderon's after the clinic rounds. They're concerned too."

"Remember the new Aliens Act passed just last year, immigrants to be ninety percent British, ten percent aliens and no single minority to be more than one percent, Kipling's:

Let the corn be all one sheaf
And the grapes be all one vine."

"The British are fair minded and it's different here. We're making a contribution. Feldmans is the mainstay of the town. They are generous to all sectors of the community including the churches. And Wolfson's Bakery and Shapiro's Butchery gave such good accounts of themselves during the flood and the others too, all of them," Sunny temporized.

"So far as we know all your relatives perished in Europe except the Norwegians. Let's face it. Huggins' own effort here for the refugees was pathetic. He quashed Cazalet's one million Jews settlement proposal for Northern Rhodesia because it would skew the population too drastically and he was worried the Jews would filter down to Southern Rhodesia, demand political rights, take over farms, businesses and banks...you know, the usual fear mongering: no different from the rest of the world."

"I'll stand on my record."

"There's so much you could do but don't be disappointed if you lose."

"Don't you believe in me?"

"Sunny, you're being unreasonable. I don't want you to go into one of your black moods if you lose."

CHAPTER FORTY-SEVEN

Competitions

The Chamber of Mines First Aid Inter-Mines Competition was held annually at the Cheetah Mine pavilion. Internal competition at all the large mines was fierce before final selection for the big event. Each mine was assigned a marquee as their lorries arrived. In due course things got under way with inspection of each team, their first aid boxes and a quiz on casualty protocol.

Meanwhile back at the Native Hospital P.Q. and his orderlies were enjoying themselves applying potions to simulate underground accidents on casualties to be presented to the teams. They joked with the 'victims' who belonged to runner-up teams, but some of them were uneasy with entertaining this very real pretense of calamity and didn't like to think of the spirits that might be offended. P.Q explained, first aid helps our brothers and ourselves. Cochineal oozed on ever-so-lifelike lacerations, mock-severed arteries were rigged to spout on cue. How quickly could a team apply a tourniquet, dress a wound and make the finish line or immobilize a broken leg, roll the patient on a stretcher or build a ladder from an assortment of gum poles and rope? A big clock ticked off the seconds. Besides time, they were also judged on expertise in application and technique as well as overall teamwork.

Lady Shirley requested to join the judges, who were medical officers from the larger mines, for a close up view. Sunny introduced her and she promised not to get in the way.

Cookie, dressed in his white starched uniform, interpreted for the different local tribes as well as those from the surrounding territories. If all else failed, he resorted to *Fanagalo*.

The other dignitaries, including the Minister of Mines and his wife, made their way to the front row in the pavilion while the European workers and their wives filed in behind and the Natives poured into the grandstand.

Through a bullhorn, P.Q., firmly in control, announced to the crowd the points gained by each team and the winners for each event. The Cheetah was the overall winner again this year. Cheers and whistles, some ironical, arose from the grandstand as Mr. Doolittle accepted the trophy on the mine's behalf from the Minister of Mines.

Sunny ushered Lady Shirley to their assigned front row seats at the grandstand.

P.Q. announced the start of the gumboot dance competition. Naked to the waist, trousers tucked into their gumboots, bandanas around their heads, a squad ran on briskly in column and opened out into a circle. Lady Shirley was clearly mesmerized by the stomping, with exaggerated high stepping, ankle slapping with the opposite hand as they raised their feet, whistling—interrupted by sudden stops in complete unison—before forming a line again, still stamping, and singing:

"Hee mahlalela
Hambu' uyo sebenza
Hee mahlalela
Hambh' uyo sebenza

Hee hee
He mahlalelea
Hambh' uyo sebenza
He mahlalela
Hambh' uyo sebenza"

Lady Shirley bent over and whispered to Sunny, "What're they singing?"

"They're saying how much they love to work at the mines...to go underground, where the jackhammers blast makes them deaf, where the dust swirls from the hanging wall and eats their lungs, and the wet footwall at the face melts their skin in the heat and gives them sores. They love to leave their tribal homeland and their families to work here for food. The mine brewed beer is good and the doctor is clever."

"But they really are enjoying themselves, aren't they? And the First Aid teams were keen as mustard and pretty good."

"I wish they'd be as keen about their jobs as they are their dancing," replied Doolittle dryly. "What they are really singing is pretty repetitive: *Loafer go and work. Yes! Loafer go and work!* They've got it right. They are lazy as hell if you really want to know the truth. They know it themselves."

"We don't pay them much do we? Perhaps Dr. Rubenstein is on the right track."

"Don't believe a word he tells you. Even his *Fanagalo* is minimal.

He relies entirely on his interpreter from Nyasaland."

"What are they singing now?" she asked, grinning broadly, clearly enjoying it all as she turned back to Sunny.

"One day we will overcome!

We will overcome!

We will overcome!

The mines, the gold and the money will be ours!

We will overcome!"

Mavourneen leaned over and said, "it's *Ishe Komborera Africa—God Bless Africa.*"

"God bless Africa? That's lovely," Lady Shirley replied. "But overcome what?" she asked.

"Us," said Sunny.

"He's pulling your leg again," cut in Doolittle. "Don't let him frighten you. We're firmly in control. The Natives aren't politically conscious at all."

"Time is not on our side," said Sunny. "Education is the key."

"Well, the first aid teams are making a rather splendid effort today," Lady Shirley observed.

But gumboot dancing became rather repetitive after a while and finally she said, "I could use a cup of tea."

"It's coming up shortly," said Doolittle. "The Mine Club has it all laid on. You'll need it. We've the tribal dancing still to get through. We only allow—even encourage—this dancing stuff to keep alive tribal loyalties—keep the unions out. It's their only recreational outlet."

It began with the thudding of big wooden drums, then the rush of warriors with headdresses rustling as they bobbed up and down, wrist and ankle rattles clicking and knobkerries clashing against their rawhide shields. "This is all so thrilling," said Lady Shirley. Their torsos, naked and well-oiled, glistened in the afternoon sun. There was not an ounce of fat on them. They wore white wooly sheepskin bracelets and calf leggings. Skirts made from the tails of animals swung to the throb of the drums. Hand slapping of thighs, foot stamping, and whistling was intermingled with chants. The chief stepped before the dancers and blew into a twisted kudu horn. The rhythm built to a frenzy.

Overwhelming sound and power came from barefoot stamping and beating of knobkerries against shields. Lady Shirley leaned over and in a stage whisper above the noise and movement said, "I can taste the musk of sweat mingled with the dust, can't you?" Wave after wave of dancers came and went. Finally, she said to Sunny, "Goodness gracious me! I do declare, I didn't realize the gulf between our cultures. Do you think we shall ever understand them?"

"Not in our lifetime or even our sons," said Doolittle leaning over. "We're only just letting go of India after three centuries—and although we are making a hash of our exit there by all accounts, nothing like that is on the horizon anywhere in Africa."

"They're restless to get that first suit of clothes, once they see it," said Mavourneen.

"A shilling a day's not going to keep them underground once they get an education," confirmed Sunny.

"It's those bloody missionaries, making trouble always," said Doolittle.

"The government should do more to shoulder the burden," said Sunny.

"Sir Harvey bagged an elephant, and Mr. Earle a buffalo," said Doolittle to Sunny.

"Congratulations, but mark my words, the days of the White man's playground are soon coming to an end."

"I heard you plan to get into municipal affairs?" Lady Shirley commented to Sunny.

"As a physician I believe public health measures eliminate the root causes of disease. It's a direct extension, application if you will, of the Hippocratic Oath."

"I wish you luck," she said. "I haven't forgotten my promise to get the Boyles anesthetic apparatus and new theatre table you need delivered to the Cheetah Native Hospital. It'll be my priority on my return."

"We're most grateful. I've already told the compound manager P.Q. He was my anesthetist and the assistant for the delivery of the twins you saw. No medical background of course, but a keen learner. Life out here offers the freedom and opportunity to stretch way beyond official duties to embrace unexpected challenges," he said as he took her hand and helped her down off the podium.

She gave his hand a squeeze.

In contrast to the tailored pastel suit, the bold African sunset was briefly splashing about its garish reds and oranges and yellows. Here was English breeding from the fine sun hat above the aquiline nose on down to the slim ankles and dainty heeled shoes she wore. But frail? Hardly. Hardy, more like it. Sunny was grateful to have her on his side.

CHAPTER FORTY-EIGHT

Poker Night

It was Mavourneen and Sunny's turn to host poker night. The Jewish women knew how to cook all right and she needed to give a good account of herself. It would be a challenge however, to stay within her housekeeping budget, knowing the balance of Palmer's goodwill was still outstanding and the disturbing added burden of O'Connor's debt to Jud that she felt Sunny had so unnecessarily assumed. But she knew where she could economize and where she could not for best effect.

On Friday, she splurged on three good wedges of cheeses—a treat Sunny was sure to enjoy. From Shapiro's Butchery she selected a variety of his specialty beef polonies. She picked up a loaf of bread from Wolfson's Bakery. Day-old it would slice easier for sandwiches. She ordered fresh sausage rolls to be delivered in the morning. She popped into Cynthia's Florist to order a small bunch of cut flowers that she'd augment with offerings from the garden and arrange herself.

Baking was where she could save. She gave Leonard the afternoon off, instructed Nanny to entertain the children and got stuck in. Her Aberdeen School of Domestic Science Cookbook held fail safe recipes. She made a Victoria sandwich cake and used her own homemade guava jam for the filling. Last minute she would add a sprinkling of icing sugar on top. Next on the list was a rich Dundee Cake with handfuls of dried fruit. She made a double batch of date loaf from the fresh shipment of dates that had recently arrived at De Leon's Dainty Fruitiers. She rolled out the pastry for savory as well as custard tartlets that she would fill last minute. Finally, she whipped up the leftover egg whites to stiff peaks for meringues—nothing wasted. She popped them in the cooling oven and left them there to dry out overnight to make the most efficient use of the oven.

Cynthia was generous with her bouquet, which arrived first thing in the morning. She arranged gladioli, dahlias and Barberton daisies in the beautiful silver rose bowl she had inherited from her grandmother and placed them on the dining room sideboard so that they were reflected in the long beveled mirror. This is where the men would play poker while the women spent the evening in the sitting room, eating, drinking and talking. And could they talk!

She popped into the garden and picked an assortment of filler flowers as well as some lovely big heads of deep blue agapanthus to float in crystal sweet dishes on the sitting room coffee tables.

She set the trolley with the fine coffee service left by the Palmers and put Leonard to work polishing the silverware on the kitchen steps with further instruction to dust the good glasses. The company would be pretty heavy handed with the liquor.

Time was running on. She bathed before she fixed, last minute, the savory canapés. She made a few plates of card sandwiches. They were time consuming and fiddly and not really worth the trouble but they did look festive on a bed of shredded lettuce, garnished with cherry tomatoes, cocktail onions and a few spicy radishes thrown in from the garden. She arranged the meat plate separately for those who were Kosher. The cheese platter had been brought to room temperature under an embroidered tea shower. Leonard would heat up the sausage rolls when the guests arrived. Everything had gone without a hitch.

Sunny was late as usual but she welcomed the guests warmly. They began to arrive promptly at seven o'clock, twelve couples in all plus Mrs. Hershl. She asked Mr. Shapiro if he would mind tending the bar in Sunny's absence. He and Sophie were belatedly attentive to their Jewish heritage, lucky to be included in the quota of one hundred and eighty Jews allowed into Rhodesia in '38. He managed the bar with German efficiency.

Mavourneen served the savories, reserving the sweets and the coffee for later. The party was lively by the time Sunny arrived home and took over the bar. With plates and glasses refilled, the men settled down to poker while the ladies withdrew to the spacious sitting room and the comfortable settees and chairs.

"Miriam, is it good to see you? Have you been hiding out at the store? Working too hard? *Ja!* So thin. Have something to eat, my dear," coaxed Sophie Shapiro.

"Has Mavourneen put out this *wonderful* feast just for the eyes? You *must* eat something." Gittel Wolfson handed Miriam a serviette and brought a plate of savories to her as she shrunk into the comfort of Mavourneen's favorite wing backed chair.

"We need for you to make sunbonnets from muslin. They sell like hot cakes at the fete, *Ja!*" went on Sophie.

"Have we missed you?" said Avigail Feldman, giving a squeeze to Miriam's bony shoulders. She could see she was struggling to maintain composure, close to tears with all the unwanted attention. But she had dressed and come out: a sign of recovery. With a pat, Avigail said, "We sent a lot cash to WIZO. We so glad you back."

"Yes, we must help Palestine. The British evacuated their women and children last month," said Molly Fisher.

"The poor dears," said Rebecca Hertzog.

"Death sentences—hangings—for Irgun leaders!" said Rivkah Feldman.

"What do you expect? Murderers! Kidnappers! Bank robbers!" said old Mrs. De Leon.

"The British betrayed us. What must we do?" said Gittel.

"That's a very good question," said Rebecca.

"An eye for an eye is not the way," said Mrs. De Leon.

"It seems like the British are sticking to the Old Testament," said Rebecca.

"Six hundred stacked like fish in the Ben Hecht boat. They see the lights of Haifa up to the Carmel, but the British ship them off to Cyprus detention camps!" said Gittel.

"You surprised? This not the first deportation," said Mrs. Hershl.

"Already more than ten thousand to Cyprus," said Rivkah.

"Where to go? Remember always Bulawayo Chronicle headline say *This not Judesia: Rhodesia for the Rhodesians,*" said Sophie.

"They've lifted the house arrest of the three hundred thousand," said Rebecca.

"The Arabs deny ever accepting the Balfour Declaration. They want majority rule. The British refuse to let our people in. So I ask you, can we establish a majority? It's never going to happen!" said Molly.

"The sandwiches will curl up. Think of all the hungry in the detention camps. Eat! Eat!" said Gittel.

"Does eating here help them there?" asked Rebecca.

These gatherings are all the same, anxiously exchanging news of Palestine, Mavourneen thought.

"Never should I have left Paris," said Miriam softly as she picked at a sandwich.

"We so glad to see you tonight," said Sophie.

"The Lucky Strike Native Store is a gold mine, never mind the small workings. Before you know it you'll find a manager. Move to town yourself. Start another business," said Leah reassuringly. "Who'd think Jud and I would own a hotel—the best in town? He started with nothing."

"We have been here since '20," tempered Mrs. De Leon. "Never anti-Semitism."

"All this trouble. Maybe they won't vote for the good Doctor," said Avigail.

"Maybe? Maybe not?" said Rivkah.

"Are the British worry about us? They worry about pro-Nazi Arab revolt, Suez Canal," said Gittel.

"What about, then, maybe, we canvas for him—have some teas? Invite all the ladies?" Rivkah argued aloud with herself. "Maybe not: maybe lay low because of the troubles?"

"Sunny will stand on his own record and his ideas for Umzimtuti," cut in Mavourneen.

"Like what I say. There's no prejudice here," said Mrs. De Leon.

"Can we change the past? We work for future—the good Doctor here—WIZO there," decided Rivkah.

"You right," agreed Avigail, supporting her sister-in-law. "They desperate for everything. We must work harder—send clothes— secondhand and new ones too. Money. Especially money."

"Who takes the money?" asked Mrs. De Leon.

"WIZO Headquarters in Tel Aviv—they know best who need what—food, blankets, clothes, everything," cut in Sophie authoritatively as chairperson of the Umzimtuti WIZO branch. "We want everyone participate. *Ja!* Double, double efforts."

"The stores they must donate," said Avigail.

"Perhaps the Indians will give too, some of them anyhow. Kasim & Sons are very good," said Molly.

"Everyone make financial contribution now, we buy materials wholesale prices. Sew fast. What you say Mrs. Hershl?" said Sophie.

"Me? I can't," pleaded Mrs. Hershl as she twisted forward out of the deep sofa.

"Lay out pattern. Cut. Is that so hard?" shot back Sophie.

"Me, in a hotel room?"

"*Ja!* So what wrong with the floor? Yedidah will show you."

"Ladino and Greek only. No English."

"She show with hands."

"And my back?" Mrs. Hershl reached for a sausage roll.

Rebecca turned away, "Poker's where the money is. I say no more ten percent. Let's make it fifty percent of kitty for WIZO—for arms."

"No arms!" said Mrs. De Leon.

"We manage without you," said Sophie.

"Sophie won't you help me to bring in the coffee?" Mavourneen asked as she rose. "We'll check on the men."

Mavourneen had removed two of the leaves from the dining room table and added two folding card tables in the adjoining alcove beside the fireplace. Mr. De Leon, a sinewy pioneer, sat opposite Mr. Uziel, a wisp of a man, nervous, with weak lungs and delicate hands. What news of the girls at Great Ormond Street Hospital she wondered? Then there was David Fisher, young, dapper, with a self-confidence gained from running his own Native store in Gokwe, a great improvement on his modest life in London she suspected. He was handsome with a full head of hair and a thin mustache above sensuous lips. He sat opposite Jud Levine. He, no doubt, would call everyone's bluff.

Jud had brought a newcomer, Saul Zellner, like Fisher, young, good looking and confident. With a housing shortage everywhere, especially in Umzimtuti with the Lime and Iron Works and a new power station going up, he lodged at the hotel. Demobbed from the English army, he had had plenty of experience playing poker waiting for the invasion.

At the second table she was pleased to see Isaac Kalderon, Miriam's husband, even though he looked sallow and tired. Nathan Wolfson, Gittel's husband, the baker, corpulent, voluble and excitable, probably wasn't a good poker player she guessed. Shapiro, Sophie's husband had taken a seat here, opposite Desmond Hertzog, Rebecca's husband. She wondered if their men also sparred.

The third table was occupied by the old trader, excitable Elazar. No doubt, Mavourneen thought, his polished *Burbank Green* Cadillac was carefully parked far from the boozers cars at the Club across the street, with no reversing required. The doyens of the community, the Feldman brothers, Avigail and Rivkah's husbands, joined him. Sunny sat at this table. "Gentlemen," she said, "coffee and sweets will be served shortly."

Mavourneen sieved the icing sugar onto the Victoria sandwich cake. Sophie wheeled in the tea trolley with the cups and saucers and came back for the cakes. Mavourneen instructed Leonard to bring in the coffee when it was ready.

The winners from the three tables were now sitting at the dining room table. The others had pulled up their chairs to watch. Mavourneen saw that Sunny was doing well, King George in his uniform, crumpled and smooth, on many ten shilling and pound notes as well as coins in his pile. Jud had done even better. She noticed the worn elbows of Sunny's jacket as he took his cigarettes from his pocket and lit one. She knew he had earned more from poker than from his meager housemanship stipend before the war. Only Sunny and Jud had not folded. They were both small men who had learned to use their fists inside and outside the ring: both fighters. She saw Jud push the whole of his winnings forward. She leaned in to hear.

"How much is that?" said Sunny.

"About seventeen pounds," said Jud.

"Call it twenty," said Sunny.

"Your twenty, and another thirty. Fifty!" said Jud.

Had Sunny really made another bid? Mavourneen frowned. That was half of what Sunny brought home from the mine every month— the balance going to Palmer's goodwill.

Sunny released the smoke through his nostrils. He looked at Jud, nodding slightly. The murmur of the women in the sitting room seeped into the dining room. "I'll see you."

Jud laid his cards down.

Sunny said, "Alright," and slipped his cards into the deck.

There was a chorus of exclamations. "*Oy vey!*" said Mr. Nathan Wolfson swinging his jowls as he did in synagogue.

"I say!" said Saul Zellner, putting his hands on his knees.

"My goodness me," said Mr. Fisher softly, sitting on his hands.

"Sunny!" said Desmond Hertzog, putting his hand to his chin.

"Doctor, Doctor!" said Mr. Shapiro, adjusting his spectacles and dropping his jaw.

The Feldman brothers looked at each other, inclined their heads, slightly pursing their lips, before Yankel exclaimed, "Oy-yoy-yoy!"

Mr. Kalderon shook his head sadly.

Mr. Uziel interlinked his fingers and gazed at them.

Mr. Elazar put his hand on his pocket that held his car keys and cleared his throat.

Mr. De Leon pushed back his chair and walked over to the sideboard. After this would they afford such a flower arrangement?

Mavourneen straightened her back, smoothed the sides of her dress and inclined her head to one side. She tightened her throat to suppress a surge of tears. The room fell silent. Jud Levine flushed, staring at the pile of money.

Sunny said, "Well, that's it. Thank you gentlemen. Winners please count your winnings so Mr. Shapiro can exact WIZO's tax. Let's join the ladies and sober up."

The men pushed back their chairs, grimacing at the simultaneous grating as the chairs slipped from carpet to concrete. Mavourneen opened the door and smiled.

As the men entered the sitting room, Sophie said, "Well, gentlemen, I hope you all lost lot money. *Ja!* The ladies think WIZO should take fifty percent of the winnings, not ten."

"Sophie comes up with terrific ideas," said Rebecca.

"I think that's a terrific idea, too, don't you, Jud?" said Desmond.

"Wait a minute!" said Jud.

"So, Jud, you in favor, starting from tonight," cut in Sophie. "You are generous, *Ja!* Mr. Wolfson, what do you say?"

"Next year in Jerusalem," said Nathan Wolfson.

Leah said moving to her husband's side, "What's going on, Jud?"

"It a very serious situation in Palestine," said Yankel Feldman.

"We all must do what we can for our people," echoed his brother Jacob.

"We so fortunate here," Mr. Elazar said.

"Jud, they're ganging up on you, aren't they!" exclaimed Leah.

Mr. Uziel said, "England! Palestine! We support good people."

"Well said, sir," said Mr. De Leon.

"Jud hasn't agreed to anything," said Leah.

Molly said, "What a surprise, the men have all agreed."

"Of course! All agree. What you expect," said Sophie.

Saul Zellner said, "It's been a splendid party. Really marvelous."

Mavourneen busied herself with cutting the cakes as the tartlets and meringues were passed. Gittel filled her plate and sampled. "My dear," she said, "have you quite outdone yourself with all these wonderful cakes? Should you not work in the bakery with my Nate, yes?"

"Doc, your wife has done you proud," Nate affirmed.

"Why thank you, indeed this is a compliment coming from a baker," said Sunny.

Mavourneen moved to the trolley, and said, "Black or white?"

"White, please," said Molly. Simultaneously, scalded milk was poured with coffee.

"Mavourneen, is your Victoria sandwich not light like feather! *Wunderful* filling," confirmed Sophie as she passed the sweets again.

"The guava tree above the chicken coop gives us wonderful fruit. Can't go wrong. I bottle them whole. Make lots of jam too. I try not to let anything go to waste."

"You must bring jam to Saturday market," said Sophie. "Sell like hot cakes, for sure."

"Doctor Rubenstein, you're a risk taker," observed Saul.

"I try and size up every situation."

"You're not a man to hedge your bets, though," he pressed.

"The risks I take are calculated."

"Doctor, what you think your chance in the election?" asked Shapiro as he sipped thoughtfully.

Sunny's throat was dry with his loss. He remembered when he'd once had to lean on his sister to cover his gambling debt. "I'm confident. Umzimtuti could be big." He cleared his throat before he went on, "but we can't expect to bring industry to town with fish fingerlings in the bath water and sanitary lanes with honey suckers. We have to make it a show place: dam the Umzimtuti, put in a filtration plant, get a proper waterborne sewer system going, light the streets. It'll be good for everyone's business. I hope you'll back me."

"Of course, Doc. We always support our own," said Mr. De Leon.

"Ambitious, no?" said Gittel.

"Doc, I'd like to know, where's the money coming from for all that?" asked Fisher.

"It's not fairy castles in the sky. I've got a financial plan to back everything. Liqueurs anyone? We have an assortment. Let me see," he said, reviewing the labels as he opened the liquor cabinet doors. "Palmer's left us fully stocked." Sweet alcohol—small consolation—oily, he thought wryly as he poured.

"Anyone got a room for Saul till the housing out at the power station is done? There isn't a room to let in the whole of Umzimtuti," said Rivkah.

"Isaac!" said Sunny turning to him, "why don't you take him in? Lucky Strike is not too far from the power station. You will be doing him such a favor. It's only temporary."

"Maybe not," said Isaac, "house, not too fancy."

"It's very comfortable, nothing to apologize about," Sunny reassured him.

"Leighfield Siding long way away."

There was a lull in the room. Mavourneen circulated the cakes again.

At the mention of her husband, Miriam emerged from the deep folds of the chair. She made her way to the trolley.

Saul stepped forward, "May I," he said, "help you?"

She wished she looked better—looked her best. She reached out with the empty coffee cup. She took in Saul's dashing good looks: tall to match her height, a full head of black hair parted perfectly down the middle. His mustache above his playful mouth was neatly groomed. She noticed his finely manicured nails, the quick pulled back to reveal perfect half-moons, as he took her cup. She lifted her haunted face to him. He smiled. "How would you like it?" he asked softly.

"Hot and strong," she said, "is what I need."

"At your service."

She smiled for the first time in a long time. "I'll talk to my husband," she said, "about taking you in. It'll be a pleasure."

Jud said, "Doc, you should get a new car, man."

"With you around do you think I can afford it?" he answered wryly. "But in any case I love my army Ford. It's still good for plenty of miles. I don't want to do anything ostentatious, it targets one."

"Well Doc, everyone can see you coming. The Army Ford in camouflage green is anything but," said the dandy Fisher.

"But it doesn't engender envy now does it?"

Ever the fears lurking, thought Mavourneen.

Rivkah said, "Doc, your wife, should I tell you, Mavourneen, she wonderful behind the wheel. Why not a car for her? A family such as yours—why you must."

"Don't go putting ideas into her head. I don't want her gallivanting around."

Mavourneen glanced at him. Rivkah was a true friend: the seed had been planted and she hadn't had to say a word. Everyone seemed to have thoroughly enjoyed him or herself. All the work had been worth it. The hour was late and she and Sunny soon saw everyone out the door.

They turned in and surveyed the sitting room. Mavourneen said, "I let Leonard go once coffee was made. I'll just take a moment to put the leftover cakes away."

Wheeling the trolley into the kitchen he followed and said, "I'll get a bottle of tonic water to wash things down."

The refrigerator was crammed with the savories of the evening, all those expensive meats, cheeses, bowls of this and that to fill the canapés and sandwiches. She watched him rummage behind them all and extract a bottle. An awkward silence followed which was broken by the fizz as he pried up the cap and it overflowed. He wiped the outside with a tea towel before he filled a glass and walked out.

It was past midnight when she finally checked on the children and turned the house lights out. It had been a long day but she was satisfied she had done her best. Suddenly the life within her stirred and she plopped down on her bed. She'd earned a good night's sleep. She lifted the turned down sheet to slip in. A letter lay on her pillow. She put it on the bedside table: it could wait 'till morning.

In the morning Sunny dressed silently and without a word he brought the tea tray to Mavourneen and laid it on her lap. He did not stay to join her. He left for Sick Parade without a word.

The tea was hot and strong. She needed it as she sipped and read:

Dear Mavourneen,

I came as soon as I could get away.

This excess you indulged in this evening was quite unacceptable. It is quite out of keeping with my values. This sort of drawing attention to yourself with material excess is why Jews are resented, envied and ultimately hated. As a Goy you have adapted very quickly to what you perceive as my material worth. I can assure you, you are mistaken. We cannot afford to waste. Modesty is what is called for, for financial as well as social reasons, given the times. Satisfaction of your desires shows little thought for our future.

You need to apologize to our guests for your excesses. Fortunately it is with our own and not the community at large. It is hoped you will learn from this.

You are demanding a new sewing machine and even a vacuum cleaner! My mother sews to this day on a treadle machine. She has never had the luxury of a vacuum cleaner. Refrain from fancy ideas.

You have a generous housekeeping allowance. Please see you stay within it.

As Ever,
Sunny.

CHAPTER FORTY-NINE

The Aftermath

The screen door slammed. Sunny pushed Bundu aside without so much as a pat and ignored Douglas on his return from Sick Parade. A black mood had descended upon him and his tuneless whistle haunted the house before he sat down silently to Sunday breakfast with Mavourneen's unopened response to his letter pressed under his side plate.

"It's a little early to start ringing everyone on a Sunday. I'll get on with the public apologies as soon as breakfast is over," Mavourneen said.

But he had not quite scraped the coral colored flesh of his paw paw segment down to the necrotic pock marked skin before those three short trills, pierced the air.

"Doctor," said Sophie Shapiro. "I want be first to ring. Tell you again, what *wunderful* evening we have last night. Your wife, she such a credit to you. Such a credit! A *wunderful* cook, a *wunderful* hostess. She so enthusiastic for WIZO. We so lucky have her one of us."

"Well, thank you. We look forward to hosting you all more often."

Sophie took the opportunity to gush on, "The men all agree to fifty percent! How did that happen, doctor?"

"A good cause calls for generosity. We appreciate your efforts for WIZO."

"Thank you."

"Who was that?" asked Mavourneen.

"Sophie. Thanking us for a *wunderful* evening."

With that he stuffed her note into his inside breast pocket. "I'm going to do hospital rounds. I shouldn't be too long," he said. "Then I have a few patients coming to the surgery around ten."

"It's Sunday. I thought we might patch things up and have a picnic with some of the leftovers with the children this afternoon," she called. "Spread the blanket on the bank of the river and relax at Umzimtuti Poort."

"I'd like to walk the gorge and see how feasible it really is to dam for a reliable water source for the town. I'll ring you later."

He bumped the fender of the car against the whitewashed stones in front of Casualty and sat cocooned as he read her note:

Dear Sunny,

Thank you for the report of my conduct. Perhaps you should make it a monthly one. Then I should know what to expect.

Thank you for your frankness re my awful party. Yes, there was too much food. None of it will be wasted. I don't think it entered anyone's head that I was trying to show off or be ostentatious. I have learned my lesson and will apologize for my vulgarity. You need never fear another such party.

I don't want another sewing machine in any hurry. I am quite prepared to save up out of housekeeping and buy it that way, eventually.

I DO NOT and never did want a vacuum cleaner. A salesman wrote inquiring that was all and I replied saying I was not interested.

Always your letters are written to me unbalanced in many ways and very cruel and illogical and ignorant. Because of that I try not to retaliate on first impulse.

Mavourneen

He folded the letter carefully. He still felt sick to his stomach from losing the game, and now he doubted himself after Sophie's phone call and Mavourneen's letter. The door to Casualty banged shut behind him. Here were people paying him seven shillings and six pence a visit to listen to their troubles and get his advice. He'd have to listen to a lot more troubles to make back the £50 never mind the lawyers fees and goodwill, and he had taken it all out on Mavourneen. She didn't deserve it.

Mavourneen meanwhile spent the morning fielding the calls from the party last night. Everyone effused over it: what a gracious home she had, comfortable and welcoming. Such a spread! She hadn't the heart to reveal her husband's misgivings. She accepted the compliments gracefully and asked if they would like some leftovers.

Rivkah suggested she take them over to the old age home. What a treat it would be for them all. She arranged to come over with her car on Monday.

Between calls, Mavourneen packed a picnic hamper. She filled the thermos with tea, packed a tin of meringues and wrapped slices of Dundee cake in greaseproof paper for dessert, milk and mashed-up guavas for Deborah.

Douglas, dressed in sturdy shoes, shorts and canvas sun hat, swung on the garden gate and waited patiently for his dad's return. But morning breeze gave way to afternoon shadows.

Mavourneen came out and said, "Douglas, let's get a few of your pals over and have a picnic at home. It looks as though your Dad's caught up. I'll see if Peter and Norman can come over to play. We'll go down to the bottom of the garden and have the picnic there. I know the fairies are waiting for us past the aloe garden in the shade of the frangipani. I'll read to you after we've eaten. It will be so much fun."

"I don't want to go down to the bottom of the garden. I want to go to the river with Dad." Douglas' blue eyes flashed angrily, his lips pouted. He passed a sweaty hand over his face and a dark stain smeared over his cheeks.

"Well he's not here. Caught up, as I said."

"I don't want my friends to come over. They're all playing with *their* Dads."

"No, really, most of them are milling around at the Club while their parents play tennis or billiards and drink at the bar. You don't want that do you? Let's put on a happy face and enjoy the garden. We didn't always have it you know. It's really rather special. Dad might even come home in time to build you a fire down there."

Suddenly memories of the happiest days of her childhood, camping with the Girl Guides, overwhelmed her. "On second thoughts," she said, "let's surprise him and get a fire going ourselves."

Before Douglas could protest she ran into the house and rummaged at the back of the pantry for her old knapsack, which contained the mementoes of those happy Guiding days. She'd hung onto the billy, the enamel mug and plate and the knife, fork and spoon set though the many moves after her marriage. She grabbed half a loaf of bread and wrapped a few eggs in newspaper. She threw in a tin of marshmallows she had made several weeks before. They'd be going stale—perfect for toasting. She dusted off and entrusted Douglas to carry her cast iron jaffle maker which he carried over his shoulder like a gun. They marched off on an expedition to the bottom of the garden.

She was sure Douglas would make a wonderful Boy Scout: this was Baden-Powell country after all. The Matopos was where he had learned his woodcraft skills from that American adventurer Burnham. The fire and woodsmoke kindled her desire to bring the movement to Umzimtuti. She would say nothing to Sunny but after the baby was born she would see to it: revive the pioneer spirit and confidence that mastery of the great outdoors would bring to boys and, most especially, to girls before they went boy-mad and the predictable writing was on the wall. She gave Deborah her bottle of milk. Then she lay back, her arms behind her head, and looked up through the feathery shade of the jacarandas as the late afternoon breeze stirred.

A scribbled note on the telephone table informed Sunny of the family's whereabouts. From the top of the kitchen steps curls of smoke guided him to the bottom of the garden. Bundu bounded up, barked and with tail held high led the way, glancing back every now and then to make sure his master was following. They passed the vegetable *hok*, a massive tangle of pumpkin vines with big trumpet shaped orange blossoms full of the promise of fruit. Mavourneen had given the turkeys to Avigail long ago. Sunny noticed the bantams, securely penned under the shade of the guava tree, were reproducing at an alarming rate. Bundu ruled the back yard now.

As the picnickers came into view Sunny was suddenly struck by the memory of his mother's efforts to give him and his sister Josie a happy time, packing a picnic basket for the day and two-tramming it to the Zoo or Zoo Lake from their home in the Southern Suburbs. She had had her hands full holding his hand on the one side and carrying the basket with the other and his older sister's arm linked through it so not to be lost in the crush of transfers. His father had never come along. He stayed home to await the afternoon issue of The Johannesburg Star: his joy. In some ways it had been a relief to be separated from his parents constant bickering. He remembered acutely that his sympathies had always been with his mother. She had scrimped on housekeeping expenses to save for his university education so it would never be in question. How he had let them down—disgraced them in the eyes of the tight-knit community—with his marriage outside the faith. They had worn black in mourning for a year.

He loved his beautiful wife so much, glorious in full blossom with the life within her. And yet Doris' visit—Mavourneen's best friend—had made him starkly aware that in every way she wasn't Jewish. He knew in his heart he could never change her. But was it too much to expect her to accept the everyday joys of motherhood and homemaking in this Shangri-La? He felt a pang of guilt at his habitual absence: was he after all a chip off the old block he loathed so much? He hardly knew his family. Mavourneen struggled to sit up as he joined her on the blanket, which only served to whet his guilt. He absorbed the cuddly wet kisses of his little daughter. He wished his love could be just as unconditional.

The family was having a whale of a time. He cast his conflicted thoughts aside to savor the earthy smells of burning wood suffused in their hair, their clothes smudged with charcoal, their fingers sticky with melted marshmallow. Douglas sat cross-legged on the ground beside the fire and waved his roasting stick at him, his mouth too full to talk. Bundu plonked back down beside Douglas, with his back legs splayed, panting in anticipation of another marshmallow. For a dog he definitely had an unusually sweet tooth. His tail swept the ground in a great arc. The billy was on the boil. Mavourneen poured Sunny a delicious cup of smoky tea and said, "Have you ever had a toasted egg sandwich?

"Your surprises never end."

"Let me show you how it's done."

"I'm game for anything. I'm sorry I've let you down again. But as usual you've covered for me. I do appreciate it," he said to Mavourneen as he kissed her and sat Deborah in his lap.

Mavourneen prepared the jaffle iron and Sunny tucked it into the embers.

While it cooked, Douglas offered him a blackened squishy marshmallow about to fall off the stick.

"Just the way I like them Douglas," he said. "Did you know charcoal is good for you? That's the best part."

"Bundu loves these," said Douglas retrieving his other stick poised above the embers, blowing on the marshmallow to cool it before he took it off the stick and offered it to Bundu on the flat of his sticky hand. Bundu's long tongue curled around it. He toyed with it in his mouth for some time like a hot potato, slobber dripping from his jaws before he swallowed it. Sunny was not sure if Bundu had finally reached his limit for sweet stuff: it was far too much sugar and air for anyone's good health.

"Douglas," he said, "Let's play hide and seek."

"Ah no," said Douglas. "You've probably got to go back to hospital or something. I got to help Mom put out the fire and carry the things."

Sunny winced.

Rivkah picked up Mavourneen with the hamper full of leftovers as planned on Monday afternoon. She hopped out of the driver's seat and made way for Mavourneen.

"Really I shouldn't," said Mavourneen. "I can't imagine when we'll be able to afford a second car. Sunny is still paying off Palmer's goodwill."

"Is the surgery always full? Soon, soon, plenty money for car. You ready. We surprise Sunny, yes."

"And so much money on Saturday on the poker."

"Jud want be mayor. Now Sunny running for council. They battle each other."

Mavourneen turned the key and the engine came to life.

Rivkah went on, "Yankel tell afterward Jud didn't behave like gentleman at the poker table. That why none of the men object when Sophie said WIZO take half the winnings."

Mavourneen pointed the car down the hill and then put the car into neutral. They coasted, gaining momentum as they descended to Main Street. She thrilled to the idea of carloads of Girl Guides camping in the bush. She just had to master parallel parking, then she'd be ready for the test.

A joyful time was had talking to the pioneer women, hungry more for company than food and what an abundance of both. There was no shortage of yarns about Umzimtuti when it was really wild. Mavourneen was entranced.

Over dinner that evening, Sunny asked Mavourneen politely how her day had gone.

"Well," she said, "wonderfully. Rivkah found a home for all the excess food. We went over without delay to deliver it."

"All that cheese and meat! To the old age home?"

"Why yes that's right. Made sure it didn't go to waste as you suggested."

"Your generosity to strangers is too much. Did you leave any of the smoked Edam for me?"

"No, no I didn't actually. We really have so much and you should have seen their faces. I plan to do it again soon with Rivkah."

He ate thoughtfully as he moved into the sitting room and turned on the BBC evening news:

...Military court sentenced Moshe Barazani to hang in Jerusalem for possession of a hand grenade.

"Hang in Jerusalem! They're letting go of India and it's going badly: so much bloodshed. Britain does not know how to bow out of Palestine gracefully either," said Sunny, as Mavourneen joined him with a tray of coffee.

"All the women were talking about the violence in Palestine on poker night: the floggings and murders on both sides," answered Mavourneen.

"Hanging a Jew in Jerusalem is going to create an uproar."

"The women have all sorts of views about Palestine but one thing they all agreed was backing you in the upcoming election. I'm sure you'll get a hundred percent turnout," she said encouragingly. "They offered to canvas for you—have some teas and invite the neighbors. Would you like that?"

"Mmm, no, actually the army Ford is a reminder, subconscious no doubt, that I volunteered for service."

"If only they knew the family furor over their cherished only son going off to war," she reminded him. "Yes, you more than proved your allegiance to King and Country. Still, it was generous of them to offer."

"For all the differences, hardliners or Anglophiles, Sephardic or Ashkenazi, you can count on their solidarity when the chips are down. But it's not about the past or about other places. It's about this *New Land, this New Life, this New Opportunity, this New Leadership, this New Industry, New Prosperity for all* after the ravages of war. How's that for a poster?" He shot Mavourneen a glance.

"A poster?"

"Well, yes. Just a thought," he said a trifle embarrassed. "You know the other candidates are doing it." Sunny knew he should value her opinion and her instincts because she was from the other camp after all: Anglican, loyal to The Royals, practical and down to earth, averse to intellectualizing. What was she really thinking?

"It's too wordy," she said. "Cut it down to *New Land, New Life, New Leadership*. All the same remember, the *Jews are not welcome here at the Lonsdale*. You were in your army uniform and it was impersonal then. This time you have so much invested personally and the hurt will be all the more searing. Promise me, no black moods if you lose."

"Everyone knows I'm a Jew, but it makes no difference. I'm a new Rhodesian with a contribution to make. I think everyone sees that, not only the Jewish community."

He was not a religious man, but he had been well-schooled in an Orthodox home, attended cheder faithfully as a boy and now despite his secular claims, suddenly the book of Joshua popped into his head, *Be strong and of good courage; be not afraid, neither be thou dismayed: for the Lord thy God is with thee whithersoever thou goest.*

He turned to the liquor cabinet and reached for the whisky and poured a sherry for Mavourneen. He settled into the comfort of the settee, lit up a cigarette and took a long deep draw. He was warm, inside and out, comfortable and confident again. She was as beautiful as ever despite the rigors of nursing, their controversial marriage, the rift with her family and now the demands and trials of two small children and another one so soon on the way. He swilled his glass and breathed in the fumes of liquor. Through the war her letters and her photograph had sustained him. But did she truly love him? Was she defying him giving away the Edam cheese or just true to her nature, which was generous to a fault? The subject was closed. He would not bring it up again.

CHAPTER FIFTY

The Smallest Municipality in the World

The open surgery door provided Sunny with plenty of facts and fiction about Umzimtuti's past and prospects. Councilors of any merit were hard to come by. Only one candidate had been nominated last year in this, the smallest municipality in the world, where nothing ever changed, including the apathy of the voters. The Town Clerk, Cameron Gordon Murray Paxton, had stepped out of the Town House to find a second nominee with less than an hour to the close of nominations. The streets were empty so he headed to Umzimtuti Hotel bar. With five minutes to spare he slapped Timmy Curtis on the back. "Timmy I have news for you. I hereby declare you an Umzimtuti councilor, elected unopposed."

Timmy, overwhelmed by the cheers of the patrons, was speechless. He wasn't much of a talker at the best of times. He was a good fitter and turner. When he arrived home with the ridiculous news, Lil, his normally happy wife, was worried.

But Timmy was not out of place at all as he took his seat at the inaugural meeting of the new council. Old Man Hardy had company. Angus Buchanan was delighted and fussed over him assured once more of automatic endorsement.

This year things would be different. The returning ex-servicemen and new immigrants were making their presence felt. The two retiring councilors seeking re-election, T.J. Llewellyn and Lucas Ramsay were joined by four aspirants, including Sunny. For the first time in Umzimtuti's history there was now municipal election excitement, canvassing, posters and even betting at the local bookie.

The odds favored the return of T.J. Llewellyn, the town's only chemist, a friendly Welshman whose only blemish was a peri-orbital spastic tic that was aggravated when he got upset and so he always avoided trouble. He was popular and president of the Sons of England Society.

Lucas Ramsay kept the books for the town council and was blessed by Buchanan. Sunny saw no threat in the other aspirants, but wasn't odds on for either vacancy. However, the open surgery door put him in touch with many voters. At the end of a consultation conversation often got around to the election.

Sophie Shapiro called Sunny at the surgery. "Doctor, you know we all behind you, but don't want us publicly canvas. *Ja!* But T.J. Llewellyn has poster *Vote Llewellyn Prescription for Progress* and Lucas Ramsay, *Ramsay will Always be Accountable.* What's yours?"

"*New Life, New Land, New Opportunity. Vote Sunny for a Bright Future.*"

"*Wunderful!* But, well, where to do I see it posted around town?"

"No, I haven't got around to making any posters yet."

"You must get your name out there. *Ja!* Time is short."

"I canvas at the surgery."

"*Ja! Ja!* But My God is everybody sick in this *dorf?*"

"True, but word gets around one way or another."

"We must do something for you. Mr. De Leon got printing press behind shop. We fire him up. Ream off bunch. Fast."

"You're very kind."

"Then, butchery boys tack posters everywhere. The others too, Wolfsons Bakery, why they must. The Fruitiers, Uziel's and of course Levine's Umzimtuti Hotel: very important. Then Rebecca, round all English stores, post those windows. We all support." She rushed on, "You in the council chamber: we must see to it. The girls form a committee. You approve, *Ja?*"

"Thank you. Please go ahead."

The posters were printed in record time. Government employees could not show political affiliation so no posters were tacked to the young jacaranda trees lining the driveway of the New Government Hospital but they were tacked to the silver oaks alongside the cemetery and down the length of Main Street and on all the pillars of the shops, from Fifth to First Street and east to west along the four avenues. The Cheetah Mine, though the lifeblood of the town, was outside of the municipal area, so mine workers were excluded from the vote. It was, indeed, the smallest municipality in the world.

Sophie was on the line, "You like?"

"What's that?"

"The posters. Could you miss?"

"Oh yes. Plastered everywhere. A thorough job. Your girls are champions— the patriotic red, white and blue a very good choice."

"*Ja!* Well, what you think? Your girls working hard for you?"

"I can't lose with all this support."

CHAPTER FIFTY-ONE

For or Against?

Mavourneen took down a half a dozen jars of guava jam to see how it would sell at the cake stall. The goodies were attractively arranged on a red, white and blue tablecloth. On the side were stacked red, white and blue flyers, with Sunny's ten-point platform itemized in big bold print. Besides the posters, Mr. De Leon had done a nice job with these too.

After the auction was over, Japie van Hoepen came over with the mealies she'd bid on. She had finally got Sunny to commit to a Sunday braai on the farm and they had all enjoyed themselves. Sunny had actually relaxed while *Ouma* fussed over him. Stephanus had taken Douglas in hand to explore the bush but she was too pregnant to ride—next time.

As Japie stacked the mealies neatly into her bicycle basket he said, "I bought a house in town—Third Street so we can sleep over now and then. We'll never forget how Doc saved *Ouma*, yes, saved her life with all that needle stuff in the spine. *Yirra jong*, I'm voting for him, man."

"We appreciate your support."

"Still trying to convince *Mevrou* and *Ouma*."

"What do they say?"

"They don't want this council stuff to take him away from doctoring. But I say we need a dam as well so we can make my irrigation scheme big. I know it in my heart, he'll be the one to get it for us."

"He'll manage both jobs."

"But I do still worry. You know you can always find someone to boss up the town, like Buchanan, but doctoring—saving a life—now that's a gift from God."

"I'm not a politician but the mayor's been in office too long—running things without getting any input from council. Sunny's got an ad out for a partner to lighten the medical load."

"Marie's right then, man, we'll get shoved off onto someone else."

"No, the patients will be better off with a partnership. It's too much for one man. He'll only take someone who's got credentials and experience...you have to be self-sufficient to manage here."

"Like farming, I suppose," he said. "Not everyone makes it, man. Things can be bitter sometimes. The weather's always against you: the bugs and the baboons, too." He wedged a few gem squash into the basket, courtesy of the farm. "*Ja nee*, after your baby's settled down, come again and ride horses. You'll always be welcome."

"We'd love to. Douglas will soon be old enough for lessons."

"You don't have to wait for that," he said. "Let me buy some of your guava jam. See if it's a patch on *Ouma's*."

"My pair of bantams have grown into a huge flock in the fowl run under the guava tree—that manure makes all the difference—still I'm sure it's no competition for *Ouma's* but it's for a good cause," said Mavourneen.

"*Ja,*" he said, "everyone needs a homeland."

CHAPTER FIFTY-TWO

Last Minute Canvassing

Sunny turned off the radio. "There's nothing on the deportation of immigrants in Palestine. Anyway, I don't think the public here takes much notice. I think I have a following from the practice. Let's hope so. I'd really like to get in."

"I know. You'd be so good for this town and really make something of it. Why don't you pop on down to the Umzimtuti Hotel and canvas? It's not too late. I'll wait up for you. It's Sunday tomorrow, let's have the kids pile into bed with us? Maybe you can read to Douglas over early morning tea. Can you remember when we last did that? He's so hungry for your attention."

"Yes, I know," but he made no commitment. "I'll see you later then."

There were lots of cars parked outside the Umzimtuti Hotel but the angel was on Sunny's shoulder. He slipped into the one available spot right in front of the white-columned entry. Jud was enthroned behind the big carved mahogany bar, working between the bottles and the till, making a handsome profit no doubt.

Sunny ordered a whisky and was much in demand. He moved easily from group to group. The farmers and ranchers were keen to get the Umzimtuti dammed. Water was short. The boreholes were deep and all too soon dry before the late spring rains came, year after year.

Everyone knew the richest seam of gold in the world was running out under the foundations of Umzimtuti's shops. The town needed to diversify if it was going to survive. How could it benefit from the Iron Works that Huggins would officially open next year? It would undoubtedly expand everyone's business. But more importantly, he explained, secondary industries would surely follow. Anticipation was the name of the game. Umzimtuti needed to be ready to vie for these when the opportunity came knocking or lose out to the bigger centers or even the town that would spring up around the Works themselves, as soon as the marshes were drained. The bar was abuzz with the excitement of dams, waterborne sewage, lights and pavements, a swimming bath and sports club for everyone not just the Cheetah mine employees. This doc had all the cures.

Nothing seemed impossible as liquor flowed freely in the blur of cigarette smoke. Sunny stood everyone to one last round before closing. "Here's to Umzimtuti! *New Land! New Life! New Opportunity!*"

"Hear, hear!"

CHAPTER FIFTY-THREE

A Plea

Sunny was dead to the world when the phone rang those damnable three short trills on the party line at one in the morning. He wanted to disembowel that thing: smash every one of those four hundred and thirty-three parts to pieces. Instantly he was alert. The other parties must be fed up sharing the line with him.

Sister Hoskins voice was shrill. "Doctor Rubenstein, we've got an obstructed labor that's come in sixty miles from the Jombe Native Reserve. The mother and fetus are in extremis."

"That's a case for the GMO."

"You've got to intercede."

"The GMO's the superintendent."

"Dr. Maxwell said give her a shot of morphia and don't ring again!"

"The GMO's in charge of the entire hospital including the Native wards. I've no authority there except at his invitation. I'm sorry but I can't just barge in."

"But you can save the mother and baby! I'll assist."

"It just isn't possible. I have to respect medical protocol. She's not my responsibility and I can't wrest a patient from a colleague. As I said, I can only step in at his invitation."

"They'll both be dead in the morning."

"The matron is the right person to support legitimate concerns of the nurses. It's very unfortunate, but there it is."

"How can you let bureaucracy stop you when two lives are at stake?"

"I'm terribly sorry." He didn't doubt Sister Alison Hoskins prognosis. She was such a competent and conscientious nurse. Even if they survived the night, Maxwell probably wouldn't be able to cope anyway. He should have been pensioned off long ago. He said again, "I'm sorry." Slowly he returned the receiver to the hook, but not before he heard the telltale click of someone on the party line listening in: news traveling faster than the speed of light. He simply must insist on a private line.

Mavourneen turned over in her bed and propped herself up on one elbow. "I heard," she said. "Long ago, you should've had it out with Matron over Maxwell's incompetency. This is the inevitable tragedy waiting to happen. You know Sister Hoskins is right of course."

He sat there with his feet over the side of his bed. He reached for his trousers slung over the white wicker chair, and got up to pull them up over his flannel pajamas. "You know how it is with the Natives, their delay in seeking help in the first place, which makes all the difference to prognosis. Compounding it is the terrible road—such a slow bumpy ride. If I intervene and she dies anyway, I'll be fully responsible, answerable to Matron and Maxwell. If they decide to take issue with my uninvited intervention—against his explicit instruction— butting in on their territory I could lose my hospital privileges at best, face a lawsuit. At worst, I could be struck off the roll."

"You're right," she said, getting out of bed and coming to his side. "Sister Hoskins having approached Maxwell, and he specifically prescribing and instructing, definitely excludes you. She's proved a fickle ally in the past: questioned your medical treatment of *Ouma* and surgical improvisation with Mrs. Biancardi. Going on her past history I wouldn't count on her to back you up in the event of a suit. Let this be a lesson. Promise me you won't let another day go by before you tackle Matron. It really is too bad it had to come to this."

"Either way, I can't win. How am I going to live with myself?"

"You can't be your brother's keeper. You've saved so many lives but this is not a life you can fight for. Come back to bed," she said, as she put her arms around him and hugged him tightly.

She was his rock and she was always right. He clung to her.

He was doing rounds in the European Hospital when Sister Hoskins advanced on him. She drummed her fists against his chest. "Murderer! Murderer!" reverberated hysterically through him and on down the corridor. "A mother and child have died because of...*You! You! You!* You beast!"

He turned away, and looked at his shoes, then he looked at her and said quietly, "I explained to you last night I can't simply ignore authority."

"You South African racist! If she had been European..."

Matron Griffin swung into the corridor. "Sister Hoskins! Please remove yourself from duty. Return to the nursing home at once, until you have regained your composure. I will deal with you later. Dr. Rubenstein, we can talk in my office. Please follow me."

Matron Griffin, a tyrant over the nurses, a force to be reckoned with by all who crossed her path, swept down the length of the corridor, her veil fluttering in the wind she created.

"Dr. Rubenstein," she said as she shut her office door and adjusted her spectacles, her brown eyes behind them dark with anger, "your familiarity with Sister Hoskins has led to this regrettable showdown in public. She's young, and full of idealism, a Sunshine girl looking for a husband in this unlikely place, no doubt. Your relationship needs to be reigned in."

"You assigned her to me to train on the Boyles apparatus which was closeted and I brought into use when I arrived. Our association has remained strictly professional. Your choice was a good one. She's an excellent nurse. I've sought her out when faced with difficult cases when I want strict and conscientious adherence to my instructions. We've worked well together. The GMO should have attended the mother and child last night and in all likelihood saved their lives. But as you well know, Dr. Maxwell doesn't seem to have the professional skills to cope with this sort of case anymore. As the matron it's your difficult task to mediate legitimate concerns of the nurses with senior management issues when they conflict with the professional responsibilities of the sisters."

"You have privileges in this hospital as a private doctor and this conversation will remain confidential. I'm fully aware of my responsibilities."

CHAPTER FIFTY-FOUR

An Unexpected Victory

Town Clerk Cameron Gordon Murray Paxton opened the Town House portal to make the official declaration of the council election results on Wednesday night two hours after the polling closed. There was no one in sight. Few no doubt expected a result so soon. Paxton turned to the mayor and candidates trooping out. "Read it oot mon, read it oot, the Municipal Act says so," ordered Mayor Angus Buchanan.

Paxton obeyed, "We have a ninety seven percent voter turnout with each voter having two votes, one for each of the available positions being contested. T.J. Llewellyn, the chemist, has topped the poll with seventy votes, yes, seventy. Archibald Rubenstein fills the second seat with sixty-seven."

Old Doc Maxwell's voice demanded, "What's all that? Repeat please."

Cameron Gordon Murray Paxton was nonplussed once more. The municipal act made no such provision.

"Och mon, Paxton, git on with it," ordered Angus Buchanan. By the end of the second reading a motley half dozen or so arrived to repeat Doc Maxwell's demand. Paxton, beside himself, yelled the announcement a third time to wild cheering and banter.

Sunny shook hands with all the candidates. Suddenly he recalled his successful debut into university politics to ban Verwoerd's pro-Nazi newspaper *Die Transvaler* in the SRC common room. But he'd paid a heavy price in lost friendships. Angus Buchanan had lost his right-hand man, Lucas Ramsey. They reluctantly shook his hand. He embraced Mavourneen gratefully. Then he shook hands with the happy patrons of the Umzimtuti Hotel bar who had drifted over and accepted their congratulations before he guided Mavourneen to the car, opened the big wide door of his army Ford and she eased in.

CHAPTER FIFTY-FIVE

A Setback at the Town House

"You've left your satchel behind," Sunny heard Mavourneen yell from the verandah just as he pulled out of the garage to attend his first council meeting. He pulled up to the garden gate and noticed she was still carrying the baby high as she waddled out and handed his satchel to him through the open window.

"Oh thanks," he said. "What would I do without you?"

She handed the satchel up and then reached in herself and briefly their lips touched. "You're always in such a hurry...Good luck."

He patted her hand clutching the open window, then he put the car into gear and said, "Don't worry, I'm prepared."

It had been a hectic day at the surgery, and as usual, just as he was leaving, there had been a child with a deep cut which needed stitching. It was uncanny, but there was always someone he could not turn away making him late for appointments.

Mavourneen, thoughtful and attentive as always, he noted, had laid out his clothes for him on his bed and he had changed quickly. He adjusted the knot of his tic into position in the rear view mirror as he rolled down the hill. He could still feel the thrill of her lips on his. How much she had enriched his life. In his youth mothers had always entrusted their daughters to him as a chaperone—never the suitor—and he had never imagined he would have a girl of his own—marry and have children. He wanted more than anything to make up for his deficiencies and come through for Mavourneen—deliver as her prince charming for once. He was confident her motion would pass. He would follow it up with his five-point plan to meet the needs of the town, to ready it for the Lime and Iron Works expansion and the secondary steel industries that were bound to follow lest they lose these to the larger neighboring centers that would vie for them too. Much was at stake. Time was of the essence. The dust from the unpaved road rose up to clog his nostrils and he sneezed when he braked momentarily at the stop sign. Turning into treeless Second Street and parking opposite the Town House, he mused *it doesn't look like much.*

He ran up the three red cement steps between the two modest columns. Cool inside, a sign *Accounts Payable* was suspended above a solid wooden counter behind which a woman was working late compiling demand notices. A few steps down and beyond was the Council Chamber behind wooden double doors. Council was about to begin the formalities without him. Five small tables were arranged in a semi-circle, each with its semi-circular leather padded chair, facing the Mayor's table on a rostrum with the Town Clerk beside him and just below, the Committee Clerk with notepad and typewriter at the ready. Quickly he placed his satchel on the vacant table, cleared his throat, nodded to the Mayor and sat down.

He glanced at the heavy wood-framed oil of the pioneer Frank Buckland on the wall beside him. He'd finagled to get this little appendage to the mine incorporated into a town to satisfy his ambition to become Umzimtuti's first mayor. He filled the frame from top to bottom with his unruly shock of white curly hair and equally undisciplined beard. His handlebar mustache cut right across the canvas. In Umzimtuti's folklore he'd grown up tough as a transport rider before the advent of rail. He'd bought up all the land around Umzimtuti and sired thirteen children. He was getting to know all the equally fecund family but they didn't have the unscrupulous acumen of their father: they depended on the land they had inherited. The council would have to buy some of that land back if it ever wanted to expand. The colorful oil outshone the black and white photograph of the upright King on the opposing wall.

Sunny opened his satchel and took out his papers.

The first business of the meeting was to elect the mayor. Since it was impossible to unseat Buchanan at this juncture, Sunny went along with the rest of the councilors, electing Buchanan unanimously to his seventh term.

Like everything else he did, Sunny had briefed himself thoroughly on Council proceedings. His list of six resolutions had been submitted for tabling on the agenda the week before.

On cue he stood up and with one hand in his trouser pocket, as was his wont, he said, "Mr. Mayor, fellow councilors, I'd like first of all to call on council to accept the State Lotteries Allocation Committee offer of funds to build a swimming bath, confirm council's acceptance of responsibility to maintain it and refer the General Purpose Committee to review the plans and drawings accepted by the State Lotteries and call for tenders."

"Do we have a seconder for the motion?" asked the Town Clerk Cameron Gordon Murray Paxton.

There was silence.

Sunny was surprised. He looked at Jud Levine who shifted awkwardly next to him. Then he looked around at Old Man Johnny Hardy the undertaker, slumped into the curve of the chair, mouth closed over his new dentures: he would disappoint him too. Annoyingly, Timmy Curtis was smiling but remained silent. He looked sympathetically at T.J. Llewellyn whose left eye ticked back and forth in agitation, but he did not utter a word.

The silence dragged on.

"Is there a seconder for the motion?" repeated Paxton.

Support from any of the councilors would have suggested that their conduct of affairs had been wanting when Mavourneen herself had presented it and he—young, aggressive and, worst of all, new was showing them up. Sunny looked again at Jud Levine.

Mavourneen had told him Jud resented his shouldering his financial burden to gracefully bring to an end his vindictive pursuit of O'Connor—a beaten man. But the aftermath of the poker game was so upsetting that they didn't discuss it and he had put it out of his mind.

"No seconder?" queried Paxton again.

"The motion falls away then," smirked Buchanan, as the gavel fell. "No further discussion."

He'd been so sure of himself. He dispensed decisive advice all day long in his consulting room, which he expected to be followed and it was. Suddenly, he realized he should have persuaded these councilmen, one by one, beforehand. Carefully he read out the first motion of his five-point plan for Umzimtuti.

Again there was no seconder.

How naive he had been to think the dictatorial mayor and the rubber stamp council wouldn't continue just because he had arrived on the scene. Every one of them was going to stonewall him. Why? His motions were so sound. Wouldn't they be open to reason and logic if only they would hear him out? The need was urgent.

Slowly, and emphatically he introduced the second motion.

Again there was no seconder.

He could not contain his anger. He felt the hair on the back of his neck rise. He reached up with his hand and smoothed his fine mop of hair straight back. Was this to be a repeat of the bitter SRC 'varsity politics over limiting irresponsible free speech and seeing to the ban of Verwoerd's inflammatory newspaper?

He presented his third motion through gritted teeth. With its rejection, it occurred to him that when he'd bailed Jud out he should have made it conditional on reciprocal support—then the O'Connor affair wouldn't have been an act of charity but an even deal. Jud resented the charity. At the time it seemed Jud had nothing of value to offer, but surely a friend if ever in need was implied? Jud's unreasonable bid up of the poker game was vindictive—all the men had witnessed it. Not one of them had come to Jud's defense when Sophie proposed upping the charitable contribution from the winnings. Would Jud ever learn that relationships were more important than money? How could he betray him like this? It was a sad disappointment.

He was calm and dignified as he went through the motions of presenting his fourth proposal. Speaking earnestly and enunciating carefully he put across his total conviction that this was the right thing to do.

There was no seconder.

Mavourneen was always intuitively right about people and she had warned him about Jud. She had encouraged him to run down to the Umzimtuti Hotel bar to canvas last minute. It had probably made all the difference in this closely contested election. But he had completely overlooked the need to lobby the councilors and get them on board with his agenda as well. Naively, he'd expected all the councilors to size up the motions on their merits. Surely, at least, the intelligent chemist T.J. Lewellyn could understand his reason and logic. What on earth was Buchanan's power over all of them?

He had erred in not including Jud in his campaign on his very own turf at his bar and made him a party to it, putting him firmly on side in public. He was spiting him now. It was incredible he'd rather keep Buchanan as an ignorant tyrant than support a progressive program that he himself could contribute to.

He was confident as he presented his fifth motion. He knew it would be rejected. He had only himself to blame. They were all ordinary men with limited vision but the fact was he'd have to work with them in the future.

Mayor Angus Buchanan rose and in his broad Scottish brogue and schoolmasterly tone said, "Councilors, as a rule, are wise and humble enough to sit it oot for six months, learning what municipal affairs and procedures are all aboot, before presuming to tell the council what to do. I suggest you do the same. Apparently your colleagues agree with me."

Reason gave way to rankle again as Sunny stood up and retorted belligerently, "Mr. Mayor, I am fully aware of council procedures. The town urgently needs to develop to take advantage of the opportunities that may soon pass us by. There is no procedural requirement that a new councilor do nothing for six months."

Miss Ida Hutchinson's tight bun bobbed at the back of her head. She had been the Committee Clerk since Umzimtuti had become incorporated as 'the smallest municipality in the world'. In all her years of service no one had ever talked back to the mayor. Her hand flew over the page as she took down the minutes in shorthand: every word would be on record.

"Councilor Rubenstein, if a motion fails it may not be tabled again for six months," said Mayor Buchanan, triumphant but riled.

Sunny calmed down, "I am fully aware of how the Council operates," he said. "I've studied the Municipal Act and the Council's rules of procedure. My ideas are fully formulated about what Umzimtuti needs and its citizens want. A six-month delay to have them debated is not in Umzimtuti's interest. I can assure you I will not be silenced. It's a pity that none of you have seen fit to view the motions on their merits. You have no idea how important the time issue is. That six-month delay might be critical in giving the other towns the head start to take advantage of the opportunities that will present *only once* stemming from the Works. The sacrifice you are making for the sake of a petty putdown is a tragedy."

But Sunny knew that the six-month waiting period could be circumvented by way of a committee recommendation. He would get on all four committees of the Council without delay. He would not be able to chair a committee as a newcomer but a breakthrough was sure to present. He would bide his time and cultivate his colleagues.

In the immediate, Mavourneen would be understanding and comforting which would make his defeat all the more searing. In medicine and surgery he seemed infallible but in his own personal relationships and most of all his marriage, where it mattered most to him, he acknowledged, he had made major misjudgments and it had cost him plenty.

But for now, the meeting was behind closed double doors and convention was broken again, as the clerk at *Accounts Payable* peered round and ventured apologetically, "I'm afraid there's an urgent call for the Doctor. Dr. Rubenstein. Colenso: I'm afraid they're very insistent..."

Good grief, the relentless call to duty, no place was sacred—for Colenso? He had never heard of them. He really needed a partner.

CHAPTER FIFTY-SIX

The Sin of Omission

This call—this interruption—annoyed Sunny, but at least it spared him the awkwardness of the customary notorious council meeting nightcap at the Umzimtuti Hotel bar.

Cocooned in the car, he turned the corner and sped uphill. The humiliation of the council meeting receded in the rear-view mirror and thoughts veered to Mavourneen. He had been utterly wrong on every count regarding the poker night they had hosted. She had put on a wonderful spread—attested to by all those present. He felt the compliments to be genuine. She had done it on a budget that had been imposed on her by his own misjudgments and making it worse, though her family had never had to worry about money, in contrast to his mother she was not a kvetch. How could he make it up to her?

He'd never had a pet as a child. He was surprised how fond he was of Bundu—his affection so unconditional and wholehearted. Douglas' rejection at the picnic weighed heavily on him. He was a wretched husband and father: he should never have had a child—and a third was almost here. He was spiraling into a black mood. It would take weeks to overcome.

He wrenched himself from his personal thoughts to focus on the job at hand. Colenso? The case didn't sound serious: two children with temperatures of 100.4°F. Probably just out from England: one of those nervous types. Darkness had already fallen. The headlights exposed the naked town, its shops shut and devoid of life. He was determined to light it. As he headed back uphill to the Cheetah, he thought, I bet this family's the type who didn't want to take time out from their routine and come in for a consultation. But come the night, especially Friday night with the weekend ahead, then fears loomed much larger than in the light of day—and the problem couldn't wait till Monday morning. The feathery arch of jacarandas in the beam of the car lights seemed ghoulish as they brushed the roof of the car.

He was getting tougher with time and necessity. But with children it wasn't so easy. Wolseley was picking up a sizable practice with the upper set, thrilled by his tales of exploits in India and penchant for name-dropping. He hoped his medical expertise was better than his limited repertoire logged in the surgical roster. Whatever his short-comings, it was a relief to have him as an alternative for the hard-to-please or nuisance patient. Remarkably, they'd successfully avoided direct contact and confrontation, despite the smallness of the community.

He swung into the Colenso's driveway, put his stethoscope around his neck, picked up the small black auriscope case and the red-and-white striped lunch tin. A nightjar called 'Good Lord deliver us'. Mrs. Colenso had the door open before he reached it. "Doctor!" she said, "You must do something!"

"What's the trouble?" he said testily as she led him into the children's bedroom.

"Well, last Friday they both had sore throats and I took them to see Dr. Wolseley at his surgery. He was very busy, you understand. He didn't have time to examine them. He was leaving shortly for the race-track in Salisbury. He gave me a prescription for penicillin. And honestly, Doctor, I've been giving it to them three times a day just like he said, but they haven't got any better. It's not ten days yet, but...I can't rouse either one of them now."

The room was dark. He put on the light. In the instant glare of the naked bulb he could see they were desperately ill.

He dropped quickly to the girl. She was comatose. Her pulse weak and slow, the skin blue. He tilted her head back, opened her mouth, pressed the tongue down with the back of a teaspoon. There was the telltale thick gray adherent membrane of diphtheria that could not be pulled away without tearing the mucosa behind it. He moved quickly to the younger boy. He too was in an advanced toxic state, also with extensive characteristic pharyngeal diphtheritic membrane.

"Mrs. Colenso, your children have diphtheria. It's very far advanced I'm afraid, with toxic myocarditis...that is, the muscle of the heart's inflamed." My God, he thought, they're on the brink of cardiac arrest! He was working fast. He opened the lunch tin and quickly extracted two vials of Digitalis, filled the syringes, injected each child.

"But their temperature is only 100.4°F," said the frightened mother.

"Diphtheria doesn't cause a high fever I'm sorry to say."

She stood there looking at her children.

"I don't have any anti-diphtheria serum with me. The injections will give them circulatory support."

He turned to her husband, standing behind her now. "Please carry the children out to my car and I'll drive you to the hospital, there is nothing more we can do here."

Night made the long drive to the New Government Hospital seem longer. My God, it would be sudden death if the vagus nerve was infected! *Even though I walk through the valley of death, I will fear no evil.* I'm going to need the angel on my shoulder.

He battled on into the small hours of the night, working first with one child and then the other.

It was too late.

The doors swung closed behind him. Rage consumed him. Routine! So much of general practice was repetitive and mundane in sophisticated European society. Wolseley that pompous *pukka sahib* had, no doubt, enjoyed too much non-military diversion in India. His primary concern was monetary: dependent on patient volume, turnover and target income; the issue of boring routine was subsumed in enjoying affluence and status. From the very moment he and Eckhart had set eyes on him at the Hospital Christmas Tea they had sensed it and moved to shut him out.

So much was trivial, symptomatic or normal, merely calling for reassurance. A sore throat was so common it only required a routine antibiotic. 'No need to look', was Cecil Wolseley's reasoning, no doubt.

To look only took a few seconds! The omission was unforgivable.

How could he possibly excuse the profession's dereliction of duty to the parents? My God! Didn't he have enough on his plate already! Should he be his brother's keeper also? The angel on his shoulder? He hadn't sensed it all day.

CHAPTER FIFTY-SEVEN

Preparations for the Royal Visit

Lady Catherine Kennedy felt overwhelmed: she hardly had time to find out who she was herself when she was inundated with telephone calls, letters, and personal calls from people who either thought they should have been invited to one or other Royal function or knew someone who should. She sent an SOS to Frances to come down from Edgar's Witchwood Farm and lend the hand extorted from her while on the rocks of the Matopos.

Frances was only too happy to oblige. Having tackled Edgar's perennial chaos in primitive conditions, she looked forward to being in a civilized house again with a few decent bits of furniture. She got stuck in at Government House with the domestic preparations. All the chairs were fitted with new slipcovers. The spruce up would continue relentlessly all the way to flower arrangements to be placed in every room at the last minute. She even managed to slip in an invitation to the ball for Edgar's young private secretary, Vincent, much to his delight.

Back at the farm briefly, over the Easter weekend, she took out three boys from the Kingsley Fairbridge Memorial College. On a whim, she decided to take them with her to Salisbury to see the lights. Vincent did the honors escorting them around in a taxi. At Edgar's suburban house, having just waved the boys off at the station on the night train back to Umtali, there was a phone call. Amongst the chaos, she had flung out an invitation to put up Sumajeri, Edgar's trusty farm cookboy. He had arrived at the Police Station and was asking for him.

Delighted, Edgar and Frances immediately popped down in the car. Along with Sumajeri had come two farmboys. He was very pleased that his *Inkósi* had come to fetch him himself and asked if their luggage could be picked up at the station as well. 'Luggage' included Mrs. Sumajeri and two more boys. It took two journeys to get them all home, with great exclamations of *Mai-weh Mai-weh* as Edgar pointed out all the lights, including a crown and the letters G.R. lit up over his own office door. No sooner home, they all asked for late passes to go back into town to have another look.

Indeed, Salisbury had outdone itself: the night scene was magical. The paths of Cecil Square outlined a giant Union Jack in lights. Huge illuminated crowns were strung across the main streets. All the shop windows were lit. Necklaces of lights were strung between the lamplights on the side streets. Larger than life size photos of The King and Queen and the two Princesses were floodlit on street corners.

Edgar parked the car outside so all the Natives could doss down in the garage. Fortunately they got on very well with the houseboys who came from the same district and were therefore, more-or-less, brothers.

The house itself was packed with Edgar's lion hunting friends, the Harrow family, as well as two Umtali schoolgirls that Frances had invited. Edgar's mad farm neighbor from the Vumba, George Hatcher, parked in the driveway with a caravan full of family. Everyone would have to scramble around each other to wash and dress for one splendid occasion after another in the small three bedroomed, one bathroomed house, spilling out into Edgar's sleeping-porch office.

The big day of the Royal's arrival was finally at hand. The wide jacaranda lined streets with equally generous pavements and a very small population made Salisbury a city for people watching. People of every color, size and shape waved a Union Jack as they lined the road all the way from the airport to Government House. The pomp and ceremony was about to begin.

CHAPTER FIFTY-EIGHT

Capital Affairs

The King's first duty was to open the Parliamentary Session. The House of Assembly was not a large building, well designed, plain but dignified. The gallery filled with the wives of the invited dignitaries. Meg Buchanan was proud and comfortable in the custom suit she wore with a hat to match and white gloves, though rumor had it some had spent as much as one hundred and fifty guineas on their outfits. There was time to look everyone over, more than twice.

In the anteroom Angus Buchanan donned the crimson ermine lined robe of Umzimtuti's mayoral office. Tall, he thought he looked well as he adjusted the heavy, ornate mayoral gold chain donated by the Cheetah Mine.

At last, the Sergeant-at-Arms knocked at the door and ushered in the mayors and judges in their robes, and finally the Members of Parliament and Ministers.

Each time someone was ushered in, everyone sprang to their feet, thinking it must be The King. In exasperation, the leader of the opposition's wife, Mrs. Smit, in the front row, turned round to no one in particular and hissed, "I don't see why we should stand for a mayor."

Mrs. Buchanan leaned forward and responded, "On a day like this one should be prepared to stand for anybody."

The old *vrou* slid back against the bench shaking her head and waggling her jewels.

Finally, there was a major stir. Everyone rose. The Princesses took their places on the balcony above the Southern Rhodesian Coat of Arms. They looked beautiful in cool, off-the-shoulder, short-sleeved frocks with long white gloves.

On the floor below, the Sergeant-at-Arms led the procession of representatives of the Armed Forces, followed by the Personal Staff of His Majesty, the Private Secretaries.

A hush and calm filled the small House after all the restlessness when, at last, The King's Most Excellent Majesty accompanied by Her Majesty The Queen, made a grand entry just as Mrs. Buchanan's program promised. The King in tropical white dress complete with sash and medals and Queen, with her tiara glittering and her white gown and long white train flowing behind her, mounted three shallow steps to the dais and turned to face the House before they took their seats on the thrones, flanked by the framed photographs of The King's coronation. They more than filled everyone's expectations.

After the ceremony, the Buchanans lunched in The House courtyard at the invitation of the Speaker, Sir Allan and Lady Welsh. With bonnie Meg at his side, his joy, but not a spring chicken any longer, he took a moment to reflect on how well he and Meg had done. He'd left Scotland as a lad, found his way to Umzimtuti, had been taken on as a hand at the Pegasus Garage and now he owned it. He had firm control of Umzimtuti. This was his seventh term. Lucas Ramsey's ouster by the little doctor niggled in the back of his mind—but he had put him firmly in his place. He was grateful to him for the decisive intervention with Claire's appendectomy. She would make her debut here as a fine young lady: sixteen—already—at the Young Peoples Governor's Ball. He had tossed aside his Scottish frugality for it: custom gowns had been commissioned for Meg and Claire. Even amongst the Royals he was confident Claire would sparkle and shine with her lovely golden curls dancing on her shoulders. He had bought Meg a five-string necklace of pearls and Claire a single strand as a last minute surprise and finishing touch to their outfits.

He gazed at the main table with the Royals, Huggins, Ministers and high officials. Whitehead, with his high-minded beliefs expounded from under the bar table all those years ago, had most certainly arrived. He was slated, the program said, to be invested by The King with an OBE later in the week.

He took a sip of port and tucked into the parfait in the tall glass with a long silver spoon. Now was the time to savor just desserts.

CHAPTER FIFTY-NINE

The Governor's Ball

Besides dressing herself, Frances helped Vincent with his first effort in evening clothes, borrowed from his father, and ended up dressing Edgar too, which was even more necessary. They still managed to get to the sweeping driveway of Government House before the Royals made their glittering entry.

The Queen and Princesses were all wearing tiaras and their gowns glittered too. The Queen stole the show by wearing the honeycomb-patterned Boucheron Tiara left to her by her mother and the Kent Demi-Parure of huge hexagonal amethysts surrounded by diamond sunrays. The pendant broach was pinned to the Order of the Garter ribbon and star across the shoulder of her white and gold lace crinoline.

The Princesses danced lots of reels which they obviously enjoyed, much to the delight of everyone, especially Claire who was quite a dancer herself. It gave her a chance to take in the Princesses' finery close up: diamonds and emeralds around Princess Elizabeth's long slender neck and Princess Margaret's oyster slipper satin crinoline embroidered with crystals spreading out from her eighteen inch waist. The same age as her, Claire was bewitched. Princess Margaret's eyes were a vivid blue in a perfect oval face—flawless without a single pimple or teenage blemish. She was a fairytale princess, in every sense, in the flesh.

But then, the fiddle orchestra, which besides fiddles included cellos, basses and accordions, along with percussion, woodwinds, piano and even a harp, wanted to show off their wide repertoire and struck up with a rather difficult reel, and the dance floor thinned.

Claire and her father were in their element. Buchanan was bursting with pride. His footwork was remarkable as he made the intricate patterns with perfect timing to the fast paced music. Princess Elizabeth did rather well whilst Princess Margaret obviously hadn't a clue and soon left the floor and flounced over to the orchestra. The music stopped. She displaced the pianist. She took her time, dramatically positioning herself at the bench of the grand piano before she began to belt out:

"Anything you can do, I can do better!
I can do anything better than you!
Anything you can be, I can be greater.
Sooner or later, I'm greater than you.
No, you're not.
Yes, I am
No you're not.
Yes, I am.
No, you're not.
Yes, I am. Yes I am!"

She was Ethel Merman and Ray Middleton all in one. The whole ballroom was entranced. It was such an unexpected turn of events. Everyone clapped. Brava! Brava! The princess bowed.

The orchestra struck up with a waltz and The King and The Queen took to the floor.

While they danced, a pouty Princess Margaret sought out The King's equerry, the tall and handsome Spitfire hero. He whispered to her and she smiled up at him, smoothed his lapel and murmured in his ear. A steward offered Champagne. The equerry asked for Roses lime juice for her. She was only sixteen.

When the waltz was over The King was breathless and The Queen steered him off the dance floor. Princess Margaret handed her glass to the equerry and went back to the piano and sang *Almost Like Being in Love*:

"What a day this has been!
What a rare mood I'm in!
Why, it's almost like being in love

There's a smile on my face
For the whole human race
Why it's almost like being in love

All the music of life seems to be

Like a bell that is ringing for me
And from the way that I feel
When the bell starts to peal
I would swear I was falling
It's almost like being in love."

The King looked on admiringly. Elizabeth was his pride, but Margaret, though she could be devilish at times, was his joy. When she finished singing, he promptly disappeared.

Frances was rather amused that this was putting a kibosh on Lady Catherine's agonizingly carefully laid out list of chosen few—although she was one of them herself— to be formally presented to the Monarchy by the ADC under strictly rehearsed Royal protocol.

The Queen was avoiding direction in quite the opposite way—strolling about and talking to anyone she found herself beside. Frances chortled as she saw Edgar's lion hunting friend Bess Harrow's son, Willie, engaged with The Queen. He couldn't have been a less worthy or more appreciative subject! What on earth were they talking about? Frances couldn't resist moving in closer to eavesdrop, when she was cut off, rather rudely, by a man dressed, she guessed, in tails and patent leather shoes for the first time in his life. He barged in without hesitation and said to The Queen, "Do you know, Your Majesty, us Afrikaner farmers have travelled nearly a hundred miles to see The King and your daughters."

The Queen turned her head and the diamonds in her tiara caught the light from a crystal chandelier and glinted. She said crisply, "And you can go and tell them that my husband and I, together with our daughters, have travelled six thousand miles to see them." With that she moved on easily with her warm smile and welcoming hand. Frances had to admire the way The Queen so easily won everyone else's heart.

Frances turned back to view the dance floor. The lovely young dancer in the exquisite ball gown was certainly making a splash again, with, presumably, her father. Who were they? Frances fingered her heirloom choker and ran a hand over her lacy sleeve as she turned her gaze again to Princess Margaret still standing on the sidelines fully engaged with the equerry: she really should perform her royal duties. She'd have to ask Lady Catherine about all this later in a post-mortem of the evening. She herself had looked forward to meeting The King, but he didn't appear again all evening: she consoled herself she would have other opportunities.

Edgar and Frances had been brought up in diplomatic circles from Belgrade to Berlin so they looked forward to a further two days of celebration in Salisbury that included Edgar's Investiture. He sat next to Princess Margaret at the intimate dinner party afterwards and they got on famously together despite his shyness with women. Then over the port he had quite a long talk with The King who had served in the Navy as a turret officer aboard the Collingwood in the Battle of Jutland in the First World War. He was a great admirer of Whitehead's grandfather who had invented the torpedo.

Edgar felt he had enjoyed more than his fair share of Royal attention and after dinner started backing into the second row of the crowd around The Queen but she said, "No, no! Come out of that second row and talk to me properly: Lady Catherine's told me all about you."

The governess! He talked about the farm.

"Rhodesia's won a special place in our hearts," the Queen said. "We'll be sure to tour again—and I'll look forward then to a visit to your farm. I shan't forget."

"Oh, no!" he said, alarmed at the thought, "it's hardly worthy of Royalty."

"We'll schedule it for a private 'day of rest'."

If only she knew the ramshackle state of his beloved Witchwood. It was only fit for bachelors—and always would be. He consoled himself—another visit was unlikely—and in any case she wouldn't remember the exchange.

CHAPTER SIXTY

Is the Town Ready for the Tea?

Mayor Buchanan had sacrificed the last day of celebrations in Salisbury to make sure every detail had been attended to for the upcoming Royal Tea and Retreat.

The small Umzimtuti Station had been whitewashed and the Dutch gable hung with wide scallops of red, white and blue bunting. Its two white columns were also wrapped in red, white and blue. The red cement verandah was polished to a mirror finish and the single wooden bench marked *Europeans Only*, freshly painted. The tree trunks lining the small parking lot were freshly whitewashed. Untamed bundu lay on the other side of the railway lines.

Six white sanitary pails of erect sword ferns, donated by Rosalind Doolittle, were set in the front. Hundreds of little Union Jacks supplied by Feldmans were on hand in the stationmaster's office.

The Railway Park on the left, usually unkempt, had been mowed and the jacaranda tree trunks whitewashed along with the summerhouse which had been re-thatched and re-floored and was now bedecked with bunting and flags.

Union Jacks showed in every Main Street shop window. Everyone breathed a sigh of relief. Mayor Buchanan was satisfied Umzimtuti was ready for The White Train's whistle stop for The Royal Tea before they proceeded on to Broderick Anderson's masterpiece, Sycamore Bend, in the Elazar's convertible Cadillac.

However, British liaison suddenly made it very clear that the Royals simply would not, under any circumstances, be seen in an American car, especially one in *Burbank Green*.

An emergency council meeting was held. Buchanan explained, "Aye, this toon's in a fine pickle, it is. My Pegasus Garage only sells Fords as ye know and Hazelrigg's Garage sells mostly Bedford trucks. But they do have a new Vauxhall in the showroom, the first import since the war."

"It's got to be something grand," said T.J. Llewellyn. "A Vauxhall won't do at all—though very nice I'll grant you."

"What about getting something from Gwelo?" said Johnny Hardy.

"Support Gwelo!" admonished Buchanan.

"We'll have to put our pride aside," tempered Timmy Curtis. "This's Royalty we's talking about, man."

"There's T & T Cars but they carry Studebaker which is American," said Jud, thinking out loud. "They've got a natty little Triumph Roadster in their showroom I've been looking at for me and my missus—too small. They have the newest Vanguard though."

"Vanguard. That's it!" said T.J., his spastic tic winking, "It's named after the world's fastest battleship that The Royals just sailed out on. That ought to do it."

"You're the one with all the smart ideas," said Buchanan sarcastically, turning to Sunny. "What do you say?"

"I can't imagine why," said Sunny irritably, "the Royals can't muck in with the rest of us. After all, they're supposed to be honoring the colonies' support in the war. This point seems to have been forgotten in all the fanfare."

"Got a resolution I can endorse then?"

"Yes of course."

"Let's have it, mon," baited Buchanan.

"The practical and cost effective choice is my old Army Ford in camouflage green: true recognition of the Empire's war contribution. You can loan me one of your Fords for the day."

"You're joking mon."

"No, I can't be without transportation."

"Well now," said T.J., "we've all heard the new Governor's a stickler for protocol. We have to keep up standards."

"The fact is, without the Empire, Britain would not have survived," said Sunny.

Buchanan ignored him. "Aye, you right, mon. Salisbury's done it right. Me and my wife, we saw it all, we did."

"The Rhodesians were famous for their disregard for protocol in the army but always came up trumps," said Sunny, obviously enjoying himself.

"We've got to find a solution," said Buchanan.

"Maybe we could suggest it. The King might like it," ventured Timmy.

"British prestige must always be supported," said T.J., winking furiously.

"It's a false pride. Britain's dead broke," declared Sunny conclusively.

"We've no alternative but to get a Rolls Royce down from Salisbury," said T.J. anxiously.

"We can't afford it," said Buchanan.

"You need the Rolls," Jud said emphatically. "I'm pulling out all the stops for The Royal Tea."

Mavourneen said, "Sunny, you know our Army Ford would never do. We love pomp and ceremony. Whenever else are we going to see a Rolls Royce on Umzimtuti's Main Street? Everyone except you and the Elazars are happy."

"Mr. Elazar has spent so much time polishing I'm surprised the *Burbank Green* hasn't worn off."

"You were right, there was lots of petty jealousy over the chauffeuring, so it's all happened for the best. All the same, I know he's so disappointed. I'll send him a jar of guava jam to cheer him up."

"I don't think it's going to be much of a consolation. I do hope they'll at least include him at the summerhouse Royal Tea."

"I'm not so sure," she said. "After all, the chauffeur is not exactly a dignitary, in normal circumstances, even if everyone thinks he's the richest man in town, and not *everyone* can be included. You know how they're sticklers for class."

"Well, we hardly fit in, but we've been invited."

Mayor Buchanan could not believe his ears, "I very much regret," said the voice at the other end of the line, "but as everyone knows, the war took a huge toll on The King's health. He's always been, well, delicate, and he has a heart condition. I'm afraid the excursion to Sycamore Bend is going to have to be scrapped."

"Scrapped! What do ye mean? Broderick Anderson has built a Royal Retreat, the moost luxurious game hide in all the world."

"I know, it's quite lovely. I did inspect it myself."

"Aye! Aye! All the wee details sorted oot."

"I'm sure."

"All the animals can be seen from the bedroom windows."

"Please understand, The King's not up to it. The Royal Tea is still scheduled for 3.47pm. All in order?"

"Aye! Aye! All in order."

The phone clicked. Angus could hear the other party line receivers going down too before the line went completely dead. News traveling faster than the speed of light, with any luck he wouldn't have to break the news to Broderick himself.

But he and Meg would still have their day as The White Train made a whistle stop of necessity while the Garratt took on water and the Royals took on tea.

CHAPTER SIXTY-ONE

A Watering Stop

There were exceptions, but everyone was expected to turn up at Umzimtuti Station for the Royal Visit. Even though it was Thursday, the shops shut. The farmers and their families travelled in from miles around. Small-workers from the hundreds of scattered gold claims in the vast surrounding district stilled their shafts, gave their boys the day off, and motored in.

The men put bush jackets, long shorts and long socks aside for suits and ties. Feldmans had run out of ladies white gloves but a special order arrived just in time. Ladies wore hats, gloves, high heels and stockings too if they could afford them. Huge excitement filled the crowd as they descended on the station and jostled for position as the women gave each other a critical once over. But everyone was in a generous mood and compliments abounded.

The BSAP unit stood to attention on the edge of the platform in starched khaki uniform and gleaming brasses. Mayor Buchanan and Town Clerk Cameron Gordon Murray Paxton were gowned in full regalia and flanked by the councilors in smart three-piece suits waiting to receive the Royal party. Ex-servicemen from the Great War wore their campaign medals, which they normally took out only on Poppy Day. Pat O'Connor always organized it, but he was nowhere to be seen.

Rhodesia's major role in the British Commonwealth's massive Air Training Scheme was represented by Rodney Caulfield from the Chancer Mine. Like the other ex-servicemen, he was not one to talk about his war effort. His wife standing behind the cordon would join him at The Tea afterwards.

Behind them the native commissioners from the surrounding districts, themselves representatives of the crown, stood aloof and unknown to most of the people on the platform. Beside them their native chiefs wearing jackets and ties held their ceremonial knobkerries and displayed the Southern Rhodesian Coat of Arms on their pith helmets and on the brass crescent-shaped insignia around their necks.

Buchanan had a proprietary air and gave the councilors to understand he was fully up with protocol, having mixed with all the panjandrums a great deal. Mrs. Buchanan stood out in a beautiful coat and skirt ensemble with butter-soft crocodile skin shoes and matching handbag. The coat was gently flared over her hips and as she moved the afternoon sun highlighted its soft sheen. Her hat, cocked at just the right angle, with a wide brim and a jaunty feather, shaded five strings of pearls.

Umzimtuti's two pioneer women stood with a representative of the Red Cross. A kilted Caledonian stood beside Old Doc Hamilton Cuthbert Howard Maxwell, Grand Master of the Freemasons. In his element, he looked very grand indeed: his gray mustache neatly trimmed, his full head of gray hair covered by his black two cornered hat with ostrich feather, black bow tie, dress coat with heavily embroidered cuffs, and hanging from his tartan collar was a medal which hung down to his full dress apron. A black cape was slung over one shoulder. The headmaster of the Cheetah Mine Native School and the Native Anglican Priest stood ready to be presented to The King alongside the Mine Manager, Mr. Doolittle and his wife.

Behind the cordons hung with Union Jacks the nursery school children fidgeted in front with their teacher and two helpers ready to whisk away any child who let the side down. Behind them stood Umzimtuti School boys in khaki shorts and shirts, sweltering beneath their maroon blazers, shaded by the brims of their felt hats, showing their blue and maroon school colors in their ties, belts and head bands. They stood in rows of course with the older and taller boys behind whispering derisory comments about what The King would think about particular small boys in front.

Beside them stood the girls in tunics, their ties neatly knotted between the white yokes of their blouses, wide-brimmed felt hats and blazers with pocket badges embroidered with the head of a cheetah and the school motto *non sibi, sed omnibus*. Avoiding the eyes of their mothers, they took ganders at the ladies standing with the men behind the matching cordon that flanked the station entrance.

Mrs. Caulfield was transfixed when she saw the Mayoress. She was wearing the outfit she had commissioned Mrs. Kalderon to make for her sister's wedding! It was haute couture all right, far superior to the suit she had bought at Barbours in Salisbury. She turned away and came face to face with Dot, the petite wife of ex-garage mechanic, short squat Bertie Carlisle, now the town foreman. She was wearing an identical acid green suit in size 2. How could Barbours have done this to her! At such a price! She curtly acknowledged Dot and Bertie and moved away from her front row spot behind the cordon. She hoped Dot had not been invited to The Tea.

The men, uncomfortable with formality, were reminded of being on the parade ground in the war as they waited in the heat of the shadeless platform. In the back rows, toddlers in smocked dresses or rompers and wide brimmed sunbonnets tied under their chins were hoisted on their fathers' shoulders for a clear view.

On the far side of the schoolchildren, ambulatory patients were seated on chairs and others were in wheelchairs. Only a skeleton hospital staff had stayed behind while most of the nursing sisters, veiled and starched, stood behind the patients. Native nursing aides stood with hands behind their backs in white-bibbed aprons with their heads swaddled in white *doeks*.

Everyone jostled in their segregated groups for a prominent spot to see and be seen. Perched above the crowd in the shady boughs of the jacarandas were the uninvited Natives who had the best and only shady view.

Everyone heard the rumble of a train beyond the freshly painted corrugated iron distance board at the approach to Umzimtuti Station, elevation 4003 feet, Latitude 20.1°S. They strained to catch the very first glimpse of The White Train and began to wave and cheer. A black Garratt appeared in the glare of afternoon sunshine but it was pulling ordinary gold and brown Rhodesia Railways coaches. The engine driver waved as it sailed right on through the station and continued on past the end of the platform to stop way beyond the water tower.

No one was quite sure what to do.

The BSAP officers held their positions at attention.

Mr. Buchanan's crimson cape billowed as he strode along the platform and jumped off the end onto the hard packed earth. The Town Clerk in his black cape followed. His tightly coiled ceremonial white wig with its two little knotted tails came unstuck.

Some of the men started chuckling. Wives said "Shhhh."

Just then they all heard a second train approach from the North, with a triumphant one long, one short, one long whistle blast from a royal blue Garratt with gold Rhodesian insignia below the engine's headlamp. The White Train was on schedule: three forty-seven, just the time for tea. A murmur went through the crowd, "that was just the pilot train."

Fifteen freshly painted ivory-white coaches trailed behind the royal blue glossy engine as the pistons steamed and it slid to a smooth stop, aligning the three air-conditioned coaches of the Royal party with the assembled people.

Hurriedly Mr. Buchanan retraced his steps, the shine of his patent leather shoes slightly dusted, as he climbed back onto the platform. The Town Clerk, close on his heels, adjusted his wig. A BSAP sergeant strode two paces to open the marked carriage door and stood to attention. He saluted as an elderly man in a gray suit: George VI, by the Grace of God, of Great Britain, Ireland and the British Dominions beyond the Seas King, Defender of the Faith, Emperor of India, appeared in the doorway, raised his fedora and paused. Everyone cheered.

Behind, Queen Elizabeth, everybody's favorite, was as lovely in person as the picture on those Black Magic chocolate boxes everywhere in town promised. She moved so easily in a softly flowing chiffon frock as she waved and descended the carriage steps in peep-toe sling back shoes. Her matronly figure and round smiling face beneath a hat with so much dash put everyone at their ease. Princess Elizabeth followed close behind in a silk sunflower-print shirtwaister, white hat black-trimmed with a large oval shaped brim with silk flowers tucked under it, covering her right ear. Princess Margaret, in solid pastel, wore an elliptical brimmed hat also with silk flowers tucked under the crown. This must be the new fashion in hats Mrs. Doolittle decided as The King's equerry and the ladies-in-waiting brought up the rear. She needed that annual trip to Harrods and Selfridges in London to keep abreast of the times.

Cheers reached a crescendo and flags became a blur as the ladies-in-waiting unfurled parasols and the procession got underway. Mayor Buchanan proceeded with all the appropriate formal presentations to The King on the platform as scheduled while Queen Elizabeth walked up to the cordon. She paused to stretch out a hand to a small school child in the front row and then reached out to a man three rows behind, pinched the cheek of a baby held out for her and greeted people at random before the procession turned to enter the portal of the Station.

Mayor Buchanan introduced Mr. Caulfield to The King. With a neck bow he responded, "Your Royal Highness." Lifting his head he recognized the equerry behind The King was none other than his RAF chum

Captain Peter Townsend!

Suddenly the crowd heard the thud of African drums. Bare feet stamped as a group of warriors from the Jombe Native Reserve, in traditional dress, rushed in from the town side. Drums pounded, feet stamped, thighs shook, headdresses waved, animal tail skirts whirled, eyes glared, heads snapped this way and that, whistles double tooted, bent legs double stamped. They rushed up to the Royal party, shields held close against their naked breasts, knobkerries thrust above their ostrich feather headdresses. They sank back, retreating with shields held low, accompanied by a deep-throated chorus, which was offset by a falsetto solo voice. Then the drums burst forth and the whirling dancing resumed as ankle and wrist ornaments of white cattle tails entwined with bells jangled as they made another rush toward the procession. Sweat glistened on their black bodies in the heat as they advanced and receded in waves.

Abruptly, at a signal from the Native Commissioner for Jombe, they drew their shields to their chests. Knobkerries thrust forward, they lunged in a final advance to within inches of the Royals. They did not flinch. All drums stilled in a heartbeat: into the void a falsetto's exclamation pierced the air.

The King raised his hand in salute.

"*Abiz! Abiz!*" was their deep-throated response. Then, they all bowed deeply before turning to run silently to the far end of the Railway Park to gather under the jacaranda trees.

The crowd had not expected this jolly good show put on by the NC. It was all too short. They cheered and clapped and the Natives in the trees whistled and shouted.

"That was a wonderful welcome," said The King, turning to the Mayor. "We are enjoying the train. It's amazing to think that not fifty years ago only foot paths crisscrossed this vast emptiness."

Buchanan bowed. "Aye, I'm happy to report we have made 2000 miles o' strip roads that costed four hundred pounds per mile, Your Majesty."

"Your school motto *not for ourselves, but for all* is so in keeping with the spirit of dedication to which we must all commit to make our Commonwealth even grander than it is today," said Princess Elizabeth.

"Aye, in the span of a man's life, we have set an example to the world hereabouts, Your Royal Highness," replied Mayor Buchanan. "As yea kin see, to quote Mr. Rhodes *Sae much to do sae little done.*

Slowly, civilization will overcome savagery. They cannot co-exist, Ma'am."

The Jombe dancers had settled down on their haunches and began to chat animatedly while they tucked into big hunks of bread spread thickly with melon and ginger jam and sipped sweet milky tea from enamel mugs, provided by the Native Commissioner's Office. The bus would return them the long sixty miles to the Jombe Native Reserve. A couple of Native policemen lounged nearby.

The Princess said, as she eyed them, "We do see hope looms ahead here with many opportunities, but challenges too."

"Aye Ma'am. Never a truer word said. One and a half million of them: one million one hundred thousand still in the Reserves and Native Areas. *Werk* is what they need. Plenty of *werk*. Aye, we'll have our very own Lime and Iron Works right here. Coal-fired power station too. Light the dark yea might say, Ma'am."

"We must all go forward together with faith and courage," said the Princess.

"Aye!" he said, "Although we have freed the world, Empire has much civilizing *werk* ahead, Ma'am."

"Yes, our ancient Commonwealth, going forward will be more free, more prosperous, more happy and a more powerful influence for good in the world—than ever before," said the Princess.

Standing behind, Fred Doolittle, wearing his Great War medals on his lapel, gave Rosalind a knowing look. More Prosperous? More powerful? Why, England was flat broke and giving up India, her jewel in the crown, in just a few months. His brother Teddy, high in the ranks of the elite core of ICS would be redundant, pensioned off before his term was up. But this was not the place or time to dwell on the fate of Empire. They were all here to celebrate it.

The Royal party was now promenading to the summerhouse in the Railway Park. Caulfield didn't have time to seek out his wife from the milling crowd. He wanted desperately to make contact with Townsend, wished they could forgo all the formalities and make off, just the two of them, to Umzimtuti's Hotel bar across the street. How could he wrench him from the Royal party? Townsend had married suddenly during the war, he remembered, children too. All the same, perhaps he could put an end to his money troubles by offering him a share in the Chancer? Surely the endless Royal protocol must seem dull after their war exploits, although Peter's position was a great honor. How could he corner him? Sound him out?

Bitumen moats protected the poles of the summerhouse from white ants and more of Mrs. Doolittle's handsome sanitary pails of sword ferns stood sentry at each corner. Tables with starched white table-cloths and chairs were set up in the shade of the jacarandas around the summerhouse for the honored guests. Cynthia's florist had delivered bowls of powder blue clusters of plumbago, Mr. Rhodes' favorite flow-er, punctuated by licks of flame lilies and dotted with red roses to link the colony to the mother country. An embroidered gossamer tea shower weighed down with bead work to keep the flies off was re-moved from the main table as the Royal Party entered the summerhouse, revealing a silver tea service and silver trays filled with petite savories and sweets.

The staff had worked through the night under the direction of Jud Levine on preliminaries for the savories, which were assembled last minute. Various salami and polony were supplied by Shapiro's butch-ery for an assortment of canapés as well as top quality meat for sausage rolls served warm, made with the very best flaky pastry from Wolfson's bakery. Cheddar fingers and devils on horseback made their appearance too. Koos Cronje had supplied the freshest leaf lettuce, ba-by carrots and bright red radishes for garnish of the savory trays as well as the cucumbers and fresh watercress for dainty sandwiches. On the side, a tray of samosas and mini curried kebabs donated by the In-dian community made a colorful plate.

Rumor had it that Queen Elizabeth had a penchant for pink. Deco-rated pink *petits fours*, powder pink meringue fingers and pink coconut macaroons were displayed along with miniature cream puffs, lemon curd tartlets and chocolate ginger nuggets commissioned from Wolfsons Bakery. Circulated by the immaculately turned out waiters, too, were small trays of Turkish delights and crystalized ginger, anoth-er reported favorite of Queen Elizabeth's supplied by De Leon's Dainty Fruitiers.

Baskets of hot scones along with guava jelly and bowls of clotted cream were delivered last minute.

Mrs. Doolittle circled the summerhouse critically. She had to acknowledge Jud Levine had done well. Who would have thought that little Jew could move in from the trading store and cater to The King, no less, in such grand style?

What outshone everything was the magnificent cake commissioned from the still massively overweight Mrs. Parker. An Imperial State Crown was encrusted with ruby, emerald and sapphire jellied sweets studded with silver balls. She had not quite been able to fit three thousand gems on it to make it entirely authentic, but it did include center front the Second Star of Africa she'd cut from a huge clear sugar crystal. There was a flaw here and there but nobody would notice. The crown nestled in a 'pillow' of fruitcake encased in marzipan and entombed in Royal icing, too. It was fit for royalty everyone agreed, and there was enough for every one of Umzimtuti's residents to have a piece.

The Queen only managed to sip half a cup of tea as she spread herself amongst the guests. The King stood with one pink meringue in hand fully engaged with Dr. Maxwell who was giving him a history of the Freemasons in Umzimtuti and explaining how the Society had been a source of inspiration to him in difficult times.

"I'm glad," said The King, "we admire you pioneers of Empire and all the challenges you face. Don't be afraid of making a mistake. Do the best you can but do not fear death." Crumbles of pink meringue settled into the green grass.

Dr. Maxwell swallowed a hot samosa whole. "Thank you," he said. "I'm feeling my age and of late I have struggled but I shall move forward to greater efforts with your encouragement and the support of the Society." They exchanged the Masonic grip before The King's attention was diverted and Dr. Maxwell went in search of a soothing cup of tea.

Princess Elizabeth ate half a scone as she circulated. Princess Margaret nibbled on one dainty cucumber and watercress sandwich as she chatted animatedly to Townsend. Caulfield did not know how to interject and rushed in with a neck bow, "Your Royal Highness."

Townsend exclaimed, "Tally-ho! If it isn't the Chancer, Rodney Caulfield! Still in one piece?"

"You know I'd never let the Jerries' shoot my big toe off."

"You're just jealous of a very honorable war wound. I got seconded to Buckingham Palace. What are you doing here?"

"I had to come back. The Chancer's only thirty miles from here, solid vein underground, virgin bundu topside. You could tally some grand wall trophies here, not just pheasants and foxes. Now that we saved the world, life is wide open with possibilities: free in friendly blue skies in my Tiger Moth. No rain or fog."

"Simply splendid country."

"I'd love to take you up. Any chance?"

"I can't. You know the Retreat's canceled, such a pity. We'll be pulling out in just a few minutes."

"Let's not lose touch."

"I'll talk to Rosemary...a holiday with the children, perhaps? Make it up to them—rather neglected I'm afraid."

"Better yet, come out and partner me."

The cake was being ceremoniously cut, but it was time for the Royals to reboard The White Train.

The crowd behind the platform cordon had stood firm to send The Royals on their way with great cheers and flag waving. Everyone felt reassured that within their hum-drum lives a splendid tradition endured. With a triumphant one long, one short, one long whistle blast, the royal blue Garratt, pulling its fifteen white coaches behind it, pulled out.

CHAPTER SIXTY-TWO

New Joy

Mavournecn had hoped her heavy framed, full-length prints of The King and Queen, which hung in the dining room, would come to life before her eyes but that was not to be.

Sunny helped her into the car. Her labor had begun. The going was slow, negotiating through the throngs of people wending their way down the hill to the Railway Station to welcome the Royals.

Mavourneen panted while a strong contraction gripped her as they crossed the railway line and sped on to the hospital. "I do so wish the baby could have waited just one more day. We're going to miss it all."

"What could be more exciting than bringing our own baby into the world?" said Sunny. "I can't say I'm sorry to miss all the congestion at the station and the pomp and ceremony. The only thing I'll miss seeing is Old Doc Maxwell all togged up as Grand Poobah."

"Everybody loves a uniform," she said, "don't make light of it. He's high up in the Sons of England Society and a Grand Master in the Freemasons."

"Sometimes he asks me to join his lodge while we scrub up, which always leads to debate in theatre."

"A uniform's all about service. Princess Elizabeth was a driver and mechanic in the ATS," said Mavourneen as she braced herself for another contraction. "She's such a role model. I just wanted the chance to have a little of their Royal magic rub off on us all."

"The King's touch, what?"

After the contraction passed and her breathing returned to normal she went on, "Everybody loves a fantasy. The Princesses staged pantomimes every Christmas throughout the war in aid of The Queen's Wool Fund. It spurred me on to master four-needle knitting for the troops on my long lonely nights on night duty. You're still wearing those socks."

"That womanizing, partying, gambling King Edward abdicating for that twice-divorced American socialite makes my point perfectly:

they're mere mortals just like everyone else." He swung up the jacaranda lined avenue to the all but deserted hospital. He had it all to himself. Emotionalism would not get in the way of clinical detachment. He was confident. Matron Griffin had supplied him with everything on the list he had compiled almost a year and a half ago: the hospital was fully equipped.

He scrubbed, gowned and gloved alongside Sister Fegan. The tissues had been badly torn in the delivery of the past two babies. It was sad how much damage to the trusting public the profession could do in the wrong hands. The two previous obstetricians had certainly not served Mavourneen well—but of course she never complained. He cut decisively down through the scar tissue to accommodate the large head that presented and eased the shoulders out. Their baby boy emerged with a lusty cry as whistles, one long, one short, one long, faintly penetrated the delivery room. The Royals had arrived. Distant cheers carried over the air.

Sister Fegan exclaimed, "Good work. I say, I bet he's over nine pounds." Sunny placed the baby between the cleft of Mavourneen's breasts and she embraced her baby while the blood drained from the placenta for a few minutes before Sunny would clamp the umbilical cord and sever it. He turned his attention to suture the episiotomy.

Satisfied, Sunny stripped off his gown and gloves. Although the head was so large, at least he had avoided exacerbating the damages of the past. An ice pack would reduce the swelling. He'd pop in, himself, frequently to manage the pain with narcotics if necessary. He'd won over Sister Fegan and he knew she'd conscientiously administer the frequent sitz baths he ordered and in between keep the incision clean and dry to avoid infection. He would see that Mavourneen's care could not be matched anywhere else in the world.

It was thrilling, as always, to bring another child into the world. But this—his very own! A son!

Sister Fegan lifted the baby from Mavourneen's chest for a thorough rub down and head-to-toe exam. "*Baie geluk!* Congratulations!" she said turning back to Mavourneen, "He's perfect in every way." Then she gently lowered the baby onto the scale before lifting him out and cocooning him tightly in a blanket. She passed him back to Sunny who slipped him between the sheets and into the cradle of Mavourneen's arms.

"You've given him a great start," Sunny said.

She caressed the baby's damp dark silken hair—just like Sunny's. Whistles, one long, one short, one long, signaling the departure of the Royals were overridden by Sunny crooning softly in her ear:

"I've got a pocketful of sunshine
And a heart full of song
And when I see you, all I want to do
Is pass it along, pass it along."

Sister Fegan smiled and slipped a cap over the baby's big head as he straightened up:

"Aaaaaaahhhhhhhhh
Raise your voice and sing
I was born without a silver spoon
But in my heart I have a golden tune...

The world can't go wrong
While you've got a pocketful of sunshine
And a heart full of song!"

"He's the splitting image of you," Mavourneen said. "What would you like to call him?"

"I've been so busy," he said, "I haven't given it much thought."

"What about George? After the King."

"I've high hopes for him, but he's not going to be king. In any case The King's got a speech impediment. Sickly. We want him to be articulate and strong."

"Peter?" she said, "you know, from *Peter Pan and Wendy.*"

"We want him to grow up, don't we? Take his place in the world. Make his mark, not fly off to *Neverland*. We've got a real, new land wide open with possibilities."

"It's a bit early," she said, "who knows where he'll find his niche," she said.

"Well," he said, taking the crying baby into his arms and rocking him he said, "he's got nothing to complain about. We're not going to dictate to him the way my parents did me. He'll be his own man."

CHAPTER SIXTY-THREE

A Whale of a Treat

As the last of the white coaches disappeared from view, the Mayor turned to the platform officials and said, "Aye! Mr. Levine has done the toon proud with a mighty royal spread. Let's give him three cheers."

The crowd was taken aback, but responded, "Hip hip hooray! Hip Hip Hooray!"

As they all turned reluctantly to depart Mayor Buchanan shouted, "The toon deserves a party. Aye, there's enough food for everyone if everyone is on their best behavior, as they should be, for a Royal Tea. Everybody follow me!"

With a flourish, his crimson and ermine cape billowing once more, he led the way back to the Railway Park. The women talked about how elegant the Mayoress looked alongside The Queen and the Princesses. Where had she got that smashing outfit? The men talked about the progress Umzimtuti had made since the turn of the century.

There were no streetlights: the party came to an abrupt end as the sun went down and darkness quickly descended.

Jud and Leah Levine stood arm in arm on the steps of the summerhouse in the darkness taking in the nighttime sounds: the rustle of the jacaranda leaves and snap of the strings of Union Jacks amongst the bunting in the evening breeze, the odd explosion of jacaranda pods broadcasting their seed while crickets rasped and a nightjar called, 'The Good Lord has delivered us'.

The kitchen staff carrying hurricane lamps from the hotel lit up the remains of the Royal Tea: there was work to be done. Leah moved to supervise the cleanup. Jud returned to the hotel to take up his place behind the bar counter and serve the men who had gravitated there to continue the festivities hard and fast.

When Jud finally closed the bar door, Leah appeared with hot cups of Ovaltine and they plopped wearily down at a bar table.

Jud said, leaning back and stretching his legs out in front of him,

"Besides our wedding and the birth of our children, I have to say this has given me my greatest joy—we have really made people happy."

"You don't have to tell me, I know," she said, "it's all gone royally over budget, but I agree it's been worth more than money can buy—not just to us, but to everyone."

"It's a shame O'Connor's laid up in the hospital again and missed all the going's on. You know how he enjoys pomp and ceremony having served with General Allenby in the Great War."

"No official pictures in *The Cleft Stick* then I suppose?" said Leah.

"It's not necessary. It's imprinted in everyone's hearts."

"I saved a wedge of Mrs. Parker's masterpiece. Why don't you take it to O'Connor and make your peace with him?"

"The good Doctor's got him on a diet."

"Royalty comes around only once in a lifetime."

"Making peace won't be a piece of cake," said Jud.

"Let's not go overboard," said Leah, pushing the melting marshmallow down into her mug and stirring.

"He's going to die and it's going to be on our conscience, like Sunny said."

"They have only themselves to blame."

"We can afford to bail him out. I could offer to buy the newspaper and leave him as editor."

"Sunny's bail out didn't help him for long."

"That was pure and simple charity." Jud took a long sip of his warm comforting Ovaltine. "We'd be silent partners."

She sat forward. "He's a big oaf to manage."

"I know how to fix his auctioneering business as well."

"What! And risk losing a bid on a bunch of carrots again?" She drained the last of her Ovaltine and flounced out.

CHAPTER SIXTY-FOUR

A Long Night

With the Royal festivities over, the almost deserted hospital returned to normal as staff and ambulatory patients drifted back. Sunny made rounds. He was regaled with Royal experiences and in return spread the news of the arrival of the new addition to his family and accepted their congratulations.

Just as he was about to depart, a succession of patients, both European and Native, with serious surgical and obstetric emergencies, were admitted. Old Doc Maxwell was calling on him for assistance in the Native obstetric ward but seemed strangely elated and not at all apologetic or offhand.

Sunny crossed back and forth between hospitals, to look after his own cases and briefly check on Maxwell and his backlog of casualty cases—a broken arm to be plastered, a cut lip to be sutured, as well as a mushroom poisoning to purge. He checked on Mavourneen and the baby and waited in the doctors' duty-room for another labor to progress.

He felt cold with fatigue. He wasn't anywhere near as fit as he'd been in the Army. He began his muscle toning exercises: popped his biceps, pulsed his triceps, rippled his pectorals, stretched the hamstrings. He moved a chair aside. Squats, sit ups, back bends and shoulder squeezes warmed him. Maxwell came and went but made no comment.

It was long past midnight when, finally, Sunny discarded gown and gloves for the last time and lit up a cigarette to suppress his hunger before he looked in once more on his wife tucked in and sound asleep and new son firmly wrapped and capped and sleeping too.

It had been a tumultuous day. Finally, the Casualty screen door banged behind him. About to hop into the car, suddenly Maxwell was at his side. "You can't go home yet. I have just admitted another obstetric emergency. I don't know exactly what has gone wrong but she is pretty dicky after the sixty miles bashing about in the old ambulance from Jombe."

Sunny was happy he could partly atone for the tragic case that had so upset Alison Hoskins.

They hurriedly scrubbed. The fetus lay immediately beneath the wall, obviously a ruptured uterus, the mother bled out and in severe shock. In the absence of ready blood, they would have to rely on electrolyte solutions: blood could come later. Surgery was Sunny's priority, but he said to Maxwell, "It's questionable she will survive the immediate ordeal."

Maxwell said, "I believe we can save her."

Sunny sighed. He'd be handicapped with Maxwell so stuck in the past, using ethyl chloride spray and ether on an open gauze mask, but once again, it would have to do. A total hysterectomy and ligature of the main uterine blood vessels in the process was the only hope. Speed was of the essence. With the decision made, the hair bristled at the back of his neck as a surge of adrenaline restored his metabolism and cast off his weariness. He felt the presence of the angel on his shoulder as he worked calmly with complete concentration: quick but methodical.

With a slash incision, the stillborn fetus and placenta popped out, the abdomen a blood bath diluted by the amniotic fluid. The rent in the womb extended in a ragged oblique sweep from the top to the bottom of the birth canal. He had never been faced with the challenge of such a complete rupture before which ruled out any attempt at repair. There was danger of hemorrhage resuming too, once the circulation was restored sufficiently for her to bleed again.

With the operation well under way Sunny realized that Maxwell was intensely devoted to monitoring the women so he could concentrate fully on the surgery and give Maxwell a running commentary to assist him in his judgement of the anesthesia from moment to moment.

Dawn was near when he and Maxwell sat down to restore their own fluid and calorie balance with a pot of hot tea and Marie biscuits in the duty room. Sunny was shaken by the experience, although accustomed to the severity of complications in Natives so often aggravated by inordinate delays. But he perceived that Maxwell, although also tired, was still strangely alert and confident.

"The King's Past Grand Master of the Freemasons, an honorary position especially created for him once he became King and had to resign as Grand Master. We had quite a chat," said Maxwell. "You know there's great power in uniforms, rituals, signs, symbols and gestures to bring out the best in people for the benefit of the community."

"I did my bit in the army—submitted to uniforms and all that brass and military discipline to keep the world free. But I believe in individual, free thought and independent action. But I tell you what—if the woman survives perhaps you should invite me to be inducted into The Lodge?" Sunny reached for a teaspoon and stirred his hot sweet tea.

Maxwell remained silent.

"We gave it our best shot. I must hand it to you Hamilton, you managed the old rag and bottle exceptionally well. But," Sunny went on, "she's so shocked and has lost so much blood I don't think she'll make it."

Maxwell said calmly, "Do not fear death." He put down his teacup. He pushed back his chair, rose, put his hand on Sunny's forearm, inclined his head and said, "I'm going to grab forty winks. Then I'll probably take a walk when the sun comes up."

Sunny drove home to take forty winks himself before the wail of the mine hooter signaled Sick Parade. After breakfast he rang the New European Hospital to check on Mavourneen and his new son. All was well.

He sped over the railway line, up Rhodes Highway and swung up the hospital avenue of whitewashed jacaranda saplings growing fast, like the country, he reflected. He walked briskly over to the Native Hospital. Maxwell was standing next to the bed of the woman from Jombe. He had kept vigil. He turned to meet Sunny's questioning eyes and smiled. He inclined his head to the patient.

She lived! Sunny picked up the woman's wrist, took her pulse and picked up the chart from its slot at the bottom of the bed. They discussed what to do. Maxwell wrote up the chart and replaced it. He put his hand on Sunny's shoulder, looked at him steadily for a moment and said, "I want you to teach me the new anesthetics."

Early morning dew still covered the green grass of the quadrangle from the maternity ward of the Native Hospital. Sunny cut across it and hastened up the whitewashed stone path to the European Hospital and entered the male ward.

Pat O'Connor had failed to win the Parliamentary by-election, though he made a remarkable medical recovery once Sunny had met his legal expenses, returning to Saturday auctioneering and newspaper editorializing. But then, the bank had come at him, pressing him to meet costs on his failed farming venture. There was the question of the mounting overheads on his small working which could not be deferred further. Bankruptcy loomed. Heart palpations returned. His medical condition was critical—again. Nancy was inebriated—again. Sunny had admitted them both, again, to hospital. He had done his best, but some people could not be helped, he thought resignedly, not for the first time, however much one tried.

He caught a glimpse of Jud Levine through a chink in the privacy curtain around Pat O'Connor's bed. He heard Jud say, "Why don't you let me see you through your business pressures and put your newspaper and auctioneering on a firm footing?"

He couldn't afford to get involved beyond the medical again. He silently backed away and the swing door closed quietly behind him. He was confident Pat would rally with a new bail-out—until the next financial crisis.

He strode into maternity to spend time with Mavourneen and his new son. Mavourneen, surrounded by the color and fragrance of congratulatory flowers of every sort, was brushing her hair a hundred times. The current refused to let it lie down: it had a life of its own. She put the brush down and sank back into the pillows. Gently, he pushed aside a strand on her forehead, and gave her a loving kiss before he stood back—she was so beautiful—and said, "I've decided we should call our baby Daniel."

"Daniel?" she said.

"We want him to grow up fearless in this brave new land."

"Yes, I agree, its wide open with so many possibilities."

"You've given him a first rate nine pound start. George Hyde-Clarendon's arriving on the 1.01 tonight. We can begin a normal family life now."

"It's something we know so little about."

"I'm my own man now. I've done it for you and the children."

"No," she said evenly, "you haven't done it all for me and the children. And now you're getting into politics."

"You started it—wanting a swimming bath for Umzimtuti instead of just a paddling pool at the bottom of the garden for the family. I picked up the gauntlet for you."

"That was noble but I want to fight my own battles," she said.

"I'm only trying to be your knight in shining armor."

"What we need is a husband and a father—even a master for Bundu—you haven't even got time for a pat on the back for him these days."

"Just give me one more chance." He took her hand as he crooned, just like Bing:

"Just one more chance
To prove it's you alone I care for
Each night I say a little prayer for
Just one more chance."

She crooned softly back:

"Just one more chance
Just one more chance"

He responded:

"I've learned the meaning of repentance
Now you're the jury at my trial
I know that I should serve my sentence
Still, I'm hoping all the while..."

She retracted her hand, pushed against the hard hospital bed and struggled to lift her shoulders high up on the pillows, pulled up the starched white sheet over her bed jacket. Her lovely blue-green eyes filled and tears stained the sheet.

He reached into his pocket and passed her a handkerchief and squeezed her free hand. After a while she said, "I'm sorry I can't be there to welcome Hyde-Clarendon. Remember to tell Leonard to make sandwiches before he knocks off. Cover them with a damp tea towel to keep them fresh."

"For you, I'll try to be the perfect host," he said. "I must run..." He cupped her face in his hands and kissed her again before he rose and said, "Oh, by the way, Lady Shirley's as good as her word. The equipment for the Cheetah Native Hospital has arrived at the station."

He turned and lifted the swaddled baby from the hospital cot, gave him a peck and then held him at arm's length and said to him, "Daniel, my boy! We're going to do a lot more than just a whitewash job on the jacarandas—and not just for ourselves, but for all."

AUTHOR'S NOTE

Diana Polisensky is a recluse living in a tree house on the edge of the Pacific. When colonialism was still respectable she was born into a medical family and grew up in a swimming pool in Africa. She crossed the Atlantic as a young woman and experienced life on all three American coasts, ending her career in genetic engineering behind the hedges at Rice University in the Lone Star State. *Whitewashed Jacarandas* marks the first installment in an epic saga chronicling the end of the colonial experience in Southern Rhodesia.

Maps, a glossary and discussion questions as well as an opportunity to comment on *Whitewashed Jacarandas* can be found on her web site: http://www.oncecalledhome.com

ACKNOWLEDGEMENTS

I am indebted first of all to my parents, Morris and Joan Hirsch. I lived a life of privileged neglect as they set an example giving of themselves wholeheartedly to town and country. The gift of their lives and then their memoirs, short stories, letters, 'bits and pieces' and photograph albums are the inspiration for this novel. Their spirit lives on in the hearts of many.

I am grateful too to my son Andrew Davis for suggesting, setting up and maintaining my weekly blog http://www.oncecalledhome.com for three and a half years, where I posted almost two hundred short stories. The response from so many of the Central and East African diaspora of full length unpublished and small press memoirs, short stories, vignettes, maps and photographs, books, articles, pamphlets and newspaper cuttings has been gratifying. Estranged families were reunited and lost friends re-connected. All have greatly enriched my work in one way or another. These contributors are acknowledged in my blog in http://www.oncecalledhome.

A special thank you is due to my Inner Circle of Readers who critiqued an early draft of the book. Their feedback was invaluable: Charles Ashman, Newt Barrett, Kate Bentley, Perry Brown, Robin Clay, James Dryburgh, Patsy LeVann, Morag Marinoni, Jane Maxim, Ric Neese, Wally Orchard, Carl Reddick, and Marilyn Southey.

Reference books that have been ever at my side are Michael Gelfand's *The Sick African*, Third Edition, Juta and Company, 1957 and B.A. Kosmin's, *Majuta, a History of the Jewish Community in Zimbabwe*, Mambo Press, Gwelo, 1981.

A big thank you to Lucy McCann at Rhodes House, Bodleian Library, Oxford University for facilitating my access to the uncatalogcd papers of Sir Edgar Whitehead including Frances Whitehead's letters. Thanks to Lucy, too, for connecting me with Rachel Clarkson who generously contributed additional Whitehead materials and connected me with John Beasant who briefly worked for Sir Edgar Whitehead as his personal assistant.

Late in the day I chanced to meet my structural editor Susan Kelly of Gomboc Words. She taught me so much in such a short space of time and made all the difference to a final rewrite and publishing.

A big thank you to my son Jonathan Davis for emergency bale-outs on computer glitches and patient computer coaching and to my brother David Hirsch for lessons on the art of conversation, historical insights and editing over the years that renewed our bond.

Last but not least I would like to thank Jan, my long-suffering husband, for enduring all the manic depressive phases of the creative process and unfailing encouragement.

A NOTE ON SOURCES

Grateful acknowledgement is made for permission to print excerpts from these evocative songs of the times:

Ac-cent-tchu-ate The Positive Lyric by Johnny Mercer Music by Harold Arlen (c) 1944 (Renewed) HARWIN MUSIC CO. All Rights Reserved *Reprinted by Permission of Hal Leonard Corporation.*

Just One More Chance Words by Sam Coslow Music by Arthur Johnston Copyright © 1931 Sony/ATV Music Publishing LLC Copyright Renewed All Rights Administered by Sony/ATV Music Publishing LLC 424 Church Street, Suite 1200, Nashville, TN 37219 International Copyright Secured All Rights Reserved *Reprinted by Permission of Hal Leonard Corporation.*

I'VE GOT A POCKETFUL OF SUNSHINE Music by ARTHUR JOHNSTON Lyrics by GUS KAHN © 1955 (Renewed) EMI ROBBINS CATALOG INC. All Rights Controlled by EMI ROBBINS CATALOG INC. (Publishing) ALFRED MUSIC (Print) All Rights Reserved. **ALFRED'S ADMINISTRATIVE SHARE: 100% WORLDWIDE.**

DON'T FENCE ME IN (from "Hollywood Canteen") Words and Music by COLE PORTER © 1944 (Renewed) WB MUSIC CORP. All Rights Reserved **ALFRED'S ADMINISTRATIVE SHARE: 100% WORLDWIDE.**

ALMOST LIKE BEING IN LOVE (from "Brigadoon") Lyrics by ALAN JAY LERNER, Music by FREDERICK LOEWE ©1947 (Renewed) THE LERNER HEIRS PUBLISHING DESIGNEE and THE LOEWE FOUNDATION PUBLISHING DESIGNEE All Rights in the U.S. Administered by EMI APRIL MUSIC, INC. All Rights for the World Outside of the U.S. Administered by EMI U CATALOG INC. (Publishing) and ALFRED MUSIC (Print) All Rights Reserved. **ALFRED'S ADMINISTRATIVE SHARE: 100% WORLDWIDE.**

"Blue Skies" by Irving Berlin © Copyright 1926, 1927 by Irving Berlin © Copyright Renewed International Copyright Secured All Rights Reserved Reprinted by Permission.

"Anything You Can Do" by Irving Berlin © Copyright 1946 by Irving Berlin © Copyright Renewed International Copyright Secured All Rights Reserved Reprinted by Permission.

And also these songs in the public domain:
"Behold the Lord High Executioner" 1885 lyrics by Gilbert and Sullivan
"I am the Very Model of a Modern Major-General" lyrics by Gilbert and Sullivan 1879
"Hatikvah" (The Hope) lyrics adapted from poem by Naftali Herz Imber 1877 music by Samuel Cohen 1888

Acknowledgement is made for the poem:
"The Tree" by Joyce Kilmer 1913

51493392R00219

Made in the USA
San Bernardino, CA
24 July 2017